STEPHEN KING'S
THE
DARK TOWER

A CONCORDANCE
VOLUME I

Robin Furth

FOREWORD BY
STEPHEN KING

SCRIBNER
New York   London   Toronto   Sydney

FOR MARK

FOR STEVE

FOR ROLAND

SCRIBNER
1230 Avenue of the Americas
New York, NY 10020

SCRIBNER and design are trademarks of Macmillan Library Reference USA, Inc.,
used under license by Simon & Schuster, the publisher of this work.

For information about special discounts for bulk purchases,
please contact Simon & Schuster Special Sales:
1-800-456-6798 or business@simonandschuster.com

DESIGNED BY ERICH HOBBING

Text set in Sabon

Manufactured in the United States of America

3 5 7 9 10 8 6 4

Library of Congress Control Number: 2003054272

ISBN 0-7432-5207-1

CONTENTS

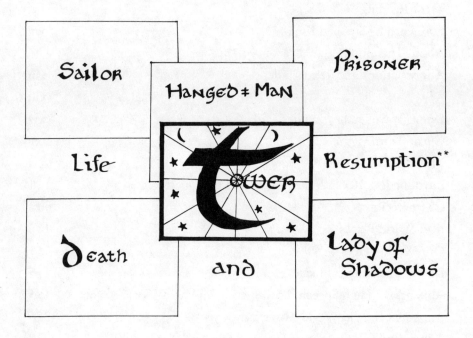

Sailor

Hanged Man

Prisoner

Life

Tower

Resumption**

Death

and

Lady of
Shadows

FOREWORD
BY STEPHEN KING

The tale of Roland of Gilead's search for the Dark Tower is a single tale, picaresque in nature (think *Huckleberry Finn* with monsters, and characters who raft along the Path of the Beam instead of the Mississippi), spanning seven volumes, involving dozens of plot-twists and hundreds of characters. It's hard to tell how much time passes "inside the story," because in Roland Deschain's *where* and *when*, both time and direction have become plastic.[1] Outside the story—in what we laughingly call "the real world"—thirty-two years passed between the first sentence and the last one.

How long were the lapses between the individual books which make up the entire story? In truth, Constant Reader, I do not know. I think the longest lapse might have been six years (between *The Waste Lands* and *Wizard and Glass*). It is a miracle the story was ever finished at all, but perhaps an even greater one that a second volume ever followed the first, which was originally published in a tiny edition by Donald M. Grant, Publishers.[2] The manuscript of that first volume, wet and barely readable, was rescued from a mildewy cellar. The first forty handwritten pages of a second volume (titled, as I remember, *Roland Draws Three*) were missing. God knows where they wound up.

Will I tell you what happens to a story when it lies fallow over such long periods of time? Will you hear? Then close your eyes and imagine a vast department store, all on one level, lit by great racks of overhead fluorescent lights. You see every kind of item under those lights—underwear and automotive parts, TVs and DVDs, shoes and stationery and bikes for the kiddies, bluejeans and mattresses (Oh look, Herbie, they're on sale, 40% off!), cosmetics and air-rifles, party dresses and picnic gear.

Now imagine the lights failing, one by one. The huge space grows

1. This was a demand of the story, but I'd be less than honest if I didn't add that it also helps to foil the often troubling questions of copy editors such as those asked by Teddy Rosenbaum, who worked on the later volumes of the cycle.

2. The stories that made up the volume were issued in *The Magazine of Fantasy and Science Fiction*, then edited by Ed Ferman.

darker; the goods so temptingly arrayed grow dimmer and harder to see. Finally you can hardly see your hand in front of your face.

That was the kind of room I came to when it was finally time to write *The Drawing of the Three*, except then the store wasn't so big—the first volume was less than three hundred pages long, so it was actually more of a mom n pop operation, do ya not see it. I was able to light it again simply by reading over the first volume and having a few ideas (I also resurrected a few old ones; I hadn't entirely forgotten what was in those handwritten pages, or the purpose of the tale).

Coming back to write the third volume (*The Waste Lands*) in the mid-eighties was harder, because the store was once again almost completely dark, and now it was much bigger. Once again I began by reading over what I'd written, taking copious notes, and filling paperback copies of the first two books with yellow highlighted passages and pink Post-it notes.

Another four years passed . . . or perhaps this time it was six. The store had once again grown dark, and by the time I was ready to write *Wizard and Glass*, it was bigger than ever. This time I wanted to add a whole new annex (call it Roland's Past instead of the Bridal Shoppe). Once again out came the books—three of them, this time—the yellow highlighter, and the packets of Post-it notes.

When I sat down to complete Roland's story in the year 2001, I knew that just re-reading and writing myself Post-it notes wouldn't be enough. By now the store that was my story seemed to cover whole acres; had become a Wal-Mart of the imagination. And, were I to write three more volumes, I'd be adding dozens of characters (I actually ended up adding over fifty), a whole new dialect (based on the pidgin English used by the natives of West Africa and first encountered by me in Richard Dooling's extraordinary *White Man's Grave*), and a back story that would—I hoped—finally make Roland's wandering present clear to the patient reader.

This time, instead of reading, I listened to Frank Muller's extraordinary audio recordings of the first four Dark Tower stories. Unabridged audio forces the reader to slow down and listen to every word, whether he or she wants to or not. It also lends a new perspective, that of the reader and the audio director. But I knew even that would not be enough. I needed some sort of exhaustive written summary of *everything* that had gone before, a Dark Tower Concordance that would be easy to search when I needed to find a reference in a hurry. In terms of the store metaphor, I needed someone to replace all the fluorescents, and inventory all the goods on offer, and then hand me a clipboard with everything noted down.

Enter Robin Furth. She came to me courtesy of my old friend and teacher at the University of Maine, Burton Hatlen. Burt is a wonderful scholar of poetry and popular fiction. He has written about Roland for several scholarly journals, and was sympathetic to what I was up to with the books (indeed, he seemed to understand what I was up to better than I did myself). So I gave him my list of requirements with some confidence (some hope, at least) that he would find the right person.

Someone who was bright and imaginative.

Someone who had read a good deal of fantasy (although not necessarily the Tower books themselves), and was therefore familiar with its rather unique language and thematic concerns.

Someone who could write with clarity and verve.

Someone who was willing to work hard and answer arcane and often bizarre questions (*Who was the Mayor of New York in 1967? Do worms have teeth?*) on short notice.

He found Robin Furth, and my wandering gunslinger had found his Boswell. The Concordance you hold in your hands—and which will surely delight you as it has delighted me—was never written to be published. As a writer I like to fly by the seat of my pants, working without an outline and usually without notes. When I have to slow down to look for something—a name in Volume III, say, or a sequence of events way back in Volume I—I can almost *feel* the story growing cold, the edge of my enthusiasm growing blunt and flecking out with little blooms of rust. The idea of the Concordance was to limit these aggravating pauses by putting Roland's world at my fingertips—not just names and places, but slang terms, dialects, relationships, even whole chronologies.

Robin provided exactly what I needed, and more. One day I walked into my office to discover her down on her knees, carefully sticking photographs to a huge piece of poster paper. It was, she explained, a "walking tour" of Second Avenue in New York, covering the avenue itself and all the cross-streets from Fortieth to Sixty-sixth. There was the U.N. Plaza Hotel (which has changed its name twice since I started writing Roland's story); there was Hammarskjold Plaza (which did not even exist back in 1970); there was the spot where Tom and Jerry's Artistic Deli ("Party Platters Our Specialty") once stood. That poster eventually went up on the wall of my writing room in Florida, and was of invaluable help in writing *Song of Susannah* (The Dark Tower VI). In addition to the "walking tour" itself, Robin had patiently winkled out the history of the key two blocks, including the real shops and buildings I'd replaced with such fictional bits of real estate as Chew Chew Mama's and The Manhattan Restaurant of the Mind. And it was Robin who discovered that, across the street from 2 Hammarskjold Plaza, there really is a little pocket park (it's called a "peace garden") that does indeed contain a bronze turtle sculpture. Talk about life imitating art!

As I say, her Concordance was never meant to be published; it was created solely as a writer's tool. But, even with most of my mind preoccupied by the writing of my tale, I was aware of how good it was, how interesting and *readable* it was. I also became aware, as time passed and the actual publication of the final three volumes grew closer, of how valuable it might be to the Constant Reader who'd read the first three or four volumes of the series, but some years ago.

In any case, it was Robin Furth who inventoried the goods I had on sale, and replaced all the dim overhead lights so I could see everything clearly and find my way from Housewares to Appliances without getting lost . . . or from Gilead to Calla Bryn Sturgis, if you prefer. That in no way makes her responsible for my errors—of which I'm sure there are many— but it *is* important that she receive credit for all the good work she has done on my behalf. I found this overview of In-World, Mid-World, and End-World both entertaining and invaluable.

So, I am convinced, will you.

January 26, 2003

ABOUT THIS BOOK

This book had its first stirrings more than twenty years ago. I was fourteen, and I was spending the summer with my grandparents in Maine. Books have always had an obsessive draw for me, and so that July I arrived with a stack of them. Top of the pile wasn't *The Gunslinger*. No. Not yet. But it was a novel called *'Salem's Lot*.

I can still remember the feeling I had when I read that book. My body was on the tiny, weedy beach of Patten Pond, but the rest of me was in the Marsten House, or crouched by Mark Petrie's side as he held up a glow-in-the-dark cross to ward off the vampire at his window. I climbed on the Greyhound Bus behind Father Callahan—my hand burned and my mouth still tasting Barlow's blood—and the two of us set off for that unknown destination of Thunderclap, a haunted place on the lip of End-World.[1]

I closed the novel, and still caught in that dream-web, I began to walk back towards home. And there, in the pine woods, with my feet deep in leaf mould and my skin still smelling of pond water, I saw myself as an adult. I was grown-up, and I was working for Stephen King. I didn't know exactly what I was doing, but I knew it had to do with books, and Father Callahan, and with that dreaded place called Thunderclap. The vision was so vivid, so convincing, and so quickly over. I held onto the feeling of it long enough to write my first horror story (it wasn't very good), but as the vision faded, I began to doubt what I had seen. I buried that vision, lost the story, and didn't think about either for two decades. That is, until one day when I went to check my mail in the English office at the University of Maine. As I was sorting through the grade sheets and memos, I felt a tap on my shoulder. It was Burt Hatlen, one of my professors. Stephen King needed a temporary research assistant, he said. Would I be interested . . .

---

1. Believe it or not, the copy of *'Salem's Lot* that I had as a teenager actually mentioned Thunderclap. I spent years wondering where that place was—it didn't sound like any city in our world. I read the book several times as an adult and never saw this reference again. Recently I asked Steve whether he had deleted Thunderclap from later editions and he told me it was never there in the first place. But it should have been. How can I explain this weird occurrence? I can't.

Sometimes, art imitates life, and sometimes life imitates art, and sometimes the two of them blend to such a degree that we can't figure out where one ends and the other begins. For months before my chat with Burt, I'd been dreaming about roses, moons with demon faces, and huge, imposing, smoke-colored Towers. I didn't think I was losing my mind, but then there was the tall, lanky, ghost-like man pacing at my writing room door. He seemed to want to get through to our world, to *need* to get through to our world, and for some reason he thought I could help him. And every time I laid out my Tarot cards, my future came out Towers.

Ka is a wheel, its one purpose is to turn, and so often it brings us back to just where we started. Twenty years had passed since I boarded that bus to Thunderclap, but in Roland's world, in the world of the Tower quest, twenty years in the past, or twenty years in the future, are only just a doorway apart. I climbed back on that Greyhound Bus only to find myself, as a young girl, still sitting behind Callahan. I'd never really disembarked in the first place.

Pere Callahan waited in Calla Bryn Sturgis, on the border of Thunderclap, and Roland had to reach him. All he needed was somebody from our world to help crack open Steve's doorway. I knew many of Steve's other works, I loved fantasy and horror, and I had those rather sinister initials that implied I might be good for writing something other than academic essays. All that remained for me to do was open Roland's biography and read that first, all-important line. *The man in black fled across the desert, and the gunslinger followed . . .*

For over two years I have lived in Roland's world—occasionally surfacing in ours—and during that time I've collected much of the myth, history, and folklore of Mid-World. Just as, when you wake up from a dream, you try to capture what you saw during your night travels, the book that follows is my attempt to capture my journey with Roland. My goal, when I started, was to make a doorway between worlds. I hope that I have, at least, made a small window.

R. F.
March 12, 2003

ABBREVIATIONS AND TEXT GUIDE

I: King, Stephen. *The Gunslinger*. 1982. New York: Plume-Penguin, 1988.

II: ———. *The Drawing of the Three*. 1987. New York: Plume-Penguin, 1989.

III: ———. *The Waste Lands*. 1991. New York: Plume-Penguin, 1993.

IV: ———. *Wizard and Glass*. New York: Plume-Penguin, 1997.

E: ———. "The Little Sisters of Eluria." *Everything's Eventual: 14 Dark Tales*. New York: Scribner, 2002.

PLEASE NOTE

1. This book went to press before a paginated copy of the new version of *The Gunslinger* was available. As a result, all *Gunslinger* page references refer to the original version of the novel. All entries that contain material drawn from the 2003 *Gunslinger* are marked with a double asterisk (**).
2. Page references are as follows:

   III:323

   (volume):(page number)

3. Although Mid-World was the name of a specific historical kingdom, in both *Wizard and Glass* and "The Little Sisters of Eluria" Roland uses this term as a general name for his world. I have followed this practice.

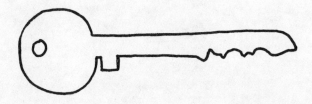

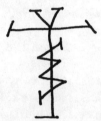

TRAVELLER, BEYOND LIES MID-WORLD

GILEAD FAIR-DAYS

WINTER

WIDE EARTH
Riddling

SOWING
(**New Earth)
(**Fresh Commala)
The Sowing Night Cotillion
called Commala
a courting rite dance
celebrating spring

MID-SUMMER

FULL EARTH
Riddling
Full Earth babies born

REAPING
Charyou Tree and burning of stuffy-guys,
Reaping lass and Reaping lad, Reap charms.
In the Outer Arc, a prize is given on Reap Day to the person or group
that collects the greatest number of rattlesnake skins.
Children planted on Reap come due on Full Earth.
This is the true Year's End.
Reap kisses
Orgy of Reap
Propitiating old gods
Reap Morn: First day of Winter

YEAR'S END

MID-WORLD MOONS

KISSING MOON
A perfect disk of silver
Moon of Romance
Shadows of lovers
On its bright skin

PEDDLER'S MOON
Late-summer moon
Huge and orange
And the Peddler, who comes out of the Nones
With his sack of squealing souls

HUNTRESS MOON
Last moon of summer, first moon of autumn
Picking apples, cutting hay
Snakes and scorpions wander east from the desert
Day moon
The huntress fills her belly
And becomes
A pallid, vampire woman
Season of Reap
The beginning of endings
Clearer and clearer on each starry night
The Huntress pulls back her bow

DEMON MOON
Blood red
Death moon
Closing of the year
Blade nose
Bone grin
Reap's scythe
Above
He grins and winks
Though a scarlet
shifting
scrim

xvi

INTRODUCTION:
ROLAND, THE TOWER,
AND THE QUEST

Spoiler's Warning: Read this essay only after you have read the first four books of Roland's saga. Otherwise, you'll get more than a glimpse of what is to come . . .

To any reader of the Dark Tower series, Roland Deschain is an instantly recognizable character. As I write this, I see him in my mind's eye, striding across the yellowing grasses of the River Barony savannah, his black hair threaded with gray, his body tall and lanky, his holster and gun belt strapped to his hips. Only one of those fabled sandalwood-handled six-shooters is with him; it rests against his left thigh. The other is back at camp, secure in the docker's clutch strapped to Eddie Dean's side. As I stare, Roland turns his head and regards me pragmatically. *If you need to talk to me,* he says, *then come.* Time may be a face on the water, but in Roland's world, water is scarce.

Roland watches as I pass through the doorway of the page. His pale blue eyes really are like those of a bombardier, both cool and assessing. By necessity, this meeting will be brief. I'm another one of Roland's secrets, and he thinks it better to keep me that way. He's not certain what level of the Tower I come from, but he knows one thing. I am mapping his travels.

Finding some shade, Roland hunkers. I hand him one of the rolling papers I've brought, and he accepts it silently. Unlacing the leather thongs of his traveling purse, he removes his tobacco poke and rolls a smoke. Despite the missing fingers on his right hand, he works the paper dexterously, licking the gummed side with a grimace. He strikes a match against the seam of his jeans and lights his cigarette. For a moment his face is illuminated with an eerie glow that makes his features look drawn and more than a little haggard. He has a few days' worth of stubble on his cheeks, and his lips are chapped. Once again I try to show him this concordance, but he waves the bound manuscript away as he exhales a cloud of smoke. As always, he thinks that my constant revisions waste

1

paper. Besides, he's only interested in the maps. But today I've brought a short piece, and this he has agreed to hear. It's my interpretation of his epic journey. Taking another deep drag, Roland rolls his hand in that gesture which means only one thing, in any world. *Get on with it.* So I clear my throat and (rather nervously) begin.

ROLAND, THE TOWER, AND THE QUEST

Roland Deschain is Mid-World's final gunslinger. Like a knight from the Arthurian legends of our world, Roland is on a quest. His "grail" is the Dark Tower, the linchpin of the Time/Space continuum, and his goal is to climb to its very top and question the god or demon who resides there. Roland's world is unraveling. The Beams that maintain the proper alignment of time, space, size and dimension are breaking down and the Tower itself is foundering. This structural instability affects all worlds, but in Roland's, the symptoms are dramatic. As the fabric of reality wears away, thinnies form and spread. These squalling mist bogs swallow all those that stumble into them, letting their captives fall into the dark no-places between worlds. As the landscape stretches, directions drift. What is west today may be southwest tomorrow and southeast the day after. A goal that lay only fifty miles away can suddenly become a hundred, or even a thousand miles distant.

As the direct descendant of Arthur Eld, King of All-World-That-Was, and as Mid-World's last *dinh*, Roland must rescue his land from annihilation. But his task is gargantuan. He must find a way to safeguard the framework, the loom, upon which the interpenetrating realities are woven. But in order to do so—in order to shore up that central Tower and the Beams which radiate out from it—he must find his way across a landscape so fragmented that neither map nor memory can help him pinpoint his destination. In fact, Roland does not even know where the Tower stands. He realizes that he must head toward a place called End-World, but where does that land lie? How can he find it? During the early stages of his journey, Roland the warrior chooses the path of the ascetic. Believing he can only reach his goal as a solitary traveler, he sacrifices all human relationships, even when it means betrayal, because he thinks such sacrifice will speed him along his way. Comrades and lovers are left behind like abandoned waterskins.

Roland believes that to climb the Tower he must have no ties holding him to Mid-World. He must be isolated, self-sufficient, cut off from the nurturing tides of relationship. Thinking in terms of conquest and battle, Roland follows the duplicitous Walter across the deserts of Mid-World, believing that this enemy will eventually lead him to his goal. Similarly, as a boy, he followed the path set for him by Maerlyn's Grapefruit, a magic ball whose evil, distorting visions tricked him into first sacrificing his lover, Susan Delgado, and then murdering his own mother.

What Roland doesn't at first realize is that, like any young knight, he is being tested. The initial path he chooses is a false start, no more than a *glammer* thrown by the enemies who want to thwart him. What their treachery exposes is that the young Roland is driven by ambition, personal glory, and revenge as much as he is by a desire to fulfill his destiny as the last warrior of the White. By tempting him to betray all that a knight should hold sacred, Roland's enemies ensure that Roland will repeat the mistakes of his fathers and either abandon his quest as hopeless or become lost in the deserts and golgothas of Mid-World which, in the end, but mirror the dry wreckage of his heart.

Roland, the young warrior, does not understand the ultimate nature of his quest. He does not realize that, as the trickster Walter says in the golgotha, he already stands so close to the Tower that worlds turn about his head.[1] Because of his own preconceptions, his inherited worldview, he does not understand that his fate, and the fate of Mid-World, are one and the same.

Roland's story is not just an adventure tale; it is one with symbolic meaning. His pilgrimage is intrinsically linked to a legend from our world, a legend which was an important influence upon the Modernists and which formed the basis for a famous poem by T. S. Eliot. That legend is the story of the Waste Land. In its incarnation in the Dark Tower series, this legend is bound to another belief, one that dates back to the time when men and women thought that their kings and queens were appointed by God. According to this worldview, the body of the king is the body of the land, and the well-being of one is indivisible from the well-being of the other. If the king is sick, in body or in mind, then the land falls to ruin. To cure the land, you must first cure the king. The one will only flourish if the other is in balance.

As above, so below. The disease of the larger is the same as that of the smaller, and they both progress according to the same principle. To understand what dries and devastates the land, what threatens the very fabric of the universe and the stability of the interpenetrating worlds, one must also understand what ails the king. All are affected by the same illness, but to cure this illness we must discover its underlying cause. And this is the true purpose of Roland's journey.

We all know that as the Beams snap, the Tower falters. But what is its

1. I:200

equivalent on the human plane? What malaise weakens the bonds of Mid-World's culture? What disease affects Roland, the foremost representative of his fragmenting world?

High Speech, the tongue of gunslingers, is a subtle and complex language. Its words are difficult to define because they are so full of nuance. Each word has multiple meanings which refer, simultaneously, to ordinary human interaction, to the web that joins the interacting individuals, and to the greater pattern of humanity's past and future movements. No human interaction, then, is meaningless. They all reflect both individual and cultural *ka*.

Ka, we know, resembles a wheel. In fact, it looks much like the wheel Roland draws in *The Waste Lands*, a wheel meant to represent The Tower, the Beams, and the Portals in and out of Mid-World. In Roland's map, the hub of the wheel is the Tower, the spokes are the Beams, and the rivets are the Guardians, who are the Portals' sentries. Some Guardians, like the Turtle, are protective, while others, like the Bear Guardian Shardik, are downright dangerous. But they all serve the Beams, the Beams serve the Tower, and the Tower is what keeps the universe united. And perhaps these Beams work like Batteries, with positive and negative charges, the one balancing the other. That would explain why the Turtle is kind and the Bear—the opposite end of the Beam—is negative. Even polarity has its place, like light and darkness. That is, as long as the whole remains in balance.

Although it would be difficult to map the wheel of *ka* in this way—it is much too big—we can, at least, map the forces of *ka-tet*, remembering that the small is a miniature of the larger. As *dinh* of his *ka-tet* and as *dinh* of Mid-World, Roland sits at the center of the wheel. The Guardians of his present *ka-tet* are his companions Jake, Susannah, Eddie and Oy. The sorcerer Walter—who plays a large part in the drawing and binding of this *ka-tet*—can also be placed as one of the Guardians, though his polarity is negative.

Just as there is a word for the pattern of *ka-tet*, there is a word for the bonds (or Beams) that hold the *tet* together. This word is *khef*. Like almost all the words of High Speech, *khef* has multiple meanings, including birth and life-force, but perhaps the most ubiquitous of these meanings is also the simplest. And that meaning is water.

As Roland knows all too well from his journey in the Mohaine Desert, a human will die much sooner from dehydration than he will from lack of food. The same can be said about the land, about society, and about the individual soul. Once again, the patterns and forces remain the same; what changes are the superficial forms. *Khef* can be literal water, the essence of life, but it can also mean emotion, the essence and bond of relationship.

Whether this bond is one of loyalty or hatred, it always binds. That is, as long as the forces of the positive and the negative remain in dynamic balance. A certain amount of conflict is necessary for growth and change, but too much of the negative—too much repellant—and the *ka-tet* ceases to exist.

The patterns of *ka-tet* can be used to describe the subtle interactions which hold a society together. Without these emotional interactions, which create dynamic and forceful cohesion, society devolves and disintegrates; it becomes a mass of warring individuals, or warring clans. The beneficial interconnectedness of the whole is lost.

The bonds of *khef* are reciprocal. Both parties must contribute or else the connection is at best unstable, at worst illusory. Each side must give of itself. The unity of *ka-tet* depends on the forces of *khef*. In order for the *ka-tet* to survive, the Guardians of *ka-tet* must remain true, but their loyalty depends, in turn, upon the truth and honesty of the center. When the center does not hold true, the fabric begins to unravel, and this is exactly what has happened to Roland's world, and what has, in turn, happened over and over in Roland's life.

Ka is a wheel; its one purpose is to turn. The spin of *ka* always brings us back to the same place, to face and reface our mistakes and defeats until we can learn from them.[2] When we learn from the past, the wheel continues to move forward, towards growth and evolution. When we don't, the wheel spins backward, and we are given another chance. If once more we squander the opportunity, the wheel continues its rotation towards devolution, or destruction. While the High Speech terms for life and relationship have multiple meanings and subtle nuances, *char*, the Tongue's word for Death, has no other meaning. *Char* is bleak and final. The wheel continues to turn, but we are forcefully removed from it. Since we each have a place in the greater pattern, breaking of *khef* rends the fabric of the All.

What can be said of individuals can also be said of societies, and Roland's society is no exception. Although Mid-World enjoyed periods of stability, its history remains predominantly a story of sacrifice and bloodshed. Although High Speech shows that unity and relationship were valued, in the everyday of life they were, more often than not, forgotten. Many of Mid-World's sins were sins against *khef*, the bonding force of *ka* and culture. In Mid-World-That-Was, the balance between positive and negative was lost; creating and maintaining *khef* became less important than the propagation of *char*. Just as the Beams began to weaken, the *khef*

---

2. As Steve mentioned when he read this essay, he first began to articulate this idea in *The Stand*.

which was meant to unite began to repel. The waters of life withdrew, and Mid-World became a desert. The result? Fragmentation and dehydration on all levels of reality, and on all levels of the Tower.

In "The Little Sisters of Eluria," Roland says that the religions of his world taught that "love and murder were inextricably bound together—that in the end, God always drank blood."[3] Upon intensive scrutiny, Roland's statement certainly seems to hold true. The Druits, the most ancient of Mid-World's people, raised the stones of the Speaking Rings in order to have temples devoted to human sacrifice. Although these practices may have drawn some of the people together, giving them a sense of unity and strength, they would have also created a blood-debt to the victim, and the victim's *ka-tet*, rending the fabric of the All. Even at this early stage of Mid-World's cultural evolution, the negative energy released by these acts began to thin reality. The forces of *char* became more powerful and the forces of *khef* were weakened. Within these circles doorways formed, but the sentries of these lesser portals were demons, not Guardians.

Although technologically advanced, the later generations of Mid-World gave little more thought to the forces of *khef*, or life-water, than their ancestors. The Great Old Ones created computerized wonders, such as Blaine, and accomplished amazing engineering and architectural feats, such as the building of Lud and the laying of the train lines deep below the Cyclopean Mountains, but even these seemingly "good" things were eventually tainted by the death-drive of their makers. Blaine developed a psychotic personality and drove the people of Lud on to Mid-World's oldest practice—human sacrifice. The city of Lud, once the gem of the Imperium, fell into the hands of diseased and warring gangs, and the train lines of the mountains seethed with Slow Mutants, those terrible creatures who were once human but who had been completely mutated by the Old Ones' poisons. No matter what grand plan they had for the future of the interpenetrating universes, the Old Ones worshipped the gods of *char*, the gods of destruction. The Old Ones' technological wizardry was focused on one endpoint, and that endpoint was the creation of more and more dangerous weapons. In this they succeeded. In fact, they succeeded so completely that they wiped out their own civilization and transformed Mid-World into a poisoned, desiccated wasteland.

As Susan Delgado says to Roland when they stand, horrified, by a line of resurrected war tankers, the ways of the Great Old Ones were the ways of death.[4] But over the course of the series we learn that the ways of death are, and always have been, the ways of Mid-World. Even during the time

3. E:147
4. IV:302

of Arthur Eld, Mid-World's greatest hero, human beings were thrown onto Charyou Tree fires to appease the gods of Reap, and in Roland's day those old ways were not completely abandoned. As we see when Susan Delgado is made into such a scapegoat, having the blame for her town's sins heaped upon her innocent head, such sacrifice and hypocrisy undermine all human relationships. No matter what their stated aims might be, such practices breed duplicity and mistrust and treachery, all of which are the opposite of *khef*.

In the more central parts of Roland's world, stuffy guys were usually burned in lieu of men and women, but life was still harsh and leaders were bred to be killers before they were taught to be statesmen. All that the ruling gunslingers had to do to justify this sacrifice of *khef* was to point west to the lands that were already torn apart by anarchy and rebellion. In Gilead, the light of civilization was championed, but its ideals of fairness, justice, compassion—of fundamental human worth whatever class or land that person might come from—were left to the gentle and the lame, like Roland's old tutor Vannay, to promulgate. Although Roland loved Vannay, by far his most influential teacher was Cort, who taught him how to survive in a world where a knife would constantly be at his back, or at his throat.

In Gilead, the sons of the aristocracy trained to be an Eye and a Hand, an aim and a trigger, before they were trained to be a heart and a mind. And often, as Roland found to his later distress, such training meant that the hand could act before the mind had time to think. Gilead's coming-of-age battles were brutal, and the cost of defeat was banishment, a complete destruction of the *khef* that linked the young gunslinger to his society. The end—the creation of a strong, fearless, hardened gunslinger elite that could keep the anarchic darkness at bay—justified both the violence and the humiliation of the means. But *ka* makes no exceptions. As one sows, so one reaps, and the harvest is not always pleasant. Those trained killers—such as Eldred Jonas—who were banished from their society became the foot soldiers of Mid-World's next apocalypse.

The gunslingers could not see that the rot eating away at the fabric of their world was also at work upon the *khef* of their city, and upon the *khef* of their personal relationships. Roland's father, Steven Deschain, is a prime example. Trained in the ways of *char*, the waters of *khef* dried up in him, and around him. He was bound to his fellow gunslingers, his fellow human hawks, but the bond he had with his wife became arid and his relationship with his magician (who also happened to be his foremost councilor) was duplicitous. Even his relations with Roland—whom he obviously loved—were gruff and distant. The situation was no better in the castle, or the kingdom. Hax, the head cook, turned traitor, as did at least some of the guards. All bonds of loyalty were broken, there was no longer a sense of cultural *ka-tet*, so many turned away to serve the forces of the enemy. Farson's propaganda about equality and democracy was only effective because it contained the grains of truth and exploited the alienation and anger of a society out of balance.

In the end, the gunslingers were destroyed and their city razed, its former castle becoming the filthy nest of a band of Slow Mutants. The forces of dissolution gained their coveted ground, and the universal waters of *khef* drew back a little more. With the fall of Gilead, the *ka-tet* of the Affiliation finally collapsed, and another part of the world stretched and unraveled.

As we have seen in the case of Steven Deschain, the reserved and isolated ruler who does not serve the greater *ka-tet* does not create the reciprocity and empathy needed to bind the parts of society into a whole. He is not behaving as a true *dinh* should. Although the disease predates him, and though he is, ultimately, another victim of the universal malaise, as the heir to the throne he carries the sins of both past kings and past kingdoms. As the center of cultural *ka-tet*, he must choose; either he must become the stable center of his kingdom and combat the malady of fragmentation or he must suffer the ultimate fate of his ancient forefathers. He can either perpetuate a cycle or pay penance, atone, and change. The disease of the land, and the disease of society, mirror the king's *ka*. In order to reverse the spin of the wheel and halt the process of dissolution, the king must look into the world-mirror but see the reflection of his own face, and the faces of his fathers.

When we first meet Roland in *The Gunslinger*, he is an anti-hero every bit as much as he is a hero. He is a man willing to sacrifice the members of his *ka-tet* in pursuit of his personal vision, just as his ancestors justified the drying of *khef* in the name of "progress" or "necessity." Susan Delgado, Roland's first and only true love, burns on a Charyou Tree fire because he will not be swayed from his quest long enough to save her. Jake Chambers falls into the abyss beneath the Cyclopean Mountains because Roland refuses to pause in his pursuit of the man in black. Even Roland's mother dies under his guns, those symbolic weapons of his fathers. As the trickster Walter hints during Roland's Tarot Reading in the golgotha, unless he, the Hanged Man, occupies the symbolic, central place of the Tower—unless he surrenders to the need of the world and focuses on the forces of *khef* which unite him to The Prisoner, The Lady of Shadows, The Sailor—his *ka* will only encompass Death, not Life. Unless he reclaims his humanity—which is, by its very definition, benevolence and respect for the needs of life—he will never reach the Tower, he will only be oppressed by its weight.

Roland, the isolated individual, is a survivor, but he is no more than a fragment of a larger, lost mosaic. He has no meaning. Like the landscape he travels, his soul has become a Wasteland. As we see in both *The Gunslinger* and the beginning of *The Drawing of the Three*, every time Roland betrays *khef*, he finds himself in an increasingly barren landscape. After his misadventures in Tull, Roland is almost killed by the parching dryness of the Mohaine Desert. After he lets Jake fall into the abyss, he finds himself first in the golgotha, an ancient bone-strewn killing ground, and then on the purgatorial beach of the Western Sea where lobstrosities devour two of his fingers and a chunk of one of his toes. It is only when Roland draws companions to him—first Jake, then Eddie and Susannah—that the landscape becomes more hospitable. At these points Roland, the isolated warrior focused only on himself and his desires, rediscovers his humanity. Significantly, it is at these points that he actually moves closer to the fulfillment of his quest. It is no accident that Roland discovers Jake at the Way Station, the place where he finds the water he needs to survive, and that with Jake he catches up with the man in black. Similarly, it is only after he has drawn Eddie and Susannah into his world (and out of their own personal hells), that he escapes the lobstrosity-infested beach of the Western Sea. And it is with Eddie and Susannah that he discovers the Bear-Turtle Beam, which will eventually lead him directly to his destination.

Unlike his ancestors, Roland is beginning to understand the relationship between his world and himself. He is beginning to learn from both his personal past and the past of Mid-World. Throughout the series, Eddie Dean accuses Roland of being a Tower-obsessed killing machine, but as Roland progresses on his journey, this accusation becomes less and less accurate. This Roland is determined to maintain his humanity despite the perils along his path. This Roland wants to live honorably, to live well and to live justly. And this is, in large part, what he strives to do over the course of the series.

In *The Gunslinger*, Roland lets Jake fall into the abyss beneath the Cyclopean Mountains, but in *The Waste Lands*, he risks his own life to save him from the Dutch Hill Mansion Demon and then from the boy-hungry gangs of Lud. When the wheel of *ka* turns and brings him back to a thinny so like the one he knew as a boy in Hambry, Roland tells his new companions about his betrayal of Susan Delgado, and then about the murder of his mother. It is almost as if he needs to confess his own sins against *khef* before he can move beyond them. This later Roland is conscious of himself and acknowledges his past mistakes. He recognizes his potential for treachery and fights against it. He is evolving, despite the twittering, goading, vindictive voice of the man in black. He is evolving from a mere warrior into a king.

Ka is destiny, but it is not just individual destiny. The sins Roland must expiate are not just his own, but those of all the rulers and cultures that came before him. *Ka* encompasses the past. Hence Roland's pilgrimage through the wastelands is also a penance for the human sacrifice of Arthur Eld's time, and for the time of the Speaking Rings. It is for the Great Old Ones and their hunger for power and their hubris, which drove them on to destroy the very fabric of the world. It's for the hierarchical inflexibility of Gilead-that-was, and the violent, destructive rebellion staged by Farson's army. It is his penance for, and his weapon against, the fragmentation generated by that gloating Prince of Chaos, the Crimson King.

Khef is what unites *dinh* and *ka-tet*, what unites king and kingdom, but it is also, ultimately, the force of the Beams and the force that keeps the multiple universes spinning like sequins around the needle of the Tower. In order to save the Tower, and in order to save all of the worlds that depend upon it, Roland must preserve the waters of *khef*. He must re-envision the world, redefine the cultural meaning of progress, and return to his lands a sense of what is truly sacred. In order to maintain the purity and strength of *khef*, he must, somehow, lessen the atrocity of Mid-World's history.

If each decision—personal, national, global—has a thousand different possible outcomes, each of those outcomes presents another possible future. Each of those futures will be different, and each will spin a unique timeline which exists only in that new-born world. But each of those future worlds remain linked, though they have no awareness of each other. Their link is the seed-moment that they came from, a seed held in the Eternal which encompasses every moment that ever has been or ever will be. They are all linked by the Tower.

In order to save the Tower, in order to ensure that there is a future for all these worlds and to ensure that more and more worlds are born, Roland must journey into the mythic history of his world—he must journey into our world. His quest, in the books to come, will be to save not a king or a kingdom but a single rose. A rose which sits in a vacant lot of a city which will someday become the technological Oz of the Great Old Ones, the foundation of their pride and the seed of their Fall. Before Roland, the great Warrior of the White, can save the Tower, he will have to risk his life to save a delicate flower whose yellow center is the womb of all worlds, and whose voice is the voice of *Yes* and of *Always*. He must save a simple rose which is, in our world, the symbol of unity and the symbol of love.

In their very imagery, the Tower and the Rose unite the symbolic male and the symbolic female, the two parts that join to give birth to the universe, and to life. In this unity they become One, which is simultaneously the center of all existence and the center of the integrated self. These two polarities, which seem so separate, bring together aggressive adventuring and passive nurturing, that within us which strives to conquer, to hold fast to high ideals, and that which is flexible enough to allow for human foibles, in ourselves and in others. They unite us with ourselves, our personal pasts, but also with the greater world. Although the Tower may reach higher than the heavens, and though the rose may sing a single aria that rises from the deepest well of the universe, both are—as Roland sees and hears in his visions and his dreams—woven of many voices and faces. The Tower and Rose unite to form the self's axis, but they also function as a brutally honest mirror, exposing where we have betrayed both ourselves and the world. The two, which are One, contain the voices and faces of Roland's betrayed loves, the reminders of his sins against *khef*. And it is these, in the final reckoning, that Roland will have to face.

Roland journeys through the purgatorial wastelands of his world as both sinner and redeemer. He is simultaneously the king, the land, and the Everyman. Through the course of his journey he must come to Know Himself. And only in this way can he begin to approach the Tower.

CHARACTERS[1]

. . . finally only three remained of the old world, three like dreadful cards from a terrible deck of tarot cards: gunslinger, man in black, and the Dark Tower.

I:140

A

ABAGAIL
In the alternate KANSAS of *Wizard and Glass*, JAKE finds a note tucked under the windshield of a camper. The note reads: "The old woman from the dreams is in Nebraska. Her name is Abagail." Somehow, BLAINE the insane Mono transported Roland's *ka-tet* to a parallel version of our world—one devastated by the genetically engineered superflu found in Stephen King's novel *The Stand*. Although Mother Abagail does not actually appear in the Dark Tower series (at least not yet), in her own particular *where* and *when* she is a champion of the White. Like Roland, this one-hundred-and-eight-year-old black woman is an enemy of the evil RANDALL FLAGG.
    IV:624

**AFFILIATION
The Affiliation was the name given to the network of political and military alliances that united Mid-World's baronies when Roland was a boy. With the IN-WORLD Barony of NEW CANAAN as its hub, the Affiliation gave military strength—and perhaps economic strength—to even the most far-flung baronies. Although Mid-World was not one united land as it had been in the days of ARTHUR ELD, the Affiliation helped to keep

---

1. Please note: The Dark Tower books contain many references to political and cultural figures from Our World. Unless these figures play an important part in the narrative, they have been relegated to Appendix III. Those people who are important to understanding the story have been included in the main Character index.

13

alive many of the more civilized ways that were under threat. It was also designed to help battle against the tides of chaos that were constantly washing over the world.

By the time Roland won his guns, the western part of Mid-World was in the throes of revolution and the Affiliation itself was under threat. Although the Affiliation served order and peace, the revolutionary and harrier JOHN FARSON claimed that the Affiliation worked against democracy and equality and in favor of Mid-World's old aristocratic order. Although Farson was a criminal and a liar, his words had their effect. By the time Roland and his first *ka-tet* reached HAMBRY, the Affiliation was already disintegrating. Many of those who once supported it had turned traitor.

Although the gunslingers of GILEAD supported the Affiliation, they thought it was small cheese compared to their own codes of culture and honor. This was eventually their undoing. Behind the Affiliation was the power of the White; its sign was Arthur's sword, Excalibur. Gilead's fall at the hands of Farson's men marked the end not only of the Affiliation but of the gunslingers as well.

In the new *Gunslinger* we find out that John Farson was actually just another one of WALTER's magical disguises, as was MARTEN BROAD-CLOAK, Steven Deschain's betraying sorcerer and counselor. Hence, the Affiliation's collapse, and the collapse of Mid-World, can be attributed to Walter's master, that ancient agent of chaos—THE CRIMSON KING.

IV:148–49, IV:150, IV:151 *(in trouble because of Farson)*, IV:163 *(gunslingers' attitude toward it)*, IV:174–78 *(general info)*, IV:180 *(and Mejis's loyalty)*, IV:181, IV:182, IV:189, IV:191, IV:199, IV:201, IV:204, IV:206, IV:211 *(hint something is wrong in Hambry)*, IV:219 *(when Gilead falls, the Affiliation ends)*, IV:221, IV:224, IV:225, IV:228, IV:229, IV:231–32, IV:250–51 *(Roland asks Susan if she supports it)*, IV:255, IV:260 *("Affiliation brats")*, IV:277, IV:302, IV:344, IV:350–51 *(implied—Inner Crescent)*, IV:359, IV:378, IV:381, IV:411, IV:417 *(and the power of the White)*, IV:423, IV:430, IV:433, IV:438, IV:501 *(Roland's ka-tet accused of being traitors)*

**AGELESS STRANGER (LEGION)

In the original version of *The Gunslinger*, we learned that the Ageless Stranger was actually just another name for the great sorcerer MAER-LYN. Like WALTER, he was a minion of the TOWER, only a more powerful one. As Walter said in THE GOLGOTHA, the Ageless Stranger *"darkles"* and *"tincts"*—in other words, he could live simultaneously in all times. If he wanted to reach the Tower, Roland would have to slay this formidable enemy.

In the new version of *The Gunslinger*, we learn something quite different about this strange being. According to Walter, the true name of the Ageless Stranger is not Maerlyn but LEGION, and he is a creature of END-WORLD. Roland must slay him in order to meet the Tower's present controller—THE CRIMSON KING. Like Roland, we don't yet know whether slippery Walter is telling the truth or is spreading lies for his own ends.

It seems quite likely that the Ageless Stranger is actually another incarnation of R.F., who is, in turn, another face of Walter. If this is the case, then Roland must battle Walter again before he reaches his final, magical destination.

I:211–12, III:261, III:387

**AILEEN OF GILEAD (AILEEN RITTER)

In the original version of *The Gunslinger*, we learned that Aileen was Roland's second important lover. He became intimate with her after his return from MEJIS but before GILEAD's fall. However, Aileen plays a smaller role in the new version of *The Gunslinger*. Instead of remembering his love for beautiful, bright-eyed Aileen, Roland longingly recalls SUSAN DELGADO of HAMBRY. In the updated *Gunslinger*, Aileen becomes Roland's dancing companion, not his beloved, and the woman his parents want him to marry, not the girl he chooses to be his lover.

I:86, I:88, I:131, I:137, I:140

ALAIN
See JOHNS, ALAIN

**ALAN
See ALLEN. See also DESCHAIN, GABRIELLE

ALBINO BEES
See MUTANTS

ALEXANDER, TRUMAN
See BALAZAR'S MEN

**ALICE OF TULL (ALLIE)

In both versions of *The Gunslinger*, Roland meets Alice when she serves him from behind the plank bar of SHEB'S honky-tonk in TULL. Although she may once have been beautiful, by the time we see her she is straw-haired and scarred. Like so many people in Mid-World, Alice has been sucked dry—both physically and emotionally—by the sterile hardpan of the desert. The overall impression she gives is of a woman who has been worn down into an early menopause. Her dirty blue dress is held at the strap by a safety pin and the livid scar corkscrewing across her forehead is emphasized, rather than hidden, by her face powder.

Although she initially reacts to him with hostility, Alice soon becomes Roland's lover. Unfortunately, she also becomes his victim. During the battle between Roland and SYLVIA PITTSON's followers, Allie's former lover SHEB uses Alice as a human shield. Like so many of Roland's other friends and confidants, Alice dies under Roland's guns.

In the new version of *The Gunslinger*, Allie still dies under Roland's guns, but before that she is the psychological victim of the MAN IN BLACK, also known as WALTER O'DIM. After he brings the weed-eater NORT back to life, Walter gives Nort a note for Allie. The note confides that Walter has planted a magical word in Nort's mind. The word is NINETEEN. If Allie says this word to him, the weed-eater will blurt out all that he saw in the world beyond.

But this message is a cruel trick, a Catch-22. Alice has always wanted to know what comes after this life, but attaining such forbidden knowledge will drive her mad. However, knowing the word, and not being able to speak it, is also guaranteed to drive her mad. In the end, Alice cannot control her curiosity and she says "Nineteen" to Nort, forcing him to spill forth all of his terrible, repressed secrets. Hence, when Roland aims his gun at her, a distressed Allie does not beg to be spared but begs to be killed so that her psychic torture will come to an end. Unfortunately for Alice, she ends up in the very place she wanted her imagination to escape—the LAND OF NINETEEN.

I:26–43 *(Nort's story 33–41)*, I:45–47, I:52–54, I:58–59 *(dies)*, I:60, I:64, I:77, I:78, I:79, I:118, I:131, I:143, I:156, II:231, III:42, III:44, III:127

**ALLEN
In the original version of *The Gunslinger*, Allen was part of Roland's *ka-tel*, or class of apprentice gunslingers, and was one of the boys who witnessed Roland's battle with CORT. In the new version of *The Gunslinger*, Allen's name is replaced with that of ALAIN JOHNS.

I:162, I:167–73 *(witnesses Roland's coming of age)*
SPELLED ALAN: II:121

**ALLGOOD, CUTHBERT
Talkative, brown-haired Cuthbert Allgood was Roland's beloved but restless childhood friend. Despite the comma of brown hair always falling over his forehead and his anarchic sense of humor, tall, narrow-

hipped Bert was quite handsome. His dark, beautiful eyes made SUSAN DELGADO wonder whether—under different circumstances—she would have fallen in love with Cuthbert rather than with Roland.

Cuthbert had a kind nature but a complex character. Although hidden behind a constant stream of jokes, Cuthbert's vision often took a dark turn. Like other apprentice gunslingers, Cuthbert was bred to be a killer, an instinct which showed itself when he secretly raged against CORT's chastisement and when he and Roland went to see HAX's hanging. (Cuthbert said he liked watching the dead man's jig.) On occasion, Cuthbert even felt a jealous rage rise up against Roland.

Although Roland loved Cuthbert more than any of his other old friends, he also found Bert's constant humor irritating. Roland often referred to Bert as *ka-mai*, or ka's fool. EDDIE DEAN, the *ka-mai* of Roland's new *ka-tet*, reminds Roland of Bert. We do not yet know whether Eddie and Cuthbert are actually paired souls, or whether Eddie is a reincarnation of Bert.

In the new version of *The Gunslinger*, we find out that Cuthbert died at JERICHO HILL—the site of the gunslingers' final battle. Cuthbert went down still blowing the HORN OF DESCHAIN. At Jericho Hill, Roland lost not just Bert but the horn of his fathers, the very horn he was meant to blow when he reached the TOWER.

In HAMBRY, Bert goes under the name **ARTHUR HEATH**. His horse is named **GLUE BOY**.

I:86, I:95, I:96–111, I:113, I:119, I:140, I:149 *(flashback)*, I:150–51 *(flashback: Cuthbert on Great Hall balcony with Roland)*, I:160, I:162, I:167–74 *(Roland's coming of age)*, I:197, II:52, II:121, II:176–77, II:207, II:231, II:355, II:394, III:33, III:41, III:60, III:124, III:242, III:268, III:270, III:278, III:346, III:377, III:417, IV:7, IV:57, IV:58, IV:59, IV:65, IV:119, IV:148 *("Mr. Arthur Heath")*, IV:151–53 *(Roland mentions him to Susan)*, IV:160–63 *(Rook skull prank and analysis of character. Physical description)*, IV:164, IV:174, IV:179–80 *(Mayor Thorin's party)*, IV:181–89 *(flashback to Sheriff Avery visit and false papers)*, IV:190–91, IV:191–210 *(Mayor Thorin's party cont., 192, raises eyebrow instead of nodding)*, IV:211, IV:218 *(physical description)*, IV:218–221 *(Travellers' Rest standoff)*, IV:224–30 *(Travellers' Rest standoff, 226–30 Sheriff Avery's office)*, IV:241, IV:245, IV:248, IV:255, IV:259–60 *("Little Coffin Hunters")*, IV:261–64 *(pigeons and message)*, IV:266–71 *(Depape learns true identity of Roland's ka-tet)*, IV:271–77, IV:282–89, IV:291 *(indirect reference)*, IV:336, IV:344–46, IV:347, IV:357–64 *(tension with Roland)*, IV:367, IV:368–69, IV:371, IV:380, IV:388–89, IV:392–93, IV:398–403, IV:408–19, IV:420, IV:426–42 *(428 described, 432 Roland's plan of attack*; *436–39 flashback to Steven Deschain and Maerlyn's Grapefruit, 439 father, Robert Allgood)*, IV:450, IV:454–56, IV:463 *(indirect reference)*, IV:465, IV:473 *(Rook's skull left by Thorin's body)*, IV:474–80 *(taken for murder)*, IV:483, IV:487, IV:500, IV:503, IV:504 *(as Sheemie's savior)*, IV:505, IV:506, IV:508–13, IV:514–19, IV:523–24, IV:525 *(mentioned)*, IV:526, IV:529–32, IV:533–35 *(Jonas discovers part of plan)*, IV:535–36, IV:539, IV:540, IV:547–48, IV:549 *(indirect)*, IV:552–60 *(attacking Jonas's company)*, IV:561 *(indirect)*, IV:573–75, IV:579–81, IV:583–84, IV:588–602 *(driving Farson's men into thinny)*, IV:608–11 *(Roland unconscious because of Maerlyn's ball)*, IV:620, IV:649, IV:658, IV:663, IV:664, E:150, E:187

   ALLGOOD, ROBERT: Cuthbert's father. I:104, IV:286, IV:436–39, IV:620

   CUTHBERT'S MOTHER: IV:282, IV:391 *(general)*

   HEATH, GEORGE: "Arthur Heath's" father.   IV:152

   THE LOOKOUT (ROOK'S SKULL): While in Hambry, Bert keeps this skull perched on the horn of his saddle. He also occasionally wears it as a comical pendant. Unfortunately, the BIG COFFIN HUNTERS use the bird to frame Cuthbert and the others for MAYOR HART THORIN's murder.   IV:119, IV:160–61, IV:163 *(lookout)*, IV:180, IV:189, IV:190, IV:191, IV:218 *(as pendant)*, IV:224, IV:227, IV:233, IV:245, IV:259, IV:261, IV:273, IV:276, IV:344–45 *(lost)*, IV:380 *(Jonas finds)*, IV:409, IV:473

AMOCO PREACHER

This hermit gained a quasi-religious following because of the wild sermons he preached while holding an ancient gasoline hose between his legs. (We don't know which was more popular among his followers—the sermons or the hose.) The words on the pump (AMOCO UNLEADED) were pretty much indecipherable, but this weird cult made AMOCO into the totem of a thunder god. They worshiped this destructive force with a mad slaughter of sheep.

   I:154, III:97

ANDOLINI, CLAUDIO

   See BALAZAR'S MEN

ANDOLINI, JACK

   See BALAZAR'S MEN

APON

   See OLD STAR

ARTHUR ELD
See ELD, ARTHUR

ARTHUR, KING
In Our World, the name King Arthur is synonymous with that of a legendary King of the Britons who oversaw the Knights of the Round Table and whose men went in search of the Holy Grail. In Mid-World, Arthur is the namesake of Roland's own illustrious ancestor, ARTHUR ELD.
I:94, III:72

AUNT BLUE
See DEAN, SUSANNAH: ODETTA HOLMES'S ASSOCIATES

AUNT CORDELIA
See DELGADO, CORDELIA

AUTHORS (OUR WORLD)
See APPENDIX III

AVERY, BONNIE
See PIPER SCHOOL CHARACTERS

AVERY, HERK
See HAMBRY CHARACTERS: SHERIFF'S OFFICE

B

BALAZAR, ENRICO
In *The Drawing of the Three*, Enrico Balazar (also known as **EMILIO BALAZAR** and **"IL ROCHE"**) is a high-caliber big shot in New York's drug world. For a very short while, EDDIE DEAN works for him as a drug runner. Although his mob is based in BROOKLYN, Balazar's headquarters are in a Midtown bar called THE LEANING TOWER. The first time Roland sees the neon sign for this bar he thinks he is approaching the TOWER itself.

Balazar is a second-generation Sicilian who looks like both a fat Italian peasant and a small-time Mafioso. However, despite his looks (and his nasty business methods), he has a quiet and cultured voice. He also has an associate's degree from the New York University Business School. One of

Balazar's passions is building houses (or perhaps I should say palaces) out of cards. In fact, he once shot a man (called **"THE MICK"**) for blowing down his creation.

In *The Drawing of the Three*, a very ill Roland and a naked Eddie Dean have a shootout with Balazar's men in the Leaning Tower. They escape after killing Balazar and his thugs. One of the most grisly weapons launched at Eddie during this fray is the decapitated head of his brother, HENRY DEAN.

II:47, II:48, II:50, II:61, II:70, II:91–92, II:96, II:100, II:106, II:107–113 *(under discussion)*, II:113–20, II:121, II:124, II:125–35, II:137, II:140, II:142–50 *(shot)*, II:156, II:179, II:204, II:205, II:206, II:244, II:309, II:349, II:369, II:398, III:17, III:51, III:67, III:68, III:180, III:262, III:340, III:346

> **TIO VERONE:** Balazar's uncle who told him never to trust a junkie.   II:118

BALAZAR'S MEN:

> **ALEXANDER, TRUMAN:** Truman Alexander died four years before our story takes place. He was one of the thugs who buried "The Mick" under a chicken house in Sedonville, Connecticut.   II:117

> **ANDOLINI, CLAUDIO:** Claudio Andolini is Jack Andolini's younger brother. He is also one of Balazar's personal bodyguards. II:113–14, II:115–20 *(watching Balazar build with cards)*, II:125–35, II:142–47 *(shot)*, II:150

> **ANDOLINI, JACK:** Jack Andolini is known to his enemies as "Old Double-Ugly." Although his bulging forehead, bulky body, and tufted ears make him look like a Cro-Magnon, he's anything but stupid. Jack is Balazar's number-one lieutenant. Unfortunately for him, Andolini meets an especially nasty end. Told by his boss to follow Eddie into the headquarters' lavatory, he ends up being pulled by Eddie onto the monster-infested beach of the WESTERN SEA, where he is devoured by LOBSTROSITIES. At least he died in the line of duty.   II:91–95 *(tailing)*, II:105 *(in truck)*, II:106–13, II:115, II:122, II:125–41 *(eaten by lobstrosities)*, II:142, II:143, II:144, II:154, II:297, III:52, III:53

> **BIONDI, GEORGE:** George Biondi is known as "Big George" to his friends and "Big Nose" to his enemies. During a game of Trivial Pursuit he gives HENRY DEAN his final deadly fix.   II:114, II:119–20, II:123–24, II:132–33, II:150–51

> **BLAKE, KEVIN:** Redheaded Kevin Blake is one of the hit men who played a final (and deadly) game of Trivial Pursuit with HENRY DEAN. During the battle he lobs Henry's decapitated head at EDDIE.   II:123–24, II:151–52, II:153

DARIO: Although he is one of Balazar's "gentlemen," during the LEANING TOWER's shoot-out he's accidentally killed by TRICKS POSTINO's incredible Rambo machine.   II:148–49

DRETTO, CARLOCIMI ('CIMI): 'Cimi Dretto is one of Balazar's personal bodyguards. Along with ALEXANDER TRUMAN he buried "The Mick" under a chicken house in Connecticut. The Mick's crime? Blowing down Balazar's house of cards.   II:113–14, II:115–20 *(watches Balazar build a house of cards)*, II:124, II:125, II:129, II:133, II:142–47 *(shot)*

    BITCH-OF-A-WIFE: II:115–16

    FATHER: II:116

    LA MONSTRA: 'Cimi's much-hated mother-in-law.   II:115–16

GINELLI: Ginelli owns both the FOUR FATHERS Restaurant and the Ginelli's Pizza truck. He is a mobster in cahoots with Balazar. II:91–95 *(his truck follows Eddie)*, II:105, II:349

HASPIO, JIMMY: II:123–24, II:150 *(shot)*

POSTINO, TRICKS: With a name like Tricks, this guy couldn't become anything other than a hit man. He is part of the deadly Trivial Pursuit game that takes place in Balazar's headquarters. II:114, II:123–24, II:132–33, II:142–49 *(shot)*, II:151

VECHHIO, RUDY: II:151

VINCENT, COL: Col Vincent is a "glorified goofer" with a big yellow-toothed grin. He smells like old sweat.   II:91–95 *(tailing)*, II:105 *(in truck)*, II:106–13, II:120, II:122, II:125–35 *(present)*

BALAZAR'S NASSAU CONNECTION:

SALLOW BRITISH MAN: This guy tries to give EDDIE DEAN poison rather than a heroin fix. He hopes to kill Eddie or at least screw up his drug run and rob him. Eddie wins out.   II:47–51, II:58

WILSON, WILLIAM: William Wilson is a soft-spoken American who specializes in strapping drugs onto smugglers. Although he doesn't know it, he shares a name with the narrator of Edgar Allan Poe's famous story entitled "William Wilson."   II:57, II:74

MICK, THE: See BALAZAR entry, above.

**'BAMA
See CHAMBERS, JAKE

BASALE, MIGUEL
See DEAN, SUSANNAH

**BEAST, THE
See GUARDIANS OF THE BEAM

BEECH, MRS.
See HAMBRY CHARACTERS: OTHER CHARACTERS

BIBLICAL FIGURES (OUR WORLD)
See APPENDIX III

BIG COFFIN HUNTERS
The Big Coffin Hunters, also known as regulators, were the harriers and outlaws that Roland, CUTHBERT, and ALAIN were forced to fight in HAMBRY. Although they initially hid their true allegiance from Roland and his friends, Roland's *ka-tet* eventually found out that the Big Coffin Hunters worked for FARSON. Despite appearances, the Big Coffin Hunters held much of the power in MEJIS (much more than the mayor, HART THORIN) and were working to bring down the AFFILIATION. The Coffin Hunters gained their name from the blue, coffin-shaped tattoos located on the webbing between right thumb and forefinger.
　　IV:65, IV:115–16, IV:142 *(as harriers and outlaws)*, IV:144, IV:154–55 *(hired by Rimer)*, IV:155 *(coffin tattoo)*, IV:177, IV:214, IV:225, IV:228, IV:234, IV:260, IV:265–66 *(tied to Vi Castas Mining Co.)*, IV:266 *(regulator tattoos)*, IV:285, IV:290, IV:292, IV:301, IV:305, IV:327, IV:342, IV:344 *(indirect reference)*, IV:347, IV:360, IV:374, IV:376, IV:424, IV:453, IV:468, IV:470, IV:472, IV:473, IV:487, IV:488, IV:498, IV:506, IV:508, IV:509, IV:546, IV:645

　　DEPAPE, ROY: Roy Depape was a twenty-five-year-old redhead who wore gold-rimmed glasses. His laughter sounded like the braying of a loud donkey. Roy was obsessed with a fifteen-year-old whore named DEBORAH who wouldn't give up working. This often put Roy in a foul humor. In fact, the standoff at The TRAVELLERS' REST was the direct result of Depape's black mood and his desire to vent his rage on innocent SHEEMIE. As punishment for the events at the Rest, ELDRED JONAS, leader of the Coffin Hunters, sent Depape to the town of RITZY. While there, Depape learned Roland's true identity.
　　Although not particularly clever, Depape had plenty of spite in him. On Jonas's orders, he killed HART THORIN and then framed Roland, CUTHBERT, and ALAIN for the murder. To incriminate the boys, he left both Cuthbert's LOOKOUT and a drawing of FARSON's *sigul* next to Thorin's corpse.   IV:65, IV:116, IV:119 *(age)*, IV:141, IV:142 *(indirect reference)*, IV:154–55, IV:172, IV:173, IV:175–76, IV:214–22 *(Travellers' Rest standoff. 214 blue coffins. 215 described)*, IV:224–32 *(Travellers' Rest standoff continued.*

230 red hair, 231 glasses), IV:265–71 *(goes to Ritzy and learns Roland's identity),* IV:271, IV:285, IV:286, IV:292 *(red hair),* IV:301, IV:305, IV:318, IV:347–49, IV:350, IV:352, IV:363, IV:371, IV:377, IV:378, IV:382, IV:385, IV:386, IV:403–5, IV:420–25, IV:451, IV:462–63, IV:472–73 *(kills Thorin. Leaves Cuthbert's Lookout and Farson's* sigul*),* IV:478, IV:480, IV:483–85, IV:487–93, IV:498–99, IV:503, IV:522, IV:528, IV:539, IV:542–46 *(present for action),* IV:553–57 *(557 killed by Roland)*

DEBORAH: Deborah was Depape's fifteen-year-old whore. Her real name was **GERT MOGGINS.** Deborah was also known as "Her Nibs," "Her Majesty," and "Roy's Coronation Cunt." Gert preferred to call herself a "cotton-gilly." IV:173 *(described),* IV:214–15, IV:266, IV:447, IV:605

JONAS, ELDRED: Eldred Jonas was the leader of the Big Coffin Hunters. He was a failed gunslinger who was lamed in one leg by CORT's father, FARDO. Like other failed gunslingers, limping Jonas was sent west, and in bitterness he took up the cause of JOHN FARSON.

Jonas had tufted eyebrows, long silky white hair, and a white mustache. Often described as a white-haired wolf, he seemed to have held some palaver with the MANNI since he knew about travel between worlds. Jonas's back was covered with scars which he said were inflicted in GARLAN. We don't know why. Jonas became CORAL THORIN's lover. Roland killed him after taking MAER-LYN'S GRAPEFRUIT from him. I:86, IV:65, IV:115–17 *(described),* IV:119, IV:121, IV:130 *(indirect reference),* IV:141, IV:142, IV:154 *(described),* IV:155, IV:172–78 *(failed gunslinger. 175 travels through "special doors" to other worlds!),* IV:191–210 *(Thorin's party. 195–97 described; 206–8; 209),* IV:211, IV:213 *(called "Il Spectro"),* IV:214, IV:220, IV:221–22 *(joins standoff at Travellers' Rest),* IV:224–32 *(227 with Sheriff Avery; 230–32 Big Coffin Hunters' palaver),* IV:235, IV:245, IV:249, IV:266, IV:269, IV:270, IV:271, IV:285, IV:286, IV:292, IV:301, IV:318, IV:327, IV:328–29 *(with Cordelia),* IV:330, IV:331, IV:336, IV:342, IV:347–53 *(349 tufted eyebrows),* IV:356, IV:358, IV:362–64, IV:367–68, IV:371–74 *(Cordelia tells him about Roland and Susan),* IV:375–80 *(as white-haired wolf; 380 finds rook's skull!),* IV:384–87, IV:388, IV:390–92 *(defaces Bar K),* IV:393–94 *(defacement continued),* IV:399–400, IV:401, IV:403–8 *(sent west by Fardo),* IV:411, IV:420–25, IV:434, IV:443, IV:448, IV:453, IV:456, IV:460, IV:466, IV:472, IV:473, IV:474, IV:478–80 *(479 Roland reveals that Jonas is a failed gun-slinger),* IV:483–85, IV:487–93, IV:496, IV:500, IV:501, IV:502,

IV:515, IV:519–23, IV:525 *(mentioned)*, IV:527–29, IV:530, IV:532–35, IV:536, IV:537–46, IV:548, IV:553–60 *(attacked by Roland's ka-tet; 559 killed by Roland)*, IV:561–62, IV:570, IV:579, IV:586, IV:592, IV:628, IV:645, IV:646, IV:649, IV:664, E:195

REYNOLDS, CLAY: Although not as sly as JONAS, Clay Reynolds—the final member of the Coffin Hunter *ka-tet*—was smarter than ROY DEPAPE. Although he walked with his left foot turned in, Reynolds was a vain womanizer who liked to swirl his fancy silk-lined cloak. He was either a redhead (see IV:173 and IV:537) or black-haired (IV:226).

Along with CORAL THORIN, Reynolds was one of the few of Roland's enemies to escape HAMBRY alive. Clay and Coral became lovers and formed a gang of professional bank robbers. Their gang was eventually trapped by a sheriff in the town of OAKLEY. Reynolds ended up dancing the hanged-man's jig.   IV:65, IV:116, IV:119, IV:141, IV:142 *(indirect reference)*, IV:154–55, IV:173–78 *(173 red hair)*, IV:214–22 *(Travellers' Rest standoff)*, IV:224–32 *(standoff continued. 226 black hair)*, IV:245, IV:265, IV:269, IV:270, IV:272, IV:292, IV:298 *(tracks and left foot)*, IV:301, IV:347–49 *(more intelligent than Depape)*, IV:352, IV:363–64, IV:367–68, IV:371, IV:377, IV:378, IV:383, IV:385–86, IV:404, IV:420–25, IV:451–52, IV:470–71 *(stabs Rimer)*, IV:480, IV:483–85, IV:487–93, IV: 521–23, IV:527–29, IV:532–35, IV:537–46, IV:548–49, IV:558, IV:565–70 *(Sheemie follows Reynolds and Susan)*, IV:585–87, IV:603–8 *(puts rope around Susan's neck. Present as she burns)*, IV:623 *(Bank robber and Coral Thorin's lover. Both killed)*

LITTLE COFFIN HUNTERS: This is the term HAMBRY folk used for Roland's *ka-tet*. Needless to say, Roland didn't like it much.   IV: 260, IV:287

BILLY-BUMBLER (GENERAL INFORMATION)

Billy-Bumblers look like a cross between raccoons, woodchucks, and dachshunds. They have black-and-gray-striped fur and lovely gold-ringed eyes. Bumblers wag their tails like dogs but are much more intelligent than canines. Bumblers are good ratters. Before the world moved on, every Barony Castle in Mid-World kept a dozen or so. Bumblers were also used to herd sheep.

In the days they lived with men, Bumblers could parrot the words they heard; some of them could even count and add. Few wild ones seem to remember how to speak, although JAKE's pet OY does. By the time Roland draws his new *ka-tet* into Mid-World, most of the Bumblers rove in wild packs. They are harmless but annoying. See entry under OY.

III:18, III:159, III:164, III:220–22, III:253, III:327
OLD GROOM FROM ROLAND'S YOUTH WHO PRAISED BUM-BLERS: III:221, III:253–54

BILLY THE KID
See GUNSLINGERS (OUR WORLD)

BIONDI, GEORGE
See BALAZAR'S MEN

BISSETTE, LEN
See PIPER SCHOOL CHARACTERS

BLAINE
See NORTH CENTRAL POSITRONICS

BLAKE, KEVIN
See BALAZAR'S MEN

BLUE
See SUSANNAH DEAN: ODETTA HOLMES'S ASSOCIATES

BORDER DWELLERS
Border Dwellers were the people who lived beyond TULL, just on the edges of the MOHAINE DESERT. Their partially submerged huts had low sod roofs and were designed to retain nighttime coolness. Dwellers burned devil grass for fuel, though they refused to look into the flames, which they believed contained beckoning devils. Their main crop was corn, though they occasionally grew peas. All of these meager crops had to be watered from deep hand-dug wells.

Many dwellers were either madmen or lepers, suffering from a disease known as the rot. The mad preacher SYLVIA PITTSTON was originally a border dweller.

I:12, I:15, I:44, II:32, III:42

**BROWN: Brown's hut was the last Roland came across before his long and almost deadly journey into the MOHAINE DESERT. Although his long, strawberry-colored hair was ringleted and wild, Brown was neither a madman nor a rotter. He lived with his pet raven, ZOLTAN, and his thin, thirsty corn crop.

In the new version of *The Gunslinger*, we learn that Brown's wife was MANNI and that he spent some time living with this sect. When Roland met him, Brown's speech was still peppered with terms such as "thee" and "thou."   I:15–22, I:64–65, I:72, I:85, III:42, IV:570, IV:628

PAPPA DOC: Pappa Doc brought beans to Brown. His name is very close to that of the Haitian despot Papa (Poppa) Doc Duvalier. I:16, I:18, I:20

ZOLTAN: Zoltan, the scrawny talking raven, was the rather sinister companion of BROWN, the redheaded Border Dweller. Zoltan's favorite sayings were "Beans, beans, the musical fruit, the more you eat the more you toot" and "Screw you and the horse you rode in on." He ate the eyes of Roland's dead mule.   I:16–22, I:64–65, I:72, I:85–86, III:41, III:42, IV:628

BRANDON
See GRAYS: GRAY HIGH COMMAND

BRIGGS, MR.
See CHARLIE THE CHOO-CHOO

**BROADCLOAK, MARTEN
Although Marten Broadcloak was STEVEN DESCHAIN's sorcerer, he was actually an enemy of the AFFILIATION. In a carefully orchestrated bit of treachery, Marten seduced Roland's mother, GABRIELLE, and then exposed the shameful affair so that Roland—raging that his father had been cuckolded and dishonored—would face his test of manhood years too early. Marten's hope was that Roland would fail his test and be sent west, into exile. To Marten's chagrin, Roland succeeded in besting his teacher CORT and won his guns at the unheard-of age of fourteen.

In *Wizard and Glass*, we learn that Gabrielle conspired to kill her husband, Steven Deschain. It seems most likely that her poisoned knife came from Marten. This plot also failed, though at the eventual cost of Gabrielle's life. (Not long after this event, Roland shot her.) Years later, Marten was delivered into Roland's hands by WALTER, the sorcerer who poses as the MAN IN BLACK.

In the new *Gunslinger*, Marten's identity takes a further twist. Marten is still Steven Deschain's sorcerer, but he is now also his foremost counselor. But unbeknownst to the elder Deschain, Marten is simultaneously his many-faced enemy.

Under the name JOHN FARSON, Marten is actually the force behind the revolutions tearing MID-WORLD'S AFFILIATION apart. He is also the penitent WALTER that Roland knew in his youth, and WALTER O'DIM, otherwise known as the MAN IN BLACK. Hence, like his alter-ego Walter, Marten is both a minion of the TOWER and an evil agent of THE CRIMSON KING.

I:86, I:94, I:95, I:106 *(as the good man)*, I:125, I:131, I:140 *(killed)*, I:151–52, I:159–61, I:164, I:167, I:172, I:173, I:175, I:205–6 *(possessed by Walter)*, I:213, II:103, II:250, II:362, III:41, III:44, III:124, III:417, IV:7, IV:65, IV:107, IV:110–12, IV:163, IV:164, IV:165, IV:223, IV:258, IV:275 *(and voice of thinny in Eyebolt Canyon)*, IV:436, IV:619 *(with Farson)*, IV:647–49 *(claims to be Flagg)*, IV:652–56, IV:665

BROWN
See BORDER DWELLERS

BRUMHALL, DR.
See KATZ: KATZ'S EMPLOYEES, CUSTOMERS AND COMPETITORS

BUCKSKIN
See JOHNS, ALAIN

BUNKOWSKI, DEWEY
See DEAN, EDDIE: EDDIE'S ASSOCIATES, PAST AND PRESENT

BUNKOWSKI, MRS.
See DEAN, EDDIE: EDDIE'S ASSOCIATES, PAST AND PRESENT

BURLINGTON ZEPHYR
See CHARLIE THE CHOO-CHOO

C

CAM TAM
See ELURIA: CHARACTERS

CAPRICHOSO (CAPI)
See HAMBRY CHARACTERS: TRAVELLERS' REST: SHEEMIE

CARTOON CHARACTERS (OUR WORLD)
See APPENDIX III

CASSIDY, BUTCH
See GUNSLINGERS (OUR WORLD)

CASSIOPEIA
In one of Mid-World's folktales, Cassiopeia causes the breakup between OLD MOTHER (South Star) and OLD STAR (North Star). Old Mother (Lydia) caught Old Star (Apon) flirting with this sweet young thing. Cassiopeia found the whole affair quite humorous.
   III:36–37

CASTNER
See TULL CHARACTERS: SYLVIA PITTSTON'S REVIVAL

CHAMBERS, ELMER
Elmer Chambers is JAKE's father. He is a TV network big shot who works at 70 Rockefeller Plaza. His job is to destroy other networks and he is very good at it. In fact, he is a self-proclaimed master of "The Kill."
   Elmer is five-foot-ten, a chain-smoker, and a coke fiend. His black crew cut bolts straight up from his head. Jake thinks he looks like a man who has just suffered some tremendous, galvanizing shock. Elmer smokes Camels.
   I:81, I:82, I:180, III:89–91, III:92, III:93, III:94, III:99, III:100, III:102, III:103, III:108, III:121–22, III:126, III:129–35, III:136, III:137–38, III:156–58, III:168, III:194, III:256, III:315, III:355, III:376, III:380, IV:21, IV:31, IV:32 (indirect), IV:80 (parents), IV:85 (parents), IV:93, IV:655

**CHAMBERS, JAKE
Jake's real name is JOHN CHAMBERS. At eleven years old, he is the youngest member of Roland's present ka-tet. Jake is small for his age and (in his previous life) was often mistaken for a girl. However, his time in Mid-World has toughened him up.
   Before being brought to Mid-World, blond, blue-eyed Jake was in the sixth grade at PIPER, his expensive private middle school. A loner, he had few friends and felt estranged from his parents, who were always too busy for him. Jake spent most of his time under the care of professional people, even though he despised all professional people. At this point in his life, Jake was dangerously close to despising himself.
   Jake first met Roland at the WAY STATION in the MOHAINE DESERT. He traveled with Roland, pursuing the MAN IN BLACK, until Roland betrayed him in pursuit of his elusive TOWER. As Jake fell into a deep river chasm below the CYCLOPEAN MOUNTAINS he

said, "There are other worlds than these." It turns out that Jake was right. There *ARE* many worlds, and alternate Jakes exist in almost all of them.

Jake gained his first entry into Roland's world after he was hit by a blue Cadillac (a 1976 Sedan de Ville) on the corner of Fifth Avenue and Forty-Third Street on May 9th, 1977, at 8:25 A.M. In *The Waste Lands*, he reentered Roland's world through a linked doorway. In our world the door existed within a haunted MANSION. In Roland's world EDDIE DEAN drew a linking door in the center of a SPEAKING RING. Jake's second Mid-World birth happened on June 1st, 1977, the day after he found both the MANHATTAN RESTAURANT OF THE MIND and the vacant LOT.

In *The Waste Lands*, Jake briefly goes by the alias **TOM DENBY**. In the new *Gunslinger*, we find out that MRS. SHAW nicknamed him 'BAMA. I:74–95, I:112–13, I:117–26, I:129, I:132–44, I:149–58, I:174–92, I:198 *(indirect)*, I:215, I:216, II:15 *(as sailor)*, II:31, II:32 *(Isaac)*, II:37, II:101, II:105, II:203, II:231, II:254, II:315–18 *(and Jack Mort)*, II:319, III:29–30, III:35–36, III:41–48, III:50, III:51, III:59, III:78, III:86, III:89–146 *(89–102 looking for magic door)*, III:149, III:151, III:152–58, III:162, III:165–70 *(169 as Tom Denby)*, III:172–73, III:175–76, III:176–78, III:179, III:180, III:181 *(coming into Mid-World)*, III:182–88, III:190–92, III:193–94 *(born)*, III:194–96, III:197, III:198–201, III:202, III:203–4, III:205–13, III:219–67, III:268, III:269, III:273–81, III:283–303 *(294 Oy almost falls off bridge; 300 Gasher)*, III:304–7, III:307–8 *(Roland follows)*, III:312–14, III:314–16 *(Roland follows)*, III:323 *(indirect)*, III:325–28, III:328–31 *(Roland follows)*, III:334–39, III:340, III:341, III:342, III:349, III:350–61, III:364, III:365–72, III:373–85 *(Roland and Jake escape Grays. Run to Blaine's cradle)*, III:389, III:393–420, IV:3–10 *(Blaine)*, IV:13–42 *(30 Edith Bunker, sex goddess; 31–35 Falls of the Hounds)*, IV:44–70 *(61 leave Blaine; 64 sound of thinny; 64 & 67 saw player, Central Park)*, IV:71–112 *(Topeka train station; 72–77 Topeka Capital Journal; 83 reflects on Forty-Sixth and Second; 86–87 roses; 87–89 Charlie the Choo-Choo in Topeka; 91 sign of Crimson King; 95 enters thinny; 97 Oz palace in distance; 106–12 Roland begins story)*, IV:335–37 *(interlude in Kansas)*, IV:414, IV:570 and 572 *(Roland's vision)*, IV:615–25 *(end of Roland's story; back in Topeka)*, IV:626–68 *(626 ruby Oxfords; 632 Green Palace; 634 gate like Wizard's Rainbow; 646 Tick-Tock; 648 Flagg; 652 Roland's matricide)*

JAKE'S ASSOCIATES, PAST AND PRESENT:

CHAMBERS, ELMER: Listed separately

CHAMBERS, LAURIE: Listed separately

CHARLIE THE CHOO-CHOO CHARACTERS: See CHARLIE THE CHOO-CHOO, listed separately

DOORMAN, JAKE'S APARTMENT BUILDING: III:129
PIPER SCHOOL STAFF AND STUDENTS: See PIPER SCHOOL CHARACTERS, listed separately
**SHAW, GRETA: Greta Shaw works as a housekeeper for the CHAMBERS family and looks like Edith Bunker. Mrs. Shaw is one of the few professional people that Jake actually likes. In fact, she qualifies as one of his "almost" friends. In the new *Gunslinger*, we find out that she nicknamed Jake 'Bama. I:81–82, III:91, III:102, III:106, III:107–8, III:129–30, III:133–37, IV:30 *(and Edith Bunker)*, IV:64 *(Central Park saw player)*
TIMMY: Timmy was one of the regulars at Mid-Town Lanes. He either worked there or was one of the bowlers. When Jake began to suffer from a split psyche, Timmy told him to go home and drink plenty of clear fluids, like gin and vodka.   III:107
CHARACTERS JAKE MEETS WHEN HE GOES TO SEE ROSE, AND THEN WHEN HE RUNS AWAY TO BROOKLYN AND MID-WORLD:
DEEPNEAU, AARON: See DEEPNEAU, AARON, listed separately
DUTCH HILL CHARACTERS:
  DELIVERY VAN DRIVER: III:204–5
  LITTLE LEAGUE PLAYERS: III:204
  WOMEN OUTSIDE OF DUTCH HILL USED APPLIANCES: III:204–5
ELI: Jake met this guy—who happened to have dreadlocks and a canary yellow suit—while he was sitting in TIMES SQUARE. III:168
GUARD AT MET: III:167
MAN WHO BUMPS INTO PROSTITUTE: III:169
MARK CROSS PEN BUSINESSMEN: Jake saw two of these guys playing tic-tac-toe on a wall. One of them was named BILLY. III:110–11
MESSENGER BOY ON BIKE: III:111
OLD MAN FROM BROOKLYN: This old guy told Jake that there was no such thing as a MARKEY ACADEMY.   III:177–78
PIPER SCHOOL CHARACTERS: See PIPER SCHOOL CHARACTERS, listed separately.
PRETTY BLACK TEACHER AT THE MET: This woman discovered Jake while he was on "French leave." She told him to rejoin his class, not realizing just how far Jake was from it.   III:166–67
TIMES SQUARE COP: While Jake was wasting time in TIMES

SQUARE, this cop pegged him as a runaway. Jake mesmerized this bluecoat with his magic key. He also hid his true identity by giving the false name TOM DENBY.   III:167–69

TIMES SQUARE PROSTITUTE: Jake wasn't certain what this woman did for a living, but he was fairly certain that she wasn't a librarian.   III:169

TOWER, CALVIN: See TOWER, CALVIN, listed separately

YOUNG PUERTO RICAN LADY: III:120

WITNESSED JAKE'S DEATH:

BLACK MAN SELLING PRETZELS: I:83, III:103–7, III:112

BUSINESSMAN IN BLUE HAT WITH JAUNTY FEATHER: This man ran over Jake with his 1976 Sedan de Ville Cadillac. I:83, III:104–6

CHICANO GUY: III:104–6

FAT LADY WITH BLOOMINGDALE'S BAG: III:103–6, III:112

TALL MAN IN NAILHEAD WORSTED SUIT: III:103–6

TOOKER'S WHOLESALE TOYS (DRIVES BY): III:104

WHITE GIRL IN SWEATER AND SKIRT: III:104–6

WOMAN IN BLACK HAT NET: I:83

CHAMBERS, LAURIE

Laurie Chambers is JAKE'S mother. She is "scrawny in a sexy way," has a cultured Vassar voice and tends to go to bed with her sick friends. In *Wizard and Glass*, she is called **MEGAN CHAMBERS.**

I:81, I:82, I:135, III:89–90, III:92, III:99, III:100, III:102, III:106, III:108, III:129–35, III:137–38, III:156, III:157–58, III:168, III:186, III:355, IV:80 *(parents)*, IV: 85 *(parents)*, IV:655 *(Megan)*

**CHARLES SON OF CHARLES

In the new version of *The Gunslinger*, Charles son of Charles is the unlucky gunslinger who "drew the black stone" and so had to act as HAX's hangman.

CHARLIE THE CHOO-CHOO

Jake bought *Charlie the Choo-Choo*—a children's book about a talking 402 Big Boy Steam Locomotive—at the MANHATTAN RESTAURANT OF THE MIND, a bookstore owned and operated by CALVIN TOWER. Charlie (whom Jake finds sinister despite his apparent friendliness) prefigures BLAINE, the insane Mono. Like Blaine, Charlie is part of the MID-WORLD RAILWAY and terminates in TOPEKA.

Throughout *Charlie the Choo-Choo*, Charlie sings this song:

> Don't ask me silly questions,
> I won't play silly games.
> I'm just a simple choo-choo train
> And I'll always be the same.
>
> I only want to race along
> Beneath the bright blue sky,
> And be a happy choo-choo train
> Until the day I die.

Charlie's nasty double, Blaine, actually likes silly games, if not EDDIE DEAN's silly questions. Both versions of the Mid-World Railway seem to be connected to the ATCHISON, TOPEKA, AND SANTA FE RAILROAD that once crossed much of the American West on our level of the TOWER.
   III:114, III:116, III:125, III:128, III:129, III:133, III:134, III:138–46, III:153, III:156, III:186, III:254, III:255, III:263, III:265–67, III:270, III:278, III:343, III:400, IV:71, IV:87–89 *(in Reinisch Rose Garden, Topeka)*

   BRIGGS, MR.: Roadhouse manager.   III:141–42

   BURLINGTON ZEPHYR: He's the 5,000-horsepower diesel engine who is supposed to be Charlie's replacement.   III:141–45, III:254–55

   ENGINEER BOB (BOB BROOKS): Charlie's driver and friend. III:139–46, III:245, III:255, III:266, IV:87–88, IV:101 *(and Eddie's bulldozer dream)*

      DECEASED WIFE: III:141, III:146

   EVANS, BERYL: Beryl Evans was the author of this sweetly sinister children's book. She also happened to share her name with one of the victims of the 1940s British serial killer John Reginald Halliday Christie. On our level of the Tower, Cristie killed both Beryl and her baby daughter. It's no wonder Beryl wrote scary books.   III:114, III:139–45, IV:71, IV:88

   MARTIN, RAYMOND: President of Mid-World Railway Co. III:141–42, III:143–46, III:255

   MARTIN, SUSANNAH: Daughter of Raymond Martin.   III:142, III:143–45, III:146

   MID-WORLD RAILWAY CO: (See this entry in the PORTALS AND MAGICAL PLACES section.)   III:139–46

CHAS
   See ELURIA: CHARACTERS

CLAYPOOL, FRANK
   See HAMBRY CHARACTERS: SHERIFF'S OFFICE

CLEMENTS, JUSTIN
Justin Clements owns CLEMENTS GUNS AND SPORTING GOODS
and is one of BALAZAR's associates. He is also known as **ARNOLD**
CLEMENTS. The police have been after him for years. His brother-in-
law, FAT JOHNNY HOLDEN, runs the shop for him.
   II:343, II:347, II:348–49, II:376

CÖOS, RHEA
   See RHEA OF THE CÖOS

COPPERHEAD
   See GRAYS: GRAY HIGH COMMAND

COQUINA, SISTER
   See ELURIA, LITTLE SISTERS OF

CORCORAN, JOHN
   See TOPEKA CHARACTERS

CORT
Cort was Roland's teacher. Like his father, FARDO, Cort trained generations of gunslingers. Described as a scarred, bald, squat man with
bowlegs and a bulging belly of solid muscle, he was a violent carouser who
frequented the brothels of GILEAD's lower town. He also happened to be
blind on one side—most likely the result of an ancient battle, brawling, or
teaching injury. Cort called the apprentices "maggots." Coming from him,
it was an almost affectionate term. His job was to train young gunslingers as killers, and he was excellent at it. In *The Gunslinger* we witness
Roland's coming-of-age battle with his teacher. If every gunslinger entered
manhood with such a fierce fight, it is surprising that Cort reached middle age at all.
   Evidently, Cort had a philosophical side. Roland believes that he often
held palaver with the mystical MANNI. He was also Gilead's finest riddler,
though he was intolerant of cheaters. During one of the Fair-Day riddling
contests, Cort stabbed a wandering singer and acrobat who had stolen the
judge's answers.
   Like his father's before him, Cort's end was not a good one. Two weeks
after Roland's *ka-tel* loaded their guns for the first time, Cort was dead.
Roland thinks he was poisoned.

I:65, I:86, I:95, I:96–100, I:104, I:107, I:108–9, I:110, I:124 *(creation of mescaline)*, I:127, I:135, I:137, I:149, I:162–73 *(Roland's coming of age)*, I:213, II:16, II:28, II:36, II:66, II:104, II:166, II:167, II:174, II:177, II:180, II:249, II:250, II:251, II:304, II:309, II:361, II:383, III:11, III:13 *(indirect)*, III:14, III:41, III:259, III:276, III:277, III:280, III:328, III:418–19, IV:8 *(Gilead riddling)*, IV:9, IV:33–34 *(knowledge of other worlds)*, IV:70, IV:107, IV:109, IV:110, IV:160 *(described)*, IV:178 *(his father lamed Jonas)*, IV:197, IV:286, IV:321, IV:325, IV:326, IV:344, IV:407 *(see Cort's father, FARDO)*, IV:436, IV:479, IV:523, IV:650, IV:664, E:163–64

FARDO: Cort's father. He, too, taught generations of gunslingers. IV:178, IV:407

****MARK:** In the new version of *The Gunslinger*, we learn that Cort's predecessor was named Mark. He died in the yard behind the GREAT HALL, stabbed to death by an overzealous student.

WANDERING SINGER AND ACROBAT: This man was cross-eyed and wore a cap of bells. Cort killed him for attempting to cheat in a riddling contest.   III:277

COUNTESS JILLIAN OF UP'ARD KILLIAN
See HAMBRY CHARACTERS: TRAVELLERS' REST

CRESSIA CHARACTERS
HIGH SHERIFF: Beheaded by Farson.   IV:163
INDRIE'S MAYOR: Beheaded by Farson.   IV:163

**CRIMSON KING, THE
Although Roland doesn't know who the Crimson King is, we do. We met him in one of Stephen King's other novels, namely *Insomnia*. If Roland is a soldier of the White, then the Crimson King is his natural enemy. This prince of chaos is a shape-shifter whose true form is red-eyed and fanged.

In the new *Gunslinger*, SYLVIA PITTSTON claims that the Crimson King is the Antichrist who will lead men into the flaming bowels of perdition. He is behind every fleshly pleasure, and is the wicked force that created the destructive machines imprinted with LaMERK FOUNDRY. However, despite her sermons, Sylvia Pittston is seduced by the Crimson King's power. Believing that WALTER is the King's angel, she lets him impregnate her with his master's demonic child. Roland removes the demon by inserting his gun into Pittston's vagina and screwing her with it. The child dies, but in response, Pittston raises her congregation against Roland.

In the new *Gunslinger*, Walter tells Roland that the Red King already controls the TOWER and that the earth has been delivered into his hand. Although the Crimson King may turn his blazing red eye toward the kingdoms of the mortal worlds, he is far from mortal himself. Roland has a larger and more powerful enemy than he ever imagined, and that enemy has opposed him from the beginning. FARSON's *sigul,* which was used to frame Roland's *ka-tet* in HAMBRY, depicted the Crimson King's red eye. This is not surprising since, in the new *Gunslinger,* we find out that Farson is actually none other than Walter, the servant of the Red King.

IV:91(*"WATCH FOR THE WALKIN' DUDE"*; *"ALL HAIL THE CRIMSON KING"*), IV:100 *(Eddie's bulldozer dream)*, IV:111 *(creature that rules Farson and MARTEN)*, IV:632, IV:666

CROSS DOG
See JESUS DOG under ELURIA CHARACTERS

CROW, JIM
See "JIM CROW"

CROYDEN, JOHN
See HAMBRY CHARACTERS: HORSEMEN'S ASSOCIATION

CUSTOMS
See DEAN, EDDIE: DELTA FLIGHT 901 CHARACTERS

CUTHBERT
See ALLGOOD, CUTHBERT

D

DARIO
See BALAZAR'S MEN

DAVID
David—named for the young boy in the biblical story of David and Goliath—was Roland's trained falcon. He was a pet, a comrade-at-arms, and a weapon. Roland used him in his coming-of-age battle against CORT. Cort said that hawks were God's gunslingers.

I:95, I:96–98, I:104, I:105, I:160, I:165–74, II:19, II:180, III:174, IV:107, IV:344, IV:547

DEAN, EDDIE (EDDIE CANTOR DEAN)

Eddie Dean is in his early twenties and has unruly black hair and hazel eyes. Originally from CO-OP CITY in BROOKLYN, the city boy Eddie has adjusted extremely well to Mid-World's landscape. He is married to SUSANNAH DEAN.

Before Roland drew Eddie through the freestanding ironwood door located on the LOBSTROSITY-infested beach of the WESTERN SEA, he entered Eddie's mind in the Our-World-*when* of 1987. At the time Eddie was a heroin addict running cocaine for the drug king ENRICO BALAZAR, in large part to keep his beloved but bullying older brother HENRY DEAN in drugs. Despite Eddie's nasty habit, Roland knew that Eddie was a born gunslinger. Early in their relationship, Roland compares him to a good gun sinking in quicksand.

Eddie is the human embodiment of the Tarot card called The Prisoner and so is an integral part of Roland's destiny—a future foretold by the sinister wizard WALTER, who is also known as the MAN IN BLACK. From the beginning of their association, Eddie reminds Roland of his old companion CUTHBERT ALLGOOD. In fact, Roland calls Eddie *ka-mai*, or *ka*'s fool, the term he often used for Bert.

Eddie is the only member of Roland's *ka-tet* who recognizes the fact that Roland may still sacrifice them all in pursuit of the TOWER. Despite this knowledge he, too, becomes addicted to the quest. In *The Waste Lands*, when our *ka-tet* is trying to draw JAKE CHAMBERS into Mid-World, we learn that Eddie has a magical skill. He is a key maker and can both create and unlock doors leading to other *when*s and *where*s. In other words, he can open portals leading to other levels of the Tower. Eddie's skill may yet prove to be a burden as well as a gift. The Tower leads to many parallel universes, not all of them pleasant.

I:130 *(Prisoner in prophecy of drawing)*, II:25 *(Prisoner)*, II:34–62 *(Prisoner's door; 38–57 Delta Flight 901)*, II:63–84, II:85–157 *(85 twenty-one years old; 85–90 Customs; 121–57 Balazar's)*, II:161–82 *(Lobstrosity Beach)*, II:201–9, II:225–305 *(235 twenty-three years old, born 1964)*, II:306–7 *(Detta thinks about him)*, II:307–12, II:315, II:316 *(Prisoner)*, II:324–26, II:327–38, II:339, II:357, II:359–61, II:367, II:371, II:379, II:386, II:387–90, II:393–99, III:11, III:12, III:13, III:16, III:18–19, III:21–86 *(25 Shardik/Mir attacks; 37 Roland's story; 51–54 dream)*, III:96, III:97 *(Prisoner)*, III:149–52, III:153–55 *(in Jake's dream)*, III:158–66, III:170–76 *(171 he is twenty-three years old)*, III:177–78 *(thirteen years old)*, III:178–82, III:183–88, III:189–90 *(drawing Jake)*, III:190–92 *(thirteen years old)*, III:193–94 *(drawing Jake)*, III:201–3, III:204, III:206–13, III:219–54, III:256–67, III:268–70, III:273–85, III:286–300 *(Gasher)*, III:302–4, III:308–12, III:316–25,

III:329, III:331–34, III:340–50, III:361–65 *(363 says Eddie was a junkie for six years. In earlier books he'd been shooting up for less than a year)*, III:372–73, III:378, III:382–85 *(Blaine)*, III:393–420, IV:3–10, IV:13–70 *(riddling; 42–45 flashback to own past; 49 decides to piss off Blaine; 51 begins to do it; 58–59 crash; 64 first thinny sound)*, IV:71–112 *(Topeka train station. 72–77 Topeka Capital-Journal and superflu; 79 Beam disappears; 87 Charlie the Choo-Choo in Topeka; 91 The Crimson King; 95 entering thinny; 97 Oz in distance; 99–101 Eddie's dream of bulldozer and rose; 102–3 discusses rose and Tower with Roland; 106 Roland begins his story)*, IV:335–37 *(interlude in Kansas)*, IV:570 and 572 *(Roland's vision)*, IV:581, IV:615–25 *(end of Roland's story; back in Topeka)*, IV:626–68 *(627 ruby Beatle-boots; 632 Green Palace; 634 gate like Wizard's Rainbow; 646 Tick-Tock; 648 Flagg; 652 Roland's matricide)*

EDDIE'S ASSOCIATES, PAST AND PRESENT:

BOY WITH BASKETBALL: This young black boy witnessed Eddie's interactions with BALAZAR'S MEN in CO-OP CITY. Thinking the boy might get into trouble if he talked too much, Eddie told the kid to forget everything he'd seen.   II:110, II:113

BUNKOWSKI, DEWEY: Dewey was one of Eddie and Henry's friends.   III:187

BUNKOWSKI, MRS.: She was Dewey's mom.   III:187

DEAN, GLORIA: Listed separately

DEAN, HENRY: Listed separately

DEAN, MRS.: Listed separately

HATHAWAY, MISS: Eddie's third-grade teacher.   II:295

KIDS FROM NORWOOD STREET (MURDERED BY MANSION DEMON): III:187

MARYANNE (MAJESTIC THEATER): See DEAN, HENRY

McGURSKY, MRS.: Eddie and Henry's neighbor.   II:175

POTZIE: Eddie Dean's cat.   II:111

UNCLE REG: Eddie's uncle. He worked as a painter on the Triborough Bridge and the George Washington Bridge.   III:292

DELTA FLIGHT 901 CHARACTERS, NASSAU TO JFK:

ANNE: Stewardess, Delta flight 901.   II:58

CABBIE: He helped Eddie make a quick getaway from the Priests of Customs.   II:90–91, II:95

CUSTOMS OFFICIALS: Roland called these guys the "Priests of Customs."   II:40, II:41, II:42, II:46, II:47, II:58, II:61–62, II:63, II:64, II:69, II:70, II:75 *(DEA)*, II:76, II:78, II:79–84, II:85–90 *(seven of them)*, II:91, II:92–95 *(following cab)*, II:96–99, II:104, II:111, II:112, II:119, II:205, II:239, II:241

DEERE: Copilot, 727 Delta flight 901.   II:74–76, II:78–84

DORNING, JANE: Stewardess, Delta flight 901. Jane Dorning was the first member of the flight crew to notice that something was not quite right with Eddie. She thought that Eddie was a terrorist. Her friend SUSY DOUGLAS realized that he was a drug smuggler.   II:38–39, II:45–46, II:52–55, II:56, II:58–60, II:61, II:64–69, II:75–76, II:78–83, II:86

> **BATTLE-AXE FLIGHT SCHOOL INSTRUCTOR:** She taught Jane how to spot potential terrorists. She was old enough to have flown with Wiley Post.   II:53–54, II:59

DOUGLAS, SUSY: Susy Douglas was also a stewardess on Eddie's fateful flight, and was friends with JANE DORNING. She spotted the cocaine bulges under Eddie's arms.   II:59–60, II:64–69, II:75–76, II:78–83

FLIGHT ENGINEER: II:75–76

McDONALD, CAPT.: Pilot of Delta Flight 901.   II:60, II:64, II:66, II:69, II:71, II:74–76, II:78–84

NAVIGATOR: II:75–76, II:78–84

OLD WOMAN EN ROUTE TO MONTREAL: II:78–79

PAULA: Stewardess, Delta flight 901.   II:53

PETER: Steward, Delta flight 901.   II:58

SALLOW BRITISH MAN: See BALAZAR, ENRICO: BALAZAR'S NASSAU CONNECTION

WILSON, WILLIAM: See BALAZAR, ENRICO: BALAZAR'S NASSAU CONNECTION

DEAN, GLORIA (SELINA DEAN)

Gloria Dean, also called Selina Dean, was EDDIE DEAN's older sister. She was run over by a drunk driver when she was six and Eddie was two. Poor Gloria was standing on the sidewalk at the time, watching a game of hopscotch.

   II:68 *(Selina)*, II:172, III:22

DRUNK DRIVER WHO KILLED HER: III:22

DEAN, HENRY

Henry was EDDIE DEAN's bossy and manipulative older brother. Eddie often refers to him as "the great sage and eminent junkie." Henry served in Vietnam and returned home with a bad knee and a worse Habit. Acne-scarred Henry was neither very attractive nor very bright, but he had one outstanding skill—he could make Eddie do whatever he wanted. Hence, he convinced Eddie to become a drug-runner for the dangerous mobster BALAZAR.

In many ways, Henry was the bane of Eddie's youth. Whenever Eddie tried to do something well—anything from playing basketball to woodcarving—Henry made fun of him for it. While under Balazar's "protection," Henry died of an overdose. One of Balazar's thugs then used Henry's head as a missile and lobbed it at Eddie.

II:41–42, II:46, II:47, II:48, II:51, II:52, II:61, II:68, II:71–72, II:77, II:81, II:86, II:87, II:88, II:95, II:97, II:99, II:106, II:107, II:108–9 *(Balazar has him)*, II:111–12, II:114, II:118–20, II:123–24, II:126–27, II:128, II:129, II:132–33, II:134, II:144–45, II:148, II:152 *(head only)*, II:154–56, II:169, II:171–76, II:178, II:206, II:207, II:209, II:233–34, II:237, II:239, II:254, II:276, II:287, II:309, II:337–38, II:398, III:21–23, III:24, III:26, III:27, III:41, III:59, III:72, III:75–76, III:84, III:85, III:150–51, III:154, III:161, III:162, III:174, III:179, III:180, III:183–88, III:189, III:190–92, III:207, III:333, III:344, III:348, IV:19, IV:25, IV:42–45 *(saying Eddie can talk the Devil into setting himself on fire)*, IV:49–50, IV:60

> MARYANNE:Maryanne was a blonde who worked at the MAJESTIC THEATER box office in CO-OP CITY. Henry probably had a crush on her, but instead of being nice he teased her until she cried.
> III:182–84, III:185, III:186

> HENRY DEAN'S KA-TET: IV:43–45, IV:60
> > BRANNIGAN, SKIPPER
> > DUGANELLI, FRANK
> > DRABNIK, CSABA (THE MAD FUCKIN HUNGARIAN)
> > FREDERICKS, TOMMY
> > McCAIN, LARRY
> > PARELLI, JOHN
> > POLINO, JIMMIE (JIMMIE POLIO): Jimmie had a clubfoot.
> > PRATT, GEORGIE
> TURNPIKIN FRIENDS: IV:90
> > CORBITT, SANDRA
> > O'HARA, BUM
> > POLINO, JIMMIE (JIMMIE POLIO)

DEAN, MRS.
Mrs. Dean was EDDIE, HENRY, and dead GLORIA's mother. She raised her kids alone, so we can assume that Eddie's father left when the children were very young. Mrs. Dean made Eddie feel like he owed his life to his older brother, who could have been great had he not had Eddie to watch out for. This was a complete family lie.

II:171–74, II:156 *(parents dead)*, II:206 *(indirect)*, II:239, III:22, III:28, III:60, III:76, III:179, III:185, III:187, III:188, III:207, III:235

MR. DEAN: Eddie has no memory of his father, since Mr. Dean deserted the family when Eddie was very small.   III:68, III:174

DEAN, SUSANNAH (ODETTA HOLMES/DETTA WALKER)

ODETTA HOLMES (the first of Susannah Dean's personalities) was the only child of the wealthy black dentist and inventor DAN HOLMES. She was named after the town of ODETTA, ARKANSAS, the place where her mother, ALICE, was born. Odetta lived in the penthouse of GREY-MARL APARTMENTS on Fifth Avenue and Central Park South. In the early 1960s, she was the only black resident at that exclusive address.

At the age of five, Odetta was hit on the head by a brick dropped out of a window by JACK MORT and slipped into a coma. As a result, her second personality, that of DETTA WALKER, gained life. Detta remained a small part of Odetta until August 19th, 1959, when Jack Mort once again entered Susannah's life by pushing Odetta/Detta in front of an approaching A train at CHRISTOPHER STREET STATION. As a result, both her legs were amputated just above the knee. After the accident, Detta had more and more waking time.

Odetta was a vocal supporter of the Civil Rights Movement and often took part in protests. In fact, some racist rednecks in OXFORD TOWN actually imprisoned her and some of her Movement friends during their time in the South. Unlike Odetta, Detta didn't believe in any movements but was full of rage against white oppression. In fact, her rage often pushed her into committing dangerous and bizarre acts.

Roland entered the mind of Odetta/Detta in the *when* of 1964, and brought her (complete with wheelchair) into Mid-World. It was in Mid-World that Detta and Odetta were forced to face each other. From their battle and eventual union arose SUSANNAH DEAN, EDDIE DEAN's lover and then wife. Susannah reminds Roland of ALAIN. Like him, she appears to have the "touch," or psychic flashes.

Because of her disability, Susannah moves through Mid-World using either her wheelchair or a piggy-back harness (the latter strapped to either Roland's or Eddie's back). When she travels to GILEAD via MAERLYN'S GRAPEFRUIT, Susannah has her legs again. This could be significant later. In TOPEKA, Eddie finds Susannah a new (and lighter) wheelchair.

At the end of *The Waste Lands* and throughout *Wizard and Glass*, Susannah suspects she is pregnant. She thinks the child is Eddie's, but it could be a DEMON's offspring, or Eddie's child corrupted by the demon she "held" in the DEMON RING. Roland realizes something is wrong with Susannah and he suspects the worst. Demonic contact always changes a person, he says, and rarely for the better. Roland and Susannah have, as yet, to palaver about this state of affairs. ("One rooster and one hen," Susannah states. She doesn't want Eddie in on the conversation.) Like Eddie, Susannah comes from a world similar, but not identical, to ours. In our world, the A train doesn't stop at Christopher Street Station.

I:130 *(as Lady of Shadows)*, II:180–81 *(Lady of Shadows)*, II:185–203 *(Detta/Odetta in 1964 New York; 201 Roland and Eddie see her through door)*, II:204–9 *(discussed by Roland and Eddie)*, II:211–12 *(discussed by George Shavers)*, II:214–20 *(George Shavers remembers)*, II:220–23, II:225–96 *(on beach. 235–38 remembers brick accident; 247–77 Detta takes over; 277–96 Odetta takes over)*, II:297, II:298, II:299, II:300–305 *(these and previous pages—Eddie and Roland discuss)*, II:305–7 *(Detta)*, II:308–12 *(discussed)*, II:315, II:316 *(Lady)*, II:318, II:320–24, II:324–26 *(Detta)*, II:327–38 *(Detta)*, II:339, II:357, II:359–60, II:367, II:379–80, II:385–90 *(Roland makes Detta and Odetta face each other)*, II:393–99, III:11–19, III:23, III:24–25, III:26, III:29–51 *(from 37, Roland's story; 43 says Susannah from 1963)*, III:54–77, III:78–86, III:96, III:97 *(Lady)*, III:136 *(Lady)*, III:149, III:151–52, III:158–65, III:170–76 *(171 says she is twenty-six years old)*, III:178–82, III:189–90 *(drawing Jake)*, III:193–94, III:196–98 *(Detta's sex wars)*, III:201–3, III:206–13, III:221–54, III:256–67, III:268, III:269, III:273–81, III:283–85, III:286–301 *(Gasher)*, III:302–4, III:308–12, III:316–25, III:329, III:331–34, III:340–50 (345 says she's from 1963), III:356, III:361–65, III:372–73, III:377, III:378, III:382–85, III:393–420, IV:3–10, IV:13–42 *(riddling; 30 Edith Bunker blunder; 31–35 Falls of the Hounds)*, IV:44–70 *(58–59 crash; 60 leave Blaine; 64 thinny's sound and saw player in Central Park "sounds Hawaiian"; 69 pains in belly and dangers of demon contact)*, IV:70–112 *(Topeka train station; 72–77 Topeka Capital Journal and superflu; 79 Beam disappears; 81 dead of Topeka and crip spaces; 82 new wheelchair for Susannah; 87 Charlie the Choo-Choo in Topeka; 91 sign of the Crimson King; 92 bullets in ears; 95 enter thinny; 97 Oz in distance; 106–12 Roland tells story)*, IV:335–37 *(interlude in Kansas)*, IV:570, IV:615–25 *(end of Roland's story; back in Topeka)*, IV:626–68 *(626 ruby cappies; 632 Green Palace; 634 gate like Wizard's Rainbow; 646 Tick-Tock; 648 Flagg; 652 Roland's matricide)*

ODETTA HOLMES'S ASSOCIATES:

   CYNTHIA: Odetta's friend.   IV:626

   FEENY, ANDREW: Odetta's chauffeur.   II:185–93, II:197, II:242, II:294, III:258

   FOLK CLUB BOYFRIEND: This young man introduced Odetta to the folk music she grew to love.   II:199

HOLMES, ALICE (SARAH WALKER HOLMES): Alice Holmes (also called ALLIE, II:200) was Odetta's mother. She was born in ODETTA, ARKANSAS, and christened her only child with the name of her home town. Alice Holmes is also called SARAH WALKER HOLMES.   II:199–201 *(Alice)*, II:235–38, II:295, II:320–24 *(and Mort)*, III:15 *(Sarah Walker Holmes)*

HOLMES, DAN: Dan Holmes was Odetta's father and the founder of the extremely successful Holmes Dental Industries. He's described as a thin black man with gray hair and steel-rimmed spectacles. Dan Holmes's wealth came from the orthodontic and cosmetic procedures he invented and patented. He did not like to discuss his early life with his daughter, though his experiences with racism in America probably fed his profound cynicism. He died in 1962.   II:199–201, II:235–38, II:320–24 *(and Mort)*, II:389, III:258, III:310–11, III:394–96

> **MURDOCK, REVEREND:** Minister of Grace Methodist Church. He once gave a sermon entitled "God Speaks to Each of Us Every Day." The subject made Dan Holmes laugh. Susannah's father believed that people put words into God's mouth and hear what they want to hear.   III:311

HOWARD: Doorman, Greymarl Apartments.   II:190–93

LEON: Odetta's friend. He was with her in the OXFORD TOWN prison. The guards called him a pinko fag.   III:15

SISTER BLUE: Odetta's maternal aunt, Sophia, who was especially fond of the color blue. Susannah traveled north with her parents to attend Sister Blue's wedding and was subsequently hit on the head by JACK MORT's brick. In revenge, the newly born Detta took her aunt's *forspecial* plate and broke it.   II:194, II:235–36, II:277, II:324, II:388, III:266, IV:650

OTHER ASSOCIATES:

DETTA/ODETTA'S "A TRAIN" ACCIDENT:

ELDERLY WHITE BUSINESSMAN: This man gave his belt to the OLD BLACK WOMAN who was trying to save Detta/Odetta's legs.   II:216

ESTEVEZ, JULIO: An ambulance worker who helped to save Detta/Odetta's life after her legs were amputated by the A train. He was deeply disturbed by her split personality. Julio belonged to the bowling team **THE SPICS OF SUPREMACY.**   II:211–12, II:214–20 *(present)*

> **BASALE, MIGUEL:** One of the guys on Julio Estevez's bowling team.   II:211

OLD BLACK WOMAN: She jumped onto the tracks to make

tourniquets around Detta/Odetta's bleeding thighs, thereby saving her life. She was later given a Medal of Bravery by the Mayor. The only other ones who helped the rescue effort were the white kid who called for an ambulance and an old businessman who loaned his belt.   II:215–16

PARAMEDICS (THE BOBBSEY TWINS): II:211, II:217–20 *(present)*

SHAVERS, GEORGE: The intern from SISTERS OF MERCY HOSPITAL who was part of the "Emergency Ride" program. He helped to keep Detta/Odetta alive during her ambulance ride. Like ESTEVEZ, he knew that there was something profoundly wrong with her mind.   II:211–20

YOUNG WHITE GUY: This young man called for an ambulance while most of the A train commuters just stood and stared. II:215

FRAT BOY: He was one of the many white boys cock-teased by vengeful Detta.   II:195–96

MACY'S EMPLOYEES:

    FLOORWALKER: II:221, II:222, II:223

    HALVORSEN, JIMMY: Halvorsen was the Macy's store detective who caught Detta shoplifting. His jiggling belly resembled a sack of potatoes.   II:221–23, II:227

    SALESGIRL #1: II:202–3, II:208

    SALESGIRL #2: II:208

DEARBORN, WILL

This was young Roland's alias in HAMBRY. It is used throughout much of *Wizard and Glass*. Since Roland is the main character in the Dark Tower series, his presence is implied in all other entries. For specific information about Roland's adventures, look up the other characters or places involved. For example, page references for his love affair with Susan Delgado are listed under DELGADO, SUSAN. See also the essay "Roland, the Tower, and the Quest" at the beginning of this Concordance.

DEBORAH

See BIG COFFIN HUNTERS: DEPAPE, ROY

DE CURRY, JAMIE

Jamie, who had a pronounced birthmark, was Roland's fellow apprentice gunslinger. Jamie swore that Roland had eyes in his fingers and so could shoot blindfolded. His last name is spelled three different ways in the books: De Curry, de Curry, and DeCurry.

I:140, I:149–52 *(Dance)*, I:156–57, I:160, I:161–62, I:167–73 *(witnesses Roland's coming of age)*, I:174, III:41, III:417, IV:7, IV:649 *(birthmark)*, IV:658, E:158

DEEPNEAU, AARON

JAKE met Aaron Deepneau at THE MANHATTAN RESTAURANT OF THE MIND. Aaron was obviously a friend of CALVIN TOWER's, though he thought Tower was cheap. Aaron was the one who explained Samson's riddle—and the importance of riddling in general—to Jake. He was also a pretty good folksinger. A rather sarcastic Tower claimed that his buddy was hanging around BLEECKER STREET before Bob Dylan could blow more than an open G on his Hohner.

Aaron was a fan of the Existentialists. When Jake met him he was reading *The Plague*.

III:115–18, III:155–56, III:279, IV:28, IV:46

DEERE

See DEAN, EDDIE: DELTA FLIGHT 901 CHARACTERS

DEIRDRE THE MAD

She was Roland's grandmother. It was from her that he inherited his particular combination of dry pragmatism and wild intuition.

III:361

DELEVAN, CARL

Carl Delevan was the overweight, cigarette-loving New York cop who patrolled the area around CLEMENTS GUNS AND SPORTING GOODS. He and his partner GEORGE O'MEARAH were fooled and then humiliated by Roland. Years later, Delevan died of a stroke while watching *The Terminator*. The reason? The Terminator reminded him of Roland.

II:343, II:346, II:347–59 *(354 unconscious)*, II:368 *(indirect)*, II:371–77, II:378, II:380

DELGADO, CORDELIA

Cordelia Delgado was SUSAN DELGADO's skinny maiden aunt. Susan's widowed father, PAT DELGADO, took her in when she had nowhere else to go, but this act of goodwill proved to be quite unwise. Within a few years Pat was dead—betrayed by one of his friends. His lands and possessions were stolen by the traitorous members of THE HORSEMEN'S ASSOCIATION and his daughter's maidenhead was essentially auctioned off by Cordelia. It seems unlikely that Cordelia participated in the plot against her brother, but she most certainly knew about it.

Although Cordelia was herself a prude, she didn't seem to have any qualms about acting as a kind of pimp for her niece. After Susan was burned on the Charyou Tree fire, Cordelia died of a stroke.

IV:125, IV:126, IV:130, IV:131, IV:133, IV:135, IV:140, IV:151, IV:152 *(story of Susan's family "madness")*, IV:166–69 *(167 personality described)*, IV:176–77 *(Jonas mentions)*, IV:191–210 *(Thorin's party: 195–203 introduced; 197 described; 202–3 whispers to Susan; 206–8 sits next to Susan)*, IV:211, IV:212, IV:235–39 *(235 described; 236 blouse incident)*, IV:240, IV:241–43 *(242–43 described)*, IV:244, IV:245, IV:249, IV:256, IV:278–79, IV:281, IV:287, IV:294, IV:303–4, IV:307, IV:308–14, IV:324, IV:328–31 *(with Jonas)*, IV:336, IV:343, IV:356, IV:361–62, IV:364–66, IV:372–74 *(tells Jonas suspicions about Susan/Roland)*, IV:375–76, IV:377–78, IV:397, IV:413, IV:426–28, IV:429, IV:459–60, IV:466–67 *(burns Susan in effigy)*, IV:495–98 *(496 has horse teeth)*, IV:503, IV:513, IV:515, IV:549–52 *(and Rhea)*, IV:563–65, IV:605–8 *(Susan burns)*, IV:624–25 *(dies of stroke)*

DELGADO, HIRAM
Hiram was SUSAN's grandfather as well as PAT and CORDELIA DELGADO's father.

IV:551

DELGADO, PAT
Red-haired, red-bearded Pat Delgado was SUSAN DELGADO's "da." He also happened to be the best drover on the WESTERN DROP. By the time Roland and his first *ka-tet* arrived in HAMBRY, Pat had already been dead for five years. Unlike many of the important men of Hambry, Pat Delgado was loyal to the AFFILIATION. FRAN LENGYLL maintained that Pat was killed by his horse, **OCEAN FOAM,** but he was actually murdered for daring to stand up to Lengyll and CROYDON's plans to turn traitor. Though Pat was honorable in life, his memory was desecrated. The men who were supposed to be his friends stole his lands, and his money-hungry sister, CORDELIA DELGADO, tried to sell his only daughter's maidenhead to the highest bidder.

IV:124–25, IV:135, IV:139, IV:140, IV:142, IV:143, IV:144, IV:146, IV:150–51, IV:156 *(remembered first appearance of thinny)*, IV:157–58, IV:168, IV:169, IV:202–3, IV:205, IV:207–8, IV:212, IV:235, IV:236, IV:237, IV:240, IV:251, IV:254–56 *(rolled on by his horse)*, IV:279, IV:282, IV:287 *(Susan thinks he was murdered)*, IV:293, IV:294 *(interest in Old People)*, IV:295, IV:301 *(friend of betrayer Brian Hookey)*, IV:309, IV:314, IV:315, IV:365, IV:457–60 *(Susan in his office)*, IV:466, IV:497, IV:504, IV:505, IV:507, IV:541, IV:551, IV:604

DELGADO, SUSAN

Although we hear of Susan Delgado, "the lovely girl at the window," as early as *The Gunslinger*, we don't find out much about her love affair with Roland until *Wizard and Glass*. Susan was Roland's only true love. He met her in HAMBRY, after he and his first *ka-tet* were sent east by their fathers, who wished to keep them far from the dangerous machinations of THE GOOD MAN, otherwise known as JOHN FARSON. At the time of their meeting, Roland was fourteen and Susan sixteen. Roland had just won his guns and had only recently lost his virginity. Susan, a drover's daughter, had lost her father and was about to lose her honor as well, thanks to her AUNT CORDELIA's financial deal with the randy mayor, HART THORIN.

Susan was probably descended from the "FRIENDLY FOLK," a sect that seemed quite widespread in Mid-World before it moved on. Like them, she used the terms "thee" and "thou" in her speech. It's quite possible that the Friends were somehow related to the MANNI, though we do not know this for certain. Although she was an excellent horsewoman (her beloved horses, **PYLON** and **FELICIA**, are also characters in the book), Susan was uncomfortable with guns. This, too, may have been owing to her family's background.

Roland first met Susan while she was on her way home from her disagreeable and embarrassing meeting with the nasty old witch RHEA OF THE CÖOS. Rhea was to check Susan's "honesty"—in other words, her virginity. In order to fulfill her upcoming duty as Mayor Hart Thorin's gilly she had to be pure—unsullied by man or demon. Ostensibly she was to bear the mayor a child (his own wife was barren) but Thorin was actually much more interested in the planting than in the cultivation of his seed.

With her waist-length golden-blond hair and gray eyes, Susan is the most beautiful woman found in the Dark Tower series. She is also "honest" in every sense of the word and gives Roland her heart freely and completely, despite the fact that her prissy and hypocritical maiden aunt has already squirreled away much of the gold given for Susan's maidenhead.

Susan's devotion to Roland did not end happily. Branded a traitor, she was burned as a Charyou Tree sacrifice. Although she didn't know it, Roland had already abandoned her, though he was forced to witness her death while lost in the nowhere dreamtime of MAERLYN'S GRAPEFRUIT.

In the years following her death, Roland frequently dreamed of Susan, often in association with the rhyme: "bird and bear and hare and fish, give my love her fondest wish." Her scent of jasmine, rose, honeysuckle, and old sweet hay was evoked by the ORACLE OF THE MOUNTAINS when she wanted to seduce him.

I:86, I:106, I:119–20, I:128, I:131, I:140, I:157, II:231, II:394, III:41, IV:65, IV:66–67, IV:68 *(physical description. ". . . bird and bear and hare and fish . . ."),* IV:79, IV:98, IV:116, IV:120, IV:122–38 *(and Rhea; 123 "Careless Love"; 123 heart vs. head; 127 sees Maerlyn's Grapefruit; 130–35 Rhea inspects her "honesty"; 133–34 Rhea's sexual touch; 134 invokes Thorin's name for protection and is ashamed; 137–38 Rhea puts spell on Susan),* IV:139–59 *(meets "Will Dearborn." He whistles "Careless Love"),* IV:162, IV:164–65 *(Roland thinks about her),* IV:166–70 *(and Cordelia. Won't lie with Thorin until Demon Moon),* IV:191, IV:191–210 *(Thorin's Party; 195 sapphire pendant, fog-colored eyes; 197–98 introduced to Roland, 208 Roland wants to shoot her; 209–10 Roland dances with her. A question of propriety),* IV:211–12, IV:213, IV:222–23 *(Roland and love/hate),* IV:233, IV:234–59 *(237–38 cheated of inheritance; 239 desire for Roland; 241 flowers from Roland; 247 Roland on Drop),* IV:277, IV:278–84, IV:285, IV:286, IV:287 *(suspects father was murdered),* IV:288–305 *(Citgo with Roland. Rhea spying),* IV:306–28 *(311–12 Thorin grabs; 316 loss of virginity; 326 Roland's rhyme to wake her from trance),* IV:329–31, IV:336, IV:342–45, IV:353, IV:356–60 *(subject of angry thoughts),* IV:361–62 *("lovely girl at the window"),* IV:364–67, IV:368, IV:370, IV:372, IV:373–74, IV:377–78, IV:388, IV:393, IV:399, IV:400, IV:401, IV:405, IV:406, IV:411–12, IV:413, IV:415, IV:416, IV:418–19, IV:426–44 *(with Roland, Cuthbert, Alain. 432 Roland's plan of attack; 435 hypnotized; 441–42 remembers Rhea and Maerlyn's Grapefruit),* IV:449–50 *(stealing firecrackers with Sheemie),* IV:452, IV:457–61 *(in father's office),* IV:463–66 *(464 intuition that Roland will desert her),* IV:466–67 *(Cordelia burns her in effigy),* IV: 474, IV:479, IV:480–83, IV:494–500, IV:502–13 *(507–13 rescues Roland's ka-tet),* IV:514–19, IV:523–26, IV:529, IV:531, IV:533–34 *(Rhea tells Jonas her location),* IV:536–46 *(taken by Jonas),* IV:548–49, IV:549–52 *(subject of discussion between Cordelia and Rhea),* IV:561–62, IV:564–65 *(Rhea and Cordelia lead crowds against her),* IV:565–70 *(Sheemie follows),* IV:571, IV:577, IV:578, IV:579–81 *(Roland decides to leave her),* IV:581–83, IV:585–87, IV:594, IV:602–9 *(Roland sees her burn in* Wizard's glass*),* IV:619, IV:622 *(Roland always dreams of her),* IV:650, IV:653, IV:655, IV:664, E:160, E:165, E:168, E:169, E:195

    GRAMMA: Susan inherited her singing voice from this grandmother.   IV:123

    MATERNAL GREAT-AUNT: She ran crazy, set herself on fire, and threw herself over the DROP.   IV:152

DEMONS/SPIRITS/DEVILS

Mid-World is a desolate land littered with the ruined machinery and leaking poisons of the GREAT OLD ONES. However, it is also a landscape haunted by the magic of a more primitive but equally dangerous people—those who knew more about demonology than they did about technology.

In each of the novels, Roland and his friends encounter "thin" places—areas where the division between the spirit world and the physical world is almost nonexistent. These places—whether circles of DRUIT STONES or cellars where men have been murdered and their bodies hidden—are the sites of human sacrifice. Hence, they function as evil magic circles. Unfortunately for unwary travelers, it is not just the magician who can conjure demons and spirits in these "in-betweens." Because of their history of violence and blood, these evil places are portals where thirsty demons can manifest whenever they scent possible prey.

Like the demons of our world, Mid-World demons seem to feed on human blood and human energy. Locked in the circles or buildings they haunt, they wait for unwary men and women to chance upon them. Drawn by the *khef*, or life force, of human beings, they come to drink. Lucky people chancing upon these beings will be able to entice a prophecy from them. Unlucky ones will lose their lives.

I:14 *(dust devils)*, I:16, I:22, I:44, I:48–52 *(Pittston's Interloper)*, I:55–56 *(Pittston's Interloper)*, I:58, I:59–62 *(Pittston's Interloper)*, I:85, I:88 *(spooks)*, I:90, I:91, I:124, I:154, I:205, II:25, II:34, II:40, II:44, II:73, II:114, II:362, II:367, III:20, III:35, III:315, IV:15, IV:63, IV:92 *(thinny as demon)*, IV:132, IV:157 *(thinny as demon)*, IV:321, IV:353 *(inside Maerlyn's glass)*

DEVIL GRASS/DEVIL WEED: Devil grass grows in the waste lands of Mid-World. It is often the only fuel in these desolate places but burning it brings its own dangers. Devils dance in the greasy flickering flames and those who watch them can be drawn into the fire. Roland thinks that the **DEVIL POWDER** (cocaine) of our world is very similar to devil grass.   I:12–13, I:15, I:23, I:28–29, I:34, I:35, I:36, I:39–40, I:44, I:51, I:118, I:119, I:138, II:40, II:65, II:73, II:100 *(devil powder)*, II:101 *(devil dust)*, II:141 *(devil powder)*, II:394, III:46, III:248, IV:268

**INTERLOPER/SATAN/ANTICHRIST: The Bible-bashing lunatic SYLVIA PITTSTON believed that Roland was the Interloper—in other words, Satan himself. In the new *Gunslinger* Roland shares this dubious honor with his eventual nemesis, THE CRIMSON KING. I:49–52, I:59; I:62

MANSION DEMON/DOORKEEPER (PLASTER-MAN): This is the demon-of-place that haunts the DUTCH HILL MANSION in BROOKLYN. It is the animating spirit of an evil house but it is also a

DOORKEEPER, or a spirit that guards the passageway between one world and another. The Dutch Hill Mansion Demon is paired with the SPEAKING RING DEMON that ROLAND, SUSANNAH, and EDDIE encounter while traveling along the PATH OF THE BEAM toward LUD. The Dutch Hill Demon keeps people from leaving Our World; the Speaking Ring Demon stops them from entering Mid-World. Although both of these demonic doorkeepers are evil, they also serve a purpose: they prevent people from leaping from one level of the TOWER to another.

Because of these two demons, JAKE CHAMBERS's second entry into Mid-World is doubly dangerous. Not only does he have to elude this Mansion Demon but he must also escape the Speaking Ring Demon who waits for him on the other side. Luckily, he has his *ka-tet* to help him make the journey.   III:190–92, III:194–96, III:198–201, III:203–11, III:219, III:234, III:263, III:265, IV:98

ORACLE (SUCCUBUS): This female demon haunts a circle of DRUIT STONES in the WILLOW JUNGLES of the CYCLOPEAN MOUNTAINS and is the first such creature we meet in the series. Like others of her kind, she feeds on desire. This weeping, sighing presence, who is described as a "demon with no shape, only a kind of unformed sexual glare with the eye of prophecy," first lures JAKE into her cold embrace and then, when she is thwarted, takes Roland. (Roland is probably the one she wants anyway.)

Unlike Jake, Roland enters the Oracle's circle willingly, and with the aid of mescaline (what CORT once called the Philosopher's Stone) makes conscious contact with the haunting presence. Roland's desire is to force the spirit to prophesy, but in order to do this he has to have sex with this star-slut and whore of the winds. During their encounter, the Oracle takes on the voice and scent of Roland's dead love, SUSAN DELGADO.

In the new version of *The Gunslinger*, the Oracle warns Roland to watch for Roses and Unfound Doorways.   I:117, I:121–32, I:138, I:215, II:25, II:40, II:315, III:173

SPEAKING DEMON (WAY STATION): When Roland descended into the Way Station's cellar, he heard this demon moaning. The sound, which soon turned into labored breathing, came from behind one of the cellar's crooked sandstone walls. Roland addressed the creature in High Speech and it responded in a low, dragging voice which resembled that of his dead lover ALICE from the town of TULL. After hearing the demon's warning about the DRAWERS and about JAKE ("Go slow past the Drawers, gunslinger. While you travel with the boy, the Man in Black travels with your soul in your pocket"), Roland punched the wall, reached in, and pulled out a human jawbone. Though this action seems violent to us, it was one of the things Roland had been taught to do when dealing with demons. As the old Mid-World proverb stated, "only a corpse may speak true prophecy." From the moment he heard that initial moan, Roland knew that a body lay behind the sandstone. Such corpses can be possessed by spirits and can prove to be powerful mojo when dealing with other demonic beings.   I:122–26, I:132, I:139, III:44, III:46, III:48, III:97, III:136

SPEAKING RING DEMON: Like the MANSION DEMON, this invisible male monster is a Doorkeeper. Roland, EDDIE, and SUSAN-NAH have to outwit it in order to draw JAKE CHAMBERS from his version of our world into Mid-World.

Like all such sexually charged Druit Stone spirits, this invisible creature's weakness is the same as its weapon. Hence, the only hope our *ka-tet* has of "drawing" Jake successfully is first to capture the Doorkeeper and then to keep him in a sexual snare long enough for the boy to pass through.

As soon as our *ka-tet* enters the circle, this raging, hungry demon senses their presence and comes toward them, disturbing the grasses to the north as it rushes forward. Since Eddie is the one drawing the magical picture of the door itself (and hence the one transgressing that ancient law against passage between worlds), he is the lightning rod drawing the force. However, as the demon rushes toward him, Susannah Dean traps it, quite literally, between her legs. Though it is agonizingly painful, Susannah manages to hold the demon long enough for Jake to be "born."

Sex with such demons has its risks, as Roland is all too aware. As the novel progresses we find that Susannah is probably pregnant, but it is all too likely that this demon—whose engorged sex is like a giant icicle—is the baby's father.   III:189–90, III:193–94, III:197–98, III:201–3, III:206–12, IV:69, IV:92

SUCKERBATS: These strange creatures live in the WILLOW JUNGLES of the CYCLOPEAN MOUNTAINS. Many of them are vampire bats. Those bitten in the night do not wake to the world of the living. I:118

SUVIA: Suvia is a female demon with eight or nine arms.   II:181

DENBY, TOM
JAKE CHAMBERS uses this alias during his NEW YORK wanderings. III:169

DENNIS
See FLAGG, RANDALL

**DESCHAIN, GABRIELLE (GABRIELLE OF ARTEN, GABRIELLE VERISS, GABRIELLE OF THE WATERS)
Born Gabrielle of Arten (IV:595), Gabrielle Deschain was Roland's mother. Despite her standing as the wife of STEVEN DESCHAIN—the last Lord of Light and the direct descendant of ARTHUR ELD, King of ALL-WORLD—she broke GILEAD's code of honor and had an affair with the court enchanter, MARTEN BROADCLOAK. Gabrielle is quite a sad character, since this affair was, at least in part, a trap set for her by the enemies of the AFFILIATION.

Despite her dislike of guns and her gentleness toward her son, Gabrielle had a dangerous side. In MAERLYN's glass, Roland saw his mother scratch his father with a poisoned knife. This terrible deed was to be done after Gabrielle falsely repented her affair and made love with her husband. Roland prevented this disaster, but later on, blinded by a different kind of *glammer*, he committed matricide by shooting her.

In the new *Gunslinger*, we learn that Gabrielle's given name was GABRIELLE VERISS, and that she was the daughter of ALAN. She was also known as GABRIELLE OF THE WATERS.

I:71–72 *(71 mistake: should say mother not father)*, I:77, I:95, I:106, I:127, I:136, I:151–52, I:159–61, I:167, I:171, I:173, I:187, I:205, III:417, IV:7, IV:107, IV:110–11, IV:223 *(and Olive Thorin)*, IV:257, IV:317, IV:439, IV:594–95 *(Roland's memory of his parents, Lake Saroni)*, IV:619, IV:620, IV:652–58 *(Roland's matricide)*, IV:661–62, IV:665–66, E:195
**ALAN (GABRIELLE'S FATHER)
ROLAND'S NURSE: III:33, III:39, III:40

DESCHAIN, HENRY
See HENRY THE TALL

**DESCHAIN, HORN OF
See HORN OF DESCHAIN

DESCHAIN, ROLAND
Roland Deschain, Mid-World's last gunslinger, is the central character of the Dark Tower series. Son of STEVEN DESCHAIN and GABRIELLE DESCHAIN, he is thirtieth in a side line of descent from ARTHUR ELD, the mythical king of ALL-WORLD. Like the rest of his line, Roland is a Warrior of the White. His quest is to find the DARK TOWER, the linchpin of the Time/Space continuum.

Since Roland is the main character of the Dark Tower series, his presence is implied in all other entries. For specific information about

Roland's adventures, look up the other characters or places involved. For example, page references for his love affair with Susan Delgado are listed under DELGADO, SUSAN. Also see the introductory essay entitled "Roland, the Tower, and the Quest," located at the beginning of this Concordance.

**DESCHAIN, STEVEN (STEVEN OF GILEAD)

Steven Deschain, the last Lord of Light, was twenty-ninth, on the side line of descent, from ARTHUR ELD, King of ALL-WORLD. (In other words, he was descended from one of Arthur's side-wives, or gillies.) Before Roland gained his guns at fourteen, Steven Deschain was the youngest apprentice to prove his manhood and win his weapons. (Steven bested CORT when he was sixteen.) After he was murdered, and after the final gunslingers were defeated at the battle of **JERICHO HILL, the last vestiges of Mid-World's decaying civilization collapsed into complete anarchy.

Steven Deschain (also occasionally called ROLAND THE ELDER) was the leader of NEW CANAAN's gunslingers. Tall, painfully thin, and with a heavy handlebar mustache, the elder Deschain's gruff looks belied his actual nobility. Like all the gunslingers, he was an aristocrat, and it was in part this class division that turned many common people against the AFFILIATION and toward the cause of the traitorous GOOD MAN, JOHN FARSON. Like his fathers before him, Steven Deschain wore the true gunslinger's six-shooters—the ones with sandalwood grips—against the wings of his hips. He passed them on to Roland after the younger man proved himself in HAMBRY.

In the new *Gunslinger*, we learn that during Roland's childhood his father managed to take control of his *ka-tet* (the *tet* of the Gun), and was on the verge of becoming *dinh* of Gilead, if not all of IN-WORLD. He was betrayed by the serpent in his bosom—his own counselor and sorcerer, MARTEN—who first seduced his wife and then raised the forces of anarchy in his lands. Although Steven didn't know it, Marten was actually a shape-shifter of multiple identities. Some of his other names were John Farson and WALTER O'DIM. In all of his incarnations, Walter/Marten/Farson served the chaotic force of THE CRIMSON KING. Hence he opposed the White and all who championed it.

I:71 *(mistake: says father, should say mother)*, I:103–6, I:107, I:109, I:110, I:111, I:151–52, I:160, I:161, I:164, I:167, I:171, I:184, I:205, I:213, I:216, II:104–5, III:11, III:50, III:276, III:375, III:377, III:415, III:417, IV:19, IV:50, IV:108–12 *(grabs Roland from a whore's bed)*, IV:144, IV:163–64 *(Roland as "son who had lived")*, IV:181, IV:183–84 *(twenty-ninth generation descended from Arthur Eld's side line)*, IV:258, IV:262, IV:270–71 *(line of Arthur Eld, son of HENRY*

THE TALL), IV:275–76 *(voice of Eyebolt Canyon thinny)*, IV:285 *(father's son)*, IV:286, IV:317, IV:436–39 *(tells of MAERLYN's Grapefruit and MAERLYN'S RAINBOW)*, IV:443, IV:464, IV:499, IV:530, IV:531, IV:570, IV:594–95 *(Roland's memory of his parents, Lake Saroni)*, IV:620–21 *(plot to kill him)*, IV:650, IV:653, IV:655–56 *(Gabrielle plans to murder him)*, IV:657, IV:665, E:195, E:206

DESMOND
Desmond was one of Roland's original gunslinger companions. When Roland sees the neon sign for BALAZAR's headquarters, THE LEANING TOWER, he calls out this old friend's name. For a moment, Roland believes that he has reached his final destination.
II:121

DEWEY
See DEAN, EDDIE: EDDIE'S ASSOCIATES, PAST AND PRESENT

DEWLAP
See GRAYS: GRAY LEADERS: TICK-TOCK

DIANA'S DREAM
Diana's Dream is a Mid-World story very close to that of "The Lady or the Tiger."
II:105–6

DOCTOR BUGS
See CAM TAM under ELURIA CHARACTERS

DOLLENTZ
See KATZ

DORFMAN
See MORT, JACK

DORFMAN, STAN
See PIPER SCHOOL CHARACTERS

DORNING, JANE
See DEAN, EDDIE: DELTA FLIGHT 901 CHARACTERS

DOROTHY (OF OZ)
See OZ, WIZARD OF

DOUGLAS, SUSY
  See DEAN, EDDIE: DELTA FLIGHT 901 CHARACTERS

DRETTO, CARLOCIMI ('CIMI):
  See BALAZAR'S MEN

E

EARP, WYATT
  See GUNSLINGERS (OUR WORLD)

EASTWOOD, CLINT
Clint Eastwood starred in a number of spaghetti westerns, including *A Fistful of Dollars* and *For a Few Dollars More*. He also directed and starred in such great gothic westerns as *Pale Rider* and *High Plains Drifter*. Roland looks a bit like Clint and is an even better shot.
  III:182

ELD, ARTHUR
Roland is thirtieth in a side line of descent from one of Arthur Eld's forty gillies. Despite his many wives and side-wives, Arthur represented the White. In story and tapestry, Arthur is often depicted as riding a white stallion and brandishing his great sword Excalibur. In fact, he was popularly known as "he of the white horse and the unifying sword." After his death, Arthur's sword was entombed in a pyramid.

  In Arthur's time, Mid-World was unified; hence, he wore the crown of ALL-WORLD. His original kingdom lay in the western part of Mid-World, in the Baronies destroyed by FARSON. Despite the glory of its memory, Arthur's reign was a brutal time. In the days of ELD, people, not stuffy-guys, were thrown on the Charyou Tree fires.
  IV:171 *(picture in Travellers' Rest. "ARGYOU NOT ABOUT THE HAND YOU ARE DEALT IN CARDS OR LIFE")*, IV:181, IV:183–84 *(and Steven Deschain)*, IV:194 *("he of the white horse . . .")*, IV:206 *(Excalibur and the Affiliation)*, IV:211 *(tapestry in Seafront. Sword entombed in a pyramid)*, IV:223 *(40 gillies)*, IV:251, IV:267–71, IV:302 *("fantastic pride" of his line)*, IV:317 *(Excalibur and crown of All-World)*, IV:350, IV:360 *(Jewels of Eld)*, IV:379, IV:382, IV:508, IV:558 *(Roland as Arthur Eld)*, IV:563, IV:580, E:206

ELI
See CHAMBERS, JAKE

ELURIA CHARACTERS
Eluria was a small town in the far west of Mid-World; it was also the setting for the story "The Little Sisters of Eluria." At the time of this tale, GILEAD had already fallen but Roland had not yet managed to track down his enemy, the evil sorcerer WALTER.

Like so many Mid-World villages, Eluria resembled one of the tumbleweed towns of the Old West. When Roland arrived, it seemed to be deserted save for a CROSS DOG (also known as a JESUS DOG), a single corpse, some SLOW MUTANTS (called the GREEN FOLK) and some strangely disturbing singing insects. After being attacked by the Green Folk, an injured Roland found himself in the hospital-tent of the *glammer*-throwing LITTLE SISTERS OF ELURIA—a tribe of female vampires. Roland fell in love with SISTER JENNA, the youngest of these strange demonic women, and she, in turn, betrayed her sisters in order to help him escape.

BOUNCER OF THE BUSTLING PIG: By the time Roland reached Eluria, the only sign of this man was his nail-spiked club, wielded by one of the Green Folk.   E:154

CAM TAM (DOCTOR BUGS): The vampiric Little Sisters posed as a religious order of hospitalers. Hence, the doctor bugs—which were only a little smaller than fat honeybees—were an important part of their disguise.

Despite the sisters' evil habits, these insects were actually healers. Although ugly and disturbing to watch, the *cam tam* ate disease and knitted broken bones.   E:146, E:147–48, E:152, E:158, E:159, E:164, E:168, E:169–73, E:174, E:178, E:179, E:180, E:183, E:185, E:193, E:197, E:198–201, E:202, E:206, E:208–9

CHAS: A free-born cattle thief destined to be tried in Eluria. However, the Little Sisters got to the town first.   E:151

CROSS DOG/JESUS DOG: The Cross Dog takes its name from the black cross upon its white chest fur. This coloration oddity saves its life, since the vampiric Little Sisters can't touch it. Despite its superficial relation to religious good, this crippled animal is a rather unpleasant creature. In fact, the first time Roland sees it, it is chewing on the bloated leg of dead JAMES NORMAN. At the end of the story, the Jesus Dog redeems itself by attacking the evil SISTER MARY. It kills her.   E:151–53, E:155, E:156, E:159, E:160, E:182, E:204–5, E:207

GREEN FOLK: Like many other tribes of SLOW MUTANTS, the

Green Folk are the descendants of human men and women exposed to the OLD ONES' toxic pollutants. In the case of the Green Folk, the poison was radium. In fact, Roland is fairly certain that the ones who attacked him still hide from sunlight in the old radium mines.

Despite their unnerving color and their tallowy skin, these shuffling, snuffling, fluorescent green Slow Mutants have a more human shape than the group Roland and JAKE met under the CYCLOPEAN MOUNTAINS. Roland thinks of them as both animate corpses and toadstools with brains. Like other Slow Mutants, the Green Folk sometimes eat human flesh. For more information on Slow Mutants, see entry under MUTANTS.   E:146, E:151, E:154–58, E:160, E:162, E:171, E:173, E:177, E:178–79, E:193, E:205

   LUMPY BALD HEAD WITH RED SIZZLING SORES: E:154–58
   MALE WITH MELTED CANDLEWAX FACE: E:154
   MR. CLUB-WITH-NAILS: This creature probably stole his nasty weapon from THE BUSTLING PIG'S dead BOUNCER. E:154–58, E:159
   MR. TOAD: Mr. Toad looks like a toad-mouthed troll.   E:155–56 (shot)
   RALPH: One-eyed Ralph wears a bowler hat and red suspenders. He is one of the mutants who attacks Roland soon after his arrival in Eluria. It seems likely that Ralph is the leader of his tribe. He is also the one that the Little Sisters try to bribe into removing JOHN NORMAN's Christian medallion.   E:155–58, E:179, E:190–92, E:193
   RED VEST WOMAN: Her saggy breasts are visible beneath her vest.   E:155–58, E:179
   SMASHER: He gave Roland's guns to the Little Sisters without telling Ralph.   E:192
   TWO-HEADED MALE: This nasty creature is the one who sneaked up behind Roland and mounted a surprise attack. Roland shot him.   E:157 (shot), E:174

LITTLE SISTERS OF ELURIA: See ELURIA, LITTLE SISTERS OF listed separately

NORMAN, JAMES: James Norman was a young, towheaded cowboy of about fourteen to sixteen. He was the brother of JOHN NORMAN and the son of JESSE NORMAN. Roland came across his drowned corpse early in his wanderings around Eluria. James wore a medallion that read "James, Loved of Family, Loved of God." SISTER JENNA placed it around Roland's neck and he continued to wear it throughout his time among the Sisters. They could not bleed him while he wore it.   E:146, E:151–58, E:162, E:164 (medallion), E:172, E:176 (Roland poses as James), E:177, E:178–79, E:184 (Roland), E:185 (Roland), E:188, E:189, E:193, E:194, E:196

NORMAN, JASON ("JASON, BROTHER OF JOHN"): The Little Sisters call Roland "Jason, Brother of John" to trick him into proving he is not really JAMES NORMAN. Perhaps that would have made the magic of his medallion less potent. Roland doesn't fall for the trick. E:184

NORMAN, JESSE: Father of John and James.   E:176, E:188

  NORMAN, MRS.: Mother of John and James. Wife of Jesse. E:162, E:176, E:188

NORMAN, JOHN: John Norman was the brother of JAMES NORMAN, and was in the bed next to Roland's in the Little Sisters' hospital tent. John warned Roland about the Sisters' evil natures. Like his brother JAMES, John wore a Christian medallion around his neck. The sisters eventually forced one of the GREEN FOLK to tear it from him. E:162–64, E:168, E:172, E:176–80, E:181, E:183, E:184, E:186, E:187, E:188, E:190–92, E:193, E:194, E:196–97, E:199, E:202, E:205

SHERIFF: By the time Roland reached Eluria, the Sheriff had long since disappeared. Like everyone else in the town, he was probably drained dry by the Little Sisters.   E:150, E:155

UNCONSCIOUS MAN: Roland sees this unconscious man dangling from one of the Sisters' white slings. Like JAMES and JOHN NORMAN, this unfortunate fellow was attacked by the GREEN FOLK while protecting a long-haul caravan. The three men were later given to the Little Sisters. This man never completely regained consciousness while under the Sisters' care. They drank his blood anyway. E:162–64, E:169–71, E:180–81, E:183, E:198

ELURIA, LITTLE SISTERS OF

This tribe of vampires posed as a holy order of hospital nuns. They dressed in billowing white habits and their crones' faces were framed by white wimples. Hanging from the bands of silk imprisoning their hair were lines of tiny bells which chimed when they moved or spoke. Upon the breast of each habit was embroidered a single, blood-red ROSE—the sigil of the DARK TOWER. Roland barely escaped their clutches. A few of them are still wandering around Mid-World.

These strange sorceresses were not actually human. When Roland grabbed SISTER MARY by the throat he found her flesh repellent. It didn't feel like solid flesh at all but something both *various* and flowing.

In their true form, the Little Sisters looked like the ghastly siblings of RHEA OF THE CÖOS, the ancient hag-witch we met in *Wizard and*

Glass. Like Rhea, they were creatures of magic and could cast a *glammer* which made them appear young and lovely. But this illusion faded quickly, especially when they were hungry. Like their own loveliness, the airy white silk pavilion in which they kept their victims—first to cure them, then to bleed them—was only a *glammer*. In reality it was a fraying canvas tent. The only truly beautiful creature ever existent in the dream-realm woven by the Little Sisters was SISTER JENNA, a twenty-one-year-old woman bound to these others by the cruelty of *ka*.

The Little Sisters were—and are—a strange order, and the reader cannot help but wonder whether they, like the mutants of Mid-World, were originally something good. Although their *cam tam* were ugly, their purpose was to heal, and the Rose they wore was a *sigul* not only of the Tower but of the White.

However, not all things that serve a purpose are comfortable to contemplate. The dark bells which Sister Jenna wore, and which Roland thought were the true *sigul* of the order, are described as *charry*. Since the High Speech root-word *char* means death, it seems likely that these quasi-mortal women were originally death-angels, or beings meant to help men avoid (or less painfully reach) death. Perhaps, as Sister Jenna said, before the world moved on, they really were an order of hospitalers, albeit supernatural ones. But sadly, the evil of the Great Old Ones poisoned not only the air and water of Mid-World, but the magic as well. Although they may have begun as creatures of the White, the evil Little Sisters now have cause to fear all religious *siguls*, even their own dark bells.   E:165–67, E:168, E:177–80, E:180–82, E:183, E:186 *(soup)*, E:188, E:190–92, E:193, E:195, E:200, E:202, E:205, E:206

SISTER COQUINA: E:165–67, E:173–77, E:177 *(indirect)*, E:180–82, E:190–92, E:197–99

SISTER JENNA: Sister Jenna was a young black-haired beauty of twenty-one or twenty-two. Unlike that of her sisters, her youth was real, not the result of *glammer*. Although Jenna was a vampire and participated in her order's grisly meals, she wished to rebel against her destiny.

Sister Jenna appeared to be a kind of vampire royalty. Although the other sisters wore bells of bright silver, the ones Jenna wore looked as though they had been smoked over a fire. These dark bells—also called charry bells—are the true *sigul* of the order, and gave Jenna special powers over the doctor bugs.

Jenna fell in love with Roland and betrayed her sisters in order to help him escape, but human love was forbidden her. After she helped Roland flee from the hospital pavilion and then elude the evil clutches of SISTER MARY, Jenna's body became *cam tam*.   E:159–61, E:162,

E:165, E:166–73, E:174, E:175, E:177, E:179, E:180, E:184–88, E:189, E:194, E:195, E:197–209

JENNA'S MOTHER: Like her daughter, Jenna's mother tried to escape her fate. She deserted her order and bore a child, presumably to a human man, though it is possible these creatures reproduce by parthenogenesis. Unfortunately, escape was not possible. Without blood to sustain her, Jenna's mother began to sicken. She returned to her sisters along with her small child. Jenna's mother died, but the Little Sisters kept and raised Jenna. E:167, E:183, E:184, E:202, E:206

SISTER LOUISE: E:165–67, E:171, E:180–82, E:183–86, E:190–92, E:200–201, E:205

SISTER MARY/BIG SISTER: Sister Mary, also called Big Sister, was the head of the Little Sisters' order. Like the others of her kind, she was actually more shade than substance.

Although she did not wear the charry bells as did JENNA, Sister Mary's dominance over her order was complete. Whenever one of them disobeyed her wishes, Sister Mary sent them to the nearby cave called THOUGHTFUL HOUSE. Sometimes she even had disobedient sisters whipped.

Out of love for Roland and despair over her fate, Jenna rebelled against Big Sister. But outside the *glammer*-filled pavilion, not even the charry bells were strong enough to defeat her enemy. In the end, it was the *sigul*-bearing CROSS DOG—not Jenna or Roland—that destroyed Sister Mary. E:165–67, E:169, E:175–76, E:177, E:180–82, E:183–86, E:187, E:190–92, E:193–95, E:196, E:197, E:201, E:202–4, E:205, E:208

SISTER MICHELA: E:165–67, E:171, E:180–82, E:188–89, E:190–92, E:200–201, E:205

SISTER TAMRA: E:165–67, E:171, E:176–77, 180–82, E:190–92, E:196, E:200–201, E:205

ENGINEER BOB
See CHARLIE THE CHOO-CHOO

ESTEVEZ, JULIO
See DEAN, SUSANNAH: DETTA/ODETTA'S "A TRAIN" ACCIDENT

EVANS, BERYL
See CHARLIE THE CHOO-CHOO

F

FANNIN, RICHARD
See R.F.

FARDO
See CORT

**FARSON, JOHN (THE GOOD MAN)
John Farson was a bandit who justified his thefts and murders with talk of democracy and equality. He wanted to overthrow the AFFILIATION and IN-WORLD's aristocracy of gunslingers. However, it seems fairly certain that Farson had no intention of setting up a democratic government in place of Mid-World's reigning order. Like THE CRIMSON KING,** whose *sigul* he used and whom he ultimately served, Farson gloried in chaos, and chaos and destruction were exactly what he brought to the civilized lands Roland knew as a boy. At the beginning of *Wizard and Glass,* Farson had MAERLYN'S GRAPEFRUIT, one of Mid-World's magic balls. Luckily for In-World, Roland stole it from him, though Roland paid a great price for this theft.

Farson began as a harrier and a stage-robber in GARLAN and DESOY. Late in his career he was known for his cruelty. According to ELDRED JONAS, Farson was dangerously insane; one of his favorite pastimes was playing polo with human heads as the balls.

Farson pretended to represent the people, and part of his appeal was religious. In *The Gunslinger,* HAX equated him with Jesus, but there was little of the savior in the Good Man. Unfortunately for Mid-World, Farson resurrected the Old Ones' robots and killing machines so that he could use them against the Affiliation. By so doing, he destroyed what was left of Mid-World's cohesion.

In *Wizard and Glass,* we found out that WALTER worked for Farson. However, in the new *Gunslinger* we find out that Farson was just one of Walter's many masks. Roland, as a soldier of the White, actually has one single enemy. But his name is LEGION.
I:101–2, I:105, I:111, II:126, III:242, IV:110, IV:111, IV:142, IV:149 *(bandit who talks of "equality" and "democracy"),* IV:151 *(began as harrier/stage-robber in Garlan and Desoy),* IV:163 *(in Cressia. Speaks out against "class slavery"),* IV:164, IV:174–78, IV:183, IV:194, IV:196

(and "Good Men"), IV:199, IV:206, IV:262–63, IV:277, IV:302–3 *(brings Death)*, IV:344 *(indirect reference)*, IV:348, IV:351 *(attacks nobility, chivalry, ancestor worship. Will use robots)*, IV:368, IV:378 *(insane, plays polo with human heads)*, IV:386, IV:402, IV:404 *(eye sigul; Farson described and compared to LORD PERTH)*, IV:421, IV:422–25, IV:430–33, IV:438 *(and pink talisman)*, IV:443, IV:470, IV:487–88, IV:489, IV:490, IV:496 *(Farson's soldiers)*, IV:501, IV:518, IV:519 *(and Horsemen's Association)*, IV:520, IV:522, IV:531, IV:538, IV:543, IV:580, IV:583 *(hand-clasping sigul)*, IV:584, IV:585, IV:589 *(his lieutenants)*, IV:590, IV:597, IV:601 *(the last of his men goes screaming into thinny)*, IV:609, IV:619, IV:621 *(Roland sees Farson's triumph in Wizard's glass)*, IV:623, IV:632

FARSON'S MEN:

  FARSON'S NEPHEW: Disguised as a wandering singer, this young man smuggled a poisoned knife into GILEAD. The knife was meant to kill STEVEN DESCHAIN.   IV:621

  HENDRICKS, RODNEY: IV:590–93, IV:594 *(general)*, IV:596–98 *(present for battle; 598 swallowed by thinny)*

  LATIGO, GEORGE: One of Farson's chief lieutenants.   IV:368, IV:371, IV:378 *(hired Big Coffin Hunters)*, IV:381, IV:404, IV:405, IV:421–25 *(blond, from Northern In-World)*, IV:470, IV:484, IV:501, IV:523, IV:528, IV:542, IV:583, IV:584, IV:589–91 *(589 we learn his first name)*, IV:592–94 *(and his men)*, IV:596–600 *(600 walks into thinny)*, IV:623

  RAINES: Bugler.   IV:591, IV:596–98 *(not named, but present for battle)*

FEATHEREX (GRAND FEATHEREX)
The Grand Featherex is a winged being that supposedly lives in the mythical Kingdom of GARLAN. Like the stork, the Featherex brings babies. In *Eyes of the Dragon*, we learn that this creature is related to the phoenix.
  II:66, IV:151

FEENY, ANDREW
  See SUSANNAH DEAN: ODETTA HOLMES

FELDON, AMY
  See TULL

FELICIA
  See DELGADO, SUSAN

FLAGG, RANDALL
See R.F.

FRANCESCA (AND ROBERT)
See HAMBRY CHARACTERS: HAMBRY LOVERS

FRANKS, JOANNE
See PIPER SCHOOL CHARACTERS

FREEDOM RIDERS
II:227

FRIENDLY FOLK
The Friends were a sect of the OLD PEOPLE. Like the MANNI, they spoke using the terms "thee" and "thou." SUSAN DELGADO may have been descended from them, since her family used these words in their daily speech. The Friendly Folk remained in IN-WORLD throughout Roland's youth.
IV:250

G

GALE, DOROTHY
See OZ, WIZARD OF

GARBER
See HAMBRY CHARACTERS: HORSEMEN'S ASSOCIATION

GASHER
See GRAYS: GRAY HIGH COMMAND

GHOSTS IN THE MACHINES
See NORTH CENTRAL POSITRONICS: BLAINE

GILEAD STABLEHAND
When Roland was a young boy, this man was badly burned in a kerosene fire. Like the patient-prisoners of the LITTLE SISTERS OF ELURIA, he was suspended above his bed rather than being placed directly upon the sheets. He eventually died, but only after two days of shrieking.
E:160

GILEAD WHORE
After his coming-of-age battle with CORT, Roland went to one of Gilead's brothels and lost his virginity. This was the lucky gal.
I:174, IV:107–12

GINELLI
See BALAZAR'S MEN

GLUE BOY
See ALLGOOD, CUTHBERT

GOOD MAN, THE
See FARSON, JOHN

GRAND FEATHEREX
See FEATHEREX

GRAYS
The Grays were one of the two bands of harriers warring over the city of LUD, and were the sworn enemies of the PUBES. Although the Grays lived in the mazes and old silos below the eastern part of the city and the Pubes lived aboveground in CITY NORTH, the Grays were the more powerful. With the help of BLAINE, the city's mad computer brain, they convinced the Pubes that they had to appease the vindictive and flesh-hungry GHOSTS IN THE MACHINES with a daily ritual of human sacrifice. The Grays signaled this horrid event by playing the god-drums (actually no more than the backbeat of the ZZ Top song "Velcro Fly") over the city's loudspeakers.

Originally, the Grays were the city's besiegers. They were led by DAVID QUICK, the outlaw prince. In our story, the Grays are led by ANDREW QUICK, also known as TICK-TOCK, who is David Quick's great-grandson.

Tick-Tock and his band don't really understand why the god-drums work, but are eager to try to control more of Lud's computers. In the end, the computers (à la Blaine) destroy both of Lud's warring factions.

The easiest way to tell the difference between Pubes and Grays is by checking the color of their headscarves. The Pubes wear blue ones while the Grays wear yellow ones. The Grays also have a taste for young boys.
III:232, III:238, III:240, III:244–45, III:298, III:304, III:307, III:309, III:318, III:321, III:322, III:350–61 *(high command)*, III:362, III:365–72, III:373–82, III:388, III:403, III:411, IV:57

GRAY LEADERS:

QUICK, DAVID: Also known as the outlaw prince, David Quick was the original leader of the Grays. He was also the harrier who organized the sundry outlaw bands besieging the city of LUD. Roland's *ka-tet* finds his giant, mummified body in a wrecked German Focke-Wulf airplane a few days' walk outside the city. David Quick was TICK-TOCK's great-grandfather. III:241, III:244, III:273–75, III:355–56, III:358 *(plane)*, III:381, III:410, IV:22 *(dead harrier)*

TICK-TOCK (ANDREW QUICK): Tick-Tock was the leader of the Grays at the time of Roland, JAKE, and OY's little visit to the CRADLE OF THE GRAYS. He was also the great-grandson of DAVID QUICK, the outlaw prince. Tick-Tock looked like a cross between a Viking warrior and a giant from a child's fairy tale. He had a heavily muscled upper body, dirty gray-blond hair that reached halfway down his back, and green eyes. He had a refined sense of cruelty and wore a coffin-shaped clock around his neck. The clock ran backward. III:298, III:305, III:313, III:314, III:326, III:327, III:336, III:338–39, III:351–61, III:365–72, III:373, III:375, III:381, III:385–90, III:394, IV:28, IV:645–47 *(in Oz; killed by Roland's ka-tet)*, IV:663

> **DEWLAP:** Once upon a time, a scrawny old man named Dewlap worked the cider presses located in a park on the far western side of LUD. In the later chaos of that city, even the cider houses were probably destroyed. By the time our tale takes place, Dewlap and his companions are no more than memories in the damaged brain of the injured ANDREW QUICK. III:386

> **FATHER:** After he was scalped by JAKE's bullet, Tick-Tock had a memory of his father taking him to see the cider presses of Lud. III:386

GRAY HIGH COMMAND:

BLACK-HAIRED WOMAN: This unnamed woman had an annoying laugh, so TICK-TOCK threw a knife at her. The blade stabbed her in the chest and she died in front of JAKE. III:352–53, III:356

BRANDON: Brandon was a short, bandy-legged man. III:353–61, III:365–72, III:374, IV:646

COPPERHEAD: Copperhead was a tall, bespectacled man in a white silk shirt and black silk trousers. He looked like a college professor in a late-nineteenth-century *Punch* cartoon. III:313, III:365–74

GASHER: The first time Roland's *ka-tet* met Gasher, he was wearing patched green velvet pants and looked like a dying, but dangerous, buccaneer. Since he was in the late stages of the nasty venereal disease known as mandrus, his face was covered with oozing sores. Gasher had gray eyes, and was bald except for a few black hairs that stuck out of his head like porcupine quills. He usually covered his head with his yellow scarf.   III:296–303 *(takes Jake)*, III:304–7, III:308, III:312–14, III:314–16 *(followed by Roland)*, III:323 *(indirect)*, III:325–28, III:328–31 *(followed by Roland)*, III:334–39, III:340, III:341, III:350–61, III:363, III:365–72, III:375, III:383, III:402, IV:23, IV:28, IV:88 *(indirectly compared to CHARLIE THE CHOO-CHOO)*, IV:100–101 *(Eddie's bulldozer dream)*, IV:646

> **GASHER'S FATHER:** When he died, he was so rotten with mandrus that the dogs wouldn't even eat him.   III:355

HOOTS: Hoots was Gasher's former lover. When we see him in the Cradle of the Grays, he is a tall skinny man in a black suit. He has a terrible, itchy rash on his face, caused by mandrus.   III:338, III:352–61, III:365–72, IV:646

TILLY: Tilly was one of the two female members of the Grays High Command. (Unfortunately, Tick-Tock murdered the other one.) She looked like a red-haired female truck driver. III:353–61, III:365–72, III:373–74, IV:646

OTHER GRAYS: After Blaine set off the city's alarms, Roland and Jake saw a number of unnamed Grays fleeing through the gang's kitchens.   III:378

> **SCRUFFY MAN IN KITCHEN:** Blaine killed this guy by dropping open an oven door and directing a blast of blue-white fire at his head.   III:376

GREAT OLD ONES
See OLD ONES

GREEN FOLK
See ELURIA CHARACTERS

**GUARDIANS OF THE BEAM (TOTEMS OF THE BEAM)
In *The Waste Lands,* Roland draws a metaphysical map of Mid-World. The map is circular and looks like a clockface, but its circumference contains twelve *X*'s rather than twelve numbers. Each *X* designates a PORTAL, or a doorway into, and out of, Mid-World. Just as the minor portals in and out of Mid-World are guarded by DEMONS, the major portals are guarded by animal totems. These twelve Guardians (divided into six pairs to guard the ends of each of the six BEAMS) are not mortal, and so exist either beyond, or outside, *ka.*

During Roland's youth, many people maintained that the Beams and Portals were natural. Others (such as HAX) stated that they were created by the OLD ONES in atonement for the great wrongs they had done to one another, and to the earth. When Roland was young, the Guardians were still revered. He sees them depicted outside HAMBRY'S MERCANTILE and then later upon the imposing CRADLE OF LUD, where they march along the roof in their Beam pairs. We are told the names of eleven of the twelve Guardians. They are BEAR, TURTLE, FISH, EAGLE, LION, BAT, WOLF, HARE, RAT, HORSE, and DOG. We also know that the DARK TOWER is guarded by a thirteenth totem, known as THE BEAST. (However, in the new version of *The Gunslinger*, we find out that it is THE CRIMSON KING, and not the Beast, that Roland will have to face when he reaches the Tower.)

As the Dark Tower fails, the Guardians sicken and die. When we meet the Bear Guardian (also known as SHARDIK, or MIR), he is coughing up white worms, a disease which (if we take a look at *The Talisman*), concurs with the breakdown of the time/space continuum.

Although the original Guardians may have been magical creatures, the one that Roland, SUSANNAH, and EDDIE find is a giant cyborg. Shardik's body was created by NORTH CENTRAL POSITRONICS, the same company that made BLAINE. When Roland was a child, he was told that each Guardian had a thinking cap, or a hat upon its head which contained a second brain. This somewhat apocryphal story was based on the fact that the North Central Positronics Guardians all had small radar dishes coming out of their skulls.

Two Mid-World sayings invoke the Guardians. They are "Bird and bear and hare and fish, Give my love her fondest wish," and "Bless the Turtle."

GENERAL INFORMATION: III:29, III:33, III:37–40 *(40 thinking caps)*, III:171, III:325, III:331, III:333, IV:222, IV:326, IV:328 *(Hambry's Mercantile)*, IV:355 *(and Reap charms)*, IV:424, IV:464, IV:529, IV:536, IV:571, IV:573, IV:606–8, IV:629, IV:667, IV:668

**BEAST, THE: In the original version of *The Gunslinger*, we learned that the Beast was the Thirteenth Guardian, that he stood watch over the DARK TOWER, and that he was the final enemy that Roland would have to face before attaining his goal. The Beast (so WALTER said) was the originator of all *glammer*, and was an even more powerful force than MAERLYN. However, in the new version of *The Gunslinger*, the Beast is not mentioned and neither is Maerlyn. Instead we learn that Roland will have to slay the AGELESS STRANGER, whose other name is LEGION, before he meets his final enemy, who is THE CRIMSON KING himself. It seems likely that the Ageless Stranger is a great sorcerer (perhaps another incarnation of the shape-shifter Walter) and that the Beast is the ugly form of the Crimson King. I:212, III:261, IV:464–65 *(and the wind)*

BAT: III:39, IV:222 *(Hambry's Mercantile)*

BEAR (SHARDIK/MIR):

DESIGN 4 GUARDIAN
SERIAL # AA 24123 CX 755431297 L 14
TYPE/SPECIES: BEAR
SHARDIK
NRSUBNUCLEAR CELLS MUST NOT
BE REPLACED**NR**

Shardik was made in the dim, unknown reaches of OUT-WORLD, where we can assume the factories of NORTH CENTRAL POSITRONICS operated. Standing seventy feet high, Shardik was the largest creature ever to walk the GREAT WEST WOODS. He was so huge that he seemed to be a moving building or a shaggy tower rather than a bear. Although Shardik had roamed the woods for eighteen centuries, Roland believed that he was actually two or three thousand years old. By the time Roland and his friends met the great bear, he (like the rest of Mid-World) was dying.

The primitive people who came across Shardik in the years following the destruction of the OLD ONES' world renamed the great bear MIR. In their language, Mir meant "the world beneath the world" (III:32). They believed him to be both a demon incarnate and the shadow of a god.

In *Wizard and Glass,* Eddie Dean had a dream-vision in which he and his friends stood before the fence surrounding the magic LOT. Written in dusky pink letters upon the fence was the following rhyme:

See the BEAR of fearsome size!
All the WORLD'S within his eyes.
TIME grows thin, the past's a riddle;
The TOWER awaits you in the middle. *(Eddie's Dream IV:100)*

Shardik is paired with the TURTLE Guardian.   *(III:11–86 section title: Bear and Bone),* III:19–21, III:24, III:25–36 *(31 shot),* III:37, III:39, III:50–51 *(backtrail and portal),* III:53–77 *(58–65 following backtrail; 65–77 clearing and portal),* III:79, III:84, III:154, III:162, III:260, III:261, III:262, III:264, III:325, III:331, III:333, III:347, III:407, IV:42 *(Eddie remembers him),* IV:222 *(Hambry's Mercantile),* IV:326, IV:481

SERVOMECHANISMS: These nasty little mechanical creatures served Shardik. Like the Guardians, they each had a radar dish coming out of their heads. After Shardik's destruction, our *ka-tet* came across this pathetic but dangerous little retinue walking round and round in a circle. The five described resemble a **TONKA TRACTOR**, a **RAT**, a **SNAKE**, a **BLOCK**, and a **BAT**.   III:65–71, III:72, III:153, III:260

DOG: The Dog is paired with the HORSE Guardian.   III:325, III:331, III:333

EAGLE: IV:222 *(Hambry's Mercantile)*, IV:126–27 *(on gold coins)*

FISH: The Fish is paired with the RAT Guardian. When JAKE ran through the CRADLE OF THE GRAYS (prodded ever onward by the malicious GASHER), he saw a huge chrome and crystal fish statue. Upon it was written a single word of High Speech. That word was DELIGHT.   III:39, III:304, III:325, III:331, III:333, IV:222, IV:326

HARE: IV:326

HORSE: The Horse is paired with the DOG Guardian.   III:325, III:331, III:333

LION: III:39, IV:222 *(Hambry's Mercantile)*

RAT: The Rat is paired with the FISH Guardian.   III:325, III:331, III:333

TURTLE: The Turtle is one of the most important Guardians, and seems to be the major totem of the city of LUD. (The STREET OF THE TURTLE, with its sculptured Turtle, leads to BLAINE'S CRADLE.) Although we have not seen him yet, we have heard the following two poems about him:

> See the TURTLE of enormous girth!
> On his shell he holds the earth.
> His thought is slow but always kind;
> He holds us all within his mind.
> On his back all vows are made:
> He sees the truth but mayn't aid.
> He loves the land and loves the sea,
> And even loves a child like me. *(III:40)*

> See the TURTLE of enormous girth!
> On his shell he holds the earth
> If you want to run and play,
> Come along the BEAM today. *(III:122)*

The Turtle is paired with SHARDIK, the BEAR Guardian.   III:39–40, III:122, III:129, III:264, III:266, III:309 *(sculpture of and street of the)*, III:310 *(voice of the)*, III:312 *(street)*, III:316 *(street)*, III:325 *(street)*,

III:331, III:332 *(street)*, III:333, III:341 *(street)*, IV:222 *(Hambry's Mercantile)*, IV:424 *("Bless the Turtle")*, IV:481 *("in the name of the turtle and the bear")*, IV:570–73 *(Roland hears the turtle's voice during his time trapped in Maerlyn's ball)*
WOLF: IV:222 *(Hambry's Mercantile)*

GUNSLINGERS (OUR WORLD)

Individuals from our *where* and *when* who come in contact with Roland Deschain are often reminded of one or more gunslingers from the Old West of the late nineteenth and early twentieth centuries. Here is a short list of those gunslingers, including a brief bio of each.

BILLY THE KID: Billy the Kid (William H. Bonney) was one of the Old West's famous outlaws. Although he was born in New York, the Kid became one of the most notorious gunslingers involved in New Mexico's cattle wars. Legend has it that he killed twenty-one men before his twenty-first birthday. True to his nickname, the Kid died young. He never saw twenty-two.   II:186

CASSIDY, BUTCH, AND THE SUNDANCE KID: Butch Cassidy was one of the most celebrated outlaws of the American West. Born Robert Leroy Parker, he took his last name from Mike Cassidy, a cowboy rustler who taught him the horse thieving trade. His first name came from his stint working for a butcher in Wyoming.

Butch Cassidy and Harry Longbaugh (known as the Sundance Kid) formed the Wild Bunch Gang, also called the Hole in the Wall Gang. Cassidy was sometimes called a "gentleman bandit" because he claimed never to have killed anyone during his raids.   II:358

EARP, WYATT: Wyatt Earp was one of the Old West's most famous lawmen and was a wiz with the six-shooter. He earned a reputation as a hard-caliber man in such towns as Tombstone and Dodge City. He and the other Earp brothers took part in the famous shootout at the OK Corral. (They fought the Clanton clan.) Earp actually wore the famous lawman's star for less than a decade. His other careers were as gambler, teamster, buffalo hunter, and railroad man. He was friends with the equally famous DOC HOLLIDAY.   II:358

HOLLIDAY, DOC: Doc Holliday was born John Henry Holliday. Although he trained as a dentist, he moved west to try to ease the tuberculosis that was killing him. Unfortunately, the drier climate didn't help much and his constant coughing drove away his clientele. As a result, he took up a new profession—gambling—and was remarkably good at it. He eventually diversified and added train robbery, despite the fact that he was friends with the lawman WYATT EARP. (Interestingly enough, the Doc occasionally served as Earp's deputy.) Like so many of the other famous gunslingers of our world, Holliday was a deadly shot with the six-gun. However, in the end it was the TB, and not the gun, that killed him. Holliday died at age thirty-six.   II:358

OAKLEY, ANNIE: Although Annie Oakley was a woman, she could shoot like Roland. From 1885 to 1902, she starred in Buffalo Bill's Wild West Show. Although she stood just under five feet tall, her aim could make a huge man tremble. As part of her act, Annie shot cigarettes from her husband's lips. She could even shoot through the pips of a playing card tossed in the air. Too bad she never met our *ka-tet*.   II:368

H

HACKFORD, DR. MORRIS
See TOPEKA CHARACTERS

HALVORSEN, JIMMY
See DEAN, SUSANNAH: OTHER ASSOCIATES: MACY'S EMPLOYEES

HAMBRY CHARACTERS
HORSEMEN'S ASSOCIATION: All of Hambry's important ranchers, stockliners, and livestock owners belonged to this local, but powerful, association. Many of the farmers belonged as well. FRAN LENGYLL—distant friend and later murderer of PAT DELGADO—was its president. Not surprisingly, SUSAN DELGADO thought them a cold lot. This association owned the BAR K RANCH, where Roland, CUTHBERT, and ALAIN stayed during their time in MEJIS. Although they pretended to be loyal to the AFFILIATION, the Horsemen's Association actually supported THE GOOD MAN. In reality, they were the FARSON Association.   IV:188, IV:199, IV:211, IV:251–52 *(something is wrong),* IV:293, IV:381 *(all traitors),* IV:424, IV:519 *(as "Farson Association"),* IV:522, IV:541

    CROYDON, JOHN (PIANO RANCH): John Croydon owned the PIANO RANCH and a good part of THE DROP. He also owned some small orchards.   IV:187, IV:188, IV:199, IV:204, IV:251, IV:341, IV:466, IV:470, IV:545 *(present 540–46),* IV:558 *(killed; present 553–58)*

    GARBER: This is the family that owned Bar K Ranch before it passed to the Horsemen's Association.   IV:188, IV:251

LENGYLL, FRANCIS (ROCKING B RANCH): Fran Lengyll, President of the Horsemen's Association, was a blocky man with pale eyes, a net of wrinkles, and wind-burned cheeks. His handshake was strong and quick.

Lengyll owned the ROCKING B RANCH. He also owned the biggest Honda generator in Hambry. Although he pretended to be loyal to the AFFILIATION, he was one of the first of Hambry's residents that Roland caught lying in aid of FARSON's rebel forces.

Lengyll's service to THE GOOD MAN extended to murder. According to Lengyll, PAT DELGADO—a loyal Affiliation man—was killed by his horse. However, this proved to be a lie. Lengyll killed him.   IV:186, IV:187, IV:188, IV:198–202, IV:204, IV:251, IV:254–56, IV:313–14, IV:355, IV:385, IV:447, IV:459, IV:460, IV:463, IV:466, IV:470, IV:473–80, IV:483, IV:484, IV:500–502, IV:522, IV:528, IV:535, IV:540–46, IV:548, IV:553–57 *(attacked by Roland's ka-tet; 557 killed)*, IV:566, IV:577, IV:582, IV:584 *(Alain has his machine gun)*, IV:589 *(machine gun)*, IV:592

RENFREW, HASH (LAZY SUSAN RANCH): Hash Renfrew, owner of the LAZY SUSAN RANCH, was a big boozer. Not surprisingly, he was even larger and blockier than FRAN LENGYLL. Renfrew's place was the biggest horse ranch in MEJIS. Like the other members of the Horsemen's Association, Renfrew was a secret supporter of THE GOOD MAN. Like Lengyll, Renfrew lied to Roland and his friends about the number of MUTIE horses born in the area.   IV:187, IV:199, IV:203–8 *(206 mentions Excalibur)*, IV:222, IV:236, IV:254 *(lies about threaded stock)*, IV:255, IV:355, IV:421, IV:459, IV:522, IV:527–29, IV:532–35, IV:537–46 *(present for action)*, IV:556–57 *(557 killed)*

RIMER, LASLO: Laslo Rimer was KIMBA RIMER's older brother. He looked like a stony-hearted preacher. Laslo owned the ROCKING H RANCH, where he secretly kept oxen. They were for FARSON's use.   IV:293, IV:561, IV:585–87

WERTNER, HENRY (BARONY STOCKLINER): Henry Wertner was the Barony's stockliner as well as a horsebreeder in his own right. He took PAT DELGADO's job after he died.   IV:187, IV:199, IV:204, IV:211, IV:341, IV:459, IV:545 *(present for action 540–46)*

WHITE, JAKE: White owned some of the apple orchards north of Hambry.   IV:199, IV:251, IV:341, IV:473–80 *(present for arrest of Roland's ka-tet)*

HAMBRY LOVERS:

ROBERT AND FRANCESCA: Robert and Francesca were lovers who made it into Hambry's folklore. Francesca tried to end their affair, so Robert dashed out her brains and then clipped his windpipe. This murder/suicide supposedly happened in the town cemetery.   IV:426

HAMBRY SEAFRONT (THE MAYOR'S HOUSE):

MORGENSTERN, CONCHETTA: A blade-faced seamstress. Her view of existence was that life was hard and that we'd all just better get used to it.   IV:292, IV:310–11, IV:313 *(blade-faced),* IV:426

RIMER, KIMBA: Kimba Rimer was HART THORIN's Chancellor. He was also the Barony's Minister of Inventory. Tall, thin, with skin pale as candlewax, Rimer reminded Roland of Doctor Death. His voice was that of either a politician or an undertaker.

According to OLIVE THORIN, Rimer looted Hambry's treasury, and what he didn't give to FARSON he kept for himself. But no matter how good he was at lining his own pockets, Rimer was even better at making enemies. Once, on account of CLAY REYNOLDS's swirling, silk-lined cloak, Rimer jokingly called the younger man *Sai Manto,* an insult that also implied homosexuality. Reynolds never forgot it. Hence, when the time came to send Rimer on to the clearing at the end of the path, Reynolds took the job gleefully. IV:133, IV:139 *(relationship to Hart Thorin),* IV:141, IV:153, IV:154, IV:175–78, IV:184 *(false papers for Roland's ka-tet),* IV:187, IV:191–210 *(Hart Thorin's party. Rimer appears on the following pages: 192–93 [gaunt as Dr. Death], 195–201 [196 joke about "The Good Man"], 204, 208),* IV:211, IV:212, IV:213, IV:250, IV:251, IV:257, IV:260, IV:301, IV:308, IV:347–53, IV:356, IV:358, IV:367–68, IV:373, IV:377, IV:381, IV:402, IV:405, IV:406, IV:425, IV:443, IV:453, IV:460, IV:470–71 *(killed by Reynolds),* IV:476, IV:482, IV:483, IV:488, IV:500–501, IV:519, IV:537, IV:564, IV:585, IV:664

THORIN, HART: Horny Hart Thorin was the Mayor of Hambry and the Chief Guard o' Barony. He was also CORAL THORIN's brother and OLIVE THORIN's husband. He and Coral co-owned Hambry's bar and brothel, THE TRAVELLERS' REST. Thorin was anything but elegant, and often acted like a buffoon. In fact, the reader wonders why Olive continued to love this skinny and twitchy knuckle-cracker, especially since he couldn't wait to take on other women.

Though he was gangly as a marsh bird, Hart Thorin conceived a passion for SUSAN DELGADO, a girl young enough to be his granddaughter. By the beginning of *Wizard and Glass*'s Mejis adventures, Thorin had already paid for Susan to become his gilly. Like other Hambry officials, Thorin allied himself with Farson, though those he sold his soul to eventually murdered him. Thorin's dog was named **WOLF**. IV:116, IV:121, IV:125, IV:126, IV:129–30, IV:131, IV:133, IV:134, IV:135, IV:136, IV:139–41 *(relationships with Susan and Rimer)*, IV:143, IV:153, IV:154, IV:168, IV:169, IV:172 *(and Travellers' Rest)*, IV:176, IV:177, IV:184 *(and Roland's false papers)*, IV:186–87, IV:188, IV:191–210 *(Party. He appears on the following pages: 193, 195–202 [195–96 described]; 197 with Susan; 203, 205–8 [Susan as his Sheevin, or side-wife]; 209)*, IV:211–13, IV:223, IV:236 *(and Susan's blouses)*, IV:237, IV:238, IV:242, IV:246, IV:250, IV:251–52, IV:278, IV:280, IV:285, IV:290, IV:299, IV:301, IV:303, IV:307, IV:308 *(Wolf)*, 311–13 *(lunges for Susan and loses his posh accent)*, IV:314, IV:317, IV:318, IV:331, IV:348 *(involved with Farson affair)*, IV:351, IV:356, IV:360, IV:373, IV:377, IV:381, IV:405, IV:424, IV:426–27, IV:434, IV:461–62, IV:465, IV:471–73 *(Depape kills him. Leaves Cuthbert's Lookout and Farson's sigul)*, IV:476, IV:482, IV:483, IV:492, IV:498, IV:500–501, IV:514, IV:519–20, IV:533, IV:537, IV:549, IV:561, IV:564, IV:569, IV:578, IV:585, IV:664

THORIN, OLIVE: Poor Olive Thorin was HART THORIN'S long-suffering wife. She was a plump, good-natured woman with an artless smile, and was one of the few people in Hambry that Roland really liked. Olive grew up a fisherman's daughter and never forgot it. Even though her husband wanted SUSAN DELGADO as his gilly, when Susan needed to be rescued it was big-hearted Olive who tried to help her. Olive was eventually killed by CLAY REYNOLDS. IV:191–210 *(Thorin's party. She appears on the following pages: 191–92 [described], 193 [described], 194, 195, 205, 208 [sad about Thorin and Susan])*, IV:211, IV:212 *(John Haverty's daughter)*, IV:223 *(parallel to Roland's mother)*, IV:238, IV:257, IV:259, IV:292, IV:324, IV:405, IV:428, IV:457, IV:461–62 *(nightmare about Roc. Premonition of husband's death)*, IV:569–70, IV:577–78, IV:581–83, IV:585–86 *(killed by Reynolds)*

HAVERTY, JOHN: Olive Thorin's father. IV:212

TOMAS, MARIA: Susan's maid. IV:292, IV:306–8, IV:428, IV:457, IV:480–83, IV:537, IV:577–78, IV:581

TORRES, MIGUEL: A Seafront servant. IV:405, IV:448, IV:481, IV:494–95, IV:522, IV:566–68, IV:578

HAMBRY SHERIFF'S OFFICE:

AVERY, HERK: Herk Avery was the High Sheriff of MEJIS and the Chief Constable of Hambry. He was a large, fat man "loose as a trundle of laundry" (IV:175). Like the other important men of Hambry, he had no real love for the AFFILIATION. IV:155,

IV:175, IV:179, IV:180, IV:181–90 *(181 described; 183–84 goes through Roland's false papers; 185 ice machines)*, IV:191, IV:192–93, IV:194, IV:197, IV:226–30 *(after standoff between Big Coffin Hunters and Roland's ka-tet)*, IV:251, IV:259–60, IV:273 *(and thinny)*, IV:295, IV:329, IV:359, IV:360, IV:362–64, IV:367, IV:423, IV:425, IV:432, IV:462–63, IV:473–80, IV:483, IV:502, IV:507, IV:508–13 *(511 Susan kills him)*, IV:517, IV:520, IV:521, IV:523, IV:564 *(Susan blamed for his murder)*

   HERK'S DEPUTIES: IV:181–90

   BRIDGER, TODD: IV:473–80 *(present for arrest of Roland's ka-tet)*, IV:508, IV:521

   CLAYPOOL, FRANK: IV:329 *(named by JONAS. Broke his leg. Jonas standing in for him)*, IV:462, IV:605

   HOLLIS, DAVE: Dave Hollis is often referred to as "Deputy Dave." Although he was only a few years older than SUSAN DELGADO, he was balding and wore a monocle. While she was attempting to rescue Roland and his friends, Susan accidentally killed him.   IV:181–90, IV:192, IV:227–30, IV:259–60, IV:363–64, IV:367, IV:431–32, IV:462, IV:473–80 *(present for arrest of Roland's ka-tet)*, IV:508–13 *(510 Susan kills him)*, IV:521, IV:564 *(Susan blamed for his murder)*

      HOLLIS, JUDY: Dave Hollis's wife. Her maiden name was JUDY WERTNER.   IV:182, IV:185, IV:189, IV:287, IV:432, IV:512

   RIGGINS, GEORGE: IV:259–60 *(name mentioned for the first time)*

HAMBRY TRAVELLERS' REST:

   CALLAHAN, BARKIE: Saloon bouncer.   IV:171, IV:172, IV:176, IV:218, IV:349, IV:451–52 *(at Citgo)*

   CAPRICHOSO (CAPI): Caprichoso was the Rest's Pack mule. SHEEMIE was the one who usually rode him. Caprichoso, in turn, liked to bite Sheemie. For page references, see SHEEMIE, listed below.

   COUNTESS JILLIAN OF UP'ARD KILLIAN: She was a whore who had royal pretensions. She maintained that she was from GARLAN.   IV:214

   MOGGINS, GERT: See BIG COFFIN HUNTERS: DEPAPE, ROY

   PETTIE THE TROTTER: Pettie was one of the Rest's whores. She actually wanted to change professions and become a bartender. IV:171, IV:173, IV:176, IV:213–14, IV:216, IV:218, IV:224–25, IV:336, IV:382–83, IV:403, IV:468–69, IV:470, IV:563–65 *(present)*, IV:605

ROMP, THE: The Romp was the name of the two-headed MUTIE elk mounted on the wall behind the Rest's bar. He had a rack of antlers like a forest grove and four glaring eyes.   IV:171–72, IV:176, IV:213, IV:214, IV:217, IV:382, IV:447, IV:468, IV:563, IV:570, IV:610

RUIZ, STANLEY: Stanley Ruiz was the Rest's barkeep. He was probably also SHEEMIE's father.   IV:214, IV:215, IV:216, IV:217 *(Sheemie may be his son)*, IV:218, IV:242, IV:382, IV:396 *(Rhea mentions him as Sheemie's father)*, IV:397, IV:447, IV:467–69 *(His two clubs: The Calmer and The Killer)*, IV:470, IV:506, IV:563 *(562–65 present for action)*, IV:605

**SHEB (SHEB McCURDY): Sheb played the piano in the Travellers' Rest. He also worked in TULL. See entry under SHEB, listed separately.

SHEEMER, DELORES: SHEEMIE'S mother. Before she died, she was probably one of the Rest's whores.   IV:217

**SHEEMIE: Sheemie was a mildly retarded young man who had black kinky hair and a sweet disposition. He was the bastard offspring of DELORES SHEEMER and (most likely) STANLEY RUIZ. After CUTHBERT ALLGOOD saved his life, Sheemie became devoted to Roland's *ka-tet*. He also loved SUSAN DELGADO. In the new *Gunslinger,* Roland remembers Sheemie and his humorous relationship with the mule CAPRICHOSO.   IV:172, IV:190 *(described)*, IV:214, IV:215–22 *(cause of standoff at Travellers' Rest; 217 maternity/paternity discussed)*, IV:226 *(end of fight)*, IV:228–29, IV:240–42, IV:244–45, IV:254, IV:287–88, IV:327, IV:336, IV:343–44, IV:382, IV:384–85, IV:389–90, IV:394–98 *(graf to Rhea. 396 she calls him "son of Stanley")*, IV:402–3, IV:413, IV:433–34, IV:443, IV:447–50 *(getting firecrackers with Susan)*, IV:497, IV:504, IV:505–7, IV:512, IV:514–19, IV:523–24, IV:525, IV:526, IV:529, IV:536–37, IV:539–40, IV:546, IV:565–70 *(following Susan)*, IV:571, IV:579–80, IV:581–83 *(583 he loves Susan)*, IV:585, IV:594, IV:624

THORIN, CORAL: Morose Coral Thorin was the Madame of the saloon and whorehouse known as the Travellers' Rest. She and her brother, Mayor HART THORIN, jointly owned the place. Fifty-five-year-old Coral was a wild-child in her youth and didn't get any better as she got older. She just became more mercenary about it. Although she was attractive in a large-eyed, weasel-headed way, she had a hard streak. Coral became ELDRED JONAS's lover. After he died and she fled Hambry, she became CLAY REYNOLDS's woman. The two of them turned to bank robbery and were eventually killed for it.   IV:171, IV:172 *(described. Fifty-five years old),*

IV:178, IV:191–210 *(Thorin's party. She appears on the following pages: 191–92, 193, 194, 203–8 [we learn on 207–8 that she despises Susan]),* IV:228, IV:249, IV:341, IV:347, IV:351, IV:380–87, IV:388, IV:389–90, IV:420–25, IV:434, IV:447–48, IV:449, IV:460, IV:466, IV:468, IV:489, IV:500, IV:505–6, IV:515, IV:519–23, IV:527, IV:532, IV:537, IV:545, IV:561–62, IV:566, IV:623 *(Becomes Clay Reynolds's lover and a bank robber. They are killed.)*

OTHER HAMBRY CHARACTERS:

ALVEREZ, MISHA: SUSAN DELGADO taught her daughter to ride horseback, but this didn't stop Misha from spitting on Susan as she was carted toward the Charyou Tree bonfire.   IV:607

BEECH, MRS.: Hers was the first mailbox on the edge of town. IV:144, IV:155, IV:158

HOOKEY, BRIAN: He owned HOOKEY'S STABLE & SMITHY, also known as HOOKEY'S STABLE AND FANCY LIVERY. IV:279–80, IV:282, IV:301 *(in on Farson plot),* IV:330, IV:336, IV:377, IV:386, IV:390, IV:427, IV:501, IV:512, IV:545 *(present for 540–46),* IV:556 *(556 killed; 553–56 present for action)*

HOOKEY, RUFUS: BRIAN HOOKEY's son.   IV:427, IV:501

McCANN, JAMIE: This whey-faced boy was to be HART THORIN's stand-in during the Reap festivities. Thorin was too old to be the Reaping Lad.   IV:292, IV:605

OLD SOONY: He owned the hut in the BAD GRASS where Susan and Roland made love, and where Susan was later captured by ELDRED JONAS. Old Soony joined the MANNI sect.   IV:534

ORTEGA, MILLICENT: She was a gossip who stared at CORDELIA and ELDRED JONAS from the window of ANN'S DRESSES.   IV:328

O'SHYVEN, PETER: The husband of THERESA O'SHYVEN, he is decribed as "a vaquero of laughing temperament."   IV:485

O'SHYVEN, THERESA MARIA DELORES: Wife of PETER O'SHYVEN, she sold rugs in Hambry's upper market. In her spare time, she licked corners in order to clean them.   IV:485–86

QUINT, HIRAM: He worked at the PIANO RANCH.   IV:451–52 *(at Citgo),* IV:484, IV:527–29, IV:532–35, IV:558 *(557–58 present for action; flees scene of attack)*

HARLEY, MR.
See PIPER SCHOOL CHARACTERS

HARRIERS
See HIGH SPEECH AND MID-WORLD ARGOT

HASPIO, JIMMY
See BALAZAR'S MEN

HATHAWAY, MISS
See DEAN, EDDIE

HAVERTY, JOHN
See HAMBRY: SEAFRONT: THORIN, OLIVE

**HAX
Hax was the head cook of Gilead's castle and the absolute ruler of the West Kitchen. He was a large, dark-skinned man with a gold hoop in his right ear. Although he loved children, he was a faithful follower of JOHN FARSON (THE GOOD MAN). To serve the cause of revolution, Hax was prepared to poison the men, women, and children of the town of FARSON. (In the new *Gunslinger*, Hax plots to poison the town of TAUNTON, not Farson.) Hax's plan was discovered by Roland and CUTHBERT ALLGOOD. Hax was hanged for his crime and both Roland and Cuthbert were allowed to watch. Roland took a splinter from the gallows tree.
   I:100–106, I:107–11 *(hanged)*, I:137, I:158, I:159, II:105, III:37–38, III:39, III:40, III:41, IV:161, IV:302–3, IV:417, IV:656
   MAGGIE: Maggie worked in the kitchens of Gilead's castle. She was HAX's assistant cook.   I:101

HEATH, ARTHUR
See ALLGOOD, CUTHBERT

HEATH, GEORGE
See ALLGOOD, CUTHBERT

HENRY THE TALL
Roland's paternal grandfather.
   IV:270–71

HOLDEN ("FAT JOHNNY" HOLDEN)
Stocky, black-haired "Fat Johnny" was the brother-in-law of JUSTIN CLEMENTS. He worked at CLEMENTS GUNS AND SPORTING GOODS.
   II:343–59, II:371–73, II:377
   MOTHER: II:356

HOLLIDAY, DOC
　　See GUNSLINGERS (OUR WORLD)

HOLLIS, DAVE
　　See HAMBRY CHARACTERS: SHERIFF'S OFFICE

HOLLIS, JUDY
　　See HAMBRY CHARACTERS: SHERIFF'S OFFICE

HOLMES, ALICE
　　See DEAN, SUSANNAH: ODETTA HOLMES'S ASSOCIATES

HOLMES, DAN
　　See DEAN, SUSANNAH: ODETTA HOLMES'S ASSOCIATES

HOLMES, ODETTA
　　See DEAN, SUSANNAH

HOOKEY, BRIAN
　　See HAMBRY CHARACTERS: OTHER CHARACTERS

HOOTS
　　See GRAYS: GRAY HIGH COMMAND

**HORN OF DESCHAIN
In the new version of *The Gunslinger,* we learn that CUTHBERT
ALLGOOD died while blowing the Horn of Deschain at the Battle of
JERICHO HILL. At this terrible battle, which brought down the AFFIL-
IATION, Roland lost not only the last of his fellow fighters but the
horn of his fathers, which he was meant to sound when he reached the
DARK TOWER.

HORSEMEN'S ASSOCIATION
　　See HAMBRY CHARACTERS: HORSEMEN'S ASSOCIATION

HOTCHKISS, MR.
　　See PIPER SCHOOL CHARACTERS

HOUNDS OF THE FALLS
During their terrifying ride on BLAINE the insane mono, our *ka-tet* saw
these magnificent stone statures jutting over a waterfall between RILEA
and DASHERVILLE. Although their bodies resembled those of enormous

snarling dogs, their purpose was to gather the force of the BEAM and transform it to electricity. Blaine used this energy to recharge his batteries. See BLAINE'S ROUTE in the MID-WORLD PLACES section. IV:32–35, IV: 41–42

HOWARD
See DEAN, SUSANNAH: ODETTA HOLMES' ASSOCIATES

I

"IL ROCHE"
See BALAZAR

IMPERIUM
See NORTH CENTRAL POSITRONICS

INTERLOPER
See PITTSTON, SYLVIA and DEMONS/SPIRITS/DEVILS

J

JAMIE
See DE CURRY, JAMIE

JENNA, SISTER
See ELURIA, LITTLE SISTERS OF

JESSERLING, PETRA
See PIPER SCHOOL CHARACTERS

JESUS DOG (CROSS DOG)
See ELURIA CHARACTERS

"JIM CROW"
Jim Crow was a character in an early-nineteenth-century plantation song found in Our World. His name was given to the set of laws and

social practices known as segregation. During her time on our level of the TOWER, SUSANNAH DEAN and other Civil Rights activists fought to oust the Jim Crow policies found in the South.

II:234, II:235, II:236

**JOHNS, ALAIN

Alain Johns was Roland's sworn brother and his fellow gunslinger. Although he is mentioned earlier, we do not meet Alain until *Wizard and Glass*, when he and CUTHBERT ALLGOOD accompany Roland to the OUTER ARC town of HAMBRY.

Alain was a big boy with a mop of unruly blond hair, bright blue eyes, and a round face. Because of his looks, many people assumed he was a dullard; however, he was actually both clever and sensitive. Like Roland's later *ka-tet* mate SUSANNAH DEAN, Alain had "the touch." Perhaps because of this mixture of empathy and psychic ability, Alain was much more stable than the volatile Cuthbert. Sadly for Alain, he was destined to die under Roland and Cuthbert's guns.

While in HAMBRY, Alain's alias was RICHARD STOCKWORTH. His horse was named **BUCKSKIN**. In the original version of *The Gunslinger*, Alain was not mentioned, though Roland spoke of a friend named ALLEN. In the new version of *The Gunslinger*, Allen's name is replaced with Alain's.

II:355 *(dies under Roland and Cuthbert's guns)*, II:394, III:15, III:33, III:41, III:60, III:262, III:276, III:279, III:280, IV:59, IV:119, IV:148 *(as Richard Stockworth)*, IV:151–53, IV:162, IV:163 *(Buckskin only)*, IV:164, IV:174, IV:179–80 *(Mayor Thorin's party; 179 Alain described)*, IV:181–89 *(Flashback to Sheriff Avery visit; 183–84 false papers. Richard Stockworth, Rancher's son, 184 described)*, IV:190–91 *(discussing Avery)*, IV:191–210 *(Mayor Thorin's party continued)*, IV:218–21 *(Travellers' Rest standoff)*, IV:224–30 *(standoff continued; 224 "the touch"; 226–30 with Avery)*, IV:241, IV:259–60 *("Little Coffin Hunters")*, IV:261–64 *(261 pigeons and message. 263 Susan's hair)*, IV:266–71 *(Depape finds out identities)*, IV:271–77, IV:280 *(gives message to Susan)*, IV:282, IV:283, IV:284–88, IV:291, IV:344–47, IV:357–61, IV:371, IV:388–89 *(the touch and premonitions)*, IV:392–93 *(the touch and senses trouble at Bar K)*, IV:398–402, IV:408–15, IV:426–42 *(428 described; 432 Roland's plan of attack; 436 speaks to Susan in her trance state; 436–39 Steven Deschain and Maerlyn's Grapefruit; 439 Christopher Johns [a.k.a. "Burning Chris"])*, IV:443 *("magic in his hands")*, IV:454–56, IV:463, IV:465, IV:474–80 *(ka-tet arrested)*, IV:482, IV:483, IV:487 *("boys")*, IV:503, IV:506, IV:508–13, IV:514–19, IV:523–24, IV:525 *(mentioned)*, IV:526, IV:529–32, IV:533–36, IV:538 *(reference)*,

IV:540, IV:547–48, IV:549 *(indirect)*, IV:552–60 *(attacking Jonas's company)*, IV:561 *(indirect reference)*, IV:573–75, IV:579–81, IV:583–84, IV:587–602 *(driving Farson's men into thinny)*, IV:609–11 *(Roland unconscious due to Maerlyn's ball)*, IV:620, IV:658, IV:663, E:186
    ALAIN'S MOTHER: IV:391 *(general)*, IV:399

JOHNS, CHRISTOPHER
Alain's father, known in his youth as "Burning Chris."
    IV:286, IV:436–39, IV:620

JOHNSON
    See TULL CHARACTERS

JOLENE
    See RITZY CHARACTERS

JONAS, ELDRED
    See BIG COFFIN HUNTERS

K

KATZ
    Katz was the forty-six-year-old owner of KATZ'S PHARMACY AND SODA FOUNTAIN. With his frail body, balding head, and yellow skin, he looked more like sixty-six. Katz hated his shop and never forgave his father for burdening him with it.
    II:333, II:362–70, II:374, II:375
    KATZ SENIOR: Katz's deceased father. Katz curses him every day.
    II:363, II:365, II:366–67, II:375
        KATZ'S EMPLOYEES, CUSTOMERS, AND COMPETITORS:
        BRUMHALL, DR.: Mrs. RATHBUN's doctor. He's a little too free handing out the Valium prescriptions.   II:364–65
        DOLLENTZ: Katz's competitor in the pharmacy business. II:365
        GUY IN LEATHER JACKET: This guy tries to sneak up on MORT/Roland with a knife. Roland shoots it out of his hand. II:368–69
        KATZ'S PIMPLE-FACED ASSISTANT: II:365–70
        LENNOX, RALPH: Security guard at Katz's.   II:365–70

RATHBUN, MRS.: She's a valium addict who harasses Katz with outdated prescriptions until he refills them.   II:363–65, II:366

KENNEDY, JOHN F.

John F. Kennedy, who was much admired by SUSANNAH DEAN, was the thirty-fifth President of the United States. During his three years in office he introduced the legislative program called the "New Frontier," which was supposed to extend Civil Rights. He was allegedly assassinated by LEE HARVEY OSWALD in November of 1963, only about four months before Susannah entered Mid-World. Two days after the assassination, Oswald was shot at point-blank range by JACK RUBY. Kennedy's successor was Lyndon B. Johnson.

II:185–87

KENNERLY

See TULL: SYLVIA PITTSTON'S REVIVAL

KILLINGTON

See NORTH CENTRAL POSITRONICS: BLAINE

KINGERY, MR.

See PIPER SCHOOL CHARACTERS

KING'S TOWN GIRL

This girl was one of the many that Roland loved and then left behind.

I:158

KNOPF, MR.

See PIPER SCHOOL CHARACTERS

KUVIAN NIGHT-SOLDIER

It seems likely that the Kuvian night-soldiers were a band of assassins.

I:200

L

LADY OF SHADOWS

See DEAN, SUSANNAH

**LaMERK FOUNDRY
In the days of the GREAT OLD ONES, LaMerk Foundry built the long and rusty bridge leading to the city of LUD. It also manufactured Lud's manhole covers. As we find out in EDDIE'S dream about the destruction of Jake's magic LOT on Second Avenue and Forty-sixth Street, LaMerk Foundry appears to be connected to that enemy of the ROSE found in our world—MILLS CONSTRUCTION AND SOMBRA REAL ESTATE. It may also have ties to the sinister NORTH CENTRAL POSITRONICS. According to SYLVIA PITTSTON in the new *Gunslinger,* the INTER-LOPER (also known as THE CRIMSON KING) was responsible for LaMerk's nasty machines.
  III:290, III:326, IV:100 *(Eddie's bulldozer dream)*

LATIGO
  See FARSON'S MEN

**LEGION
  See AGELESS STRANGER

LENGYLL, FRANCIS
  See HAMBRY CHARACTERS: HORSEMEN'S ASSOCIATION

LENNOX, RALPH
  See KATZ

LESTER THE LOBSTER
  See LOBSTROSITIES

LITTLE COFFIN HUNTERS
  See BIG COFFIN HUNTERS

LITTLE SISTERS OF ELURIA
  See ELURIA, LITTLE SISTERS OF

LOBSTROSITIES
These critters, which live on the beaches of the WESTERN SEA, look like a cross between scorpions and giant lobsters. They are four feet long, have bleak eyes on stalks, and sharp, serrated beaks. Every time a wave comes, they assume "The Honor Stance" by holding their claws up in the air and then wait until the water crashes over them. They are most vicious at night, and are responsible for eating two of Roland's fingers and some of

his toes. They constantly murmur *Dad-a-chum? Did-a-chick? Dum-a-chum? Ded-a-Chek?*

II:15–21, II:26, II:28–29, II:31, II:32, II:44, II:55, II:93, II:94, II:99–101, II:107, II:135, II:139, II:140–41, II:161–65 *(Eddie and Roland eat them)*, II:167–68, II:206, II:228, II:230, II:238, II:245, II:248, II:253, II:254, II:258, II:267, II:273, II:283, II:286, II:293, II:294, II:297, II:359–60, II:387–90, II:394, III:13, III:52, III:78, III:79, III:150, IV:23, IV:63 *(indirect)*, IV:68

LORD PERTH
See PERTH, LORD

LOUISE, SISTER
See ELURIA, LITTLE SISTERS OF

LUD CHARACTERS
See GRAYS and PUBES

LUDDITES
Inhabitants of the City of LUD. See PUBES and GRAYS. In Our World, a Luddite is a person who opposes increased industrialization and/or new technology. The term comes from the nineteenth-century workers who destroyed the machines which they thought were stealing their jobs. In Mid-World's Lud, the Luddites have to worry about the machines stealing their lives.

LYDIA
See OLD MOTHER

M

MAD DOG OF GILEAD
EDDIE DEAN tells BLAINE the insane Mono that Roland used to be called the Mad Dog of Gilead.
III:415, IV:5

**MAERLYN
Maerlyn is the wizard responsible for the creation of the thirteen sinister magic balls known as MAERLYN'S RAINBOW. He is also known as the

AGELESS STRANGER. In the original version of *The Gunslinger*, we learned that Maerlyn and the BEAST are the final obstacles Roland will have to face before he climbs the DARK TOWER.

In the old version of *The Gunslinger*, we learned that WALTER was once the servant of this strange mage who lives backward in time and who *"darkles"* and *"tincts."* However, in the new version of *The Gunslinger*, Walter mentions neither Maerlyn nor the Beast. Instead, he speaks only of the Ageless Stranger and his own evil master, THE CRIMSON KING.

I:212, III: 261 *(Ageless Stranger)*, III:387, IV:649

MAERLYN'S RAINBOW: See DOORWAYS BETWEEN WORLDS in the PORTALS section.

MAGGIE
See HAX

MAN IN BLACK
See WALTER

**MANNI
The Manni are a religious sect who know how to travel between worlds. A tribe of them once lived outside GILEAD. Roland suspects that his old teacher CORT held palaver with these people, and so knew something about jumping the time/space continuum. ELDRED JONAS also knew about Manni beliefs.

In the new version of *The Gunslinger*, we learn that Manni holy men can achieve a clinical detachment from their own bodies, attaining a complete division between the mind/spirit and the physical self. They can even watch their bodies die without becoming emotionally upset. Also in the new *Gunslinger*, we learn that a tribe of Manni-folk lived in the dens to the north of the MOHAINE DESERT.

As well as having their own philosophy, the Manni have their own poetic tradition. The lines "Beyond the realm of human range/ A drop of hell, a touch of strange" come from a Manni poem. BROWN, the BORDER DWELLER, married a Manni woman and lived among them for a while. Although he left their settlement, he still retained their habit of using "thee" and "thou" in his speech.

IV:34, IV:175 *(and Jonas)*, IV:534

MARIA
See HAMBRY CHARACTERS: SEAFRONT

MARK
See CORT

MARK CROSS PEN BUSINESSMEN
See CHAMBERS, JAKE

MARTEN
See BROADCLOAK, MARTEN

MARTIN, MR. RAYMOND
See CHARLIE THE CHOO-CHOO

MARY, SISTER
See ELURIA, LITTLE SISTERS OF

MARYANNE
See DEAN, HENRY

McCURDY, SHEB
See SHEB (SHEB McCURDY: PIANO PLAYER)

McDONALD, CAPTAIN
See DEAN, EDDIE: DELTA FLIGHT 901 CHARACTERS

McGURSKY, MRS.
See DEAN, EDDIE

MERCY
See RIVER CROSSING CHARACTERS

MERLIN
Although the MAERLYN of Roland's world is different from the mythical Merlin of the Arthurian legends, in *The Gunslinger* Roland seems to be aware of the existence of both these magicians. He even compares MARTEN, the wicked magician of his father's court, to Merlin.
    I:94, III:261, III:387

MICHELA, SISTER
See ELURIA, LITTLE SISTERS OF

MID-WORLD RAILWAY CO.
See CHARLIE THE CHOO-CHOO

MIGUEL
See HAMBRY CHARACTERS: SEAFRONT

MILL, AUNT
See TULL CHARACTERS

MILLS CONSTRUCTION AND SOMBRA REAL ESTATE
Mills Construction is the company that is going to build the TURTLE BAY LUXURY CONDOMINIUMS on the site of JAKE's vacant LOT on Forty-sixth Street and Second Avenue. EDDIE DEAN's dream suggests that they are connected to LaMERK FOUNDRY in Mid-World.
III:121, IV:100

> SKANK, BANGO: Graffiti artist who defaced the sign for Turtle Bay Condominiums.   III:121

MIR
See GUARDIANS OF THE BEAM: SHARDIK

MOGGINS, GERT
See BIG COFFIN HUNTERS

MONTOYA, DR. APRIL
See TOPEKA CHARACTERS

MORGENSTERN, CONCHETTA
See HAMBRY CHARACTERS: SEAFRONT

MORT, JACK ("THE PUSHER")
Despite the fact that he was a professional CPA, the prim Jack Mort had a very nasty hobby. He liked to "depth-charge" people. In other words, he liked to kill them. Mort dropped the brick that hit five-year-old ODETTA HOLMES on the head. Years later, he pushed her in front of the A train at CHRISTOPHER STREET STATION.

Like WALTER, Mort is a man of many disguises. Dressed as a priest, he shoved JAKE CHAMBERS in front of a Cadillac on Fifth Avenue. Quite understandably, Mort is the human embodiment of the Death card found in Walter's Tarot pack. He is also the destination of the magic door labeled "The Pusher."

Jack Mort divides the world into "Do-Bees" and "Don't Bees." Do-Bees get away with their crimes while Don't Bees get caught. This extremely unpleasant character (who also happens to come in his pants when he kills) keeps a scrapbook of his murders. His gold-rimmed glasses, blue eyes, and expensive address (he lives at 409 Park Avenue South), fool people into thinking he is not a psychopath. But not only is Mort psychologically imbalanced, he is also a fairly easy target for demons/demonic presences who want to use a mortal agent to do their dirty deeds. When Mort killed Jake, he was actually no more than the pawn of Walter, also known as the MAN IN BLACK. Underneath his business suits, Jack Mort wears women's underwear.

II:315–26, II:339–59 *(Roland in control)*, II:360–86 *(Roland in control. Mort dies)*, II:389, III:15, III:59–62 *(62 dark hair. In Book II said to be blond)*, III:103–6 *(and Jake's death)*, III:261, III:262, III:266

> **MORT'S ASSOCIATES:**
>
> **BALD MAN WITH GLASSES:** This guy works in Mort's office. II:326, II:339
>
> **CURD-FACED TEENAGE GIRL:** After missing his opportunity to push Jake in front of a car, a very angry Mort shoves this girl out of his way.   II:317–18
>
> **DORFMAN:** Jack Mort handles the difficult Dorfman account. II:326, II:340, II:350
>
> **FAT MAN WITH GLASSES:** This man works in Mort's office. II:339–40
>
> **FRAMINGHAM, MR.:** Mort's boss.   II:382

MUFFIN, BILL
    See RIVER CROSSING CHARACTERS

MURDOCK, REVEREND
    See DEAN, SUSANNAH: ODETTA HOLMES'S ASSOCIATES: DAN HOLMES

MUTANTS
Although the GREAT OLD ONES and their destructive culture disappeared many generations before the rise of GILEAD, the poisons they left in soil, water, and air remained. We cannot be certain whether these destructive ancients engaged in all-out chemical and biological warfare, but it seems probable. Mid-World is full of genetically mutated beings which are commonly referred to as "muties." In the case of domestic animals (and even some wild ones), muties can be carefully bred until they breed true. However, this process is slow. "Threaded stock," or those that have bred true, are extremely valuable.

The most horrific mutants of Mid-World are actually the SLOW MUTANTS. These physically disgusting beings were once men and women, although they often bear little resemblance to their human forebears. The Slow Mutants that infest the old underground railway systems of Mid-World and the ruined kitchens of Gilead's castle have green, phosphorescent skin. Their mutations are as varied as they are horrible.

Some have insect eyes, others have suckered tentacles. Many of them are nocturnal, preferring dark places to light ones. The Slow Mutants Roland meets in ELURIA are known as the GREEN FOLK.

III:223, IV:13–14, (Candleton), IV:115 (men of Mid-World and mutant sperm), IV:140 (babies), IV:203

> **ANIMALS, BIRDS, REPTILES:**
>> **GENERAL:** IV:14 (muties and threaded stock), IV:123 (werewolves), IV:203
>> **DRAGON-BIRDS AND PTERODACTYLS:** III:406, IV:13
>> **EROMOT:** Rhea's poisonous pet snake. See RHEA OF THE CÖOS.
>> **HAMBRY MUTANT HORSES:** IV:203, IV:254, IV:359 (muties)
>> **MUSTY:** Rhea's six-legged tomcat. See RHEA OF THE CÖOS.
>> **MUTANT DOE AND FAWNS:** IV:14–15
>> **RAVEN:** IV:15
>> **ROMP, THE:** See HAMBRY CHARACTERS: TRAVELLERS' REST
>> **SNAKES IN LUD'S WASTELANDS:** III:413, IV:3
>> **SUCKERBATS:** See DEMONS/SPIRITS/DEVILS
>> **TRIPOD-STORKS IN LUD'S WASTELANDS:** III:407
>> **WASTELAND MONSTROSITIES:** Roland's ka-tet sees these whitish, leaping creatures while zooming through LUD'S WASTELANDS in BLAINE's Barony Coach.   III:407
> **INSECTS:**
>> **ALBINO BEES:** Roland's ka-tet came across these mutant bees while they were on their way to LUD. These insects were truly terrible to see—they were sluggish, snowy white, and made poisonous honey. Even their hive looked as if it had been melted by a blowtorch.
>>
>> Roland believes that the bees' mutation was a result of the Great Poisoning, which destroyed so much of Mid-World. (See GREAT POISONING in the HIGH SPEECH AND MID-WORLD ARGOT section.)   III:283–84, III:286, III:311
>> **GIGANTIC BEETLES:** These are found in the WASTELANDS beyond LUD.   III:413, IV:3, IV:13
>> **SPIDERS:** Roland found these rather disgusting creatures in the cellar beneath the WAY STATION. They had eyes on stalks and as many as sixteen legs.   I:89
> **SLOW MUTANTS:** These guys are going to have a hard time getting dates.   I:137, I:157–58, I:175–80, II:379, III:33, III:171 (subhuman things under mountains), III:223, III:245
>> **GREEN FOLK:** See ELURIA CHARACTERS

TOTAL HOGS: This desert tribe of Slow Mutants held the Blue Bend of MAERLYN'S RAINBOW fifty years before Roland and his *ka-tet* arrived in HAMBRY.   IV:437

VEGETABLES: See RHEA OF THE CÖOS

N

NASSAU CHARACTERS
See DEAN, EDDIE

NEW YORK CUSTOMS
See DEAN, EDDIE

**NINETEEN

One of the most immediately striking changes made in the new *Gunslinger* is the addition of three front pages. On the first is a quote from the novel *Look Homeward, Angel*; on the second is the lone number 19; and on the third is the single word RESUMPTION. These are all vital clues about the nature of Roland's quest, and about what he is going to find over the course of the three final books of the series.

In the new *Gunslinger,* we find out that the number 19 is a magic number. After WALTER O'DIM resurrects the weed-eater NORT in the dried-up town of TULL, he implants a secret door in Nort's memory and imagination. That door, which holds back the secret horrors of the after-life, is locked. But the lock has a key, and the key is 19. In a letter written to Roland's lover ALICE, Walter confides the nature of Nort's door, what Alice will find when she opens it, and the numerical key to the lock. Driven on by a maddening curiosity, Alice speaks the word 19 and pays the price for it. Nineteen is the key to the Land of Death.

NORDITES
The blond people of Northern IN-WORLD are known as Nordites. Rumor has it that their chief sports are incest and reindeer fucking.
IV:422, IV:583

NORMAN, JAMES
See ELURIA CHARACTERS

NORMAN, JESSE
See ELURIA CHARACTERS

NORMAN, JOHN
See ELURIA CHARACTERS

NORT
See TULL CHARACTERS

**NORTH CENTRAL POSITRONICS
North Central Positronics was one of the nasty companies set up by the arrogant GREAT OLD ONES. This company and its affiliates created the technology that eventually destroyed the world. They were responsible for the highly complex computers which controlled entire cities (as well as their stockpiles of weapons and poisons), and the cyborg GUARDIANS which guarded the portals in and out of Mid-World. It seems highly likely that, through North Central Positronics, the Great Old Ones merged technology and magic. It seems even likelier that these arrogant ancestors believed that they could re-create the fabric of the multiverse and bend it to suit their fancy.

In the new version of *The Gunslinger,* we learn more about North Central Positronics's unsavory history. One hundred generations before the world moved on, humanity made enough technological advances to chip a few splinters from the great pillar of reality. The company at the forefront of these discoveries was (of course) North Central Positronics. But these so-called technological advances, wondrous as they seemed, were accompanied by little or no insight into the true nature of the universe. Instead, they were seen only in the flat but false light of science. This was where both the Old People, and their glorious company, fell short. They had no perspective, only an arrogant and dangerous drive toward what they labeled "progress." The water pump in the WAY STATION may have been created by North Central Positronics, but so were the insane SHARDIK and the murderous BLAINE, who liked to play evil god to the people of LUD. A sinister company indeed.
III:34, III:54, III:75

BLAINE: "Now, although the unthinkable machinery which maintained the Beams had weakened, this insane and inhuman intelligence had awakened in the rooms of ruin and had begun once more, although as bodiless as any ghost, to stumble through the halls of the dead." (III:373)

Our *ka-tet*'s nasty adventure with Blaine the insane Mono was prefigured by the story of CHARLIE THE CHOO-CHOO and also by JAKE CHAMBERS's crazed English essay entitled "My Understanding of Truth." This nasty, overly sophisticated train was created by the sinister NORTH CENTRAL POSITRONICS. He was therefore a distant cousin of SHARDIK and the other cyborg GUARDIANS.

Despite superficial appearances, Blaine was not just a train. He was in fact the GHOST IN THE MACHINES—LUD's city-wide computer intelligence so feared by the PUBES and the GRAYS. This fear was not unfounded since Blaine was completely psychotic. He suffered from a computerized form of split personality disorder (he was composed of nasty "Big Blaine" and terrified "Little Blaine"). While a horrified Little Blaine watched, Big Blaine committed terrible crimes such as destroying his companion mono PATRICIA (she was crying all the time) and gassing the residents of Lud. Big Blaine, whose logic and reasoning twisted long ago, agreed to take Roland and his friends southeast along the path of the BEAM to his termination point in TOPEKA. His price was a riddling contest. If the *ka-tet* won, Blaine would deliver them safely to their destination. If they lost, Blaine would kill them when he killed himself. Obviously, our *ka-tet* was at a severe disadvantage since Blaine had access to information on all levels of the TOWER. However, EDDIE DEAN succeeded in defeating Blaine with the Eddie specialty— bad jokes.   III:52, III:53, III:98, III:140, III:239, III:245–49 *(Blaine/Patricia)*, III:254, III:255–56, III:263, III:267, III:286, III:288–89, III:303, III:309, III:322–25, III:332–34, III:340–50 *(cradle)*, III:361–65, III:372–85 *(373–82 voice in Cradle of the Grays with Roland and Jake)*, III:389, III:393–420, IV:3–10 *(Roland refuses to riddle, so Blaine turns on "visual" mode; 3–6 Roland challenges, 6–9 Roland bargains)*, IV:13–42, IV:44–63 *(45 transteel piers are yellow and black, like Portal of the Bear; 49 Eddie decides to piss off Blaine; 56 Blaine blows circuit; 58–59 crash; 61 leave Blaine; 62 standing on Blaine)*, IV:642–43

"GHOSTS IN THE MACHINES": Every time the PUBES of LUD heard the god-drums, they drew lots to see who among them should be sacrificed. The Pubes believed that there were ghosts living in the machines under the city. If these ghosts were not appeased, they would take over the bodies of the dead, rise up, and eat those left alive. As JEEVES of the Pubes said, "There are a great many machines under Lud, and there are ghosts in all of them—demonous spirits which bear only ill will to mortal men and women. These demon-ghosts are *very* capable of raising the dead . . . and in Lud, there are a great many dead to raise" (III:322). Although the Grays ran the god-drum machines that incited the Pubes' frenzied sacrifice, they also believed that the city's computers were haunted by demonic spirits. When you think about it, they were right. III:322–23, III:336, III:347, III:364, III:373, III:400

IMPERIUM: III:398

LITTLE BLAINE: III:347–49, III:361, III:363, III:364, III:377 *(voice)*, III:398, III:409, III:413, IV:35, IV:52, IV:54, IV:55

PASSENGER KILLINGTON: While he and SUSANNAH were in the CRADLE OF LUD, EDDIE DEAN imagined the station as it must once have been. He even imagined he heard a loudspeaker calling for this particular passenger.   III:342

PATRICIA: Blaine's female twin. She was blue and traveled northwest. Blaine fried her circuits because he was tired of hearing her cry all the time.   III:245–49 *(speaking of Blaine, probably mean Patricia),* III:288–89, III:342, III:346, III:410–11, III:412, IV:4

SHARDIK: See GUARDIANS OF THE BEAM

**NOT-MAN
When Roland was young, he saw a Not-Man, or an invisible man, hanged for the crime of rape. Evidently, he was very good at sneaking up on people.

O

OAKLEY, ANNIE
    See GUNSLINGERS (OUR WORLD)

OCEAN FOAM
    See DELGADO, PAT

ODETTA
    See DEAN, SUSANNAH

**O'DIM, WALTER
    See WALTER

**OLD MOTHER
Old Mother is Mid-World's name for the South Star; she is married to OLD STAR. Her other name is **LYDIA.** The Universe was created when Old Mother and Old Star had a crockery-throwing fight over Old Star's flirtation with CASSIOPEIA. The other gods stepped in to break up the row but the two of them haven't spoken since. As a flirtatious gesture of respect, Roland called AUNT TALITHA of RIVER CROSSING by this name. In the new *Gunslinger,* Roland looks up and sees Old Mother in the desert sky.
    III:12, III:36–37, III:86, III:181, III:231 *(Aunt Talitha),* III:232 *(Aunt*

Talitha), III:239 *(Aunt Talitha)*, III:250 *(Aunt Talitha)*, IV:33, IV:98, IV:105, IV:154

OLD ONES (GREAT OLD ONES)

The Old Ones (also known as the Great Old Ones) were the ancient people of Mid-World. Their era was long gone even by the time of ARTHUR ELD. The Old Ones had a god-like knowledge of technology and the workings of the universe but they were also a violently destructive people.

As a horrified SUSAN DELGADO said when she found out that FARSON was trying to resurrect the Old Ones' war machines, "The ways of the Old People [were] the ways of death" (IV:302). This certainly seems to be true. As far as we can tell, their computers and killing machines were responsible for the incredible catastrophe that poisoned Mid-World. Farson's resurrection of these instruments of war succeeded in destroying Mid-World's civilization a second time.

However, even the most destructive cultures often contain less chaotic elements. According to HAX, these technologically advanced people created the twelve PORTALS and the twelve GUARDIANS. They did so to make up for the crimes they'd committed against nature.

III:37–39, III:46 *(larger than men)*, III:73, III:240–41, III:244, III:245, III:246, III:284, III:288, III:297, III:342–43 *(faces on Blaine's Cradle)*, III:362, III:399, IV:23, IV:35 *(possible carvers of the Hounds of THE FALLS OF THE HOUNDS)*, IV:120, IV:294 *(called Old People by Susan)*, IV:295, IV:296, IV:302 *(their ways were the ways of death)*, IV:430 *(their weapons)*, IV:431, IV:484 *(as devils)*

OLD PEOPLE OF THE WEST WOODS

Although the GREAT OLD ONES are sometimes called the Old People, the Old People of the West Woods were a much later and much more primitive culture—one which probably arose after the Great Old Ones destroyed most of Mid-World's cities. Roland and his *ka-tet* found the Old People's primitive remains while they camped in this mixed forest located east of the WESTERN SEA.

This forest-dwelling tribe hunted with bows and arrows and lived in awe of SHARDIK, the great bear GUARDIAN. Shardik thought of them as trap-setters and forest-burners, but they regarded him as both a demon and the shadow of a god. They called him MIR, which meant "the world beneath the world."

III:19–21, III:29

**OLD STAR (NORTH STAR. Also called APON)

Old Star (also called **North Star**) is another name for the wickedly flirtatious husband of OLD MOTHER (South Star). The two of them had a knock-down-drag-out fight over his tête-à-tête with CASSIOPEIA. The universe was created from the crockery they threw at each other, but the two of them haven't spoken since. In the new *Gunslinger,* Roland sees Old Star in the sky.

III:12, III:36–37, III:86, III:179, III:181, IV:33, IV:98, IV:105, IV:166, IV:531

OMAHA
A one-eyed gambler who died with a knife in his throat at a Watch Me table.

IV:72

O'MEARAH, GEORGE
O'Mearah was one of the New York cops who patrolled the area in front of CLEMENTS GUNS AND SPORTING GOODS. His partner's name was CARL DELEVAN. The two of them were hoodwinked by Roland while Roland was in JACK MORT's body.

II:343, II:346, II:347–59 *(354 unconscious),* II:368 *(indirect),* II:371–77, II:378, II:380

ORACLE
See DEMONS/SPIRITS/DEVILS

ORTEGA, MILLICENT
See HAMBRY CHARACTERS: OTHER CHARACTERS

OSWALD, LEE HARVEY
See KENNEDY, JOHN F.

OUR WORLD: POLITICAL AND CULTURAL FIGURES
See APPENDIX III

OY
Oy is JAKE CHAMBERS's pet BILLY-BUMBLER (or perhaps Jake is Oy's pet boy). Oy approached our *ka-tet* while they traveled on the BEAM leading toward LUD. When Jake first found Oy—or when Oy first woke Jake by licking his face—the bumbler had some bites on his body. It seems likely that he was chased away from his own pack because he talked too much. Like the best Billy-Bumblers, Oy is intelligent and faithful. He can count, add, and communicate. He is completely devoted to Jake.

Unfortunately, there is a good chance that Oy will come to an unhappy end. During Roland's journey in MAERLYN'S GRAPEFRUIT, he had a vision of Oy impaled upon the topmost branch of a crooked tree.

III:219–22, III:224, III:226–54, III:255–67, III:273–81, III:283–85, III:286–300 *(294 almost falls off Send Bridge)*, III:302, III:303, III:307–8 *(follows Jake)*, III:314–16 *(follows Jake)*, III:328–31 *(follows Jake)*, III:339–40 *(follows Jake)*, III:344, III:358–61, III:367–72, III:373–82, III:382–85 *(Blaine)*, III:389, III:393–420, IV:3–10 *(afraid of Blaine's "visual mode")*, IV:13–42, IV:44–47 *(present for Blaine blowout)*, IV:71–112 *(present for entry into Topeka. 88 Jake dreams about Oy and train)*, IV:335–37 *(Interlude in Kansas)*, IV:572 *(in Roland's vision, he is impaled upon a branch)*, IV:615–25 *(back in Topeka)*, IV:626–68 *(626 ruby booties; 632 Green palace; 634 gate like Wizard's Rainbow; 646 Tick-Tock; 648 Flagg; 652 Roland's matricide)*

OZ, WIZARD OF

The story of *The Wizard of Oz,* which tells the tale of **DOROTHY,** **TOTO,** the **COWARDLY LION** and the **TIN WOODSMAN,** is mentioned quite often in the Dark Tower series. Like JAKE, SUSANNAH, and EDDIE, Dorothy Gale was blown from a world much like ours to one where witches and magic are real. In *Wizard and Glass,* our *ka-tet* actually visits an emerald palace where the evil wizard RANDALL FLAGG poses as the Great and Terrible Oz.

II:229 *(Dorothy)*, III:59, III:408, IV:629–30, IV:643–46

P

PAPPA DOC
See BORDER DWELLERS: BROWN

PATRICIA
See NORTH CENTRAL POSITRONICS

**PAUL
The only thing we know about Paul is that Roland thinks of him while at the WAY STATION. Paul's name is cut from the new version of *The Gunslinger.*
I:86

PAULA
  See DEAN, EDDIE: DELTA FLIGHT 901 CHARACTERS

PERTH, LORD
"So fell Lord Perth, and the countryside did shake with thunder." The story of Lord Perth comes from Mid-World's folklore. Perth was a giant and his fate was much like that of the colossal warrior in the biblical tale of David and Goliath. When eleven-year-old JAKE CHAMBERS mentioned this story to the huge and wicked TICK-TOCK, Tick-Tock became enraged. He considered the story unlucky. This isn't surprising since it proved to be a foretelling of his own fate.
  III:274–75, III:356–57, IV:89, IV:90, IV:294, IV:404, IV:422, IV:452, IV:571, IV:647

PETTIE THE TROTTER
  See HAMBRY CHARACTERS: TRAVELLERS' REST

PIPER SCHOOL CHARACTERS
Before entering Mid-World, JAKE CHAMBERS attended PIPER SCHOOL—an exclusive NEW YORK CITY middle school. He hated it. Below is a list of Piper School students and employees. For more information about Piper, see PIPER SCHOOL in the OUR WORLD PLACES section.
  AVERY, BONNIE: Jake's English teacher. She gave him an A+ on his very strange essay, "My Understanding of Truth."   III:94–100, III:101, III:135–36, III:195, III:417
  BISSETTE, LEN: Len Bissette was a very kindhearted French teacher. III:91–93, III:99, III:101, III:131, III:134, III:135–36
  DORFMAN, STAN: A Piper student and one of Jake's "almost" friends.   III:101
  FRANKS, JOANNE: Piper's school secretary.   III:92, III:93, III:94, III:101
  HARLEY, MR.: Headmaster and teacher for spoken arts.   III:93, III:94, III:101, III:131
  HOTCHKISS, MR.: Piper's school shrink.   III:134
  JESSERLING, PETRA: Student.   III:96
  KINGERY, MR.: Science teacher.   IV:82
  KNOPF, MR.: Geometry teacher.   III:101, III:106
  STEVENS, BELINDA: Student.   III:101
  SURREY, DAVID: Student.   III:97, III:100

**PITTSTON, SYLVIA
Sylvia Pittston was TULL's psychotic Bible-bashing preacher. Before the

events of *Wizard and Glass* took place, Pittston traveled through HAMBRY. Originally a DESERT DWELLER, she came to Tull from the dry wastes on the edge of the MOHAINE DESERT. When Roland confronted her in Tull, she was living in a shack behind her church. Pittston wore the burlap dress of a penitent.

Pittston was a huge but sexually alluring woman. She weighed about three hundred pounds but had large dark eyes and rich brown hair. Pittston's revivals were so intense that they were almost erotically ecstatic. ALICE believed that Pittston had a hoodoo on the town and that her religion was evil. Roland believed that when the MAN IN BLACK (WALTER) passed through Tull, he had sex with this preacher and left a demon inside her. Roland's theory proves to be right.

When Roland visited Pittston's shack, she was sitting in her rocker waiting for him. She believed that Roland was Satan (the INTERLOPER) and that the Man in Black was an angel. Roland removed Pittston's demon by making her come with the barrel of his gun, but in revenge, Pittston set the townspeople on him. Roland ended up killing everyone in Tull.

In the new *Gunslinger,* Roland has an eerie sense of déjà vu when he hears Pittston preach, almost as if he had heard her preach before. In this version, Walter once again comes to Pittston pretending to be an angel, but this time he admits that he serves THE CRIMSON KING, the very evil being that Pittston pretends to preach against. Pittston allows Walter to implant the Red King's child inside her, but Roland removes it in the same way he removed the demon in the earlier version of the novel. In the new *Gunslinger,* as in the old, Pittston dies under Roland's guns.

   I:47–52, I:53, I:54–56, I:58–63, I:124, I:131, III:42, IV:381–82 *(she came through Hambry)*

PLASTERMAN
   See DEMONS/SPIRITS/DEVILS: MANSION DEMON

POLITICAL AND CULTURAL FIGURES (OUR WORLD)
   See APPENDIX III

POSTINO, TRICKS
   See BALAZAR'S MEN

PRISONER, THE
   See DEAN, EDDIE

PUBES
The Pubes (short for pubescents) were the original defenders of LUD,

although the sickly bunch we meet in *The Waste Lands* were probably descended from one of the later bands of harriers that overran the city. The Pubes' archenemies, the GRAYS, live in underground silos beneath eastern Lud. The Pubes live aboveground in CITY NORTH, but are no healthier for it. You can tell a Pube from a Gray because the Pubes' head-scarves are blue. (The Grays' are yellow.)

The Pubes are convinced that there are GHOSTS IN THE MACHINES below the city, and that if these demonic spirits aren't appeased they will animate the bodies of Lud's many dead and rise up to eat the living. Although the Grays also fear the machine ghosts, they use the god-drums (actually the backbeat of ZZ Top's song "Velcro Fly") to drive the Pubes into a paranoid frenzy of human sacrifice. The grisly method the Pubes use to choose their victims is reminiscent of Shirley Jackson's story "The Lottery."

SUSANNAH and EDDIE battle the Pubes on the STREET OF THE TURTLE. In the end, two of this gang (MAUD and JEEVES) reluctantly agree to lead them to BLAINE'S CRADLE. The Pubes believe that of all the ghosts in the machines, Blaine is the most terrible. Little do they know that psychotic Blaine is actually *all* of the ghosts in the machines.

III:229, III:230, III:238, III:240, III:244–45, III:254, III:270, III:308–12 *(dead)*, III:316–25, III:327, III:329, III:337, III:358, III:373, III:380, III:402, III:411, IV:57

PUBE CHARACTERS:

ARDIS: He was electrocuted by BLAINE.   III:323–24, III:344, III:346, III:348, III:361

BLONDE WOMAN WITH MANGE: III:320

FRANK: III:321

JEEVES: Eddie nicknames this guy Jeeves because of his bowler hat. Along with Maud, Jeeves leads Eddie and Susannah to BLAINE'S CRADLE.   III:322–25, III:332–33, IV:75, IV:621

LUSTER (DWARF): Luster reminds Eddie and Susannah of Little Lord Fauntleroy.   III:317–18, III:321, IV:75

MAN IN SILK-LINED CAPE AND KNEE-BOOTS: III:319

MAN WITH BLUE ASCOT AND RED HAIR TUFTS: This guy reminded Eddie of Ronald McDonald.   III:319–20

MAN WITH HAMMER: III:319

MAUD: Maud is a heavyset woman who is very fond of Winston. She is one of the two who leads Eddie and Susannah to BLAINE'S CRADLE.   III:318–20, III:321, III:322–25, III:332–33, III:334, IV:75

SPANKER/SPANKERMAN: Spanker was the leader of the Pubes, but when the god-drums started up, his stone was pulled from the

hat and it was his turn to dance from the hangman's rope.   III:317,
III:321, IV:75
TOPSY THE SAILOR: III:321
WINSTON: Winston wore a kilt and brandished a cutlass. He was
killed by Eddie and Susannah.   III:318–19, III:320, III:321, III:324,
III:332, IV:75

PYLON
   See DELGADO, SUSAN

Q

QUEEN OF BLACK PLACES
   IV:493 *(Rhea of the Cöos compared to her)*

QUICK, ANDREW (Listed as TICK-TOCK)
   See GRAYS: GRAY HIGH COMMAND

QUICK, DAVID
   See GRAYS: GRAY HIGH COMMAND

QUINT, HIRAM
   See HAMBRY: OTHER CHARACTERS

R

RALPH
   See ELURIA CHARACTERS: GREEN FOLK

**RANDOLPH
Young Roland's friend. Randolph doesn't appear in the new *Gunslinger*.
   I:140

RATHBUN, MRS.
   See KATZ: KATZ'S EMPLOYEES, CUSTOMERS, AND COMPETI-
TORS

RAVENHEAD, PIET
Signed identity papers stating that ALAIN was actually RICHARD STOCKWORTH of PENNILTON.
IV:183

REED, JAMES
Signed identity papers stating that Roland was actually WILLIAM DEARBORN of HEMPHILL.
IV:183

RENFREW, HASH
See HAMBRY CHARACTERS: HORSEMEN'S ASSOCIATION

REYNOLDS, CLAY
See BIG COFFIN HUNTERS

**R.F.
The letters R.F. are the initials of Roland's multi-faced archenemy (present writer excluded). This nasty being occasionally takes other initials, including W.O. (Walter O'Dim), M.B. (Marten Broadcloak), and J.F. (John Farson). The new *Gunslinger* hints that R.F. and the AGELESS STRANGER may be the same being as well. While they palaver in THE GOLGOTHA, Walter tells Roland that the Ageless Stranger's real name is LEGION. R.F. is an agent of Chaos (but we are much nicer in our female incarnations).
IV:663–64, IV:666

> **FANNIN, RICHARD:** In his form as Richard Fannin, R.F. is described as being inhuman. He has blue-green eyes but blue-black hair that looks like a raven's feathers. Fannin must be a fairly imposing figure, since even TICK-TOCK, leader of the murderous GRAYS, is afraid of him.
>
> Fannin's hand has no lines on it, which makes us wonder if he is mortal at all. He claims not to be MAERLYN, but he is obviously a sorcerer of extreme power. Like all of R.F.'s selves, Fannin glories in destruction.   III:385–90
>
> **FLAGG, RANDALL:** Randall Flagg is another incarnation of R.F. He is a demon posing as a man, and is capable of turning men into dogs. In *The Stand* (a related novel), Flagg is also called the Walkin' Dude, an epithet that Roland's *ka-tet* sees spray-painted on a road sign in the alternate TOPEKA. He was also the nasty sorcerer found in the novel *Eyes of the Dragon*. When Roland encountered Flagg for the first time, he was pursued by **DENNIS**

and **THOMAS,** two characters from *Eyes of the Dragon.*   II:362, IV:648–50

**RHEA OF THE CÖOS (RHEA OF CÖOS HILL/RHEA DUBA-TIVO/WEIRDLING OF THE CÖOS)

Rhea of the Cöos was a nasty old bad-smelling hag. She was also a witch. Rhea lived on the Cöos (a hill outside of HAMBRY) with her two mutant pets, ERMOT and MUSTY.

Like the men of the HORSEMEN'S ASSOCIATION, Rhea played a part in the defeat of the AFFILIATION. At the beginning of *Wizard and Glass*'s Hambry adventures, the BIG COFFIN HUNTERS entrusted the evil magic ball known as MAERLYN'S GRAPEFRUIT to Rhea's keeping. This magical ball was FARSON's prize and secret weapon, but it was also vampiric. Rhea used the ball to spy on people (including Roland) but in the end the ball made her even more crazily malicious than she was at the beginning of the tale. By the end of *Wizard and Glass,* Rhea is a sore-covered specter. However, she is still a formidable enemy.

Rhea was attracted to pretty young women, but even before her journeys in the pink Bend o' the Rainbow her desires had a malicious edge, especially when her advances were rebuffed. It was in large part Rhea's vindictiveness that landed pretty SUSAN DELGADO on the Charyou Tree fire. In the new version of *The Gunslinger,* Roland bitterly remembers the part Rhea played in Susan's death.

IV:65 *(indirect—"crone on the hill"), IV:115–21 (115 description of her hut and Cöos hill; 118 described), IV:122–38 (122 left side of her face is frozen; 130 inspects Susan's "honesty"; 133–34 touches Susan's clit; 137 parallel between Susan's sexuality and her hair; 137–38 spell on Susan to make her cut her hair), IV:140–41, IV:146, IV:154, IV:157 (and Susan), IV:159, IV:166–70, IV:177 (keeper of glass), IV:202, IV:212, IV:228 (cures), IV:235, IV:246, IV:249, IV:290–91 (sees Roland and Susan. She's being eaten by Maerlyn's ball), IV:299, IV:300, IV:311, IV:319–20, IV:324, IV:325–26, IV:335, IV:343, IV:353–54 (Susan must die), IV:355–56, IV:374–75, IV:384 (Rhea Dubativo), IV:389–90, IV:394–98 (repercussions of using Maerlyn's ball. Message for Cordelia), IV:403, IV:411 (note to Cordelia), IV:413,*

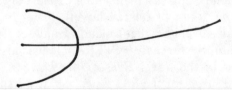

IV:415–19, IV:420, IV:424–25, IV:426, IV:434, IV:436, IV:440–42, IV:443, IV:449, IV:452–53 *(aging because of Maerlyn's glass)*, IV:485–93 *(493 as Queen of Black Places)*, IV:495, IV:496, IV:498–99, IV:519, IV:527–29, IV:532–35, IV:536, IV:540, IV:541–44, IV:545, IV:546, IV:549–52 *(and Cordelia)*, IV:563–65, IV:570, IV:571, IV:587, IV:602, IV:603–8 *(burning Susan)*, IV:622, IV:628–29, IV:649, IV:650, IV:656–58, IV:662, IV:666, E:165, E:166

MUTANT PETS:
ERMOT: Poisonous snake. Has four pairs of fangs.   IV:115, IV:117, IV:290–91, IV:299, IV:356, IV:396–97, IV:417–18 *(killed by Roland)*, IV:419, IV:452, IV:488, IV:492, IV:533, IV:602, IV:657, IV:658
MUSTY: A six-legged tomcat with a split tail. He had gray-green eyes which were the same color as Rhea's.   IV:115–21 *(116 described)*, IV:123, IV:124, IV:291, IV:320, IV:353–54, IV:356, IV:383–85, IV:452, IV:453, IV:485, IV:486
MUTANT VEGETABLE GARDEN: IV:415

RIGGINS, GEORGE
See HAMBRY CHARACTERS: SHERIFF'S OFFICE

RIMER, KIMBA
See HAMBRY CHARACTERS: SEAFRONT

RIMER, LASLO
See HAMBRY CHARACTERS: HORSEMEN'S ASSOCIATION

**RITTER, AILEEN
See AILEEN OF GILEAD

RITZY CHARACTERS
JOLENE: Whore.   IV:267–68
OLD MAN: A weed-eater who told DEPAPE that Roland was descended from ARTHUR ELD. Depape killed him after he shared this information.   IV:267–71

RIVER CROSSING CHARACTERS
Although River Crossing was once a very busy town, since the beginning of the LUD wars her aging citizens have lived in relative isolation. In order to disguise their town from passing looters, they hide their gardens behind clumps of weeds and let the facades of their buildings go to ruin. However, to friendly folk passing through, they are extremely generous.

By the time we meet them in *The Waste Lands*, most of the citizens of River Crossing are positively ancient. Their leader is the matriarch TALITHA UNWIN. Like Roland, Talitha speaks the High Speech. When she sees Roland she proclaims, "Behold ye, the return of the White! After evil ways and evil days, the White comes again! Be of good heart and hold up your head, for ye have lived to see the wheel of *ka* begin to turn once more" (III:232).

GENERAL REFERENCES (ALL CHARACTERS): III:257, III:258, III:270, III:276, III:284, III:288, III:385

GENERAL CHARACTERS NOT LISTED BELOW: (unnamed women, man with crutch)   III:233–36

BILL AND TILL: See TUDBURY, BILL AND TILL, below.

MERCY: Mercy was one of the first people that Roland's *ka-tet* met in River Crossing. Like almost all of the other townspeople, Mercy is very old. Twenty-five years before the beginning of our tale she was blinded by harriers who said she was looking at em pert. Mercy is married to Si.   III:229–36, III:246, III:247–51, III:288

MUFFIN, BILL, AND HIS BOY: Bill Muffin and his son saw the bridge over the RIVER SEND. Bill eventually died of blood sickness.   III:241, III:248

SI: Si is Mercy's husband. He assures her that Roland and his friends are gunslingers, not harriers. He and his wife were the first two people Roland's *ka-tet* met in River Crossing.   III:229–51, III:288

GREAT GRAND'DA: III:243

TALITHA, AUNT: Aunt Talitha's full name is **TALITHA UNWIN**. She is the matriarch of River Crossing as well as its oldest citizen. Roland calls her OLD MOTHER. Talitha gives Roland her cross and asks him to lay it at the foot of the DARK TOWER.   III:231–51, III:263, III:274, IV:14

GRANDFATHER AND GREAT-GREAT GRANDFATHER: III:232

TUDBURY, BILL AND TILL: These two old twins are albino. III:231–51, III:252

RIVERS, LUCAS
Signed identity papers stating that CUTHBERT ALLGOOD was actually ARTHUR HEATH of GILEAD.
   IV:183

ROBERT AND FRANCESCA
   See HAMBRY CHARACTERS: HAMBRY LOVERS

ROBESON
Robeson was one of GILEAD's guards. Like HAX, he was a traitor who supported FARSON.
I:101–3, I:105 *(indirect)*

ROLAND THE ELDER
See DESCHAIN, STEVEN

ROMP, THE
See HAMBRY CHARACTERS: TRAVELLERS' REST

ROSE, THE
JAKE CHAMBERS discovered this magical dusky-pink rose in the vacant LOT on Second Avenue and Forty-sixth Street where it was growing amid a clump of alien purple grass. Although he doesn't know it, the Rose is the *sigul* of the TOWER itself.

This magic flower hums like a great open chord, inexpressively lonely and inexpressibly lovely. It is full of faces and voices. Jake believes that it is the key to everything; Roland suspects that it is the Tower itself.

Throughout the Dark Tower books, roses are extremely significant. The Dark Tower of END-WORLD sits amid a sea of shouting red roses, the LITTLE SISTERS OF ELURIA wear an embroidered rose upon their white flowing habits, and a model of CHARLIE THE CHOO-CHOO sits in REINISCH ROSE GARDEN in the alternate TOPEKA. As Eddie states within the *glammer* of his dream-vision, "First the key, then the rose! Behold! Behold the opening of the way to the Tower!" (III:49). The following entries contain references to all roses.

III:49 *(Eddie's vision in the jawbone fire),* III:50, III:51, III:52–53 *(field of),* III:54–55, III:56 *(field of),* III:98, III:124–29, III:130, III:132, III:155, III:158, III:177, III:205, III:262, III:264–65, III:267, III:280 *(fire like roses),* IV:48 *(hope compared to it),* IV:83 *(Jake's reflections upon it),* IV:86–87 *(Reinisch Rose Garden, Topeka),* IV:100–101 *(Eddie's bulldozer dream),* IV:102, IV:103, IV:429–30 *(Thorin mausoleum),* IV:447 *(field of roses and Dark Tower),* IV:552 *(Rhea dreams of it),* IV:572 *(and Roland's vision),* IV:667, E:165, E:175

RUIZ, STANLEY
See HAMBRY CHARACTERS: TRAVELLERS' REST

S

SHARDIK
See GUARDIANS OF THE BEAM: SHARDIK

SHAVERS, GEORGE
See DEAN, SUSANNAH

SHAW, GRETA
See CHAMBERS, JAKE

**SHEB (SHEB McCURDY: PIANO PLAYER)
In the new version of *The Gunslinger,* we find out that the two piano players named Sheb—one in TULL, one in HAMBRY—are actually the same man. In both stories he works in bars owned by women. (Though Tull's local honky-tonk bears his name, the place actually belongs to Sheb's former lover, ALICE.)

Sheb of Hambry, and later of Tull, is described as a small, useless man with one gold tooth. He is in love with Alice, Tull's bar owner, though she thinks of him as a gelded dog. Jealous that Roland monopolizes Alice's attentions, he tries to assault Roland with a knife. Later, during the town's surprise attack on the gunslinger, Sheb uses Allie as a human shield. In the new version of *The Gunslinger,* Roland recognizes Sheb as the man he met in MEJIS.

I:26–29, I:34–38, I:40, I:45–47, I:47–52, I:58, I:59, I:60, II:126, III:42, IV:171–72, IV:213, IV:216, IV:226, IV:349, IV:382–83, IV:403, IV:453, IV:468, IV:505, IV:563, IV:570, IV:628

SHEEMER, DELORES
See HAMBRY CHARACTERS: TRAVELLERS' REST

SHEEMIE
See HAMBRY CHARACTERS: TRAVELLERS' REST

SI
See RIVER CROSSING CHARACTERS

SILICON VALLEY COKE-HEADS
These guys supply high-tech police equipment to BALAZAR'S MEN.
II:125

SISTER BLUE
See DEAN, SUSANNAH: ODETTA HOLMES'S ASSOCIATES

SISTER COQUINA
See ELURIA, LITTLE SISTERS OF

SISTER JENNA
See ELURIA, LITTLE SISTERS OF

SISTER LOUISE
See ELURIA, LITTLE SISTERS OF

SISTER MARY
See ELURIA, LITTLE SISTERS OF

SISTER MICHELA
See ELURIA, LITTLE SISTERS OF

SISTER TAMRA
See ELURIA, LITTLE SISTERS OF

SKANK, BANGO
See MILLS CONSTRUCTION AND SOMBRA REAL ESTATE

SLOW MUTANTS
See MUTANTS

SMASHER
See ELURIA CHARACTERS: GREEN FOLK

SOOBIE
See TULL CHARACTERS: **KENNERLY, JUBAL

SOPHIA (SISTER BLUE)
See DEAN, SUSANNAH: ODETTA HOLMES'S ASSOCIATES

SPICS OF SUPREMACY
See DEAN: SUSANNAH: OTHER ASSOCIATES

STAUNTON, ANDREW
A New York City foot patrolman. His partner is NORRIS WEAVER.
II:380–84, III:262 *(indirect)*

STEVENS, BELINDA
    See PIPER SCHOOL CHARACTERS

STOCKWORTH, RICHARD
    See JOHNS, ALAIN

STUFFY-GUYS
The red-handed stuffy-guys are a leftover of one of Mid-World's more unsavory practices. In the time of ARTHUR ELD, human beings were sacrificed during the harvest festival of Reap. In the more civilized days of Roland's youth, stuffy-guys—or human effigies—were set onto the Reap bonfires in lieu of actual people. The stuffy-guys had heads made of straw and white, cross-stitched eyes. In their arms they carried baskets of produce.
    IV:355, IV:361, IV:373, IV:415, IV:417, IV:446–47 *(propitiating old gods)*, IV:449, IV:466–67 *(Cordelia burns Susan in effigy)*, IV:501, IV:502, IV:505, IV:507, IV:605 *(Susan placed among them on the fire)*

SUCCUBUS
    See DEMONS/SPIRITS/DEVILS

SUCKERBATS
    See DEMONS/SPIRITS/DEVILS

SURREY, DAVID
    See PIPER SCHOOL

SUSAN
    See DELGADO, SUSAN

T

**TAHEEN
The taheen are found in the new version of *The Gunslinger*, but not the old. These strange hybrid creatures are part man and part either animal or bird. In the new *Gunslinger*, Roland sees a taheen with a man's body but a raven's head wandering in the MOHAINE DESERT. According to the BORDER DWELLER BROWN, the taheen is searching for a place called ALGUL SIENTO.

TALITHA, AUNT
See RIVER CROSSING CHARACTERS

TAMRA, SISTER
See ELURIA, LITTLE SISTERS OF

**THOMAS OF GILEAD (THOMAS WHITMAN)
The Dark Tower series contains references to two different characters named Thomas. One was a gunslinger companion of Roland's youth who witnessed Roland's coming-of-age battle against CORT. The second was a young man from the novel *Eyes of the Dragon*. This second Thomas (who met Roland only briefly) was in pursuit of RANDALL FLAGG. (For pages including references to Flagg's pursuer, see entry under R.F.)

In the new *Gunslinger*, we learn that Roland's friend Thomas had the last name Whitman.

I:162 *(Roland's childhood friend)*, I:167–73 *(witnesses Roland's coming of age)*

THORIN, CORAL
See HAMBRY CHARACTERS: TRAVELLERS' REST

THORIN, HART
See HAMBRY CHARACTERS: SEAFRONT

THORIN, OLIVE
See HAMBRY CHARACTERS: SEAFRONT

TICK-TOCK
See GRAYS HIGH COMMAND: TICK-TOCK (ANDREW QUICK)

TILLY
See GRAYS HIGH COMMAND

TOMAS, MARIA
See HAMBRY CHARACTERS: SEAFRONT

TOPEKA CHARACTERS
CORCORAN, JOHN: *Topeka Capital Journal* correspondent.   IV:74
HACKFORD, DR. MORRIS: Doctor at Topeka's St. Francis Hospital and Medical Center. He reports on superflu.   IV:74

MONTOYA, DR. APRIL: Doctor at Stormont-Vail Regional Medical Center. She reports on superflu.   IV:74

TOPSY
Roland's horse in "Little Sisters of Eluria."
    E:146–54

TOPSY THE SAILOR
    See PUBES

TORRES, MIGUEL
    See HAMBRY CHARACTERS: SEAFRONT

TOTAL HOGS
    See MUTANTS: SLOW MUTANTS

TOTEMS OF THE BEAM
    See GUARDIANS OF THE BEAM

TOWER, CALVIN
Calvin Tower is the bibliophile who owns THE MANHATTAN RESTAURANT OF THE MIND. He sold JAKE CHAMBERS copies of *CHARLIE THE CHOO-CHOO* and *Riddle-De-Dum*—both clues to Jake's destiny in Mid-World. Whether he is conscious of it or not, Calvin Tower serves the will of the BEAM and of the DARK TOWER itself.
    III:114–18, III:119, III:277, III:281

TRAINS
    See CHARLIE THE CHOO-CHOO

TUDBURY, BILL AND TILL
    See RIVER CROSSING CHARACTERS

TULL CHARACTERS
Tull had a population of thirty-nine men, fourteen women, and five children. Roland ended up killing all of them except the weed-eater NORT. (Poor Nort was crucified by the townsfolk.) For information about the town of Tull, see TULL listed in the MID-WORLD PLACES section.
    I:23–24, I:26–29 *(barflies)*, I:33, I:34–39 *(barflies)*, I:40 *(barflies)*, I:47–52 *(barflies and others at Pittston's revival)*, I:58–65 *(attack Roland)*, I:78
    ALICE: See ALICE OF TULL, listed separately.

BALD MAN WITH KNIFE: This guy tried to attack Roland in SHEB's bar. I:27–28

BOYS PLAYING MARBLES: In the new *Gunslinger,* these boys are described. One has a scorpion's tail poking out of his hatband, one has a bloated and sightless eye, and the youngest has a large cold sore on his lip. The youngest one is named **CHARLIE and is scorned by his companions for giving directions to Roland.   I:24, I:25–26

CASTNER: He owned Tull's Dry Goods emporium.   I:47–52

   SLAT-SIDED WIFE: I:47–52

**FELDON, AMY: One of Tull's barflies. At NORT's wake, ZACHARY threw her skirts over her head and drew zodiacs on her knees. In the new *Gunslinger,* we find out that Amy was a whore and that Zachary drew Reap charms on her knees, not zodiacs. I:34–39, I:61

JONSON: Jonson was one of the born-again sinners attending PITTSTON'S revival.   I:51–52

**KENNERLY, JUBAL: Kennerly was a skinny, incestuous livery owner who was plagued with daughters. In the new *Gunslinger* we learn that he buried two wives and that his first name was Jubal. I:24–25, I:33, I:40, I:42–45, I:47–52, I:57–58, I:61, I:64

   DAUGHTERS (GENERAL): I:33 *(second-eldest),* I:43–45, I:47–52, I:58, I:61

      BABY GIRL: I:43, I:44

      KENNERLY, SOOBIE: One of Kennerly's overly sensual daughters. She liked to suck her thumb.   I:43–45, I:57–58, I:61

   KENNERLY'S FATHER: I:44

LADIES IN BLACK SLACKS: I:24

MILL, AUNT: She was a barfly who had a broad belly and a quavery voice. She sang at NORT's funeral. Mill was one of PITTSTON's followers. Like everybody else in Tull, she was killed by Roland.   I:34–39, I:61

**NORT: Nort was Tull's resident weed-eater. Once he had a honey wagon, but drink and then weed killed off his desire to do anything but chew his way to oblivion. Before his first death, Nort already resembled a walking corpse. He looked like a man made of coat hangers and had green-coated teeth—green and smelly as his stinking pants. By the time Roland arrived in town, Nort had already died of weed and had been resurrected by the MAN IN BLACK. Thanks to the magic of the man in black, the resurrected Nort addressed Roland in High Speech. Nort's second death was a crucifixion. In the new

Gunslinger, WALTER (the man in black) places a locked door in Nort's imagination. Behind this door lurk the secrets of the afterlife. The key to the door is the number NINETEEN.   I:18–19, I:20 *(indirect)*, I:26–30, I:31–41 *(Nort's story)*, I:42, I:63, II:40, III:42

OLD MAN WITH STRAW HAT: He was the first person Roland saw when he entered Tull.   I:24, I:62

PITTSTON, SYLVIA: Listed separately.

SHEB (PIANO PLAYER): Sheb was Tull's piano player, and though the local honky-tonk bore his name the place actually belonged to ALICE. Sheb was also once a piano player in the HAMBRY saloon called the TRAVELLERS' REST. See SHEB, listed separately.

YOUNG BOY AND GIRL: I:24

**ZACHARY: One of the barflies at SHEB's. He liked to draw zodiacs on girls' knees, although in the new *Gunslinger* he draws Reap charms instead of zodiacs.   I:34–39

TURTLE
See GUARDIANS OF THE BEAM: TURTLE

U

UNWIN, TALITHA
See RIVER CROSSING CHARACTERS

V

**VANNAY, ABEL
Vannay was one of Roland's tutors. He told Roland that a boy who could answer riddles was a boy who could think around corners. Unlike the warrior CORT, limping Vannay was a gentle man. In the new version of *The Gunslinger*, we find out that Vannay taught his students about the poisons used by the OLD ONES. Vannay had a son who was very clever.
III:276, IV:326, IV:650, IV:664, E:195

**VANNAY'S SON: As was stated above, this boy was extremely intelligent. We don't yet know his name or what happened to him.

VECHHIO, RUDY
See BALAZAR'S MEN

VERONE, TIO
See BALAZAR, ENRICO

VI CASTIS COMPANY
This is the name of the corrupt mining company that destroyed all of the freehold mines north of Ritzy. The BIG COFFIN HUNTERS were part of this conspiracy.
IV:265

VINCENT, COL
See BALAZAR'S MEN

W

WALKER, DETTA
See DEAN, SUSANNAH

WALKIN' DUDE
See entry under R.F.
IV:91

**WALTER (MAN IN BLACK, WALTER O'DIM)
The Dark Tower series begins with Roland's pursuit of the man in black. We find out at the end of the original version of *The Gunslinger* that the man in black is actually the sorcerer Walter, a figure from Roland's childhood and the one who finally delivered the treacherous MARTEN into Roland's hands.

Walter's magic is extremely powerful. He brings the weed-eater NORT back to life and can alter his own appearance. (In other words, he never has to wear the same face twice.) Although a sorcerer, Walter often functions as a kind of trickster, leading Roland into the darkest regions of his own soul. It is Walter who tempts Roland to let JAKE fall into the abyss below the CYCLOPEAN MOUNTAINS, and it is often Walter's taunting voice that Roland hears in his head, mocking and deriding his desire to live—and pursue his quest—honorably.

Among Walter's infernal skills is that of prophecy. In the bone-strewn wastes of the GOLGOTHA he reads Roland's future with a deck of Tarot cards. During this reading he foretells the drawing of the Three, and tells Roland the perils he will have to face on his way to the TOWER. Walter also gives our gunslinger an overwhelming vision of the universe, and a sense of the immensity of the Tower itself. At the end of the first book of the series, Roland wakes up from a short sleep to find that he has aged a decade and that Walter is only a pile of bones. Roland takes Walter's jaw as a talisman.

In the new version of *The Gunslinger* we learn some surprising things about Walter. First, Walter is actually all of Roland's enemies. Under different magical disguises he was MARTEN, he was JOHN FARSON, and he was the penitent Walter whom Roland remembered from his youth. Walter serves THE CRIMSON KING, whom we met in the related Stephen King novel entitled *Insomnia*. The Crimson King is an agent of chaos and is, by his very nature, opposed to the White, which Roland and his line represent. Hence, so is Walter. Walter maintains that the Red King rules the Tower, and that Earth has been given into his hand. It yet remains to be seen whether Walter is telling the truth.

One of the most interesting things added to Walter's palaver is the theme of RESUMPTION, a word which we see on one of the new opening pages of the revised *Gunslinger*. Roland believes that his quest for the Tower has been continuous, but Walter implies that it has not. He says that Roland never learns, and that he never remembers. This casts Roland's frequent sense of déjà vu in a new light. Perhaps Walter and his master have Roland caught in some kind of time loop, and are playing with him the way a cat plays with a mouse.

I:11–14, I:16–17, I:20–21, I:23, I:29, I:30, I:33–39 *(Nort's story)*, I:42, I:54–56 *(Pittston)*, I:58, I:64, I:73–74, I:76–77, I:78–79, I:82–84, I:86, I:87, I:90, I:93, I:94, I:95, I:112–13, I:119, I:122, I:130, I:131, I:136, I:137, I:138, I:139, I:140, I:142–43, I:149, I:174, I:176–77, I:184, I:186, I:190–216, II:15, II:16, II:20, II:25, II:30, II:31, II:36, II:40, II:55, II:101, II:104, II:316, II:318, II:319, II:324, II:397, III:38, III:41, III:42, III:43, III:46–47, III:48, III:59–62, III:94, III:103–6, III:107, III:172, III:226, III:261, III:417, IV:7, IV:65, IV:106, IV:404–8, IV:421, IV:423 *(and The Good Man)*, IV:597, IV:624 *(the dark man in the west)*, E:146, E:209

WEAVER, NORRIS
New York City foot patrolman. His partner is ANDREW STAUNTON. II:380–84, III:262 *(indirect)*

WERTNER, HENRY
See HAMBRY CHARACTERS: HORSEMEN'S ASSOCIATION

**WHEELER'S BOY
Like many of the figures from Roland's past, we don't know much about
this gunslinger apprentice. The only bit of information we're given is that
STEVEN DESCHAIN thinks he is brighter than Roland. This character
is cut from the new version of *The Gunslinger*.
    I:105

WHITE, JAKE
   See HAMBRY CHARACTERS: HORSEMEN'S ASSOCIATION

WHITMAN, THOMAS
   See THOMAS OF GILEAD

WILSON, WILLIAM
   See BALAZAR, ENRICO: BALAZAR'S NASSAU CONNECTION

WIZARD OF OZ
   See OZ, WIZARD OF

Z

ZACHARY
   See TULL

ZOLTAN
   See BORDER DWELLERS: BROWN

MID-WORLD PLACES[1]

My world is like a huge ship that sank near enough shore for most of the wreckage to wash up on the beach. Much of what we find is fascinating, some of it may be useful, if ka allows, but all of it is still wreckage. Senseless wreckage.

Roland Deschain
IV:71

For the gunslinger it had been a stranger death yet—the endless hunt for the man in black through a world with neither map nor memory.

I:140

A

**ALGUL SIENTO
See ALGUL SIENTO in the PORTALS section

ALL-WORLD
In the time of Roland's semi-mythical ancestor, ARTHUR ELD, all of the kingdoms of the land—whether part of IN-WORLD, OUT-WORLD or MID-WORLD—were united under one high king who wore the crown of All-World upon his brow. This king was Arthur, Warrior of the White and the first Lord of Light. Like the great King Arthur of Our World, Arthur

---

1. **NOTE ON MID-WORLD DIRECTIONS:** In the original version of *The Gunslinger*, Roland follows Walter (the Man in Black) due south through the Mohaine Desert and the Cyclopean Mountains. In the 2003 edition of the book, Roland follows Walter southeast, both of them drawn toward the force of the Bear-Turtle Beam. For a detailed account of how this alters Mid-World's geography, see MID-WORLD MAPS located at the end of this Concordance.

Eld wielded a magical sword called Excalibur. Arthur reigned during a kind of Golden Age that came (we believe) after the nuclear and chemical destruction wreaked by the OLD ONES.

Even in Roland's youth, when the IN-WORLD Baronies still stood and the gunslingers maintained relative peace by exerting their strength through the fragmenting AFFILIATION, the unity of Arthur Eld's All-World was only a myth. FARSON (who we believe was the pawn for an even greater destructive force) warred in the west, drawing over to his side many of the embittered, failed gunslingers originally sent to the western lands in disgrace.

IV:317

**ARROYOS
In the new version of *The Gunslinger*, we find out that there are arroyos in the hardpan of the MOHAINE DESERT.

ATCHISON
See ATCHISON, TOPEKA, AND SANTA FE RAILROAD in the OUR WORLD PLACES section. See also KANSAS in that section and KANSAS in the PORTALS section.

B

BACK COURTS
See NEW CANAAN, BARONY OF: GILEAD

BAD GRASS
See MEJIS, BARONY OF

BAR K RANCH
See MEJIS, BARONY OF: HAMBRY

BAYVIEW HOTEL
See MEJIS, BARONY OF: HAMBRY

BEAMS
See BEAMS in the PORTALS section

BIG EMPTY
In the town of RIVER CROSSING, the elderly residents refer to the waste lands beyond LUD as the Big Empty. SUSANNAH DEAN thinks that all of Mid-World's barren lands are a "Big Empty," and confronting that desolation turned Roland in on himself. See also WASTE LANDS and DRAWERS in the PORTALS section.

    III:226, III:243

BLAINE'S ROUTE
Our desperate *ka-tet* boarded the slo-trans mono BLAINE in LUD, just after EDDIE and SUSANNAH's shootout with the PUBES and JAKE's escape from TICK-TOCK, leader of the GRAYS. Blaine's track led southeast, roughly along the PATH OF THE BEAM, in the direction of the DARK TOWER. Although Blaine claimed that he could take our group closer to their final destination, none of them were certain whether they would be able to disembark this Barony Coach alive.

Although probably originally endowed with a polite personality by the GREAT OLD ONES (who in retrospect were much less than great), over the centuries Blaine's personality fragmented into its component parts, finally evincing some of the cruelty of its Makers. The resulting monstrosity—which our *ka-tet* battled in a life-or-death riddling contest—consisted of a frightened LITTLE BLAINE as well as a nasty Big Blaine, who seemed to believe he served the people of Lud best by killing them.

Blaine's route led through the surreal WASTE LANDS and terminated in an alternate version of Our World's TOPEKA, one afflicted by the terrible superflu found in Stephen King's novel *The Stand*.

Blaine was obviously created to transport the Great Old Ones onto other levels of the Tower, and is an example of the sinister technology created by NORTH CENTRAL POSITRONICS. For more discussion on the subject of trains between worlds, see the ATCHISON, TOPEKA, AND SANTA FE RAILROAD in the OUR WORLD PLACES section.

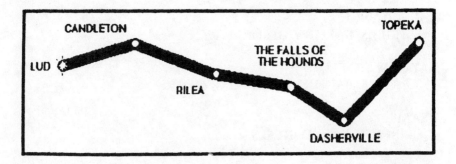

CANDLETON: This was the first official stop on Blaine's route. Luckily for our folks the train didn't actually stop here, otherwise they would have been exposed to the killer radiation levels still pulsing from a nearby Ground Zero.

Although described as "a poisoned and irradiated ruin," Candleton is not completely dead. Trundling along the corridors of the CANDLETON TRAVELLERS' HOTEL are turtle-sized beetles, birds that look more like small dragons, and blind, bloated, mutant rats.   III:404, III:416, IV:13–14, IV:15

    CANDLETON FOUNTAIN: IV:13–14

    CANDLETON TRAVELLERS' HOTEL: IV:13–14

    ELEGANT BEEF AND PORK RESTAURANT: IV:13

DASHERVILLE: Dasherville was the stop before Topeka on Blaine's run.   III:404, IV:36

FALLS OF THE HOUNDS: The Falls of the Hounds was actually a torrential waterfall guarded by two giant stone sculptures shaped like ferocious dogs. (The dogs actually protruded from a point about two hundred feet below the place where the torrential, brawling river tumbled over its drop.)

It was at the Falls of the Hounds that Blaine switched to battery power. His batteries were fired up by the electric-blue energy zapping from the giant hounds' eyes.   III:404, IV:31–33, IV:34–35, IV:41, IV:653

RILEA: Rilea was the stop after Candleton on Blaine's run.   III:404, IV:15, IV:16, IV:22, IV:26

TOPEKA: Topeka was Blaine's termination point. It also happened to be located in an alternate version of our KANSAS. See KANSAS in the PORTALS section.

**BLUE HAVEN/BLUE HEAVEN
See ALGUL SIENTO in the PORTALS section

BLUFFS
See MEJIS, BARONY OF

BORDER (BORDER DWELLERS)
The Border Dwellers live in this transitional desert area bordering the waterless waste land of the MOHAINE DESERT. This region was one of the first in which time grew soft.

    BROWN'S HUT: I:15–22, I:64–65, I:72

C

CANDLE, THE
See MEJIS, BARONY OF: HAMBRY: CITGO

CANDLETON
See BLAINE'S ROUTE

CENTRAL PLACE
See NEW CANAAN, BARONY OF: GILEAD

CHURCH OF THE BLOOD EVERLASTING
See RIVER BARONY: RIVER CROSSING

CITGO
See MEJIS, BARONY OF: HAMBRY

CLEAN SEA
See MEJIS, BARONY OF: HAMBRY

**COACH ROAD
This is the two-rut track that Roland follows during *The Gunslinger*. It runs from PRICETOWN (though it probably began much farther back) through TULL, past BROWN's hut and then into the wastes of the MOHAINE DESERT. Before the world moved on, this road was one of Mid-World's highways. The deserted WAY STATION, where Roland met Jake, was once a stopping place for the coaches that traveled along this artery.

Like most of the amenities of organized culture, by the time of *The Gunslinger* Mid-World's coach service had almost disappeared. A few still ran between Pricetown and Tull, but none ventured into the deadly regions of the desert. In the new *Gunslinger*, we find out that bucka wagons also used this road. In this version of the story, the Coach Road runs southeast, like the BEAR-TURTLE BEAM, not due south.

I:11–16 *(Roland on it)*, I:22–24

CÖOS, THE (HILL)
See MEJIS, BARONY OF: HAMBRY

CRADLE OF LUD
See RIVER BARONY: LUD

CRAVEN'S UNDERTAKING PARLOR
See MEJIS, BARONY OF: HAMBRY

CRESSIA
Cressia was one of the Baronies located west of GILEAD. Its Barony Seat was **INDRIE**, a city burned to the ground by FARSON'S harriers. Fearful for their lives and afraid to join the thousands already slaughtered by THE GOOD MAN (including Indrie's mayor and high sheriff, who were beheaded by the rebel forces), Cressia repudiated the AFFILIATION and bowed to Farson. It later became one of his strongholds.

When Roland challenged CORT and underwent an early test of manhood against his father's wishes, he thought that his father was far away in this distant Barony searching for one of MAERLYN'S glass balls. He was wrong. Cressia was famous for one of its sayings: "If ye'd steal the silver from the dining room, first put the dog in the pantry" (IV:175).

IV:110, IV:163, IV:164, IV:175, IV:619 *(Marten joins Farson here)*
INDRIE: IV:163

CYCLOPEAN MOUNTAINS[2]
The first foothills of the Cyclopean Mountain Range can be seen from the dry wastes of the MOHAINE DESERT. The WILLOW JUNGLE, where JAKE was almost trapped by the demonically sexual ORACLE OF THE MOUNTAINS, is located here among the first tumbling rises of granite and grasses.

These mountains are one of the many physical barriers which Roland and Jake have to traverse in order to pursue the MAN IN BLACK, also known as WALTER. At first, their path winds through a much more hospitable landscape than the desert which Roland traversed earlier in *The Gunslinger*. Trees grow there, and there are rabbits to hunt and eat. However, as their experience with the sexual demon of the SPEAKING RING showed, Roland's world contains sinister magic, much of it manipulated by the very sorcerer they pursue.

As Jake and Roland climb higher toward the mountain pass, following the burned-out ideograms left by their elusive and dangerous quarry, the way becomes steeper and less accessible, at times no more than a narrow

2. For Book II, I have only listed direct references to the Cyclopean Mountains. However, whenever action takes place on LOBSTROSITY BEACH, which borders the WESTERN SEA, these mountains are on the horizon.

V cut into the mica- and quartz-veined granite. Just before the mountains rise to their most inaccessible icy heights, the path zigzags into a canyon. There, our two friends follow a taunting Walter into the black cleft of a waterfall cave. Little do they know it, but they are eagerly awaited by the band of SLOW MUTANTS who nest in the deserted mountain subway system left by the OLD ONES.[2]

I:11, I:44, I:56, I:65, I:72, I:92, I:112–34 *(foothills)*, I:134–44, I:149–58 *(Gilead story 149–52)*, I:174–216, II:31, II:32, II:168, II:177, II:231, II:232, II:242 *(foothills)*, II:275 *(hills)*, II:286 *(brakes)*, II:291–97 *(they reach beach)*, II:300–312, II:315 *(abyss)*, II:327, II:367, II:379, II:394, III:36, III:42, III:48, III:97, III:109, III:180, III:195 *(indirect)*, III:223, III:260, III:407

D

DARK TOWER
See DARK TOWER in the PORTALS section

DASHERVILLE
See BLAINE'S ROUTE

DEBARIA
Debaria is the location of a women's retreat, quite possibly a religious one. While Roland is in HAMBRY, his mother, GABRIELLE DESCHAIN, supposedly goes to Debaria to pray for his safe return. However, it seems highly likely that her lover MARTEN BROADCLOAK—and Gabrielle's complicity in his plot to overthrow the aristocratic gunslingers—is the real reason for her sojourn. Gabrielle's attempted assassination is foiled, but it seems quite probable that she was schooled in the ways of deceit while in Debaria.
IV:619, IV:620, IV:655

DELAIN
JOHN NORMAN, the young man Roland meets while imprisoned by the LITTLE SISTERS OF ELURIA, comes from Delain. This kingdom is derisively known as Dragon's Lair, Liars' Heaven, and the home of tall tales. It also happens to be the setting for the novel *Eyes of the Dragon*.
E:188

DESATOYA MOUNTAINS
The town of ELURIA is located in the Desatoya Mountains. Like so many
of the landscapes found in the Dark Tower series, both the mountains and
the towns dotted through them resemble the landscape of the American
Southwest.
    E:146

DOORS: MID-WORLD TO NEW YORK
    See DOORWAYS BETWEEN WORLDS in the PORTALS section

DOWNLAND BARONIES
    See GREATER KINGDOMS OF THE WESTERN EARTH

DRAGON'S GRAVE
The Dragon's Grave was a bottomless crack in the earth named for the
great bursts of steam that erupted from it every thirty to forty days.
Roland knew of it as a boy, so it is most likely located near GILEAD-that-
was.
    III:37

DRAGON'S LAIR
    See DELAIN

DRAWERS
    See DRAWERS in the PORTALS section

DROP, THE
    See MEJIS, BARONY OF: HAMBRY

DRUIT STONES
    See DOORWAYS BETWEEN WORLDS in the PORTALS section

E

ELD
Eld was the name of the ancient land ruled by Roland's ancestor,
ARTHUR ELD, who later became king of ALL-WORLD. Eld was
located northwest of GILEAD, in the northwesternmost reaches of the

AFFILIATION. By the time of Roland's trials in HAMBRY, those ancient lands were already being burned and looted by FARSON and his men.
    IV:181

ELURIA

Eluria is a small town located in the DESATOYA MOUNTAINS. It is also the setting for the short story "The Little Sisters of Eluria." Like many of the places in Mid-World, it looks like a town out of the old American West. Along its High Street are quite a few wooden shop fronts, including a mercantile, a smithy, a Gathering Hall, a church (complete with bell tower), a livery, a market, and a sheriff's office. It also has a single hotel (GOOD BEDS HOTEL), and two saloons, one of which is called THE BUSTLING PIG. When Roland arrives during the heat of Full Earth, the place has been deserted for about two weeks. The only living (or once living) beings Roland finds are the CROSS DOG, a single corpse, and some sweet-singing insects.

Although there are no people to be seen, the town's gates are still strung with garlands of dried flowers and the church doorway with tiny silver bells—decorations which Roland finds both disturbing and eerie. Soon after his arrival he discovers that the town is not completely deserted after all. It is inhabited by the mutant GREEN FOLK and the vampiric LITTLE SISTERS OF ELURIA.
    E:146–58, E:159, E:166, E:173, E:178–79, E:181, E:190, E:193, E:201, E:205, E:209

HOSPITAL (RUN BY LITTLE SISTERS): See LITTLE SISTERS' HOSPITAL in the PORTALS section

LEXINGWORTH: This is where Eluria's citizens hang criminals. E:151

RADIUM MINES: The foul-looking muties known as the GREEN FOLK inhabit the radium mines outside Eluria.   E:154

RUINED HACIENDA: This is where the Little Sisters live during their time in Eluria.   E:200, E:201

THOUGHTFUL HOUSE: In "The Little Sisters of Eluria," the tyrannical SISTER MARY tells Roland that Thoughtful House is a "home for contagion," a place where the sick are brought to recover. But like so much that is said in the white tents of the sinister Little Sisters, this is a lie. Thoughtful House is not a house at all but a small hillside cave where Sister Mary sends disobedient members of her order to endure a kind of solitary confinement. The lovely and rebellious SISTER JENNA is forced to spend much time here. E:175, E:185, E:194, E:201, E:206

END-WORLD
 See END-WORLD in the PORTALS section

EYEBOLT CANYON
 See MEJIS, BARONY OF: HAMBRY

F

FALLS OF THE HOUNDS
 See BLAINE'S ROUTE

**FARSON (TOWN OF)
In *The Gunslinger* we learn that when Roland was a boy, the AFFILIA-
TION's enemy JOHN FARSON (also known as THE GOOD MAN),
planned to poison this town. Given the fact that this rather nasty character
bears the town's name, it seems likely that he—or his ancestors—originated here. In the new *Gunslinger,* the town of Farson is replaced by the
town of TAUNTON.
 I:101, I:102, I:105, I:108

**FARSON ROAD
Farson Road is the name given to the coach road that runs between
GILEAD and the town of FARSON. GALLOWS HILL is located here. In
the new *Gunslinger,* the Farson Road becomes the TAUNTON ROAD.
 I:106–11

**FOREST o' BARONY
 See NEW CANAAN, BARONY OF

FOREST TREES
 See PASS o' THE RIVER

G

GADDISH FEEDS
 See KANSAS: TOPEKA in the PORTALS section

GAGE BOULEVARD
See KANSAS: TOPEKA in the PORTALS section

GALLOWS HILL
Gallows Hill is located on the FARSON ROAD. HAX, Gilead's traitorous head cook, is hanged here.
   I:106–11, IV:161

**GARLAN
Garlan is a distant kingdom which seems almost mythical to many of the people we meet in the Dark Tower series. According to AUNT TALITHA of RIVER CROSSING, the people of Garlan have brown skin. It is also supposed to be the home of that strange baby-bearing bird, the GRAND FEATHEREX.
   Garlan also has more sinister associations. According to the novel *Eyes of the Dragon*, the nasty sorcerer R.F. once lived there, and we can guess that he learned much of his nasty magic—and knowledge of poisons—in that place. Not surprisingly, the poison coating the knife intended to kill Roland's father came from this kingdom. ELDRED JONAS—Roland's enemy in *Wizard and Glass*—received a terrible whipping in Garlan. In the new *Gunslinger*, we find out that this kingdom is located west of GILEAD, and that it is a tobacco-growing region.
   II:66, III:231, III:242, IV:214, IV:480 *(Jonas scarred here)*, IV:621 *(poison from here)*

GAUNTLET
See GREAT ROAD, THE.

GILEAD
See NEW CANAAN, BARONY OF

GILEAD, BARONY OF
See NEW CANAAN, BARONY OF

GLENCOVE
See TAVARES

GOLGOTHA, THE
See GOLGOTHA in the PORTALS section

GRAYS' CASTLE/GRAYS' MAZE
See RIVER BARONY: LUD

GREAT HALL (HALL OF THE GRANDFATHERS)
See NEW CANAAN, BARONY OF: GILEAD

GREAT ROAD
There are many Great Roads in Mid-World. Like the Roman roads of our world, they are the leftovers of an earlier civilization, namely that of the OLD ONES. Although these byways were once major highways, by the time of *The Gunslinger* their broken surfaces are covered with years of dirt. However, many of them still have intact subterranean drainage systems. Most of the Great Roads follow the PATH OF THE BEAM.
IV:653

GREAT ROAD TO LUD: III:159–65, III:170–76, III:178–82, III:189–90, III:223–32 *(directly mentioned on 224, 225, 226, 228, 230)*, III:240, III:243, III:273–89 (ka-tet *on it;* 273 *Quick's airplane; directly mentioned on 283, 286, 287)*

GAUNTLET: This is the term Jake uses for the fortifications around the Great Road just outside Lud.   III:286–89

THROUGH HAMBRY: One of Mid-World's Great Roads runs from the BARONY OF NEW CANAAN to the BARONY OF MEJIS. Along its course it passes through the town of HAMBRY. It runs east-west.   IV:182 *(runs from New Canaan to Mejis)*, IV:266, IV:271, IV:375, IV:377, IV:379 *(leads to Citgo)*, IV:402–3, IV:498, IV:610

GREAT WEST WOODS
The Great West Woods of OUT-WORLD are located north of the CYCLOPEAN MOUNTAINS and just east of the WESTERN SEA. Roland, EDDIE, and SUSANNAH recover here after their long journey along LOBSTROSITY BEACH, a trial we read about in *The Drawing of the Three*. These woods are the home of the GUARDIAN SHARDIK, also known as MIR. It is the home of the PORTAL OF THE BEAR and the place where our *ka-tet* picks up the PATH OF THE BEAM. In the SHOOTING GALLERY (a clearing in the woods), Roland teaches both Eddie and Susannah the ways of the gunslinger.
II:395–99, III:11–21, III:23–51 *(setting)*, III:53–86, III:149–53 *(Eddie's Dream)*, III:158–65, III:170, III:247, III:347

SHOOTING GALLERY: III:11–19, III:36, III:163

GREATER KINGDOMS OF THE WESTERN EARTH
When Roland was a boy he saw a map of the Greater Kingdoms of the Western Earth. It depicted GILEAD, the DOWNLAND BARONIES, which were overrun by riot and civil war the year after he won his guns, and showed the hills, the desert, and the mountains which stretched all the

way to the WESTERN SEA. At the time the map was made, one thousand miles lay between Gilead and the Western Sea. However, as the BEAMS disintegrated, distances within Mid-World shifted and grew. It took Roland many years to cross that distance.
    III:74

GREEN HEART
    See MEJIS, BARONY OF: HAMBRY

H

HALL OF THE GRANDFATHERS
    See NEW CANAAN, BARONY OF: GILEAD

HAMBRY
    See MEJIS, BARONY OF

HAMBRY CEMETERY
    See MEJIS, BARONY OF: HAMBRY

HAMBRY CREEK
    See MEJIS, BARONY OF: HAMBRY

HAMBRY POINT
    See MEJIS, BARONY OF: HAMBRY

HAMBRY POST OFFICE
    See MEJIS, BARONY OF: HAMBRY

HANGING ROCK
    See MEJIS, BARONY OF

HATTIGANS
    See RITZY

HEMPHILL
Hemphill was a small town located near GILEAD-that-was. Roland's HAMBRY alter ego, Will Dearborn, supposedly grew up there.
    IV:148, IV:183, IV:201

HENDRICKSON (TOWN)

Hendrickson was one of the many towns attacked by THE GOOD MAN.
  I:104

HOOKEY'S STABLE AND SMITHY

  See MEJIS, BARONY OF: HAMBRY

I

IL BOSQUE

Il Bosque is a forest west of MEJIS. Roland, CUTHBERT, and ALAIN
travel through it after Susan's death and after Roland's disastrous magical journey through MAERLYN'S GRAPEFRUIT.
  IV:610–11

IMPERIUM

  See NORTH CENTRAL POSITRONICS in the CHARACTER section

INDRIE

  See CRESSIA, BARONY OF

**IN-WORLD

Roland's world is often described as having two parts, IN-WORLD and
OUT-WORLD. These terms are relative to one another. To the citizens of
HAMBRY who live far from the hub of civilization, GILEAD is "In-
World." Hence, Roland and his youthful *ka-tet* are called the "In-World
boys." Hambry is an Out-World Barony because it is far from NEW
CANAAN.

  The terms *In-World* and *Out-World* may also be metaphorical references to the metaphysical map of Mid-World which Roland draws in *The
Waste Lands*. According to this map, Mid-World is shaped like a circle,
with the DARK TOWER at its center and the BEAMS radiating out from
it and terminating in twelve PORTALS. Just as the Tower is the center of
the Universe, Gilead and the In-World Baronies are the centers of human
culture. Backwaters such as MEJIS are on the Outer Crescent of the "civilized" world. See also the MID-WORLD entry (this section) and the
END WORLD entry (PORTALS section). In the new version of *The
Gunslinger*, Roland refers to himself as being from In-World.

III:375, IV:145 *(Roland's* ka-tet), IV:183, IV:192, IV:207, IV:347, IV:363, IV:379, IV:388, IV:422 *(Northern In-World and Reindeer fucking)*, IV:503, IV:506, IV:557, IV:583 *(and Nordites)*
INNER ARC: Home of the Inner Baronies.   IV:196
INNER BARONIES: IV:145, IV:295
INNER CRESCENT: IV:302
INNERS: IV:360

J

**JERICHO HILL
Jericho Hill was the site of the gunslingers' last stand against their enemies. During this battle CUTHBERT ALLGOOD died and Roland lost the horn of his fathers—the horn he was meant to blow when he reached the DARK TOWER.

JIMTOWN
See RIVER BARONY

K

KAMBERO
This is one of the villages located in the far western regions of Mid-World. It is probably even farther west than ELURIA.
E:193

KANSAS
See KANSAS in the PORTALS section

KASHMIN, BARONY OF (KASHAMIN, BARONY OF)
Before the complete destruction of the AFFILIATION and of culture as Roland knew it, the Kashmin province was famous for its rugs. Sumptuous Kashmin carpets adorned the halls of GILEAD. They also lined the floors of the CRADLE OF THE GRAYS.
III:350 *(Kashmin)*, IV:654 *(rugs from Province of Kashamin)*

KING'S TOWN
This is one of the hundreds of towns Roland traveled through on his search for the DARK TOWER. Twelve years before he met JAKE (and not long after the fall of GILEAD), Roland had a girl here. She was one of the many he deserted in order to pursue his quest.
   I:158

L

LaMERK FOUNDRY
   See LaMERK FOUNDRY in the CHARACTERS section

LANDING, THE
   See RIVER BARONY

LAZY SUSAN RANCH
   See MEJIS, BARONY OF: HAMBRY

LEXINGWORTH
   See ELURIA

LIARS HEAVEN
   See DELAIN

LOBSTROSITY BEACH
   See WESTERN SEA

LUD
   See RIVER BARONY: LUD

M

MEJIS, BARONY OF
Mejis (more specifically, the Barony Seat of HAMBRY) is the setting for most of *Wizard and Glass* (IV:115–331; IV:341–611). Mejis's Barony color is a deep orange-red, as can be seen on the official sash worn by

Mayor HART THORIN. Located east of GILEAD and on the edge of the desert, Mejis is considered one of the quiet backwaters of the OUTER ARC, or OUTER CRESCENT. Like much of Mid-World, it resembles areas of the American West. Its citizens breed horses and, in the areas closest to the sea, they also fish.

STEVEN DESCHAIN, Roland's father, sends Roland and his two friends to Mejis in order to keep them safe from JOHN FARSON, who is destroying the lands farther west. Little does he know that THE GOOD MAN'S poison has spread as far as the Outer Arc. Mejis is no longer loyal to the AFFILIATION, and the final battle of Mid-World is destined to take place in this quiet Barony. Within two years of Roland's trials in Mejis, the light of the IN-WORLD BARONIES will be snuffed out and the world, as Steven Deschain knew it, will no longer exist. (Below are some of the direct references to Mejis's character, customs, etc.)

IV:68, IV:99 *(east of Gilead)*, IV:144, IV:149, IV:151, IV:161, IV:162 *(end of the world)*, IV:164 *(Steven Deschain thinks it's safe)*, IV:179 *(the smells of it. Loyal to the Affiliation)*, IV:180, IV:187, IV:193, IV:195, IV:201, IV:206, IV:214, IV:221, IV:232, IV:244, IV:256, IV:269, IV:271, IV:316, IV:336, IV:341, IV:342 *(orchards north of Hambry)*, IV:351, IV:355 *(and Reap)*, IV:391, IV:410, IV:414, IV:423, IV:426, IV:431, IV:434, IV:436, IV:445, IV:447 *(Out-World Barony)*, IV:451, IV:456, IV:461, IV:471, IV:473–74, IV:480, IV:485, IV:486, IV:500, IV:502, IV:506, IV:507, IV:521, IV:546, IV:547, IV:555, IV:605, IV:620, IV:624, IV:627, IV:650, E:160

BAD GRASS AND AREAS WEST OF HAMBRY:

BAD GRASS: This is the freeland west of Hambry and is located on the edge of the desert waste lands.   IV:271, IV:324, IV:343, IV:344, IV:394, IV:474, IV:499, IV:523–26 *(setting)*, IV:529–35 *(setting)*, IV:536–49, IV:552–60

BLUFFS: The bluffs are six miles beyond the long grassy DROP at the edge of HAMBRY. HANGING ROCK is located here. IV:272

CÖOS: The Cöos is a ragged hill five miles from the town of HAMBRY, ten miles from EYEBOLT CANYON. To the northwest of it is the desert, the BAD GRASS, HANGING ROCK, and EYEBOLT CANYON. RHEA, the weirdling of the Cöos, has her hut here below the crest of the hill.   IV:115–38, IV:166, IV:168, IV:246, IV:290, IV:299, IV:343, IV:394–98, IV:414, IV:415–19 *(setting)*, IV:420, IV:448, IV:449, IV:452–53 *(setting)*, IV:657, IV:662

EYEBOLT CANYON: A short, steep-walled box canyon shaped like a chimney lying on its side. A THINNY has eaten its way into

the far end of it. Roland destroys his enemies by laying a trap for them in Eyebolt Canyon.   IV:115, IV:118 *(and thinny)*, IV:156 *(described)*, IV:272–76 *(described)*, IV:324, IV:351, IV:394–95 *(described)*, IV:422, IV:431, IV:432, IV:454–56, IV:470, IV:547, IV:580, IV:590–602 *(Latigo's men are trapped here)*, IV:622–23
HANGING ROCK: IV:272, IV:324, IV:368, IV:371 *(Latigo's men come here)*, IV:386, IV:394, IV:407, IV:422, IV:432, IV:456, IV:484, IV:503, IV:522, IV:530, IV:532, IV:536, IV: 547, IV:555, IV:573, IV:579, IV:583, IV:584, IV:589–91 *(setting)*
HAMBRY (BARONY SEAT OF MEJIS): Hambry is a beautiful town located on the edge of the CLEAN SEA. From High Street you can see the bay, the docks, and the many-colored boathouses. The newer buildings are adobe, the older ones are brick and are reminiscent of GILEAD's Old Quarter. Hambry has two markets—an upper and a lower. The lower market smells fishy but is cheaper.

Roland associates Hambry with the smell of sea-salt, oil, and pine. Its citizens are fishermen and horsebreeders. Although Hambry is picturesque, it is full of hidden dangers. The THINNY of Eyebolt Canyon is the most visible; however, other dangers lurk. As Roland soon realizes, "in Hambry, the waters on top and the waters down below seem to run in different directions" (IV:205). Although they declare their allegiance to the AFFILIATION, the politically powerful men of the town have (metaphorically speaking) sold their souls to FARSON, also known as THE GOOD MAN. Although the gunslingers of NEW CANAAN do not know it, the destruction of their world will begin here, in a Barony they can barely recall.

In Hambry, Roland faces the first true trials of his manhood. He also discovers MAERLYN'S GRAPEFRUIT, the pink sphere of MAERLYN'S RAINBOW.

General Pages: IV:115–331, IV:341–611.

Specific References: IV:65, IV:79 *(and thinnies)*, IV:115, IV:142, IV:144 *(mailboxes)*, IV:145, IV:153 *(dinner of state)*, IV:180–89 *(180–81 description of bay; 182 five hundred miles from In-World; 183 and "old ways"; 186 four hundred wheels from Gilead)*, IV:190, IV:193, IV:200, IV:205, IV:206, IV:219, IV:220, IV:238, IV:239 *(beauty of it)*, IV:244, IV:254 *(few muties in Outer Baronies)*, IV:261, IV:263, IV:267, IV:271, IV:276, IV:282 *(upper and lower markets)*, IV:284, IV:293 *(and game of Castles)*, IV:300, IV:305, IV:402, IV:426, IV:430, IV:446, IV:451, IV:453 *(lower market)*, IV:461, IV:467 *(lower market)*, IV:484, IV:504, IV:506, IV:521, IV:550, IV:569, IV:570, IV:584, IV:603, IV:605

ANNE'S DRESSES: IV:328

BAR K RANCH: A deserted spread of land northwest of town. It was once owned by the GARBER family; now it belongs to the HORSEMEN'S ASSOCIATION. Roland's *ka-tet* stays in Bar K's bunkhouse during their time in Hambry.   IV:175, IV:188, IV:199, IV:211, IV:233, IV:260–64 *(260 described)*, IV:274, IV:276, IV:277, IV:286, IV:288, IV:294, IV:305, IV:352, IV:357–60, IV:368, IV:378, IV:388–89, IV:390–92, IV:393–94 *(Jonas is there)*, IV:398–402 *(Roland's* ka-tet *finds Jonas's mess)*, IV:403, IV:431, IV:450, IV:473–80, IV:484, IV:502, IV:574

BAYVIEW HOTEL: Located on High Street.   IV:447, IV:502

CANDLE, THE: The gas-pipe of Citgo.   IV:295, IV:363.

CITGO: An oil patch filled with 200 steel towers, 19 of which still ceaselessly pump oil. They have existed for more than six centuries.   IV:135, IV:145–48, IV:157, IV:159, IV:176 *(Jonas tells Depape to cover tankers)*, IV:185, IV:186, IV:214 *(Reynolds and Depape camouflage)*, IV:281, IV:285, IV:289–304 *(289 orange grove nearby; 295 "the candle")*, IV:300–301 *(tankers)*, IV:319, IV:345, IV:363, IV:378–80, IV:385–86, IV:390, IV:395, IV:411, IV:421, IV:430, IV:432, IV:451, IV:480, IV:483–85, IV:515–19

CLEAN SEA: This is the sea located east of Hambry.   IV:145, IV:151, IV:164, IV:231–32, IV:233, IV:341, IV:441, IV:479, IV:521–22

CRAVEN'S UNDERTAKING PARLOR: IV:381

DROP, THE (WESTERN DROP): This long, grassy slope stretches for thirty wheels toward the sea. It is used as a horse meadow and belongs to JOHN CROYDON. Part of it is known as TOWN LOOKOUT. SUSAN DELGADO's house is visible from here (IV:284).   IV:125, IV:133, IV:140, IV:153, IV:160–65, IV:170, IV:188, IV:191, IV:205, IV:234, IV:239–40, IV:246–59 *(too many horses)*, IV:261, IV:271–72, IV:276, IV:281, IV:284, IV:288, IV:293, IV:301, IV:311, IV:324, IV:346, IV:352, IV:358, IV:361, IV:368, IV:371, IV:378, IV:400, IV:402, IV:414, IV:423, IV:427, IV:446, IV:459, IV:502, IV:503, IV:522, IV:525, IV:529, IV:532, IV:548, IV:566, IV:568, IV:608, IV:635

GREAT ROAD: Listed separately

GREEN HEART (also PAVILION, MANAGERIE, RED ROCK): Green Heart is a pavilion located on HILL STREET, fifty yards from the jail and TOWN GATHERING HALL. It is the site of the Reap Dance. The stone wall at the back contains the red rock where Roland and SUSAN agree to leave notes for each other. Susan is eventually burned here.   IV:147, IV:327, IV:351, IV:343 *(red rock)*, IV:355, IV:370, IV:371, IV:372–74 *(Jonas and Cordelia)*, IV:381, IV:434, IV:462, IV:505, IV:507, IV:605–8 *(Susan burned)*

HAMBRY CEMETERY: Hambry Cemetery is the site of the famous murder/suicide of ROBERT AND FRANCESCA. Roland, CUTH-BERT, ALAIN, and SUSAN DELGADO meet to palaver here. IV:426, IV:428–36, IV:495, IV:514–15

HAMBRY CREEK: See also WILLOW GROVE below.   IV:311

HAMBRY JAIL: See SHERIFF'S OFFICE, BARONY JAIL below

HAMBRY MERCANTILE STORE: Located on South High Street. The porch has a line of carved totems depicting seven of the twelve GUARDIANS OF THE BEAM. They are BEAR, TURTLE, FISH, EAGLE, LION, BAT, and WOLF. People often hang Reap Charms from them.   IV:222, IV:245, IV:328, IV:342 *(rattlesnake skins),* IV:355 *(Reap Charms hang from the Guardians),* IV:447

HAMBRY POINT: The point is located two miles from the TRAV-ELLERS' REST.   IV:216

HAMBRY POST OFFICE: Although it is an Out-World Barony, Hambry has a postal service.   IV:181

HOOKEY'S STABLE AND SMITHY/HOOKEY'S STABLE AND FANCY LIVERY: IV:279–80, IV:282, IV:330, IV:344, IV:376, IV:512, IV:514–15

LAND OFFICE: IV:181

LAZY SUSAN RANCH: This ranch belongs to RENFREW and is the largest one in Mejis.   IV:187, IV:205, IV:208, IV:355, IV:421

MENAGERIE: See GREEN HEAR, above

MILLBANK, THE: Food served here.   IV:259

ORANGE GROVE: See CITGO above

PIANO RANCH: Owned by CROYDEN.   IV:187, IV:191, IV:215 *(Her Nibs is here),* IV:344, IV:451, IV:558

ROADS:

   CAMINO VEGA: Crosses HIGH STREET.   IV:329

   GREAT ROAD: (runs east/west) See GREAT ROAD, listed sep-arately.

   HIGH STREET: The TRAVELLERS' REST is located here. IV:171, IV:180, IV:189, IV:224, IV:329, IV: 381, IV:447, IV:505

   HILL STREET: GREEN HEART and the SHERIFF'S OFFICE are located here.   IV:180, IV:327, IV:371, IV:507, IV:605

   SEACOAST ROAD (BARONY SEA ROAD): IV:271, IV:370, IV:402, IV:581

   SILK RANCH ROAD: IV:602, IV:603

ROCKING B RANCH: Owned by LENGYLL.   IV:186 (genera-tor), IV:187, IV:199, IV:355

ROCKING H RANCH: This is LASLO RIMER's place.   IV:262 *(has oxen),* IV:293

SEAFRONT: This is Mayor HART THORIN's house. "Come in

peace" is inscribed above the door.   IV:153, IV:158, IV:162, IV:179–80, IV:191–210 *(193–94 interior described)*, IV:222, IV:234, IV:278, IV:279, IV:292, IV:306–8, IV:310–13, IV:328, IV:350, IV:367, IV:376, IV:391, IV:403, IV:405, IV:420, IV:428, IV:443, IV:448–49, IV:453, IV:457, IV:460, IV:468, IV:480–83 *(action here)*, IV:494–95 *(action here)*, IV:496, IV:498, IV:499, IV:506, IV:519–23 *(setting)*, IV:537, IV:542, IV:552, IV:561–62, IV:566–70, IV:577–78, IV:579, IV:582

SEVEN-MILE ORCHARD: IV:370

SHERIFF'S OFFICE, BARONY JAIL: This dual-purpose building is located on Hill Street, overlooking the bay.   IV:180–90 *(descriptions of office. Sheriff goes through Roland's false papers)*, IV:226, IV:259–60, IV:327 *(jail)*, IV:329, IV:362–64, IV:367–68, IV:371, IV:501, IV:502, IV:507, IV:508–13, IV:520, IV:523, IV:537

TOWN GATHERING HALL: IV:181, IV:185, IV:227–30, IV:500–502 *(setting)*, IV:562

TOWN LOOKOUT: Located on THE DROP.   IV:284

TRAVELLERS' REST: Located on HIGH STREET, the Rest is Hambry's bar and whorehouse. It is owned by CORAL THORIN and her brother, HART THORIN. Hart never sets foot in the place, but Coral runs it. The Travellers' Rest is the site of a showdown between Roland's *ka-tet* and the BIG COFFIN HUNTERS.   IV:144, IV:170–78, IV:190, IV:213–22, IV:224–26, IV:232, IV:241–42, IV:244–45, IV:286, IV:287, IV:342 *(and rattlesnake skins)*, IV:347–53, IV:355, IV:366, IV:367, IV:380–87, IV:389, IV:403–5, IV:420–25, IV:447 *(cotton-gillies)*, IV:451, IV:500, IV:502, IV:505, IV:506, IV:512, IV:527, IV:562–65 *(setting)*

WILLOW GROVE: Roland and SUSAN DELGADO make love here. It is Susan's favorite place, and eerily prefigures the WILLOW JUNGLE in which Roland later encounters the succubus, or ORACLE OF THE MOUNTAINS.   IV:311, IV:315–19, IV:321–23, IV:343, IV:435, IV:436, IV:537

ONNIE'S FORD: IV:306, IV:311

ORCHARDS NORTH OF HAMBRY: IV:341

SANTA FE: There is a sign for this city at BLAINE's termination point in TOPEKA. However, there is also a Santa Fe in Mejis. For more information on the significance of Santa Fe to the series, see ATCHISON, TOPEKA, AND SANTA FE RAILROAD in the OUR WORLD PLACES section.   IV:68

WASTE LANDS: There are waste lands beyond Hambry. But later on, when Roland and his new *ka-tet* reach the city of LUD, they find much nastier ones.   IV:271

**MID-WORLD

MID-WORLD was originally the name of an ancient kingdom, one that tried to preserve culture and knowledge in a time of darkness. Although not as large as ARTHUR ELD's united kingdom of ALL-WORLD, it was still sizable. Mid-World's ancient boundaries—which our *ka-tet* stumbles across during their travels in *The Waste Lands* and *Wizard and Glass*—stretched from a marker near the edge of the GREAT WEST WOODS to TOPEKA, the city where BLAINE the insane Mono terminates his run. The city of LUD (much like a ruined version of our NEW YORK) was once Mid-World's greatest urban center.

In Roland's youth, the great city of GILEAD tried to keep Mid-World's traditions alive and in many ways thought of itself as Mid-World's successor. Hence, Roland sometimes refers to his world as Mid-World, a term which includes both the IN-WORLD BARONIES, such as NEW CANAAN, and the farthest reaches of OUT-WORLD, including forgotten ruins such as ELURIA.

In *The Waste Lands,* Roland draws a metaphysical map of Mid-World which (in this case) is meant to encompass all the known lands of his reality. According to this map, Mid-World is shaped like a sequin impaled upon a central needle. The center of the needle—or the hub of the earthwheel—is the DARK TOWER, or the nexus of the time/space continuum. Radiating out from the Tower are the BEAMS, the invisible high-tension wires which both hold all of the multiple universes together and maintain the divisions between them.

The term *Mid-World* is reminiscent of both Middle Earth—Tolkien's magical world—and Midgard, the realm inhabited by human beings in both Norse and Anglo-Saxon mythology. Interestingly, the Dark Tower does not exist in Mid-World at all but in the fey region known as END-WORLD—a place which is both the center of all things and a land far beyond the known Baronies.

In the new version of *The Gunslinger,* we learn that Roland has been searching for the old Kingdom of Mid-World for a very long time. He has heard rumors that green lands still exist there, but he finds it hard to believe.

III:153 *(Mid-World Railway),* III:154, III:163–64, III:177, III:256, III:266, III:267, III:334, III:347, III:375, III:410, III:419, III:420, IV:66 *(Mid-World ends near Topeka),* IV:71, IV: 445, IV:447, E:147, E:165, E:198

MID-WORLD LANES
See MID-WORLD LANES in the PORTALS section

MID-WORLD RAILWAY
See MID-WORLD RAILWAY in the PORTALS section

MILLBANK, THE
    See MEJIS, BARONY OF: HAMBRY

**MOHAINE DESERT
In *The Gunslinger*, Roland crosses this desert in pursuit of WALTER. The Mohaine is described as "the apotheosis of all deserts, huge, standing to the sky for what might have been parsecs in all directions. White; blinding; waterless; without feature save for the faint, cloudless haze of the mountains which sketched themselves on the horizon and the devil grass which brought sweet dreams, nightmares, death." It is a harsh and unforgiving place that steals youth and sucks moisture from the very soul. The town of TULL is located near the desert and BORDER DWELLERS live on the edges of this waste land, but nothing can live within its desiccated heart.

In pursuit of the MAN IN BLACK, Roland crosses this desert on foot, making his way along the old COACH ROAD, which winds through PRICETOWN and TULL. He stops briefly at BROWN's hut (the final human habitation), then travels across the hardpan until he reaches the WAY STATION, where he meets JAKE. The final leg of this journey (from Brown's hut to the Way Station) almost kills him. Much of Mid-World has been reduced to desert, but the Mohaine seems to be, by far, the worst. In the new version of *The Gunslinger*, we find out that the Mohaine is haunted by at least one TAHEEN—a hybrid creature with a raven's head and a man's body.

I:11–22, I:30, I:31, I:42, I:44, I:45, I:52, I:65–81 *(72–81 Way Station)*, I:83–95 *(83–92 Way Station)*, I:119, I:124, I:127, I:134–35, I:209, II:40, III:43, III:101

N

NEW CANAAN, BARONY OF (also known as GILEAD BARONY [IV:595])
The Barony of New Canaan shares its name with the biblical land of milk and honey. Before the fall of the AFFILIATION it was a green, sweet land—one that tried to keep alive the ideals of hope, knowledge, and light. Roland remembers his home city of Gilead as a jewel set amid New Canaan's green-gold fields and serene, blue rivers. Unlike many of the OUT-WORLD baronies, New Canaan (the hub of IN-WORLD) still had running electricity.

I:136, IV:108, IV:148, IV:153, IV:182, IV:190, IV:199, IV:266–67, IV:289 *(apple orchards)*, IV:350

**FOREST o' BARONY: The warped pines that grow here are used to make gallows trees.

GILEAD: At the time Roland sets out for HAMBRY, Gilead is Mid-World's last great living city. Ancient and walled, it is the Barony Seat of New Canaan, one of the INNER BARONIES of western Mid-World. Gilead is known as the green land, and its city is divided into two separate towns. The filthy maze-like streets of **LOWER TOWN** (frequented by CORT) contain brothels. From the high, pennon-fluttering battlements of the castle, you can view the vendors of the brick and wrought-iron Old Quarter.   I:94, I:96–111, I:149–52, I:158–74, III:152, III:207, III:242, III:349, III:375, III:410, III:411, III:414, III:415, III:416, III:417, III:418, III:419, IV:6–9, IV:15, IV:48, IV:49, IV:50, IV:93 *("green land")*, IV:107–12 *(brothels of lower town. Roland visits a whore)*, IV:119 *(western barony)*, IV:164, IV:194, IV:201 *(and outlying towns of Hemphill and Pennilton)*, IV:213, IV:219, IV:266, IV:289, IV:350, IV:357, IV:388, IV:389, IV:402, IV:405, IV:415, IV:436, IV:464, IV:474, IV:499, IV:536, IV:547, IV:564, IV:570, IV:584, IV:587 *(Roland of Gilead)*, IV:603, IV:611, IV:621 *(Roland sees its fall in Wizard's glass)*, IV:624, IV:644, IV:651, IV:652, IV:653, E:159, E:170, E:171, E:172, E:195, E:198, E:202

    CENTRAL PLACE: This ancient part of Gilead consists of 100 stone castles.   I:137

    BACK COURTS AND FIELDS: Women play Points in the main castle's Back Courts. These courts seem to be adjacent to the fields where CORT trains young gunslingers in archery and falconry.   I:96–100, I:137

    BARRACKS: This is where young gunslinger apprentices live, away from their parents. The apprentices' nickel guns (given once they pass their coming-of-age battle against CORT) are stored in the vaults below.   I:171

    CORT'S COTTAGE: I:162–64, I:170, I:172

    EXERCISE YARD: I:161

    GABRIELLE'S APARTMENTS: I:159–61, IV:654–58

    GATHERING FIELDS: E:160

    GREAT HALL (CENTRAL HALL, HALL OF THE GRANDFATHERS, WEST'RD HALL): The Spring Ball, also known as ****the Sowing Night Cotillion, was held in Gilead's Great Hall. It was a grand place with great balconies and a central dancing area illuminated by electric flambeaux. Roland saw his mother dance with the traitorous MARTEN BROADCLOAK

here. In the new version of *The Gunslinger*, Roland calls it the
WEST'RD HALL.   I:137, I:150–52, I:156, I:164, I:166, III:276,
III:417–18, IV:7–8, IV:150 *(electric lights)*, IV:178, IV:193–94,
IV:405, IV:436, IV:547, E:160

GREAT HOUSE KITCHENS (WEST KITCHENS): This was
HAX's domain.   I:100–103, I:109, I:137, E:187

MAIN RECEIVING HALL: I:103–6

ROLAND'S CHILDHOOD ROOM: This room had a window
of many colors.   I:71–72

ROYAL COURT GARDENS: II:300

SQUARE YARD: Apprentice gunslingers proved themselves
here. It sits just east of the Great Hall, and was the site of Fair-
Day Riddling.   I:164, I:166–74, IV:436 *(east of Great Hall)*,
IV:436–39

WEST-TOWN: This is the merchant area in the western part of
Gilead.   I:159

LAKE SORONI: This lake was located in the northern part of the
Barony. When Roland was still a small child, his parents brought him
here.   IV:595

NONES
See NONES, listed in the PORTALS section

NORTHWEST BARONIES
BLAINE'S twin mono PATRICIA headed to the Northwest Baronies. We
are not told any of their names.
    III:342

O

OAKLEY
CLAY REYNOLDS and CORAL THORIN escaped the carnage of
HAMBRY and set off to become outlaws. They became lovers and
formed a gang of bank robbers and coach thieves. They were eventually
killed by the sheriff of Oakley.
    IV:623

ONNIE'S FORD
See MEJIS, BARONY OF

ORACLE OF THE MOUNTAINS
See STONE CIRCLES in the PORTALS section

ORANGE GROVE
See MEJIS, BARONY OF: HAMBRY

OUT-WORLD (OUTER ARC/OUTER CRESCENT/OUTER BAR-ONIES/THE OUTERS)
Roland's world is often described as having two parts, IN-WORLD and OUT-WORLD. These terms are relative to one another. To the citizens of HAMBRY, who live far from the hub of civilization, GILEAD is "In-World." Hence, Roland and his youthful *ka-tet* are called the "In-World boys." Hambry is an Out-World Barony because it is far from NEW CANAAN.

The terms *In-World* and *Out-World* may also be metaphorical references to the metaphysical map of Mid-World which Roland drew in *The Waste Lands*. According to this map, Mid-World is shaped like a circle, with the DARK TOWER at its center and the BEAMS radiating out from it and terminating in twelve PORTALS. Just as the Tower is the center of the Universe, Gilead and the In-World Baronies are the centers of human culture. Backwaters such as MEJIS are on the Outer Crescent of the "civilized" world. See also the MID-WORLD entry (this section) and END-WORLD entry (PORTALS section).

IV:213, IV:295, IV:350 *(Crescent)*, IV:359 *(Outer Crescent)*, IV:436, IV:447, IV:506, IV:653

P

PASS o' THE RIVER (TOWN)
A Mid-World town whose bar, **FOREST TREES,** had a female bartender.
IV:382

PENNILTON
Mr. RICHARD STOCKWORTH (ALAIN's alias in HAMBRY) was supposed to have come from this town.
IV:148, IV:183

PIANO RANCH
See MEJIS, BARONY OF: HAMBRY

PORLA
The people of RIVER CROSSING believe that the civil wars of Mid-World began in either this land or in GARLAN.
   III:242

PORTALS
   See PORTALS section

PRICETOWN
Roland passes through Pricetown on his way to TULL. He buys a mule here.   I:22, I:23, III:42

R

RADIUM MINES
   See ELURIA

RAILROAD (SUBWAY)
Jake and Roland meet SLOW MUTANTS here. See also CYCLOPEAN MOUNTAINS.

RILEA
   See BLAINE'S ROUTE

RITZY
The down-and-out town of Ritzy is located 400 miles west of MEJIS. It is a one-road mining village on the eastern slope of the VI CASTIS MOUNTAINS, fifty miles from the VI CASTIS CUT. Once there were freehold mines in the foothills, but they were regulated out by the VI CASTIS COMPANY.
   IV:265–271, IV:348, IV:391, IV:527, IV:545
   BEAR AND TURTLE MERCANTILE & SUNDRIE ITEMS: IV:265
   HATTIGAN'S SALOON: IV:266, IV:267–69
   SIX ROARING BARROOMS: IV:265
   TOWN GATHERING HALL/JAILHOUSE: IV:265
   VI CASTIS COMPANY STORE: IV:265
   VI CASTIS CUT: IV:265 *(fifty miles from Ritzy)*
   VI CASTIS MINES: IV:265–66

VI CASTIS MOUNTAINS: IV:265, IV:527
VI CASTIS (TOWN): Farson will refine CITGO oil here.   IV:431

RIVER BARONY

This is the Barony that contains JIMTOWN, RIVER CROSSING, and LUD. It takes its name from the RIVER SEND which flows through it. III:240, III:379 (West River Barony)
BARONY CASTLE AND VILLAGE: III:242–43
GREAT PLAINS OF RIVER BARONY: III:170 *(not named yet)*, III:281, III:407
JIMTOWN: A village near River Crossing.   III:228, III:240, III:309, III:346
**LUD: Lud was once the major city of River Barony. For many years after River Barony erupted in civil war, Lud held out against its besieging harriers. It remained the last fortress; a final refuge of the latter world.

For more than a hundred years, Lud has been torn apart by constant warfare. The major players in this ongoing battle are the PUBES, who are the descendants of the besieged artisans who stayed in Lud to defend their homes, and the GRAYS, who are the great-great-grandchildren of the attacking harriers. By the time our *ka-tet* has the misfortune of traveling through Lud, all of the city's occupants are mad. The Pubes practice human sacrifice to appease the god-drums operated by the Grays (with the help of Lud's sadistic computer BLAINE) and the Grays have dwindled to a gang of murderous, disease-ridden lechers hiding like rats in mazes below the city.

Children, especially boys, are sought out in the decaying and decadent city of Lud. They can be trained as fighters and can be used for sexual gratification. In the new version of *The Gunslinger,* we learn that 2,000 years before our story, Lud resembled NEW YORK CITY.   III:164, III:170–72, III:181 *(drums)*, III:195, III:222–23 *(drums)*, III:226, III:228, III:233, III:238, III:239–45, III:240, III:242, III:248, III:254–55 *(drums)*, III:256–57, III:263, III:267, III:268 *(drums)*, III:269–70, III:274, III:281, III:282 *(drums)*, III:285, III:287, III:289–302 *(cross bridge)*, III:302–404 *(drums 312, 313, 314, 315, 316, 317; land of drums, 321, 329, 332–33, 411; 404 leaving on Blaine)*, III:405, III:406, III:408, III:410, III:411, IV:16, IV:23, IV:25, IV:28, IV:34, IV:35, IV:62, IV:66, IV:75 *(drums)*, IV:76 *(drums)*, IV:663
APPLE PARK: TICK-TOCK, leader of the GRAYS, remembers visiting this park on the west side of Lud when he was a child. His father took him there to see the ciderhouse and apple press.   III:386
CITY NORTH: The PUBES occupy City North. It is here that they

practice human sacrifice in response to the god-drums.   III:308–12, III:316–25 *(321 named)*

CRADLE OF LUD/BLAINE'S CRADLE: The Cradle of Lud is a magnificent structure of blinding white stone. Despite the fact that its builders died off hundreds of generations before, the walls still clean themselves with endless streams of water. Marching around the Cradle's roof are the GUARDIANS OF THE BEAM, two by two. The roof's corners are guarded by dragons but on its peak, towering sixty feet above an already imposing edifice, is a golden statue of a gunslinger.

The Cradle of Lud—which was the GREAT OLD ONES' equivalent of Grand Central Station—is the home of BLAINE, the insane Mono. Praise the Imperium!   III:303, III:316, III:322–25 *(Eddie and Susannah make Pubes bring them here)*, III:329, III:331–34, III:340–50, III:360–65, III:372–73, III:381, III:382–85, III:393–400, IV:67, IV:71, IV:75

GRAYS' CASTLE/GRAYS' MAZE/CRADLE OF THE GRAYS: This winding mess below the city looks more like a trash midden than the headquarters of the GRAYS. In order to build it they dragged old cars, old computers, and even sculptures and fountains from other parts of the city. This varied pile acts as a kind of barrier, but one full of tripwires and booby traps. Located in the eastern part of Lud, the Cradle of the Grays is essentially the kingdom of the very nasty ANDREW QUICK, also known as TICK-TOCK. From here the Grays operate the god-drums, whose frenzied beat drives the PUBES to sacrifice each other.   III:304–8, III:312–16, III:325–31, III:334–40, III:350–61 *(357 named)*, III:365–72, III:373–78, III:378–82, III:385–90, IV:647

GREAT ROAD TO LUD: See GREAT ROAD

GREAT WALL OF LUD: III:405

HANGING FOUNTAIN: III:313–14, III:328–29

LUD BRIDGE: See SEND RIVER

PLAZA OF THE CRADLE: III:331–34, III:341

SEND BASIN NUCLEAR PLANT: Lud computers control this area as well.   III:379

STREET OF THE TURTLE: See also GUARDIANS OF THE BEAM.   III:309–12, III:316–25, III:331–34, III:341

RIVER CROSSING: River Crossing is the last outpost of civilization in River Barony. Its citizens are ancient but this does not stop them from trying to keep the old ways alive. Over the years they have had to keep their gardens and well-tended homes and meeting places secret from the harriers who pass through, burning, killing, and blinding as they go.

River Crossing is ruled by the matriarch AUNT TALITHA. The old folks of this town tell our *ka-tet* everything they know about the lay of the land, give them a wonderful meal, and then send them on their way toward LUD. Talitha gives Roland her silver cross and asks him to lay it at the foot of the TOWER.   III:225–45, III:245–51, III:253, III:254, III:257, III:258, III:270, III:276, III:284, III:288, III:309, III:310, III:329, III:383, IV:14, IV:31, IV:52

> **CHURCH OF THE BLOOD EVERLASTING:** III:227, III:232–45, III:232–49
> **LANDING, THE:** III:227, III:240
> **RIVER ROAD:** III:228

TOM'S NECK: A town located near River Crossing.   III:240
WEST RIVER BARONY: BLAINE (who is actually the computer-brain behind all of Lud's computers) controls this area.   III:379

ROCKING B RANCH
See MEJIS, BARONY OF: HAMBRY

ROCKING H RANCH
See MEJIS, BARONY OF: HAMBRY

S

SANTA FE
See MEJIS, BARONY OF

SEAFRONT
See MEJIS, BARONY OF: HAMBRY

SEND BASIN NUCLEAR PLANT
See RIVER BARONY: LUD

SEND RIVER
The Send River flows through RIVER BARONY. Roland's *ka-tet* travels along the Send River through much of *The Waste Lands* and then crosses it in order to enter LUD. (Below are some specific references.)
   III:170–71, III:176, III:223, III:241, III:256, III:283, III:285, III:288–302, III:310, III:311, III:363, IV:28, IV:31, IV:53, IV:100
   SEND RIVER BRIDGE (CROSSING TO LUD): Eddie and Susannah

think that the Send River Bridge resembles the GEORGE WASH-INGTON BRIDGE in NEW YORK CITY. This bridge was made by LaMERK FOUNDRY.   III:241–42, III:256–57, III:268, III:285, III:287, III:288–303, III:380

SEVEN-MILE ORCHARD
See MEJIS, BARONY OF: HAMBRY

SHARDIK'S LAIR
See BEAM PORTALS in the PORTALS section

SHAVÉD MOUNTAINS
The Shavéd Mountains are located northwest of GILEAD. FARSON intended to battle the AFFILIATION here.
   IV:378, IV:430, IV:465

SHEB'S
See TULL

SPEAKING RINGS
See DOORWAYS BETWEEN WORLDS in the PORTALS section

SQUARE YARD
See NEW CANAAN, BARONY OF: GILEAD

STONE CIRCLES
See DOORWAYS BETWEEN WORLDS in the PORTALS section

T

**TAUNTON
In the new version of *The Gunslinger,* it is the people of Taunton, and not the people of FARSON, that HAX and THE GOOD MAN's followers try to poison.

**TAUNTON ROAD
In the new version of The Gunslinger, GALLOWS HILL is located on the Taunton Road. Taunton Road replaces the FARSON ROAD.

TAVARES
Tavares is a town located up the coast from HAMBRY. One of its bars (**GLENCOVE**) had a female bartender who eventually died of the pox.
IV:382

TEJUAS
Tejuas is an unincorporated township located 200 miles west of ELURIA. The NORMAN brothers were headed here when their caravan was attacked by the GREEN FOLK.
E:178, E:193

TEPACHI, BARONY OF
People from Tepachi have an accent similar to that of the people in the nearby Barony of MEJIS.
IV:269

TERRITORIES
The Territories are mentioned by Calvin Tower in *The Waste Lands* as he sells Jake *CHARLIE THE CHOO-CHOO* and *Riddle-De-Dum!* "Consider it my gift to a boy wise enough to saddle up and light out for the territories on the last real day of spring." The Territories, which are a parallel world to our earth, are found in *The Talisman*, by Stephen King and Peter Straub. Every human being in our world has a "twinner" in the territories.
III:116

THINNY/THINNIES
See THINNY/THINNIES in the PORTALS section

THOUGHTFUL HOUSE
See ELURIA

THUNDERCLAP
See THUNDERCLAP in the PORTALS section

TOM'S NECK
See RIVER BARONY

TOPEKA
See KANSAS: TOPEKA in the PORTALS section

TOWER
See DARK TOWER in the PORTALS section

TOWN GATHERING HALL
See MEJIS, BARONY OF: HAMBRY

TRAVELLERS' REST
See MEJIS, BARONY OF: HAMBRY

**TULL
The sand-colored, pitted buildings of TULL are located south of PRICE-TOWN and just north of the MOHAINE DESERT. The town consists of four roads—the COACH ROAD and the three that cross it. Since it is located on the line of the Coach Road, we can assume that Tull was once more prosperous. Now it consists of a boarded-up grocery, a livery, a tailor, a church, a barber, a dry goods emporium, and a bar called SHEB'S.

Like so many of Mid-World's towns, Tull—located on the floor of a circular, bowl-shaped hollow—is reminiscent of the Old West. It is in Tull that Roland meets his lover ALICE. It is also where he meets the formidable (and dangerously crazy) SYLVIA PITTSTON. Thanks to Pittston's treachery, Roland ends up killing everyone in the town, including Allie. In the new version of *The Gunslinger,* we find out that there's an old train yard near Tull.
I:15, I:18–19, I:20–21, I:22–64, I:77, I:78, I:86, I:90, I:118, I:124, I:131, I:143, I:156, II:40, II:126, II:145, III:42, III:44, IV:72, IV:628
SHEB'S: Sheb's is Tull's single honky-tonk. Despite its name it actually belongs to ALICE. Within its batwing doors it has a sawdust floor, spittoons, and tipsy-legged tables. The bar is a plank resting on sawhorses. At the back people play interminable games of Watch Me while SHEB bangs away on his piano.   I:22, I:23, I:26–43, I:45–47, I:52–54, I:58, I:61, I:63, I:64, II:40, II:126, II:145, II:264

TURTLE, STREET OF THE
See RIVER BARONY: LUD

V

VI CASTIS CUT
See RITZY

VI CASTIS MOUNTAINS
See RITZY

W

WASTE LANDS
See WASTE LANDS in the PORTALS section, and MEJIS, BARONY
OF in this section

**WAY STATION
The Way Station, where Roland finds JAKE, was once a stopping point for
the Coach lines that ran across the MOHAINE DESERT. By the time our
story takes place it has been deserted for years. The station consists of two
buildings (a stable and an inn) surrounded by a fallen rail fence whose
wood is so fragile that it's rapidly thinning into desert sand. Luckily for
both Jake and Roland, the station's water pump still works. (In the new
version of *The Gunslinger* we find out that this pump was made by
NORTH CENTRAL POSITRONICS.) In the building's cellar, Roland
faces down the SPEAKING DEMON.
   I:72–81, I:83–92, I:93, I:122, II:319, III:43–46, III:47, III:48, III:59,
   III:60, III:62, III:91, III:106–7, III:128, III:132, III:263, IV:106
   CELLAR: I:87–88

WEST RIVER BARONY
See RIVER BARONY

WEST-TOWN
See NEW CANAAN, BARONY OF: GILEAD

WEST WOODS
See GREAT WEST WOODS

**WESTERN SEA
Throughout *The Gunslinger,* Roland pursues the MAN IN BLACK south
and then southwest through the MOHAINE DESERT and the CYCLO-
PEAN MOUNTAINS (in the new *Gunslinger,* he follows his enemy
southeast). At the end of his journey he finds himself at THE GOLGO-
THA, just three miles from the Western Sea, which is the setting for the
next book in the series. The Western Sea is a terrible, barren place. Its
waters are the color of dirty undergarments and its yellow, gross-grained
beaches are littered with no-color shells and rocky protrusions. The tide

line crawls with man-eating LOBSTROSITIES and its horizons seem endless and hopeless. The sea's LOBSTROSITY BEACH is a terrible place, but it is through the magical BEACH DOORS, found here, that Roland draws EDDIE DEAN and SUSANNAH DEAN into his world. In the new version of *The Gunslinger,* we find out that the Western Sea is the edge of the world.

I:44, I:214, II:15–21, II:26–36, II:44, II:55–56, II:62–63, II:72–74, II:76–78, II:79–82, II:92–94, II:99–105, II:135–43, II:154 *(indirect),* II:156–57, II:161–82, II:201–9, II:225–312, II:327–38, II:359–60, II:371, II:387–90, II:393–94, III:12, III:47, III:261, III:407, IV:42, IV:96

LOBSTROSITY BEACH: II:15–21, II:26–36 *(setting),* II:44, II:54, II:55–56, II:62–63, II:72–74, II:76–78, II:79–82, II:92–95, II:99–105, II:135–43, II:154 *(indirect),* II:156–57, II:161–82, II:201–9, II:225–312, II:327–38, II:359–60, II:387–90, II:393–94, III:13, III:36, III:316

**WEST'RD HALL
See NEW CANAAN, BARONY OF: GREAT HALL

WILLOW GROVE
See MEJIS, BARONY OF: HAMBRY

WILLOW JUNGLE
This wild jungle is located in the foothills of the CYCLOPEAN MOUN-TAINS. (It is sometimes also called the WILLOW GROVE, although the main Willow Grove is in HAMBRY.) After the dry hardpan of the desert, the Willow Jungle's wet lushness is a relief. However, this dangerous jungle is the home of vampiric SUCKERBATS and the demonic ORACLE OF THE MOUNTAINS who tries to destroy first JAKE, and then ROLAND, with its sexual *glammer.*

I:117–34, III:172–73

WIND
Wind is a town even less ritzy than RITZY. It is located fifty miles from Ritzy and the VI CASTIS MOUNTAINS.

IV:266

OUR WORLD PLACES

Go then. There are other worlds than these.
Jake Chambers
I:191

ALABAMA
  MONTGOMERY: II:199
    WOOLWORTH'S: II:199

ALASKA
  ACHIN' ASSHOLE: This is another place Eddie made up.   II:396

AMHIGH
  See DRAWERS in the PORTALS section

APPALACHIAN TRAIL
The Appalachian Trail is a continuous footpath that runs from Mount
Katahdin in central Maine to Springer Mountain in Georgia, a distance
of approximately 2,160 miles. EDDIE DEAN imagines that the trail is
overrun by bomber-joint-smoking hippies carrying packsacks like
Roland's.
  II:77

AQUINAS HOTEL
  See BAHAMAS

ARIZONA
  BLACK FORK: III:115

ARKANSAS
  ODETTA: Odetta Holmes's mother, ALICE HOLMES, was born

151

here. Hence Odetta (later called SUSANNAH DEAN) was christened with this name.   II:199

ATCHISON
See KANSAS. See also ATCHISON, TOPEKA, AND SANTA FE RAILROAD (below) and KANSAS in the PORTALS section.

ATCHISON, TOPEKA, AND SANTA FE RAILROAD
The Atchison, Topeka, and Santa Fe Railroad Company (originally called the Atchison and Topeka Railroad Company) was founded in 1859 by Colonel Cyrus K. Holliday of KANSAS, one of the founders of the town of TOPEKA. The railroad changed its name in 1863 because of its planned expansion. By 1887 the railroad extended all the way to Los Angeles. Known as "The Atchison" in the East and as "The Santa Fe" in the West, it was one of the major railroads serving the Southwest United States.

Our *ka-tet* stumbles across a sign for the Atchison, Topeka, and Santa Fe at BLAINE's terminating point in an alternate Kansas. Roland assumes—quite rightly—that the three names designate three towns. However, because he does not know the history of railroads in our *where* (or in this Topeka's alternate *when*) he does not understand the full significance of these places or of the towns he sees listed on the departures board, namely DENVER, WICHITA, and OMAHA.

All of the listed towns were linked—directly or indirectly—by the AT&SF. Obviously, Atchison, Topeka, and Santa Fe were part of the service's main run. Denver was also served by the Atchison line, and Wichita could be reached by one of the railroad's branch lines. Although Omaha was actually accessible by the Union Pacific Railroad, the Union Pacific and the Atchison, Topeka, and Santa Fe were linked in 1881, completing the second transcontinental railroad.

Hence, what we learn from Roland's sojourn in the alternate Topeka is that not only do the GREAT ROADS of Mid-World follow the BEAM but so do the great railroads. Also, it seems that these railroads can be used not only to cross continents, but to jump from one level of the TOWER to another. Blaine and his fellow locomotives and slo-trans engines are portals every bit as much as the other doorways in and out of Mid-World. The GREAT OLD ONES, aided by the technology of their sinister company, NORTH CENTRAL POSITRONICS, learned how to bridge the time/space continuum.
IV:68

ATTICA STATE PRISON
See NEW YORK (STATE)

B

BAHAMAS
EDDIE DEAN'S little trip to the Bahamas almost ends in disaster and incarceration. Although he is dressed like a college kid, Eddie goes to Nassau so that he can smuggle packages of cocaine for the drug king ENRICO BALAZAR. At this point in our story (namely, at the beginning of *The Drawing of the Three*), Eddie is a heroin addict under the thumb of his older brother, the great sage and eminent junkie HENRY DEAN. Roland saves Eddie's bacon three times: first by helping him evade the CUSTOMS police, second by coming to his aid against Balazar and his thugs, and finally by spiriting Eddie off to LOBSTROSITY BEACH. There, on the shore of the WESTERN SEA, Eddie comes down off the Horse, only to become addicted to Odetta Holmes (aka Detta Walker/SUSANNAH DEAN) and another potent drug—Love.
  II:42, II:86, II:87, II:112, II:176
  NASSAU: Eddie goes to Nassau to pick up Balazar's cocaine. While there he stays at the **AQUINAS HOTEL.**   II:47, II:47–51 *(hotel)*, II:57 *(flashback to hotel)*, II:58, III:346

BEAMS
  See BEAMS in the PORTALS section

BEIRUT
  See LEBANON

BERMUDA TRIANGLE
  See PORTALS section

BOGOTÁ
  See COLOMBIA

BONDED ELECTROPLATE FACTORY
  See NEW YORK (CITY OF): BROOKLYN

BOSTON
  See MASSACHUSETTS

BRENDIO'S (SHOP)
See NEW YORK (CITY OF): MANHATTAN

C

CALIFORNIA
III:284
DISNEYLAND: II:169
MID-WORLD AMUSEMENT PARK: See MID-WORLD AMUSE-
MENT PARK in the PORTALS section.
SILICON VALLEY: II:125

CANADA
MONTREAL: One of the little old ladies on EDDIE'S disastrous
Delta flight from NASSAU to NEW YORK was headed to Montreal.
II:78–79

CAPE CANAVERAL
See FLORIDA

CASTLE AVENUE
See NEW YORK (CITY OF): BROOKLYN

CHEW CHEW MAMA'S (RESTAURANT)
See NEW YORK (CITY OF): MANHATTAN

CHINA
III:287

CHRISTOPHER STREET STATION
See NEW YORK (CITY OF): MANHATTAN

CLEMENTS GUNS AND SPORTING GOODS
See NEW YORK (CITY OF): MANHATTAN

COHOES STREET
See NEW YORK (CITY OF): BROOKLYN

COLOMBIA
  BOGOTÁ: II:58

COLORADO
  IV:32
  DENVER: One of the towns that could be reached by the ATCHI-SON, TOPEKA, AND SANTA FE RAILROAD. See that entry.
  IV:72

CONEY ISLAND
  See NEW YORK (CITY OF): BROOKLYN

CONNECTICUT
  MYSTIC: III:32
  SEDONVILLE: Somewhere in this town, buried under a chicken house, is an Irishman shot dead for blowing down one of BALAZAR's card houses.   II:117

CO-OP CITY
  See NEW YORK (CITY OF): BROOKLYN and NEW YORK (CITY OF): BRONX

CUBA
JANE DORNING—one of the stewardesses on EDDIE's Delta flight from NASSAU to JFK—harbors a fear of being hijacked by Cubans.
  II:54

CUSTOMS, NEW YORK
  See NEW YORK (CITY OF): QUEENS

D

DAHLIE'S (DAHLBERG'S)
  See NEW YORK (CITY OF): BROOKLYN

DENBY'S DISCOUNT DRUG
  See NEW YORK (CITY OF): MANHATTAN: TIMES SQUARE

DENVER
See COLORADO. See also ATCHISON, TOPEKA, AND SANTA FE RAILROAD.

DETTA'S SEX HAUNTS
See DRAWERS in the PORTALS section

DISNEYLAND
See CALIFORNIA

DISNEY WORLD
See FLORIDA

DODGE
See KANSAS

DOORS: NEW YORK TO MID-WORLD
See DOORWAYS BETWEEN WORLDS in the PORTALS section

DRAWERS
See DRAWERS in the PORTALS section

DUTCH HILL
See NEW YORK (CITY OF): BROOKLYN

DUTCH HILL MANSION
See DOORWAYS BETWEEN WORLDS in the PORTALS section

DUTCH HILL PUB
See NEW YORK (CITY OF): BROOKLYN

DUTCH HILL USED APPLIANCES
See NEW YORK (CITY OF): BROOKLYN

E

EASTER ISLAND
III:24

ECUADOR
IV:86

**ENGLAND
Walter claims that he lived in England hundreds (and perhaps a thousand) years before the GREAT OLD ONES crossed the ocean to the land Roland now inhabits. In the new version of *The Gunslinger,* the direct reference to England is cut.
  I:211
  LONDON: IV:34

F

FIFTH AVENUE AND FORTY-THIRD STREET
  See NEW YORK (CITY OF): MANHATTAN

FLORIDA
  BUSCH GARDENS: River Crossing's garden (located behind THE CHURCH OF THE BLOOD EVERLASTING) reminds EDDIE of Busch Gardens.   III:233
  CAPE CANAVERAL: When Susannah sees the missiles lining the GREAT ROAD leading to LUD, she thinks about the Redstones fired from Cape Canaveral.   III:287
  DISNEY WORLD: II:334, III:73, III:91
  FLORIDA KEYS: II:227

FOUR FATHERS RESTAURANT
  See NEW YORK (CITY OF): BROOKLYN: GINELLI'S PIZZA

G

GEORGIA
  II:198

GINELLI'S PIZZA (FOUR FATHERS RESTAURANT)
  See NEW YORK (CITY OF): BROOKLYN

GREAT PLAINS
III:171

GREAT SMOKIES
SUSANNAH DEAN/Odetta Holmes's AUNT BLUE had her honeymoon in these mountains.
II:236

GREYMARL APARTMENTS
See NEW YORK (CITY OF): MANHATTAN

GUYANA
The Reverend Jim Jones had his flock commit mass suicide here.
III:378

H

HAITI
II:58, II:186

HENRY'S CORNER MARKET
See NEW YORK (CITY OF): BROOKLYN: DUTCH HILL

I

IRELAND
II:371

ITALY
II:133 *(Old Country)*
PISA (LEANING TOWER OF): See LEANING TOWER OF PISA, listed separately.
SICILY: II:114

K

KANSAS
See also KANSAS in the PORTALS section and WIZARD OF OZ in the CHARACTERS section.   II:229 *(Dorothy)*, III:139–45 *(Charlie the Choo-Choo)*, III:258, III:287 *(concrete silos)*
 ATCHISON: Atchison is a town in Kansas famous for being the birthplace of both Amelia Earhart and the ATCHISON, TOPEKA, AND SANTA FE RAILROAD.   IV:68
 DODGE: In the late nineteenth and early twentieth centuries, Dodge had a reputation as a rowdy frontier town.   III:258, III:373
 TOPEKA: In the children's story *CHARLIE THE CHOO-CHOO*, Topeka is the MID-WORLD RAILWAY's final destination. It also happens to be BLAINE'S destination. See entry under ATCHISON, TOPEKA, AND SANTA FE RAILROAD. See also KANSAS in the PORTALS section and BLAINE in the CHARACTERS section. III:139–45, IV:68
 WICHITA: A town in Kansas accessed by a branch line of the ATCHISON, TOPEKA, AND SANTA FE RAILROAD. Roland sees a sign for it in the alternate TOPEKA. See entry under ATCHISON, TOPEKA, AND SANTA FE RAILROAD. Also see KANSAS in the PORTALS section.   IV:72
 WIZARD OF OZ: KANSAS: See KANSAS in the PORTALS section

KATZ PHARMACY AND SODA FOUNTAIN (SUNDRIES AND NOTIONS FOR MISSES AND MISTERS)
 See NEW YORK (CITY OF): MANHATTAN

L

LEANING TOWER
 See NEW YORK (CITY OF): MANHATTAN. See also DARK TOWER in the PORTALS section

LEANING TOWER OF PISA

The Leaning Tower of Pisa, whose official name is Torre Pendente di Pisa, is an Italian bell tower which was built between A.D. 1173 and 1350. As can be deduced from its name, it lists to one side, a problem that architects through the ages have not been able to rectify.

The Dark Tower series refers to this famous tower in two different contexts. First, in *The Drawing of the Three,* we learn that the neon sign marking BALAZAR's bar and headquarters is in the shape of this historic monument. Much to EDDIE DEAN's alarm, the first time Roland sees this sign he thinks he has arrived at his destination—the DARK TOWER itself.

The next time we see the Leaning Tower it takes the form of a photograph (or as Roland would say, a *fottergraf*) pasted to the last page of JAKE CHAMBERS's English Comp essay entitled *"My Understanding of Truth."* Jake was so dazed and distressed when he wrote the essay that he no longer remembers either writing it or covering his Tower with black crayon scribbles.

II:121

LEBANON
BEIRUT: IV:87

LOT, THE
See LOT, THE, in the PORTALS section

M

MACY'S
See NEW YORK (CITY OF): MANHATTAN

MAGIC SHOP
See NEW YORK (CITY OF): MANHATTAN

MAJESTIC THEATER
See NEW YORK (CITY OF): BROOKLYN

MANHATTAN RESTAURANT OF THE MIND, THE
See NEW YORK (CITY OF): MANHATTAN

MANSION, THE
See DOORWAYS BETWEEN WORLDS in the PORTALS section

MARKEY ACADEMY
See NEW YORK (CITY OF): BROOKLYN: MARKEY AVENUE

MARKEY AVENUE
See NEW YORK (CITY OF): BROOKLYN

MASSACHUSETTS
BOSTON: II:348
    MUSEUM OF SCIENCE: II:348

METROPOLITAN MUSEUM OF ART
See NEW YORK (CITY OF): MANHATTAN

MICHIGAN
II:169

MID-TOWN LANES
See NEW YORK (CITY OF): MANHATTAN

MILLS CONSTRUCTION AND SOMBRA REAL ESTATE
IV:100

MISSISSIPPI
II:188, III:220, IV:67
OXFORD: Oxford was made famous (or infamous) by the Bob Dylan song "Oxford Town" and by the events upon which the song was based. In 1962 there were riots on the University of Mississippi campus based on the university's forced acceptance of its first black student, James Meredith. Meredith, whose acceptance at the university had been rescinded once it was discovered that he was dark-skinned, had fought for reacceptance for over a year before the Fifth U.S. Circuit Court of Appeals ruled that the state could not deny him admission based on color. Meredith was escorted to campus by Federal Marshals but the city of Oxford erupted in violence. Before the National Guard could arrive, two students had been killed.

SUSANNAH DEAN's three-day incarceration in a Mississippi jail (which she refers to as a short season in hell) came about because of her participation in the nonviolent civil rights movement. Like Meredith's antagonists, Susannah's captors were racists abusing their legal power. II:187–90, II:193, II:233–34, II:236–37, II:238, II:241, II:242, II:243, II:258, III:15

MISSOURI

In the children's story *CHARLIE THE CHOO-CHOO*, the talking train CHARLIE travels through the state of Missouri, tooting his horn.
III:255, III:256
MISSOURI PLAINS (THE BIG EMPTY): III:140, III:255, III:383
ST. LOUIS: III:139–45, III:255

MONTGOMERY
See ALABAMA

MONTREAL
See CANADA

N

NASSAU
See BAHAMAS

NEBRASKA
See also NEBRASKA in the PORTALS section
BUTTFUCK: Believe it or not, this place doesn't really exist. EDDIE DEAN just pretends it does.   III:331
OMAHA: A town in Nebraska served by the Union Pacific Railroad. The Union Pacific was joined with the ATCHISON, TOPEKA, AND SANTA FE in 1881, creating the second transcontinental railroad. See ATCHISON, TOPEKA, AND SANTA FE RAILROAD.   IV:72

NETWORK, THE
See NEW YORK (CITY OF): MANHATTAN

NEVADA
Beneath the mountains of this state there are concrete bunkers containing ICBMs.
III:287
RENO: III:241

NEW JERSEY
II:115, III:55
ATLANTIC CITY: II:131, III:316
ELIZABETH: When Odetta Holmes (later SUSANNAH DEAN) was a child, her AUNT BLUE got married in Elizabeth, New Jersey. Five-year-old Odetta went to the wedding, but on the way to the train station JACK MORT (who was hiding in an abandoned building at the time) dropped a brick on her head. Odetta went into a coma for three weeks and her second personality—that of the venomous Detta Walker—was born.   II:234–38, II:320–24, III:266
MEADOWLANDS: Eddie once saw a concert here.   III:55
NEW JERSEY TURNPIKE: I:180
NUTLEY: See DRAWERS in the PORTALS section

NEW MEXICO
SANTA FE: Santa Fe was one of the stops on the ATCHISON, TOPEKA, AND SANTA FE RAILROAD. It is also the name of a town in Roland's world. See MEJIS, BARONY OF: SANTA FE in the MID-WORLD PLACES section, and SANTA FE in the PORTALS section. IV:68

NEW YORK (STATE)
ATTICA STATE PRISON: II:372
LONG ISLAND SOUND: EDDIE DEAN's plane from the BAHAMAS flies over Long Island Sound before landing at JFK AIR-PORT. II:58
NEW YORK CITY: See NEW YORK (CITY OF)
NIAGARA FALLS: IV:32
UTICA: In the children's story CHARLIE THE CHOO-CHOO, Charlie's replacement, a BURLINGTON ZEPHYR, was built in Utica. III:141
WESTCHESTER: II:345

NEW YORK (CITY OF)
New York City is the original home of the three human members of Roland's present ka-tet: JAKE CHAMBERS, SUSANNAH DEAN, and EDDIE DEAN. (OY, Jake's pet BILLY-BUMBLER, is from Mid-World.) The Portal of the TURTLE and the Portal of the BEAR connect Mid-World to this city of Our World.

Throughout the series we are told that the urban ruins of Mid-World bear a strong resemblance to the thriving metropolises of our world. In The Gunslinger, the subway system beneath the CYCLOPEAN MOUN-

TAINS reminds Jake of New York's subways. Later, in LUD, the bridges and buildings of that war-torn city make our *ka-tet* think of Manhattan. It seems quite probable that Roland's world is actually one of Our World's many potential futures, but it is a future in which nuclear disaster has already taken place. The first time Roland hears Jake talk about the skyline of this city he thinks it is like a myth out of prehistory. BLAINE the insane Mono knows New York City well. He calls it the Barony of New York.

I:79–84, I:123 *(Jake's when of 1977)*, II:45, II:50 *(See JFK Airport entries)*, II:90–99, II:105–22, II:123–57, II:172–76 *(Susannah's when of 1964)*, II:185–201, II:202–9 *(Susannah's 1964)*, II:211–20 *(Susannah's 1959)*, II:220–23 *(Susannah's when)*, II:230, II:237–38, II:315–26 *(New York 1977)*, II:339–59, II:360–86, III:11 *(indirect)*, III:22 *(state of)*, III:43, III:45, III:51, III:72, III:89–146, III:154–58, III:164, III:165–70, III:171, III:176–78, III:182–88, III:190–92, III:220, III:225, III:238, III:261, III:336, III:340, III:349, III:350, III:355, III:361, III:363, III:365, III:375, III:376, III:377, III:402, III:409, III:417 *(Barony of)*, III:419, IV:7 *(Barony of)*, IV:9–10, IV:20, IV:22, IV:36, IV:45, IV:46, IV:47, IV:48, IV:51, IV:52, IV:53, IV:63, IV:77

BRONX: II:110

> **CO-OP CITY:** In our *where* and *when*, Co-Op City is an ethnically diverse housing cooperative located in the northeasternmost corner of the Bronx. In Eddie's version of New York, Co-Op City is located in BROOKLYN. (On II:110 it is said to be in the Bronx.)

BROOKLYN: For many years EDDIE DEAN lived in Co-Op City, which—in his version of New York—is located in Brooklyn. As he points out to Jake when the two of them meet in a dream version of New York, Brooklyn also contains his world's version of the portal of the BEAR.   III:154, III:165, III:168, III:169, III:170, III:176–78, III:179, III:182–88, III:190–92, III:265

> **BROOKLYN AVENUE:** III:190
>
> **BROOKLYN VOCATIONAL INSTITUTE:** III:179

CASTLE AVENUE: JAKE travels along Castle Avenue while looking for MARKEY AVENUE. He thinks that his doorway into Mid-World will be there. It's not, but it does lead him to the MAJESTIC THEATER and a thirteen-year-old EDDIE DEAN.   III:176–78

COHOES STREET: Home of the Bonded Electroplate Factory. II:172

> **BONDED ELECTROPLATE FACTORY:** EDDIE and HENRY DEAN smoked here.   II:172

CONEY ISLAND: II:117 *(mirror maze)*, II:169, III:350, III:372

CO-OP CITY: In EDDIE DEAN's version of New York, Co-Op

City is located in Brooklyn rather than the BRONX. (This is one of the many time/space variations found on different levels of the TOWER.) Eddie and his brother, HENRY, lived in this big cooperative located between CASTLE and BROOKLYN AVENUES. II:95, II:105–13, II:241, III:23, III:154, III:170, III:176–78, III:179, III:182–88 *(Dean family apartment 187, 188)*, III:190–92 *(Dean family apartment 192)*

DAHLIE'S: This was one of HENRY DEAN's hangouts. Dahlie's (also called **DAHLBERG'S**) sold Hoodsie Rockets and Popsicles. III:76, III:187, IV:43, IV:54, IV:60

DUTCH HILL: JAKE'S search for a doorway into Mid-World leads him to Dutch Hill and its terrible Haunted MANSION. When Jake enters The Mansion he is attacked by the MANSION DEMON.   III:161–62, III:189, III:191–92, III:262, III:344

> **DUTCH HILL LITTLE LEAGUE FIELD:** III:204
> **DUTCH HILL PUB:** III:204
> **DUTCH HILL USED APPLIANCES:** III:192, III:204–5
> **HENRY'S CORNER MARKET:** III:204
> **RHINEHOLD STREET:** The terrible haunted MANSION (which JAKE enters in order to find his doorway into Mid-World) is located on this street.   III:75, III:189, III:190, III:192, III:195, III:204, III:344
> > **DUTCH HILL MANSION, THE:** See DOORWAYS BETWEEN WORLDS in the PORTALS section.

GINELLI'S PIZZA (FOUR FATHERS RESTAURANT): Ginelli's is a front for BALAZAR's illegal empire.   II:91

MARKEY AVENUE: On his travels through Brooklyn, JAKE travels along Markey Avenue.   III:161, III:165, III:178

> **MAJESTIC THEATER:** The Majestic movie theater is located on the corner of Markey and BROOKLYN AVENUES. EDDIE DEAN used to watch Westerns here. His brother, HENRY, liked to tease the ticket girl.   III:182–84
> **MARKEY ACADEMY:** This place doesn't actually exist. III:167, III:177–78
> **MARKEY AVENUE PLAYGROUND:** EDDIE and HENRY used to play basketball here. It has since been replaced by the JUVENILE COURT BUILDING.   III:161, III:165, III:185–88
> > **JUVENILE COURT BUILDING:** III:161

NORWOOD STREET: Some kids from this street were mysteriously killed at the DUTCH HILL MANSION.   III:187

PROJECTS: EDDIE, HENRY, and their mom lived in the projects when Eddie and Henry were young.   II:68

RINCON AVENUE: Once upon a time there was a candy store on Rincon Avenue. EDDIE and HENRY DEAN filched comic books from it.   II:172

EAST RIVER: III:102

EAST RIVER DRIVE: III:301

MANHATTAN: *(directly named)* II:345, III:23, III:122, III:171, III:345

BELLEVUE: II:176, II:241

BLOOMINGDALE'S: III:45, III:103, III:106, III:107

BLEECKER STREET: III:118, III:155

BRENDIO'S: JAKE passes Brendio's on his way to school. Some of the mannequins in the window are dressed in Edwardian clothes. Others are "barenaked."   I:82, III:103

CENTRAL PARK: II:187, II:189, II:200, II:237, IV:64, IV:67

CHEW CHEW MAMA'S (RESTAURANT): See SECOND AVENUE below

CHRISTOPHER STREET STATION: In SUSANNAH DEAN's version of New York (yet another level of the DARK TOWER) the fabled A train stops at Christopher Street Station. Unfortunately, Odetta Holmes/Detta Walker happened to be waiting at this stop at the same time as the evil JACK MORT. Mort pushed her in front of the train. Luckily Susannah (and her many selves) survived; however, her legs (or what was left of them) had to be amputated just above the knee.   II:215–17, II:380–86

CLEMENTS GUNS AND SPORTING GOODS: This shop is located on Seventh Avenue and Forty-ninth Street. While occupying JACK MORT'S body, Roland visits Clements so that he can restock his dwindling supply of live rounds. Besides buying ammo, Roland causes general havoc.   II:342–59, II:371–73

DENBY'S DISCOUNT DRUG: See TIMES SQUARE below

DUNHILL'S: This shop sells expensive lighters.   II:382

EMPIRE STATE BUILDING: III:350

FIFTH AVENUE AND FORTY-THIRD STREET/THE PUSH-ING PLACE: On one level of the TOWER, JAKE is killed here by a 1976 Sedan de Ville. JACK MORT (who pushed Jake in front of incoming traffic) dubs it "The Pushing Place."   II:315–18, III:104–6

FIRST AVENUE POLICE SHOOTING RANGE: III:157

FOUR SEASONS RESTAURANT: II:191

GEORGE WASHINGTON BRIDGE: The SEND BRIDGE, located just outside of LUD, resembles the George Washington Bridge. III:256, III:292

GIMBEL'S: II:191, III:45

GRACE METHODIST CHURCH: The REVEREND MURDOCH preached here. SUSANNAH's father didn't agree with his sermons. III:311

GRAND CENTRAL STATION: III:331

GREENWICH VILLAGE: II:190, II:199, II:211, II:378, III:350 *(East Village)*

GREYMARL APARTMENTS: The Greymarl Apartments are a Victorian block of flats located on Fifth Avenue and Central Park South. Odetta Holmes (one of SUSANNAH DEAN's earlier selves) lived in the penthouse apartment.   II:189–93, II:200, II:226 *(Odetta's apartment),* II:255 *(Odetta's apartment)*

HUNGRY I: Odetta Holmes (later SUSANNAH DEAN) really liked this coffee house.   II:218

JAKE CHAMBERS'S APARTMENT: The Chamberses' family apartment is located on Fifth Avenue, three and a half blocks farther up than the PUSHING PLACE. Hence it is probably on Fifth and Forty-sixth or Fifth and Forty-seventh.   I:81, III:102, III:107–8, III:129–46, III:155–58, III:165

KATZ PHARMACY AND SODA FOUNTAIN (SUNDRIES AND NOTIONS FOR MISSES AND MISTERS): Katz Pharmacy is located at 395 West Forty-ninth Street, and has been at that address since 1927. (It was founded by the present owner's father.) While searching for Keflex, Roland causes complete havoc here. As KATZ says, Roland commits the first penicillin hold-up in history.   II:333, II:358, II:360, II:361–70, II:373–77

LEANING TOWER: The Leaning Tower is a midtown saloon. It is also BALAZAR's place of business. The first time Roland sees its neon sign he is convinced that he has reached the DARK TOWER. II:91, II:107, II:112, II:113–22, II:123–57 *(135–43 Western Sea as well),* II:204, II:205, II:309, II:369, III:67, III:68, III:99, III:100, III:180, III:262, III:340

LOT, THE: See PORTALS section

MACY'S: II:99, II:196, II:202–9, II:221–23, II:226, II:227, II:228, II:243, II:255, II:336, III:45

MAGIC SHOP: See SECOND AVENUE below

MANHATTAN RESTAURANT OF THE MIND, THE: See SECOND AVENUE below

METROPOLITAN MUSEUM OF ART: The Met appears to exist in all the New Yorks on all levels of the TOWER. It is located on Fifth Avenue.   III:166–67

**MID-TOWN LANES: JAKE bowls here. This bowling alley is mentioned in the new version of *The Gunslinger.*   III:107, III:168

MISS SO PRETTY (SHOP): III:166

MORT'S HOME: 409 Park Avenue South.   II:349

MORT'S OFFICE: Mort's accountancy firm is located on Sixth Avenue, also known as the Avenue of the Americas.   II:324–26, II:339–41

NETWORK, THE: JAKE's father, ELMER CHAMBERS, is a high-powered executive at this TV network, where he is an acknowledged master of "The Kill." The Network offices are located at 70 Rockefeller Plaza.   I:81, I:82, III:90, III:91, III:102, III:168, IV:32

NEW YORK HARBOR: III:90

NEW YORK UNIVERSITY: II:115, II:174

PAUL STUART (SHOP): III:166

PIPER SCHOOL: Listed separately

PORT AUTHORITY: II:42

PUSHING PLACE: See FIFTH AVENUE AND FORTY-THIRD STREET

RADIO CITY: III:122, III:350

REFLECTIONS OF YOU: See SECOND AVENUE below

REGENCY TOWER: II:41

ST. ANTHONY'S: II:359

SAKS: II:191

SECOND AVENUE: III:51–53, III:77–78, III:79, III:118–20

CHEW CHEW MAMA'S: Chew Chew's can be found at Second Avenue and Fifty-second Street. Both EDDIE and JAKE see BALAZAR here, dressed as a bum. The restaurant's name is especially sinister because (as Jake points out) it is reminiscent of CHOO-CHOO and CHARLIE, the nasty train.   III:119

LOT, THE: See PORTALS section

MAGIC SHOP: This magic shop exists only in EDDIE DEAN's dream version of New York. He imagines it sits on Second Avenue and Fifty-second Street, the location of CHEW CHEW MAMA'S. In Eddie's sleep vision, ENRICO BALAZAR sits in front of the store dressed as a bum. In the window is a sign that reads HOUSE OF CARDS. Quite appropriately, the window display is of a tower built of Tarot cards.   III:51–52

MANHATTAN RESTAURANT OF THE MIND, THE: This bookstore is located on Second Avenue and Fifty-fourth Street. It's run by CALVIN TOWER, probably with a little help from his sidekick, AARON DEEPNEAU. These two characters are mysteriously connected to both the Territories of *The Talisman* and Roland's world. It's here that JAKE buys both *CHARLIE THE CHOO-CHOO* and *Riddle-De-Dum! Brain Twisters and Puzzles for Everyone!*   III:112–18, III:119, III:128, III:155, IV:18 *(as bookstore)*, IV:46

PAPER PATCH: III:120

REFLECTIONS OF YOU: This shop's display window is full of mirrors. In his dream-vision of New York, EDDIE sees himself reflected in these mirrors but his image is actually dressed like JAKE. Later, on his way to find the ROSE, Jake also sees himself reflected in these mirrors.   III:77, III:119

TOM AND GERRY'S ARTISTIC DELI: Tom and Gerry's is located on Second Avenue and Forty-sixth Street, which is part of TURTLE BAY, Manhattan. In JAKE's *when*, Tom and Gerry's has already been demolished. However, the magical ROSE grows in the vacant lot left behind. (See LOT, THE, in the PORTALS section.) III:52, III:77–78, III:79, III:119–20, III:123, III:177, III:262, III:264, IV:83 *(Jake's vision)*, IV:100–101 *(Eddie's dream)*

TOWER OF POWER RECORDS: As JAKE passes by this shop on his way to the ROSE (which he actually hopes is a portal to Roland), "Paint It Black" is belting out of the doorway. Not surprisingly, the lyrics are about doors.   III:119

TURTLE BAY: JAKE's magic LOT is located in an area of Manhattan once known as Turtle Bay. Since the Turtle is one of the GUARDIANS OF THE BEAM, it seems that this area of New York—and the magical ROSE that lives here—is protected by the TURTLE.   III:122

> **TURTLE BAY LUXURY CONDOMINIUMS:** The Turtle Bay Condos are a project planned by MILLS CONSTRUCTION AND SOMBRA REAL ESTATE, an evil company that has no interest in building housing. What they really want to do is own the magic Lot so that they can destroy the Rose that grows there.   III:121, III:264, IV:100

SISTERS OF MERCY HOSPITAL: II:211–12, II:214–20

SPARKS: A restaurant that EDDIE and HENRY like to go to.   II:47.

STATUE OF LIBERTY: I:79, III:349

TIMES SQUARE: While searching for a doorway into Mid-World, JAKE stops here to rest and is accosted by an officer of the law. He uses his magic key to mesmerize the cop and escape.   III:167–69

> **DENBY'S DISCOUNT DRUG:** This shop is located in TIMES SQUARE. JAKE sits across the street from it during his search for a doorway into Mid-World. Denby is part of the pseudonym Jake gives to the policeman he mesmerizes with his magic key.   III:169

TOOKER'S WHOLESALE TOYS: III:104 *(exact location not mentioned)*

QUEENS: III:168, III:265
JFK AIRPORT: In order to deliver his cocaine packages to the nefarious BALAZAR, EDDIE has to pass through CUSTOMS at JFK airport. He manages to do so, but only because of Roland's intervention. **(Please note: On the following pages, JFK is mentioned. I have also listed pages where it is the setting, even when Eddie's plane is sitting on the runway.)**   II:57, II:68, II:70–76, II:78–79, II:80, II:81, II:82–84, II:85–90, II:91, II:92, II:96–99, II:118–19, II:127, III:161

CUSTOMS: The Customs officials found in *The Drawing of the Three* suspect that EDDIE DEAN is carrying drugs, so they search for them in rather personal places. Since the packages are on LOBSTROSITY BEACH, they can't arrest him. (For Customs page references, see the listings under EDDIE DEAN in the CHARACTERS section. For CUSTOMS located at Forty-third Street, see II:118, II:119, and II:127.)

RIKERS ISLAND: Rikers Island is the U.S.'s largest penal colony. There are ten jails on the island. Had EDDIE DEAN been caught carrying BALAZAR's coke, he would have ended up at Rikers.   II:112

TRIBOROUGH BRIDGE: The Triborough Bridge is a major New York traffic artery. It connects Manhattan, Queens, and the Bronx. III:171, III:292

NUTLEY
See DRAWERS in the PORTALS section

O

ODETTA
See ARKANSAS

OMAHA
See NEBRASKA. See also ATCHISON, TOPEKA, AND SANTA FE RAILROAD.

OXFORD TOWN
See MISSISSIPPI

P

PENNSYLVANIA
PHILADELPHIA: Known to those who live there as Philly, this city figures prominently in a song JAKE CHAMBERS sings to scare away the GHOSTS IN THE MACHINES. It goes, "My girl's a dilly/She comes from Philly."   III:336

PERU
II:371

PHILADELPHIA
See PENNSYLVANIA

PIPER SCHOOL
This is Jake's exclusive school, located on East Fifty-sixth Street, between Park and Madison Avenues, Manhattan. It is Private and Nice and most of all, White. Jake hates it.
    I:81, I:82, III:89–102, III:106, III:110, III:119, III:126, III:131 *(indirect)*, III:134, III:135, III:136, III:156, III:183, III:225, III:358 *(Jake calls it a "Cradle of the Pubes")*, IV:30 *(Piper and Blaine)*, IV:62, IV:626

PORT AUTHORITY
See NEW YORK (CITY OF): MANHATTAN

PUSHING PLACE
See NEW YORK: MANHATTAN

Q

QUINCON
II:58

R

RED WINDMILL, THE
See DRAWERS in the PORTALS section

REFLECTIONS OF YOU
See NEW YORK (CITY OF): MANHATTAN

RIDGELINE ROAD
See DRAWERS in the PORTALS section

RIKERS ISLAND
See NEW YORK (CITY OF)

RINCON AVENUE
See NEW YORK (CITY OF): BROOKLYN

ROUTE 88
See DRAWERS in the PORTALS section

RUSSIA
III:31

S

SANTA FE
See MEJIS, BARONY OF: SANTA FE in the MID-WORLD PLACES section. See also NEW MEXICO (this section) and ATCHISON, TOPEKA, AND SANTA FE RAILROAD (also this section)

SPAIN
"The rain in Spain falls mainly on the plain." This rhyme is heard in both Our World and Mid-World, although Mid-World's version is quite a bit longer.
    I:71, I:73

SUNNYVALE SANITARIUM
This is where we will probably all end up one day. Jake has an especial fear of it.
III:91, III:92, III:93, III:99

SWEDEN
III:100

T

TEXAS
The band ZZ Top was originally from Texas.
II:396, III:254

TIMES SQUARE
See NEW YORK (CITY OF): MANHATTAN

TOM AND GERRY'S ARTISTIC DELI
See NEW YORK (CITY OF): MANHATTAN. Also see LOT, THE, in the PORTALS section

TOOKER'S WHOLESALE TOYS
See NEW YORK (CITY OF): MANHATTAN

TOPEKA
See ATCHISON, TOPEKA, AND SANTA FE RAILROAD in this section. See also KANSAS in the PORTALS section

TOWER OF POWER RECORDS
See NEW YORK (CITY OF): MANHATTAN

TRIBOROUGH BRIDGE
See NEW YORK (CITY OF)

TURTLE BAY, MANHATTAN
See NEW YORK (CITY OF): MANHATTAN

TURTLE BAY CONDOS
See NEW YORK (CITY OF): MANHATTAN

U

U.S. CUSTOMS
  See NEW YORK (CITY OF): QUEENS: JFK AIRPORT

USSR
  III:287

V

VIETNAM
EDDIE DEAN's older brother, HENRY DEAN, fought in the Vietnam
War and got part of his knee shot off. It was while recovering from this
injury that Henry became addicted to morphine, which led to his later
heroin addiction.
  II:169, II:174, II:207, II:239, II:242, II:337–38

W

WASHINGTON, D.C.
  II:114
  GEORGETOWN: II:114

WICHITA
  See KANSAS. See also ATCHISON, TOPEKA, AND SANTA FE
RAILROAD.

WOOLWORTH'S
  II:64
  Also see ALABAMA

WYOMING
  IV:32

PORTALS AND MAGICAL PLACES

All is silent in the halls of the dead. All is forgotten in the stone
halls of the dead. Behold the stairways which stand in darkness;
behold the rooms of ruin. These are the halls of the dead where
the spiders spin and the great circuits fall quiet, one by one.
                                                        III:76–77

> *Beyond the reach of human range*
> *A drop of hell, a touch of strange . . .*
> Line from a Manni Poem
> I:127

A

**ALGUL SIENTO (BLUE HEAVEN)
In the new version of *The Gunslinger,* we see a TAHEEN bird-man in the
MOHAINE DESERT. According to the BORDER DWELLER named
BROWN, the taheen is lost. He is looking for a place called Algul Siento.
We do not yet know what this place is or where it is located.

ATCHISON
    See KANSAS in this section. See also KANSAS in the OUR WORLD
PLACES section and ATCHISON, TOPEKA, AND SANTA FE RAIL-
ROAD in the OUR WORLD PLACES section.

B

BEACH DOORS:
    See DOORWAYS BETWEEN WORLDS in this section

BEAM PORTALS
  See PORTALS OF THE BEAM

**BEAMS, PATH OF THE
In *The Waste Lands,* Roland draws a metaphysical map of his world. According to this map, Mid-World is shaped like a wheel. The hub of this earth-wheel is the Thirteenth Gate, known in Mid-World as the DARK TOWER. The spokes radiating out from this hub are the BEAMS.

There are six Beams, which connect twelve PORTALS. Each Beam is like an invisible high tension wire, affecting both gravity and the proper alignment of time, space, size, and dimension. Their purpose is to bind the multiverse together while simultaneously holding the separate worlds—which spin upon the Tower like sequins upon a needle—apart. As the Beams break down, and as the Tower becomes unstable, the effects are felt in all worlds. The coherence of the time/space/size continuum weakens and THINNIES appear.

Although the Beams may not be visible in all worlds, they affect all of them. In *The Waste Lands,* JAKE follows the path of the Beam to THE MANHATTAN RESTAURANT OF THE MIND and later to THE MANSION. While Jake follows the Beam in his version of our earth, Roland, EDDIE, and SUSANNAH follow the same Beam from its origin at SHARDIK'S LAIR through the GREAT WEST WOODS and finally on to the GREAT ROAD, which leads southeast toward the decaying and dangerous city of LUD. Along the Path of the Beam, Roland, Susannah, and Eddie use a magical SPEAKING RING—one of the places where the divisions between worlds are thin—to draw Jake into their *where* and *when.* Perhaps the fact that they are on the path of the BEAR/TURTLE Beam makes this drawing easier. In the new version of *The Gunslinger,* Roland follows WALTER (the MAN IN BLACK) southeast. Both of them are drawn in the direction of the Bear/Turtle Beam.

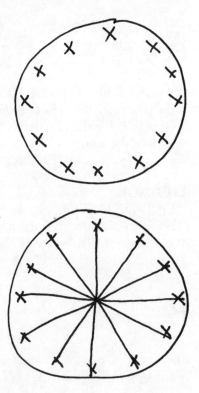

  III:39, III:73–77, III:80–86, III:122, III:130, III:149–52, III:155,

III:158–65 (following the Beam. Direct references on 158, 164), III:166, III:170–76, III:178–82, III:191, III:194, III:219–32 (following. Directly mentioned on 232), III:238, III:243, III:253–70 (following the Beam. Directly mentioned on 262, 264, 266, 269), III:273–301 (leave the Beam. Directly mentioned on 285), III:309 (Street of the Turtle corresponds to Beam), III:310–12, III:331, III:337 (Grays tunnel follows it), III:349, III:350, III:400–420 (Blaine follows path of the Beam. Directly mentioned on 404), IV:3–61 (Blaine follows path of the Beam. Directly mentioned on 14, 34 electricity at Fall of the Hounds, 49), IV:62–78 (ka-tet follows Beam through Topeka. Directly mentioned on 72), IV:79 (ka-tet falls off the Beam), IV:96, IV:659–68

BERMUDA TRIANGLE
EDDIE thinks that DAVID QUICK's Nazi airplane arrived from our world via a time/space warp similar to the Bermuda Triangle. Eddie calls this huge doorway between worlds the Roland Zone. The THINNIES, found in both the Alternate KANSAS where BLAINE terminates and in the HAMBRY of Roland's youth, also make Eddie think of the Bermuda Triangle. As is purported to happen in the Triangle, people, animals, and machinery can disappear into a thinny and never be seen again.
   III:275, IV:86

D

**DARK TOWER, THE
The Dark Tower is a looming gray-black edifice which is simultaneously the center of all the universes and the linchpin of the time/space continuum. All worlds and all realities are contained within its many levels. In its spiraling windows are flashes of electric-blue fire. Its very stairs murmur with the voices of the lost (or damned) souls trapped within it. Located in a sea of red ROSES, it is the focus of Roland's long and arduous quest. The room at the top of the Tower may contain God, or it may be empty.

The Line of ELD, of which Roland is the last, is sworn to protect the Tower. Yet a terrible illness affects this structure, one that is often compared to a cancer. As this cancer spreads, THINNIES appear and the divisions between worlds soften.

The Tower is held in place by a network of magical magnetic force-rays known as the BEAMS. There are six Beams. They cross at the Tower and terminate in twelve PORTALS. Each Portal has an animal GUARDIAN.

Although some believe that the Tower, Beams, Portals, and Guardians were magical things that preceded the destructive technology of the GREAT OLD ONES, it seems fairly certain that the Old Ones re-created the world according to their own laws, seeking to replace outmoded magic with machinery. Yet machinery, like Man, is mortal. Hence the Beams, Portals, and mechanical Guardians are breaking down. If the weakening Beams collapse and the Tower falls, all creation will blink out of existence.

The Tower and its sea of roses are located on the edge of END-WORLD, just beyond the demon-haunted realm of THUNDERCLAP. It is guarded by the BEAST, the originator of all *glammer*. Sometimes the diseased Tower cries out in the Beast's monstrous voice. If Patrick Danville—the little boy found in the novel *Insomnia*—has true visions of Mid-World, when Roland reaches the Dark Tower, he will have to face THE CRIMSON KING, who is trapped on one of its balconies. Interestingly, in the new version of *The Gunslinger*, we are told that Roland's final enemy is going to be the Crimson King, not the Beast. Perhaps they are the same being.

I:80–81, I:113, I:130, I:136, I:140, I:151, I:184, I:191, I:200, I:201, I:202, I:204, I:205, I:206, I:207, I:209, I:212, I:213, I:214, I:216, II:30, II:40, II:55, II:101, II:113, II:120–21, II:155, II:156, II:166, II:170, II:177, II:206, II:231, II:307, II:308, II:310, II:311, II:332, II:333, II:362, II:393, II:395–99, III:39, III:40–41, III:49, III:52–53, III:56, III:70, III:71, III:72, III:73–77, III:78, III:82, III:83, III:155, III:158, III:172, III:176, III:191, III:212, III:232, III:238, III:250, III:252, III:262, III:264, III:267, III:268, III:285, III:349, III:389, III:400, III:409, III:410, III:411, IV:9, IV:17, IV:19, IV:27 *(image of Tower's many levels)*, IV:30 *(worlds as levels of the Tower)*, IV:63, IV:66, IV:78–79 *(and thinnies)*, IV:86 *(structural weakness and thinnies)*, IV:86 *(destiny)*, IV:102–3 *(and roses)*, IV:164 *(Roland as a boy, thinking it is the center of all things)*, IV:437, IV:447, IV:552 *(Rhea dreams of it)*, IV:572–73 *(great description)*, IV:580–81, IV:588, IV:601, IV:617, IV:618, IV:621, IV:624, IV:635, IV:648, IV:649, IV:651, IV:658, IV:664, IV:666, IV:667, IV:668, E:157, E:161, E:165, E:207

FIELD OF SHOUTING RED ROSES: III:52–53 *(Eddie's dream)*, III:54–55, III:78, III:83, III:267, E:207 *(implied)*

DOORWAYS BETWEEN WORLDS
GENERAL: III:43, III:52 *(Eddie's dream door—Tom and Gerry's)*, III:62 *(Walter's door)*, III:261, III:275

BEACH DOORS: These doorways were created by the magical tension between Roland and WALTER, otherwise known as the MAN IN BLACK. They are made of ironwood, and stand, without any visible support, on the LOBSTROSITY-infested beach of the WESTERN SEA. The first door Roland comes to during his slow, feverish crawl up LOBSTROSITY BEACH is that of THE PRISONER. It leads him to the heroin-addicted EDDIE DEAN. The second door leads Roland to the LADY OF SHADOWS, also known as ODETTA HOLMES and DETTA WALKER—two women in one body. When these two personalities unite, the Lady of Shadows becomes Roland's *ka-tet* mate SUSANNAH DEAN. The final door, called THE PUSHER, leads Roland to the evil JACK MORT. At different times, Mort tried to kill both Susannah Dean and JAKE CHAMBERS. Hence, he is tied to Roland's *ka-tet*.

Although Roland doesn't meet any of these characters until *The Drawing of the Three,* their coming is predicted by Walter, who tells Roland's fortune while the two of them palaver in the dead zone of THE GOLGOTHA.   III:38, III:62, IV:44

> **DOOR #1 (THE PRISONER):** II:32, II:33–40, II:44, II:54, II:55, II:62–63, II:72 *(72–82 it is present)*, II:82, II:92–95, II:99, II:100–102, II:135–43, II:156–57, II:259, II:268–69, III:41
>
> **DOOR #2 (THE LADY OF SHADOWS):** II:178 *(Roland sees)*, II:179–82, II:245, II:256–57, II:259, II:268–69, II:306, III:41
>
> **DOOR #3 (THE PUSHER):** II:259, II:268–69, II:286–96 *(looking for it)*, II:300–12, II:325, II:328, II:329, II:332, II:385–87
>
> **JAKE'S DOOR (DOOR #4: THE BOY):** Although JAKE is the third member of Roland's *ka-tet,* he is not drawn through one of the Beach Doors. Instead, he is drawn through a magical doorway that EDDIE DEAN creates in a SPEAKING RING located on the GREAT ROAD between the GREAT WEST WOODS and the city of LUD. See THE MANSION below and STONE CIRCLES, listed separately.

GREEN PALACE: See GREEN PALACE, listed separately.

MAERLYN'S RAINBOW (THE BENDS o' THE RAINBOW): See MAERLYN'S RAINBOW, listed separately.

MANSION, THE: Located on RHINEHOLD STREET in DUTCH HILL, BROOKLYN, this haunted Mansion sits only one mile from where EDDIE DEAN grew up in CO-OP CITY. It also happens to sit on the PATH OF THE BEAM. Like many magical places, The Mansion is not really a mansion at all but a portal between worlds that shifts shape from reality to reality and TOWER level to Tower level. In JAKE's world it most certainly looks like an imposing building, but in

Roland's world it is the haunted force within a SPEAKING RING. All that Eddie has to do to let Jake pass through this portal—and be born into Mid-World—is to connect these two thin places with a drawn door. Unfortunately, the door is locked and both Eddie and Jake need copies of the key.

Just as the PORTALS OF THE BEAM are protected by GUARDIANS, all other portals, in our world or Mid-World, are protected by demons. In order to cross over into Mid-World and join Roland's *ka-tet*, Jake must face The Mansion's demon. The Mansion's demon is the animating spirit of the house, a spirit of place, and parallels the demon which Susannah battles sexually in the Speaking Ring. See also STONE CIRCLES in this section and DEMONS/SPIRITS/DEVILS in the CHARACTERS section.   III:75–76, III:161–62, III:185, III:187–88, III:189, III:190–92, III:194–96, III:198–201, III:203–4, III:205–6, III:207, III:208–9, III:210–11, III:262, III:344, III:348, III:399, IV:98

JAKE'S DOOR (MANSION VERSION): See also STONE CIRCLES: JAKE'S DOOR.   III:200–204, III:205–12, III:219

PORTALS OF THE BEAM: See PORTALS OF THE BEAM, listed separately. See also GUARDIANS OF THE BEAM in the CHARACTERS section.

SHARDIK'S LAIR: See PORTALS OF THE BEAM, listed separately. See also GUARDIANS OF THE BEAM in the CHARACTERS section.

STONE CIRCLES: See STONE CIRCLES, listed separately

THINNIES: See THINNIES, listed separately

TRAINS BETWEEN WORLDS: See BLAINE'S ROUTE in this section. See also NORTH CENTRAL POSITRONICS: BLAINE in the CHARACTERS section, and ATCHISON, TOPEKA, AND SANTA FE RAILROAD COMPANY in the OUR WORLD PLACES section.

DRAWERS
According to SUSANNAH DEAN (previously Odetta Holmes/Detta Walker), the Drawers are places that are spoiled, useless, or both. However, they are also places of power. In many ways they resemble a psychic trash midden. The Drawers are a kind of WASTE LAND.

I:90, II:327, III:44–46, III:82, III:264, III:347, III:377, III:407

DETTA AND *FORSPECIAL* PLATE: II:194–96

DETTA'S SEX HAUNTS: These locations (RIDGELINE ROAD outside NUTLEY, ROUTE 88 outside AMHIGH, and THE RED WINDMILL) were places where Detta Walker vented her rage against white men. The negative force of her emotion, and the experiences she had in these places, transformed them into a kind of psychic Drawers. III:196–97

E

**END-WORLD
This is the fey region that exists beyond Mid-World. It contains both THUNDERCLAP and the DARK TOWER. According to the LITTLE SISTERS OF ELURIA, the ashes of the dead blow out toward this dream place. Once, hundreds of years before our *ka-tet* traveled in his Barony Coach, BLAINE had monitoring equipment in End-World. However, it has been down for more than eight centuries. When Roland and his friends reach the border between Mid-World and End-World, the first part of their journey will be complete.

In the new *Gunslinger*, Sylvia Pittston states that when God casts out the unrepentant from his palaces, he will send them to the burning place beyond the end of End-World. End-World must be a terrible place. Even the sorcerer WALTER states that to speak of things in End-World is to speak of the ruination of one's own soul.
III:412, IV:66, IV:580, E:184

G

GOLGOTHA, THE
Roland and the MAN IN BLACK (WALTER) hold palaver here in this ancient killing ground located on the western slopes of the CYCLOPEAN MOUNTAINS. To Roland, the golgotha is "the place of the skull." Its floor is dusty with bonemeal and contains the skeletal remains of many small animals. It is here that Walter tells Roland's fortune, and it is here that Roland experiences a ten-year-long night as well as a tremendous vision of the multiverse.
I:197–216, II:20, III:47 *(indirect)*, III:48

GREEN PALACE, THE
This palace, which FANNIN/FLAGG maintains is in Oz, is actually

located along the I-70 THINNY in the ALTERNATE TOPEKA, which Roland's *ka-tet* must travel through at the end of *Wizard and Glass*. R.F. probably created it as a kind of practical joke. Like the buildings of Oz's Emerald City, it is entirely green.

The Green Palace is made of glass. Its gate is made of twelve colored bars (six on each gate wing). They represent the twelve bends of MAER-LYN'S RAINBOW. The central bar (which is broad instead of flat and round) is dead black. All of the bars contain strange little life-forms. The Green Palace hums like a THINNY, but the sound isn't as unpleasant.

IV:97 *(in distance)*, IV:103–5, IV:626, IV:632–51 *(632 hums)*, IV:659, IV:660, IV:662, IV:666

H

HAUNTED MANSION
See DOORWAYS BETWEEN WORLDS

HIDDEN HIGHWAYS/ HIGHWAYS IN HIDING
These are the hidden highways (both in Our World and in Mid-World) that lead us on to our destinies. JAKE follows one of these from his apartment door to CO-OP CITY in BROOKLYN and then to the haunted MANSION. The BEAMS are also "hidden highways."

III:83, III:122, III:158

J

JAKE'S DOOR (DOOR #4: THE BOY)
See STONE CIRCLES. For more information, see DOORWAYS BETWEEN WORLDS: MANSION

K

KANSAS
Kansas is frequently mentioned in the Dark Tower series, usually in conjunction with *The Wizard of Oz*. However, it does not become part of the plot until *Wizard and Glass*. The Kansas we enter in Book IV of the Dark Tower series is both subtly and not so subtly different from our Kansas. Unlike the Kansas of Our World, this Kansas seems still to use the old ATCHISON, TOPEKA, AND SANTA FE RAILROAD. Its former residents drove Takuro Spirits and ate at Boing Boing burgers—cars and fast-food joints we've never heard of—but worse yet, they've all been wiped out by the superflu, the same disease that killed most of America's population in Stephen King's novel *The Stand*. This Topeka seems to suffer from the worst diseases of both Mid-World and Our World. Like HAMBRY, it contains a THINNY. (See MID-WORLD RAILWAY in this section.)

II:229 *(Dorothy)*, III:139–45 *(Charlie the Choo-Choo)*, IV:62–112, IV:335–37, IV:615–51, IV:658, IV:660
ATCHISON: IV:68
KANSAS MUSEUM OF NATURAL HISTORY: IV:75
PHILLIP BILLARD: IV:75
TOPEKA: This is where Mid-World ends and END-WORLD begins (IV:66). The first part of Roland's quest ends here.   III:199, III:266, III:400, III:404, III:409, III:411, III:413, III:419, IV:62–112, IV:335–37, IV:615–25
  BERRYTON ROAD: IV:74
  BOING BOING BURGERS: IV:92, IV:617
  CRADLE OF TOPEKA: Like an outdoor LUD. Looks Western. IV:67, IV:72
  FORBES: IV:75
    FORBES FIELD: IV:74
  GADDISH FEEDS: Grain-storage tower.   IV:95
  GAGE BOULEVARD: IV:83, IV:84
    GAGE BOULEVARD AMTRAK STATION: IV:75
  GAGE PARK: IV:86–91
  HEARTLAND LANES: IV:92
  HEARTLAND PARK RACE TRACK: Disposal pit for superflu dead.   IV:74

KANSAS TURNPIKE: See ROUTE I-70
OAKLAND BILLARD PARK: Disposal plant for superflu dead. IV:74
REINISCH ROSE GARDEN: IV:86, IV:87–89 *(and* Charlie the Choo-Choo*)*
ROUTE I-70: IV:62, IV:63, IV:71, IV:91–112 *(*ka-tet *follows. Directly mentioned on 92, 94, 104),* IV:623, IV:625, IV:629, IV:635, IV:660
SOUTHEAST SIXTY-FIRST STREET: IV:74
ST. FRANCIS HOSPITAL AND MEDICAL CENTER: IV:74
STORMONT-VAIL REGIONAL MEDICAL CENTER: IV:74
TOPEKA STATE HOSPITAL: IV:92
TOPEKA ZOO: IV:89
WAMBEGO: IV:75
KAW RIVER NUCLEAR PLANT (KAWNUKE): IV:75
WICHITA: IV:72

L

**LAND OF DEATH (LAND OF NINETEEN)
This is the place that the weed-eater NORT of TULL journeyed to. Unlike most people, he came back again. After the sorcerer WALTER raised Nort from the dead, he sealed Nort's memories of the Land of Death behind an imaginary door, or blockade. This door could only be opened—and Nort's memories released—by uttering the word NINE-TEEN. ALICE OF TULL is the unlucky person who does so. What she learns drives her mad. See NINETEEN in the CHARACTERS section.

LAND OF NINETEEN
See LAND OF DEATH, above.

LAND OF THE DRUMS
The PUBES of LUD believe that they must sacrifice one of their own each time they hear the god-drums pounding out over the city's loudspeakers. If they don't give a life, the GHOSTS IN THE MACHINES will animate the city's many corpses and rise up to eat the living. It is thought that once a Pube is sacrificed, he or she journeys to the Land of the Drums. We can assume that the Land of the Drums isn't a very nice place since the Ghosts must be there, beating their hungry instruments.

Although the Pubes don't know it, the god-drums are actually no more than the backbeat of the ZZ Top song "Velcro Fly." They are operated by the city's rival gang, THE GRAYS, with a little help from BLAINE the insane computer brain.

III:317

LITTLE SISTERS' HOSPITAL

When Roland awakes in the Little Sisters' Hospital he believes he is in a vast and airy pavilion of white silk, one hung with tiny silver bells. However, like the beauty of the LITTLE SISTERS OF ELURIA, the pavilion's loveliness is no more than a *glammer*. In reality it is an old, fraying canvas tent so thin and worn in places that it lets in the light of the Kissing Moon.

E:158–99, E:200–201

LOT, THE

JAKE's magic lot is located on the corner of Forty-sixth Street and Second Avenue. It was once the home of TOM AND GERRY'S ARTISTIC DELI. Now it is a waste land containing a single, beautiful wild ROSE. According to the sign, TURTLE BAY CONDOMINIUMS are coming soon. In the remaining books of the series, Roland and his friends must find a way to protect both the Rose and the lot. Since the Rose and the Tower are actually one force in two forms, the future of the interpenetrating worlds hangs on the outcome of this mission.

III:121–29, III:264, IV:83 *(Jake's vision of empty lot),* IV:100–101 *(Eddie's dream)*

M

MAERLYN'S RAINBOW (THE BENDS o' THE RAINBOW): There are thirteen glass balls in the Wizard's Rainbow, one for each GUARDIAN and one for the TOWER and the BEAST. The balls are for scrying. Some colors look into the future; others look into alternate worlds. Still others look far into Mid-World. The balls show where one may find the secret doors between worlds, and sometimes they act as doorways themselves. All of the balls are alive and hungry. A person begins by using them, but in the end, he or she is used by them and sucked dry.

The Wizard's Rainbow is a corruption of the pure energy of the White. If the White represents wholeness, and the best human beings can strive for in ideal and action, the colors represent the baser emotions—or the fallen emotions of a fallen world. For example, the Pink One resonates with sexual energy, but it is desire, possessiveness, and cruelty without the higher emotions that true love can instill in us. Not surprisingly, the gate of the sinister GREEN PALACE is made to resemble Maerlyn's Rainbow. The gate's two wings consist of six colored bars each; one for every bend. The central bar (which is broad instead of flat and round) is dead black.

Few of Maerlyn's balls still exist. They never stay in one pair of hands for very long, and, as STEVEN DESCHAIN points out, even enchanted glass has a habit of breaking. Three or four of the bends o' the Rainbow are probably still rolling around. They are:

THE BLUE: Fifty years before Roland's first *ka-tet* set off for MEJIS, this Bend o' the Rainbow was in the possession of a desert tribe of SLOW MUTANTS called the TOTAL HOGS.

THE GREEN: This one is thought to be hidden in the city of LUD.

THE ORANGE: This ball was last seen in the ruined city of DIS.

THE PINK: This one, also known as **MAERLYN'S GRAPEFRUIT,** was in Farson's possession until Roland stole it at the end of *Wizard and Glass*. Like the other bends o' the Rainbow, the pink ball is alive. On the lid of its box (now lost) was the High Speech motto I SEE WHO OPENS ME. The Grapefruit's energy is sexual, and its color is often described as labial pink. It is one of the balls that expose people's secrets.

BLACK THIRTEEN: This final Bend o' the Rainbow may also still be in existence. However, it is unlucky even to speak of Thirteen, as it may hear its name called and roll the speaker away to unknown worlds. Even STEVEN DESCHAIN, the last Lord of Light, seemed wary of it.

GENERAL REFERENCES FOR ALL THE BALLS: IV:116–21, IV:122, IV:134, IV:141, IV:164, IV:290–91, IV:299, IV:319–20, IV:325–26, IV:335, IV:353–54, IV:356, IV:374–75, IV:378, IV:413, IV:424–25, IV:437–39 *(Steven Deschain describes)*, IV:442, IV:443, IV:452–53, IV:485–93 *(Jonas takes from Rhea)*, IV:528 *(voice of the ball)*, IV:532–33, IV:536, IV:542–44, IV:545–46, IV:558–60 *(Roland takes ball from Jonas)*, IV:570–75 *(Roland's vision; he's trapped within the glass)*, IV:579–81 *(Roland decides to leave Susan)*, IV:601–2, IV:604–11, IV:618–21, IV:634–35 *(gate of Green Palace)*, IV:648–58 *(650 the Grapefruit; 652 Roland's matricide)*

MANSION, THE
See DOORWAYS BETWEEN WORLDS

MID-WORLD AMUSEMENT PARK
In the children's story *CHARLIE THE CHOO-CHOO*, the talking train Charlie is given a nice retirement taking children round and round

on a track located in CALIFORNIA's Mid-World Amusement Park. The Mid-World Amusement Park doesn't exist in Our World. However, a version of it exists in the alternate TOPEKA that Roland's *ka-tet* reaches after their catastrophic ride on BLAINE the insane Mono. In the alternate Topeka, a rather sinister Charlie resides in the REINISCH ROSE GARDEN.

III:145

MID-WORLD LANES

When JAKE is accosted by an officer of the law in TIMES SQUARE and is asked for some identification, he offers to show his Mid-World Lanes membership.

III:168

MID-WORLD RAILWAY (KANSAS-TO-TOPEKA LINE)

We first learn about the Mid-World Railway through the children's book *CHARLIE THE CHOO-CHOO*, which JAKE CHAMBERS finds in THE MANHATTAN RESTAURANT OF THE MIND. Despite the fact that it was written for kiddies, Jake finds the story (and the main character, a talking train) extremely sinister. Jake senses that Charlie is a force of destruction, and that the Mid-World Railway has only one ultimate destination—the Land of Death.

Jake's vision of a killer train on a death-track prefigures the actual Mid-World Railway that exists on Roland's level of the TOWER. In Roland's world, Charlie is replaced by the talking Mono BLAINE, though their routes are very similar. In Roland's world, *char* means "death." Hence, Charlie (like Blaine) is literally a killer train. Roland, Jake, and their *ka-tet* survive Blaine only to find a toy version of Charlie's railway in the alternate TOPEKA. (For more information on the children's book, see entry under CHARLIE THE CHOO-CHOO listed in the CHARACTERS section.)

CHARLIE THE CHOO-CHOO VERSION: III:139–46, III:266
BLAINE'S VERSION: III:267

MORDOR

This realm of darkness and death can be found in J.R.R. Tolkien's famous trilogy, *The Lord of the Rings*. SUSANNAH thinks about Mordor and the Cracks of Doom as she rides through the Waste Lands beyond LUD.

III:406

N

**NA'AR
When WALTER reads Roland's cards in the new version of *The Gun-slinger*, he calls him the Hanged Man, plodding ever onward toward his goal over the pits of Na'ar. Na'ar sounds a lot like Hell. It is probably a MANNI term.

NEBRASKA
In *Wizard and Glass* we find out that ABAGAIL—the champion of the White found in King's novel *The Stand*—lives in an alternate version of Nebraska.
    IV:624

NONES
The Moon Peddler comes from the Nones bearing his sack of squealing souls.
    IV:274

O

OZ
    See WIZARD OF OZ in the CHARACTERS section. See also THE GREEN PALACE in this section.

P

PATH OF THE BEAMS
    See BEAMS, PATH OF THE

**PLACE OF BURNING DARKNESS
    See END-WORLD

PORTALS OF THE BEAM

In *The Waste Lands,* Roland draws a metaphysical map of Mid-World. This map is shaped like a wheel. At the center of the wheel is the DARK TOWER, also known as the THIRTEENTH GATE. The twelve power points on the rim of this wheel are known as PORTALS. These Portals are actually twelve doorways leading into and out of Mid-World. The six BEAMS, which connect opposite Portals and which pass through the nexus of the Dark Tower, are like high-tension wires. They can be seen and felt by those who pass near them.

According to HAX, when the GREAT OLD ONES re-created the world, they made twelve Guardians to watch over the twelve Portals. These GUARDIANS OF THE BEAM, also known as TOTEMS OF THE BEAM, had animal shapes. Although we have met MIR/SHARDIK, the cyborg Bear Guardian, it seems highly likely that the Beams, Guardians, and Dark Tower existed before the technology of the Great Old Ones came into being.

The portals are not the only doorways into and out of Mid-World, but they are the most powerful ones. Their health is intrinsically tied to the health of Mid-World and the time/space continuum of all worlds. As the alterations the Old Ones made to the fabric of reality begin to unravel, THINNIES appear. Thinnies are like extremely nasty portals. We don't know where they lead, but it seems likely that they transport their victims to the demon-haunted emptiness between worlds. Like BLAINE's termination point in TOPEKA, the Portals of the Beam are marked with yellow and black stripes. See also GUARDIANS OF THE BEAM, located in the CHARACTERS section.

III:37–40

PORTAL OF THE TURTLE: III:264

SHARDIK'S LAIR/SHARDIK'S PORTAL: III:51, III:65–77 *(one of six paths to the Dark Tower),* III:78 *(bone-littered clearing),* III:81, III:84, III:153, III:154, III:162, III:260, III:262, III:264, III:394, III:407, IV:42 *(Eddie's memory)*

R

REINISCH ROSE GARDEN

See KANSAS in this section

S

SHARDIK'S LAIR
See PORTALS OF THE BEAM in this section and GUARDIANS OF THE BEAM in the CHARACTERS section.

STONE CIRCLES
These circles of standing stones (also known as **DRUIT STONES**) are called **SPEAKING RINGS**. They are the haunts of spirits and oracles. In these demonic places the boundaries between the visible and invisible worlds are thin. The first Speaking Ring we see is the ORACLE OF THE MOUNTAINS, found in *The Gunslinger*. The second one we see is in *The Waste Lands,* along the PATH OF THE BEAM. It is through this second Speaking Ring that our *ka-tet* draws JAKE CHAMBERS into Mid-World.

We don't know who created the Stone Circles, or whether they predate the technological rule of the GREAT OLD ONES or came during the post-apocalyptic dark age that followed. However, we do know that Roland sees them as ancient, mysterious, and dangerous—hence they must pre-cede the rise of GILEAD and the IN-WORLD BARONIES by many hundreds of years. Although we do not know who lifted these heavy stones and made them reach toward the sky, we do know that human sac-rifice was often practiced within them, and possibly contributed to their sinister energy.

GENERAL REFERENCES: II:367 *(Druit Stones)*
ORACLE OF THE MOUNTAINS: The Oracle of the Mountains is the name Roland gives to the speaking-ring succubus that he and Jake encounter in the WILLOW JUNGLE located in the foothills of the CYCLOPEAN MOUNTAINS. Although this demoness originally tried to draw Jake into her circular lair, Roland thwarted her, saving Jake from almost certain death. In the end, Roland offers himself to this hungry succubus so that he can force her to make a prophecy. Roland uses mescaline, a drug which CORT once called the Philosopher's Stone, to draw the demon, but after he has extracted information from her he must pay her sexual tithe. The oracle uses *glammer* to con-jure the scent and voice of Roland's lost love, SUSAN DELGADO. I:121–22, I:124, I:126–32, I:134, I:138, II:315, III:172–173, IV:68
SPEAKING RING ALONG THE PATH OF THE BEAM: It is through

this second Speaking Ring that our *ka-tet* (namely EDDIE DEAN) draws JAKE CHAMBERS into Mid-World. Sketching a doorway in the dirt of a Druit Stone circle that they encounter on the GREAT ROAD to LUD, Eddie makes a magical door—one which can be unlocked by a key he carved while traveling.

Eddie's magical door is actually a portal connecting Mid-World to the haunted DUTCH HILL MANSION, located in a part of BROOK-LYN no more than a mile or so from Eddie's old family apartment. Hence, Eddie is drawing Jake from the world of his own childhood every bit as much as he draws him from a real city.

Like all portals between worlds, these two connected doorways are not unguarded. SUSANNAH DEAN must hold the Speaking Ring Demon in a sexual tangle while Eddie works his magic. Roland, in turn, must dive through the door into Jake's world to save him from the clutches of the terrible MANSION DEMON. Also see JAKE'S DOOR (THE BOY) below.   III:173, III:181, III:182, III:189–90, III:193–94, III:195–98, III:202–3, III:206, III:207–8, III:209–10, III:211–13, III:258, III:262, IV:69

JAKE'S DOOR (DOOR #4: THE BOY): Like all portals, THE BOY (DOOR #4) has a different form in each world. In Our World, it appears to be a haunted house called THE MANSION. In Mid-World, it exists within a Speaking Ring. (The Mid-World version of the door is actually drawn by Eddie within the Speaking Ring.) Obviously, places of sinister power in one world are also places of sinister power in all of the others.   III:202, III:205–12, III:219

T

THINNY, THINNIES

Thinnies are places where the fabric of existence has almost entirely worn away. These cancerous "sores on the skin of existence" have increased in number since the DARK TOWER began to fail (IV:66). Thinnies can exist only because the multiverse itself is sickening. In fact, as thinnies spread over the earth, disease spreads among humans and other creatures.

Thinnies look like silvery, shimmering water and make a nauseating, atonal squalling. In many ways they seem like fluidly animate demons, especially since they have both a kind of body and a definite, malign presence. Sometimes their liquefying element spreads, develops arms, and snatches birds out of the air. These liquid/ether demons are like monstrous sirens, singing hungrily, always willing to whisper our secret fears to us so that they can lure us into their dead embrace. They can be found in TOPEKA and HAMBRY. (The Hambry thinny has a green hue.)

> IV:64 (sounds Hawaiian, doesn't it?), IV:66 (waste lands beyond Lud are another kind of thinny), IV:67, IV:68 (parallel between thinnies, lobstrosities, and god-drums), IV:70 (hear it), IV:78 (thinnies as doors), IV:92 (enter thinny), IV:93, IV:95 (enter it and feel nauseated), IV:96 (like an entombment, an unclean purgatory), IV:118 (Eyebolt Canyon), IV:155–57 (voice), IV:261, IV:272–76 (Roland and his ka-tet face it), IV:281, IV:336, IV:371, IV:395, IV:422, IV:432, IV:433 (Roland's war plans against Farson), IV:454–56 (voice of thinny), IV:595–601 (Farson's men driven into it), IV:622–23, IV:632, IV:634, IV:660

THUNDERCLAP

The fey realm of THUNDERCLAP sits on the lip of END-WORLD. It is described as a land of dead fields, deserted villages, blasted trees, and dead soldiers. From here come the pale warriors; all clocks run backward in this land of death, and the graveyards vomit out their dead. Thunderclap is a land of vampires, and a place where those who are bitten by vampires, such as Father Callahan of the novel *Salem's Lot,* are damned to travel. Roland will have to pass through Thunderclap on his way to the TOWER. It is here that Roland and his friends will face FLAGG once more.

> IV:570–73, IV:580, IV:628, IV:666

TOPEKA
See KANSAS

TOWER
See DARK TOWER

W

WASTE LANDS

The Waste Lands are those desolate lands located beyond LUD. These horrible areas—too poisoned to support life as we know it but full of mutants and monsters—are man-made. It seems that they were the result of one of the GREAT OLD ONES' wars. We already know that BLAINE, the computer mind of LUD, has access to chemical and biological weapons, but what was unloosed upon the Waste Lands was worse than these. It was, Blaine assures EDDIE, even worse than a nuclear catastrophe. See also DRAWERS.

III:109 *(little "w")*, III:248, III:405–20 *(travel through via Blaine)*, IV:3, IV:13–14 *(and Candleton)*

**WEST END OF THE WORLD
The West End of the World is an almost unreachable place. Hence the expression, "Where else would I be? The West End of the World?" At the end of the new *Gunslinger,* we learn that the WESTERN SEA is the western edge of the world.

III:339

APPENDIX I:
HIGH SPEECH, LOW SPEECH, AND MID-WORLD ARGOT

CONTENTS

INTRODUCTION

High Speech (also called "The Tongue") was the ancient, ritualized language of Mid-World. Low speech—also called the common tongue or the vulgate—was the speech of everyday interaction, but High Speech was the language of gunslingers. It was also the language of ritual and magic.

Although not confined to the courts of Gilead (Sylvia Pittston of Tull and Aunt Talitha of River Crossing both speak the Tongue), it was, primarily, bound to the hierarchies and courtly codes of In-World. While we can assume that Fair-Day Riddling was conducted in low speech, and while the common tongue contained many fascinating terms and phrases, the spiked letters of High Speech carried the heart of Roland's culture. With one notable exception (explained in the pages that follow), each word in the Tongue had multiple meanings. These meanings were so varied and so diffuse that they were (and are) difficult to explain to outsiders.

Like other sacred languages, the words and phrases of High Speech imply an entire philosophy of life, and the speaking of it was ritualized. Gunslinger apprentices were not allowed to utter its words publicly until after they had won their guns. To do so before proving themselves in the yard behind the Great Hall was considered an affront to all that their culture held sacred. As was said earlier, High Speech was the language of gunslingers, but it was also the language used to address spirits, demons, and *dinhs*. If the glorious history of Roland's world is now no more than the wreckage of a sunken ship, then High Speech is one of the sacred relics that washed up on the shores.

> **PLEASE NOTE:** I have tried to give at least one page reference for each term so that the reader can view the entries in the context of the story. Since the new version of *The Gunslinger* was still in manuscript form when this book went to press, I was unable to include page references for new terms.

HIGH SPEECH TERMS

AN-TET: The term *tet* refers to people linked by the same destiny or goals. *An-tet* implies an intimate emotional link. It can also imply sexual intimacy. To sit together *an-tet* is to sit in council. In *Wizard and Glass*, Roland refers to the first time he and Susan made love as the first time they were together *an-tet*. Given the profound link between Roland and Susan (she appears and reappears to him in dreams and visions throughout the Dark Tower series), the term *an-tet* is appropriate. A mere sexual encounter does not necessarily imply *an-tet*.   IV:439

CHAR: Most words in High Speech have multiple meanings. However, *char* is an exception to this general rule. *Char* has one meaning only, and that is death. *Char* is the root of many Mid-World terms, including *Big Charlie Wind, charry* and *Charyou Tree*.   III:270

CHARYOU TREE: "Come Reap." Obviously, *Charyou Tree*'s original meaning had to do with sacrifice.   IV:447

****COMMALA:** *Commala* is a Mid-World term for rice. It is also an alternate name for the festival dance known as the Sowing Night Cotillion. The Commala is the courting rite of New Earth, a festival also known as Sowing and Fresh Commala.

****COTILLION (SOWING NIGHT COTILLION):** See COMMALA above.

****DAN-DINH:** The term *dan-dinh* has many meanings. To speak *dan-dinh* is to open your heart and your mind to another. This term also means Little Leader.

DARKLES and TINCTS: These terms are applied to Maerlyn, otherwise known as the Ageless Stranger. Although their exact definitions are not given, they are used in conjunction with Maerlyn's ability to live backward in time and to live, simultaneously, in all times.   I:212

DINH: A *dinh* is a leader or king. Roland is the *dinh* of his *ka-tet*. Roland asks his *ka-tet* whether the Wizard of Oz was a great *dinh*—a Baron or a king.   IV:558, IV:630

GUNNA: The term *gunna* appears to mean all one's worldly goods. This is the definition that Eddie surmises, as he watches Roland pack their *gunna* and prepare for another day's travel.   IV:103

GUNSLINGER LITANY: See GUNSLINGER LITANY in the MID-WORLD SAYINGS section of this appendix.   III:14, III:68

**HOWKEN: The act (and art) of hypnotizing someone, usually using a bullet as a focusing point.

KA: Like many words in High Speech, *ka* has multiple meanings and so is difficult to define precisely. It signifies life force, consciousness, duty, and destiny. In the vulgate, or low speech, it also means a place to which an individual must go. The closest terms in our language are probably *fate* and *destiny*, although *ka* also implies karma, or the accumulated destiny (and accumulated debt) of many existences. We are the servants of *ka*. We are also the prisoners of it. As Roland knows, *ka* is a wheel; its one purpose is to turn, and in the end it always returns to the place it began. In this sense, it is reminiscent of the major arcana card, The Wheel of Fortune.   II:178

**KA-BABBIES: Young *ka-tet* mates.

KA-MAI: In Book IV of the Dark Tower series, Cuthbert refers to himself as Roland's *ka-mai*. Roland thinks of Eddie Dean as *ka-mai* as well, another link uniting the personalities of Cuthbert and Eddie. *Ka-mai* means *ka*'s fool. It implies a constant joker (the kind Roland is obviously drawn to and easily angered by), yet the addition of *ka* adds another dimension to this term. One must remember that in Shakespeare's plays, it is often the fool who speaks the most profound truths. Sometimes jest is serious, or cuts to the heart of a matter which otherwise could not be addressed at all. Cuthbert and Eddie, both referred to as *ka-mai*, often have insights that Roland would neither grasp nor face on his own. It is Eddie, alone among the *ka-tet* traveling to the Tower, who realizes that

Roland's potential for treachery and betrayal still exists. He jokes about it, yet he states it clearly enough, and directly to Roland. The gift of *ka-mai* is a necessary one on the road to the Tower. It is as necessary as the gift of the touch.   IV:42, IV:282

**KA'S BOOK: The Book of Destiny.

KA-TEL: A *ka-tel* is a class of apprentice gunslingers. Roland was the youngest of his *ka-tel*, yet he was the first to win his guns.   IV:106

KA-TET: Literally speaking, *ka-tet* means "one made from many." *Ka* refers to destiny; *tet* refers to a group of people with the same interests or goals. *Ka-tet* is the place where men's lives are joined by fate. *Ka-tet* cannot be changed or bent to any individual's will, but it can be seen, known, and understood. The philosophers of Gilead stated that *ka-tet* could be broken only by death or treachery. However, Roland's teacher Cort maintained that neither death nor treachery was strong enough to break the bonds of *ka-tet*, since these events were also tied to *ka*, or fate. Each member of a *ka-tet* is a piece of a puzzle. Each individual piece is a mystery, but when put together, the collected pieces form a greater picture. It takes many *ka-tets* to finish one picture, or one historical tapestry. *Ka-tets* overlap, often sharing members. Individuals can also be partial members of a *ka-tet*, as Roland states when he pursues Jake through the underground mazes of Lud. Unlike the billy-bumbler Oy, who follows Jake by instinct as much as by sense of smell (members of the same *ka-tet* are drawn to one another), Roland believes he is not a complete member of Jake's destiny-bound group. He can share thoughts, but his destiny is slightly different from those of his companions. This may be because Roland is from a different world, but this explanation is not complete. After all, Oy is also from a different world, and is part of a different species.

A *ka-tet* is not always bound by love, affection, or friendship. Enemies are also *ka-tet*. Although usually referred to as positive or at least inevitable, the forces of *ka/ka-tet* can cast a sinister shadow over our lives. For Jake, Eddie, Susannah, and Roland, the *ka-tet* holding them together also binds them to the Dark Tower and the vacant Lot on Forty-sixth Street and Second Avenue. This place, where Tom and Gerry's Artistic Deli once stood, is the "secret heart" of their *ka-tet*.   III:259, III:264

KHEF: In the original tongue of the Old World, *khef* meant many different things, including water, birth, and life force. It implied all that was essential to existence. At the beginning of the original *Gunslinger*, we learn that one can progress through the *khef*. When we meet Roland, he has "progressed through the *khef* over many years, and had reached the fifth level." Those who attain the higher levels of *khef* (levels seven and eight) are able to have a clinical detachment from their bodies. The physical self may thirst, but the mind remains separate, a spectator.

Khef is both individual and collective. It implies the knowledge a person gains from dream-life, as well as his or her life force. *Khef* is the web that binds a *ka-tet*. Those who share *khef* share thoughts. Their destinies are linked, as are their life forces. Behind the multiple meanings of this word lies a philosophy of interconnectedness, a sense that all individuals, all events, are part of a greater pattern or plan. It also implies that through rigorous training (similar to that endured by gunslingers) the self can progress upward, rising tier to tier, until the body, if not one's ultimate destiny, is under the control of mind and will.

An individual's *khef* is often more complex than he or she realizes. In psychological terms, *khef* accounts for all parts of ourselves, even those aspects we wish not to see. It may also account for our other selves, those "twinners" (to borrow a term from *The Talisman*) who are our manifestations in other realities, or on other levels of the Tower. Our fates, for good or for evil, are the result of both our own and our shared *khef*. Like Roland, who must face the fact that betrayal of those he loves is part of his destiny, we must realize that we are capable of both good and evil actions. Susannah Dean—the woman who emerged from the dual personalities of Detta Walker and Odetta Holmes—experiences this firsthand. While riding through the blasted lands beyond the city of Lud, "the dark side of her personality, that side of her *khef* which was Detta Walker" drank in the vision of complete destruction. Her other personalities—Susannah Dean and Odetta Holmes—reject the hateful horrors shown by Blaine's sadistic "visual mode," but Detta rejoices in them. The part of her that has experienced rage and pain identifies with the violence of it, and is somehow pleased by it.   III:260, III:407, IV:29

POL-KAM: The *pol-kam* is a dance, faster and lighter than a waltz, danced in the Great Hall of Gilead. Roland associates it with the courtesans, the jewel-like eyes of his lover Aileen, and the bright, shining electric lights of Gilead.   I:137

SAI: Although used in low speech, *Sai* appears to be a form of address that originated in High Speech. (Nort, Tull's weed-eater, used this term when he spoke to Roland in the Tongue.) *Sai* is a term of respect and can be roughly translated as "sir" or "madam."   IV:143, IV:145

SILL: To desire or to yearn. If used patronizingly, it means that the yearner longs for something childish. It is a word with many subtle innuendos.

TET: A group of people with the same interests and goals.

****WURDERLAK:** When Roland meets with Walter in the golgotha, he fears that his guilt over Jake's death has made him into a *wurderlak,* or a kind of shape-shifter. As he says, "He was a *wurderlak,* lycanthropus of his own making, and in deep dreams he would become the boy and speak in strange tongues." This term is cut from the new version of *The Gunslinger.* I:192

MID-WORLD ARGOT AND ROLAND'S VERSIONS
OF OUR WORDS

AMOCO: In Mid-World, AMOCO: LEAD FREE is a legend of unknown meaning. Roland once met a hermit who gained a religious following by placing an Amoco gasoline hose between his legs and preaching wild, guttural, sullen sermons. Amoco became the totem of a thunder god who was worshipped with a half-mad slaughter of sheep. I:154

ASTIN: This is Roland's pronunciation of "aspirin." II:98, II:102

BIG CHARLIE WIND: The Big Charlie Wind is a death wind. Mercy, from River Crossing, refers to the Big Charlie Wind that "came and almost blew the steeple off the church." III:248

BIG-HAT STOCK: Good, threaded stock. IV:206

****BOCKS:** Dollars. It is the currency used in Tull.

****BOLT AND BAH:** Crossbow and bolt. Although Roland's *ka-tel* trained with the bolt and bah, this weapon tends to be used by those without access to guns.

BOOBYRIGGED: This is a term from Lud and is used by Tick-Tock. It means boobytrapped. III:354

BORDER DWELLERS: Border Dwellers are the men and women who live on the edges of the Mohaine Desert. They burn devil grass and live in huts with sod roofs. Their diet consists of corn, beans, and peas. See also BORDER DWELLERS in the CHARACTERS section.

BRAIN-STORM: A stroke.   IV:625

BRAKES: The Brakes are those tangled areas of mixed vegetation and woody bushes that exist in the low hills near the Western Sea.   II:286, II:296

**BUCKAS: Bucka wagons. Probably a bit like old covered wagons. Like the coaches, bucka wagons once followed the Great Road through the Mohaine Desert.

BUGGER-MAN: This is the Mid-World term for the Bogeyman.   II:286

BULLDINK: This term is used in River Crossing and is the equivalent of "bullshit."   III:248

BUX: Roland-speak for dollars (bucks).   II:345

CAMISAS: Spanish for shirts. Used in Hambry.   IV:237

CARVERS: Five shot revolvers.   IV:393

CATACLYSM: See GREAT POISONING in this section

CHEEFLET: This is Roland's pronunciation of the antibiotic Keflex.   II:157

**CLAN-FAMS: Extended family units, or clans. Many of these inbred groups live on the borders of the Mohaine Desert.

CLEARING AT THE END OF THE PATH: This is a euphemistic, but comforting, term for death.   III:380

CLOUTS: Cloth that can be used for headscarves or diapers.   IV:127, IV:448

**COMMALA: A Mid-World dance also known as the Sowing Night Cotillion. See entry under HIGH SPEECH TERMS.

CONVERSATIONAL: A Conversational is a political event. In every Barony of Mid-World, the week leading up to Fair-Day is full of Conversationals, which are like political luncheons. Important people come from all corners of a Barony to meet and palaver. The main Conversational takes place on Fair-Day itself.　IV:456–57

COOZEY: Jonas calls Roland a "coozey little brat."　IV:484

CORPSE-LAMPS: This is the name Roland gives for the lights he sees floating in the underground river located below the Cyclopean Mountains.　I:153

CORVETTE: In the Barony of Mejis, a corvette is a small leather purse, big enough for a few coins. It tends to be carried by women rather than men, but men occasionally use them as well. Literally speaking, corvette means "little packet." As can be seen, however, a more practical definition is "little purse."　IV:283

COSY: This term is from Lud. Gasher tells Jake "you've got a cosy look about you." Cosy seems to mean clever or full of guile.　III:299

COTTON-GILLIES: *Cotton-gilly* is a fancy term for a common whore. A gilly (or sheevin) is a side-wife taken by a man who already has a legal wife. She is a mistress, but one who will be faithful to the man she serves. A cotton-gilly goes with whoever has enough ready cash. Gert Moggins of the Travellers' Rest uses this term for herself and the other girls.　IV:447

COTTONWOOD: This is a tree that grows near the desert beaches of the Western Sea. Eddie makes a travois out of it in order to drag Roland north.　II:167

CRADLE: A station or homeport. It can also mean headquarters.　III:303, III:316

CRIP SPACES: This term is actually used by Eddie, king of good taste. It refers to the handicapped spaces in a parking lot.　IV:81

CROSSTREE: Gallows tree from which men are hanged.　I:111

CRUNK: Dialect spoken by Mejis *vaqueros*.　IV:575

CUCHILLO: Spanish for knife. The term is used in Hambry.　IV:365

CULLY: This word seems roughly equivalent to the British term "lad." We hear it in Lud and then again in Hambry. When Roland pulls his revolver on Gasher, Gasher replies, "Put it away, my cully . . . Put it away, my dear heart. Ye're a fierce trim, ay, that's clear, but this time you're outmatched." Susan calls Cuthbert "cully" when she gives him a corvette with a note in it for Roland. Later, Coral Thorin uses the term when she addresses her lover, Eldred Jonas. It can be used negatively as well. Rhea calls Roland a "murdering cull" after he shoots Ermot, her pet snake. IV:418

CUNNING: As in "a cunning little baby." Sweet, clever, amazing, perfectly made.   IV:140

DAB HAND: To have a "dab hand" at an activity means that you are good at it. The term is used in Hambry.   IV:182

DANCE OF THE EASTERLING: See MID-WORLD HOLIDAYS in APPENDIX II

DEMON MOON: See MID-WORLD MOONS at the beginning of this Concordance.

DEUCIES: This term is used by the Pubes of Lud. It is a negative term and seems to imply that the person being described is either cowardly or foolish.   III:319

DEVIL DUST/DEVIL POWDER: This is Roland's term for cocaine. It reminds him of devil grass. See DEMONS/SPIRITS/DEVILS in the CHARACTERS section.

DEVIL GRASS: Devil grass is a narcotic weed that grows in the waste lands of Mid-World. It is both poisonous and addictive. Those who become addicted to the grass are usually too poor to afford alcohol. They begin by smoking this nasty weed and end up chewing it. Chewers have green teeth and a rank stench. Devil grass gives its users dreams, nightmares, then death. It kills faster than liquor. Border Dwellers use devil grass for fuel since they have little else to burn. It gives off a greasy light and many believe that beckoning devils dance in the flames. See DEMONS/SPIRITS/DEVILS in the CHARACTERS section.

DIM, THE: *Dim* has several meanings. Sorcerers and witches can make themselves *dim*, or difficult to see. When a person is *dim* he or she is not invisible, merely shadowy. "The dim" is like déjà vu. When Susan meets with Roland she feels the dim—or the sense that she has met him before—and feels faint.   IV:256, IV:416

DIPOLAR: According to Tick-Tock, the computers of Lud run on either dipolar or unipolar circuits.   III:355

DJINNI: An evil genie.   III:315

DOCKER'S CLUTCH: This is Roland's term for a gunholder. He uses it for both hidden gunholders (like the one under the counter at Clements Guns and Sporting Goods) and shoulder holsters.   II:351, III:13

DOCKEY: Chicory. In River Crossing, they make coffee from Dockey. III:237

DOLINA: A kind of blanket found in Hambry.   IV:282–83

'DOWNERS: One of Gilead's mealtimes. Marten (a secret glutton) put sugar in his coffee in mornings and at 'Downers.   II:103

DROGUE AND FORWARD: Mid-World cowboys hired to protect caravans will ride drogue-and-forward to protect their convoy. In other words, they will ride before and behind.   E:178

DUST-DEVILS: These dust whirlwinds gyrate over the hardpan of the Mohaine desert.   I:14

ELAPHAUNTS: Roland heard of these great creatures when he was a child. They are supposed to bury their own dead.   II:29

FAIR-DAY GOOSE: The person who won one of Gilead's Fair-Day Riddling contests was awarded a prize goose.   III:276–77

FAIR-DAY RIDDLING: In Gilead-that-was, riddling was taken very seriously. Riddling contests were held during each of the seasonal festivals, especially during the festivals of Wide Earth and Full Earth. Riddles were considered to be full of power and were thought to make the crops grow stronger.   III:276–77, III:416–17

FAKEMENT: It can mean an event or a scene. It can also mean a falsehood.   III:317, III:337

FARO: One of the games (along with Watch Me) damned by Sylvia Pittston during her Tull sermons.   I:50

FEAST OF JOSEPH FAIRTIME: People could buy captive tubes of swamp gas at this fair. The swamp-gas tubes looked something like neon.   I:186

FIN DE AÑO: The end-of-the-year celebration. Reap Night.   IV:136

FIREDIM: A sparkling jewel that reflects light. They come in a variety of colors. Some are red, like rubies; some are green, like emeralds. Tick-Tock's eyes sometimes glow like firedims.   II:39–40, III:359

FIREDIM TUBES: In Lud, they call neon tubes "firedim tubes."   III:366

**FOT-SULS: Roland's version of Jake's word for the phosphorescent man-made "fossils" embedded in the rock below the Cyclopean Mountains. It probably refers to neon tubing.

FOTERGRAFFS (FOTTERGRAFFS, FOTTERGRAFS): Technically speaking, this is not a Mid-World term at all but Roland's rather garbled version of our word "photograph."   II:344, II:345, IV:74

**FRESH COMMALA: Another term for the season of Sowing, also known as New Earth. See COMMALA in the HIGH SPEECH section, GILEAD FAIR-DAYS at the beginning of this Concordance, and MID-WORLD HOLIDAYS in APPENDIX II.

FULL EARTH: One of Mid-World's seasonal festivals. See GILEAD FAIR-DAYS at the beginning of this Concordance and MID-WORLD HOLIDAYS in APPENDIX II.

**GILLY: A gilly is a concubine or mistress. Its plural form is gillies. Arthur Eld had forty gillies, and it is from one of these women that Roland is descended. Although many great men of Mid-World had gillies and many more were born of gillies, there is a certain disgrace attached to this state of being. In Mid-World, where mutations abound and where sterility is common, gillies are seen as necessary if not necessarily respectable. Roland is shocked to find out that Susan Delgado will soon be Hart Thorin's gilly. Susan receives disapproving stares from the women of Hambry because of the "service" she is about to render the town's mayor. In the new version of *The Gunslinger,* this word is spelled "jilly." IV:207

GLAMMER: Enchantment and magic.   I:211

GOLGOTHA: A place of the skull, or a dead place.   I:197

GRAF: An apple beer that seems to be a specialty of Mid-World. It is offered to Roland, Susannah, Eddie, and Jake when they visit the elderly people of River Crossing. It is also served in Hambry. Mid-World is full of orchards (both Roland and Tick-Tock have memories of them), so it makes sense that the world's drink of choice is a kind of hard cider. III:234

GRAYS: See GRAYS in the CHARACTERS section.

GREAT FIRE: See GREAT POISONING, below

GREAT POISONING: Also known as the OLD WAR, THE GREAT FIRE, and THE CATACLYSM. This horrific event took place more than a thousand years before the grandparents of the River Crossing folks were born. It caused the animal, plant, and human populations to give birth to muties, and it made great swaths of land turn into waste land. It was the beginning of all Mid-World's troubles.   III:284–85

GREEZY: This is Lud-speak for "greasy."   III:327

**GROW BAG: A grow bag is a magic bag that grows what you need. During his palaver with Walter in the golgotha, Roland wonders whether his grow bag will grow tobacco.

GUARD o' THE WATCH: This is Roland's term for officers of the law. He uses it for both the guards of his world and the police of Our World. I:109

GUIJARROS: In Spanish this means cobbles or pebbles. Both the stone walls and the cracked *guijarros* of Rhea's roof are slimed with mold. IV:394

GULLYWASH: This is Gasher-speak and is probably part of Lud's slang. It seems to mean penis.   III:298

GUNNA: See entry under HIGH SPEECH

HACI: Short for *hacienda* or house.   IV:191

HAI: This is the term Roland uses to call his hawk, David.   I:169

HARRIERS: The harriers of Mid-World are like outlaws or bandits. They rob, loot, murder, and destroy. The Grays are harriers, as are the Big Coffin Hunters. Harriers blinded Mercy of River Crossing with a branding iron because, they said, she was "looking at em pert."   III:226, III:230

HEART-STORM: See BRAIN-STORM

HILE: Roland greets Blaine by saying "Hile, Blaine." Blaine returns with "Hile, Gunslinger." This verbal exchange makes Susannah Dean think of Hitler, but it is actually a formal Mid-World greeting. Strangely, this term is also used to call animals.   IV:21, IV:261

HONOR STANCE: This is the term Cort uses for a boxer's opening stance. The lobstrosities of the Western Sea beach stand like this whenever there is an approaching wave.   II:16

HOWLERS: This is Roland's term for sirens.   II:153

HUBBERWOMEN: Hubberwomen are magical or fey women.   E:177

HUNTRESS MOON: See MID-WORLD MOONS at the beginning of this Concordance.

IRONWOOD: In "The Little Sisters of Eluria," we are told that this tree is also known as the seequoiah. Its wood is extremely hard and durable. In fact, it's too hard to burn. The three doors which Roland finds on Lobstrosity Beach, next to the Western Sea, are made of ironwood. Cort's stick was also made of this durable material.   E:151

JESUS DOG (CROSS DOG): This is the term used to describe dogs with a cruciform shape upon their chest fur. As Roland finds out when he faces the Little Sisters of Eluria, they can prove extremely useful when confronting vampires. (See ELURIA CHARACTERS in the CHARACTERS section.)

**JILLY-CHILD: A young jilly or gilly. See entry under GILLY.

KISSING MOON: See MID-WORLD MOONS at the beginning of this Concordance.

KUVIAN NIGHT-SOLDIER: It seems likely that the Kuvian night-soldiers were a band of assassins.   I:200

LAST TIMES: This is Sylvia Pittston's term for the End of the World. I:50

MAGDA-SEEN: This is Roland's misinterpretation of the word *magazine,* and it doesn't make any sense to him. He can't figure out what Magda must have seen.   II:61

MALHABLADA: This is a Spanish word which means "woman who speaks badly," or, in the case of Susan Delgado, a woman to uses bad words.   IV:237

MANDRUS: Mandrus's common name is "whore's blossoms." It is a venereal disease (endemic in cities such as Lud) that appears to have quite a lot in common with syphilis. The oozing sores apparent in the later stages of the disease are particularly horrific.   III:297

MANTO: In Hambry, a manto is a cloak. In other places, it is a slang term for a homosexual. Kimba Rimer once jokingly called Clay Reynolds "*Sai* Manto," referring to his cloak, but Reynolds later murdered him for doing so.   IV:471

MEGRIMS: Fears. Fantasies. As Susan walks to Rhea's hut for the first time, she sings to keep "the worst of her megrims away."   IV:123

MESCALINE: We have this in Our World too. Cort called mescaline the Philosopher's Stone. Cort maintained that the old gods pissed over the desert and made this hallucinogen. The use of drugs (usually to communicate with speaking demons) was part of a gunslinger's training. (I:124–25, I:127) See APPENDIX II: MID-WORLD DRUGS.

METAL/METALED: To Roland, a road covered with asphalt is a "metaled road."   III:287

MID-SUMMER: One of Gilead's Fair-Days. See GILEAD FAIR-DAYS at the beginning of this Concordance, and MID-WORLD HOLIDAYS in APPENDIX II.

MOTHER-ROOT: Umbilical cord.   III:175

MOZO: Spanish for porter. Used in Hambry for male servents.   IV:278

MUTIES: This is the Mid-World term for mutants. For more information, see MUTANTS in the CHARACTERS section.

NECK-POPPED: Hanged.   I:105–6

**NEW EARTH: The season corresponding to deep spring. See GILEAD FAIR-DAYS at the beginning of this Concordance. See also MID-WORLD HOLIDAYS in APPENDIX II.

OLD WAR: See GREAT POISONING

OUTLANDERS: To the Pubes, outlanders are people not from Lud. III:321, III:322

PALAVER: To talk or hold counsel. *Palaver* tends to mean the exchange of important ideas. Roland and the Man in Black make palaver in the golgotha. Roland and his *ka-tet* hold palaver with the elderly residents of River Crossing.   I:197

PAÑUELO: Handkerchief. A Spanish term used in Hambry. IV:374

PARD: Short for "pardner." We use this term in Our World too. It means partner or comrade.   E:179

PATRONO: A term used in Hambry which means employer or boss. It is very similar to the Spanish word "patrón."   IV:237

PEDDLER'S MOON: See MID-WORLD MOONS at the beginning of this Concordance.

PERT: Means impertinent or impertinently. (Mercy of River Crossing is blinded with a branding iron for looking "pert" at some harriers.) However, it can also mean smart, leaning toward "smart-ass." Coming from the right person, however, it can be meant somewhat admiringly. Gasher refers to Jake as "pert," implying that he has a smart mouth but is also quick-witted and gutsy.   III:328, III:351, III:356–57

PETTIBONE: An alcoholic drink.   IV:251

PIG-BACK: Roland's term for "piggyback." III:57

POINTS (WICKETS): This game was played in Mid-World with croquet balls. I:96

POISONING, THE: See GREAT POISONING above

POKE: A small bag for carrying meat, tobacco, or other substances. We use this term in Our World as well. I:21

**POKEBERRIES: Along with corn, this is one of the crops grown between Tull and Pricetown.

POPKIN: A sandwich. II:45

POSSE: Roland's term for New York police. II:342

PROVING HONESTY: A physical exam used to verify physical and spiritual purity. The examiner checks virginity and looks for suck marks (left by demons). IV:132

PUBE: See PUBES in the CHARACTERS section.

PULING: Crying, moaning, and making a fuss. II:155, III:173

PULER: A young man. Cort uses this term to address Roland. We hear it again in Hambry. I:163

QUESA: A dance similar to a simple reel. IV:209

QUICKPIT: Pit of quicksand. III:251

REAP: The festival of Reap (also known as Charyou Tree) is the harvest festival and the time of harvest sacrifice. In the days of Arthur Eld, it was celebrated with human sacrifice. By Roland's time stuffy-guys, and not people, were thrown onto Reap fires. During the season of Reap, people decorate their houses, and their stuffy-guys, with Reap charms. Reap charms can also be painted on the body or worn like pendants. See entries under STUFFY-GUYS in the CHARACTERS section, MID-WORLD HOLIDAYS in APPENDIX II, and GILEAD FAIR-DAYS at the beginning of this Concordance.

ROSILLO: Susan Delgado calls her horse Pylon a *rosillo*.   IV:239

ROT, THE: A disease which often affects the Border Dwellers of the Mohaine Desert. It sounds a bit like leprosy. People suffering from this disease are called "rotters."   I:18

RUSSEL: A slang term that means to take a woman by force.   II:46

SALIG: A salig looks like a crocodile or alligator and lives in the swamps of Mid-World.   IV:70

SAI: See SAI in the HIGH SPEECH section.

SANDAY: In Mejis, this is the traditional cowboys' day of rest.   IV:282, IV:287

SAWSEE: This is Roland's confused term for "seesaw."   III:38

SECRET CODE: This code is used by gunslingers when they communicate by carrier pigeon. The phrase below means "Farson moves east . . . Forces split, one big, one small. Do you see anything unusual."   IV:262

$$\square \mathsf{LL} \mathsf{OL} \mathsf{(J} \square \mathsf{JC} \mathsf{\backslash\!\!\!/OI} \square \mathsf{R}$$

SELLIAN DIALECTS: Roland used to speak the Sellian dialects, but he has forgotten all but the curses.   III:259

SERAPE: Worn in Mejis and New Canaan by both men and women. It is a bit like a poncho or cape.   IV:282, IV:365

SHEEVIN (SEEFIN): Literally speaking, *sheevin* means "quiet little woman." In practice, it means side-wife or mistress.   IV:207

SHIPMATE'S DISEASE: Roland and Eddie suffer from this even though they are on dry land. It is caused by nutritional deficiencies brought on by a lack of fruit and greens.   II:268

**SHOOT-UP MONEY: Money gained from the gun. It can be money earned by a hired gunman.

SIDE LINE OF DESCENT: Descended from a gilly. The line of Deschain is a side line of descent. In other words, Roland's ancestor was born to one of Arthur Eld's side-wives.   IV:184

SIGUL: A *sigul* is a sign, symbol, or insignia which is secret and full of meaning. It often has religious, political, or magical significance.   III:353

**SILFLAY: To graze. This term comes from the novel *Watership Down*.

SILK-ARSE GENNELMAN: This is a crass Lud-term for somebody who is well-bred.   III:354

SILVA COMPASS: This is a kind of compass used in Roland's world. In *The Gunslinger,* one of the Border Dwellers gives Roland a stainless-steel Silva compass and bids him give it to Jesus.   I:15

SINGLET: A piece of clothing worn by Cort when he battles the apprentices.   I:167

**SISSA: Sister.

SLO-TRANS ENGINES: Blaine's engines are slo-trans engines. Slo-trans technology was supposed to be immune to malfunction, but this is obviously not the case, since Blaine himself admits that he is going mad. IV:14

SLUMGULLION: This is a derogatory term for a man.   III:249

SNOOD: A headcovering worn by women in Mid-World, especially when they are in formal attire.   IV:194

SOFT: Go forward carefully, slowly. Keep your emotions under control. III:278, IV:67

SOMBRERA/SOMBRERO: The wide-brimmed hats worn in Hambry. IV:365

SOWING: One of Gilead's Fair-Days. It is also known as **New Earth and **Fresh Commala. See GILEAD FAIR-DAYS at the beginning of this Concordance. See also MID-WORLD HOLIDAYS in APPENDIX II.

SOWING NIGHT COTIL': See COMMALA

**SPARK-LIGHTS: "Spark-lights" (also known as filament lights) are electric flambeaux or electric lights. It is a Hambry term. In the new *Gunslinger* we find out that the Coach Road leading from Pricetown to Tull was once lined with spark-lights. By the time Roland passes through, they are all dead.   IV:150

SQUINT: We hear this term in both Lud and Hambry. Like "cully," it is usually used when talking to—or about—young men. However, it seems more pejorative. This term can also have sexual connotations. In boy-loving Lud, Gasher tells Roland that he must hand over the squint, meaning Jake.   III:298

STAR WHISKEY: This is the best whiskey found in Tull.   I:41

SWAMP-GAS TUBES: These tubes looked a bit like neon. They were sold at Feast of Joseph fairtime.   I:186

SWEETCHEEKS BERRY: This is Gasher's term for a boy-virgin. III:325

SWEETMEATS: This is a Lud term for testicles.   III:354

TACK-SEES: Roland's term for taxis.   II:341

TATI JACKETS: Jackets worn by musicians in Hambry. They can be found in Our World too.   IV:194

THANKEE SAI: "Thankee sai" is the polite term for thank you. Its equivalent is "thank you, sir," or "thank you, madam." These words are accompanied by three brisk taps upon the throat with the fingers of the right hand. At the beginning of *Wizard and Glass* we learn that when addressing men, one should use the left hand and tap the breastbone. However, this seems to be extremely formal. When Roland and his young friends are in Hambry, they use their right hands and tap their throats when thanking elders of either sex.   II:52, IV:21

THINKING CAP: In Roland's world, as in Our World, children are sometimes told to put on their thinking caps. On Roland's level of the Tower this is based on a story about the Guardians. Supposedly, each Guardian carried an extra brain on the outside of its head, in a hat. This apocryphal tale had a true basis. The Guardians have radar dishes sticking out of their skulls.   III:40

THREADED STOCK: Threaded stock is normal stock, or those animals born without mutations. Threaded stock can be born of threaded stock, but they can also be born from late-generation muties. (In Mid-World, they describe this process by saying the bloodlines are clarifying.) Despite what the Horsemen's Association wants Roland to believe during his stay in Hambry, there are few muties left in the Outer Arc. Even in the area outside Candleton (an area hard hit by the mutating disaster), threaded stock is on the increase.   IV:14, IV:203

TOOTER FISH: This is Roland's term for tuna fish. He thinks it's tasty. II:45–46

TOUCH, THE: The ability to read minds, and also to see into the past or the future. It is similar to ESP. In the new *Gunslinger,* it is described as half empathy, half telepathy.   IV:224, IV:388

TRAINING, THE: All apprentice gunslingers must undergo "the Training." In Roland's time, Cort was in charge of this arduous process. Before Cort, his father, Fardo, taught the apprentices (IV:407). For the most part, apprentice gunslingers were the sons of gunslingers. In other words, they belonged to the aristocracy of Mid-World. However, it is entirely possible that very young boys who showed promise were allowed to enter this small elect group.

The Training culminated in a rite of passage, enacted in the Square Yard, just beyond the Great Hall of Gilead. Eighteen was the usual age for this passage of an apprentice into manhood, although it could happen as late as twenty-five. Those who had not faced the all-or-nothing test by that age usually slipped into obscurity as freeholders. The litany and ritual of this rite were strictly observed, and had not changed for centuries. The apprentice entered the yard by the west entrance, which faced the barbarian forests. The teacher entered from the east, which faced the Great Hall and all of its symbolic civilization. The apprentice and his teacher faced one another from opposite ends of the yard and engaged in a ritual colloquy:

> "Have you come here for a serious purpose, boy?"
> "I have come for a serious purpose, teacher."
> "Have you come as an outcast from your father's house?"
> "I have so come, teacher."
> "Have you come with your chosen weapon?"
> "I have so come, teacher."
> "What is your weapon?"

The final twist in this traditional interplay was intended to give the teacher a slight advantage. He could adjust his battle plan by knowing his student's method of attack. It also meant that in order to move from childhood into manhood, the student had to be both wily and quick.

Only those who bested their teacher were permitted to exit through the east gate. Those who failed (and many did) were sent west, as exiles. In the end, the all-or-nothing aspect of the Training proved to be one of the Affiliation's weaknesses, since embittered failures, such as Eldred Jonas, took up the cause of John Farson, Gilead's great enemy.

The apprentice who won his guns was not yet entitled to the sandalwood-handled firearms of a true, mature gunslinger. Instead, he was given an apprentice's guns, which were less ornate than those he would wear later in life.   I:100

TRIG/TRIGGERS/TRIGGIE: Clever. A word used in both Lud and Hambry. It implies both craftiness and untrustworthiness.   III:327

TRIG COVE: This term can be translated roughly as "clever bastard." It can be used affectionately. For example, Gasher calls Tick-Tock "a trig cove."   III:298, III:356

UNIPOLAR CIRCUITS: See DIPOLAR CIRCUITS, above

VAQUERO (VAQ): Spanish for cowboy. This term is used in Hambry. IV:507

WATCH ME: This is a Mid-World card game. People usually place bets, so it can be rather dangerous. Players are often killed at Watch Me tables. The phrase "Watch Me" can mean "you have a deal."   III:278, III:366, IV:17

**WAY OF THE GUN: This is another term for the Training.

WEE SHIM: A small child.   IV:458

WEED-EATER: Somebody addicted to chewing devil grass.   I:26, I:35

WENBERRY: Wenberries are like strawberries.   III:279

WERY: This is Gasher's way of pronouncing "very."   III:299

WHEELS: An archaic form of measurement still used in Gilead. In *The Waste Lands*, Blaine tells us that a distance of 8,000 wheels is roughly equivalent to 7,000 miles. That means that there are about 1.143 wheels to a mile. However, in *Wizard and Glass* a tricky Blaine tells us that 900 mph is the same as 530 wheels per hour. In this second instance one wheel is equal to 1.7 miles. Either Blaine is being sneaky or he has blown more circuits than he thinks.   IV:148

WHITE, THE: The White is the force of good. When Aunt Talitha of River Crossing learns that Roland is a gunslinger, she says to her companions, "Behold ye, the return of the White! After evil ways and evil days, the White comes again! Be of good heart and hold up your heads, for ye have lived to see the wheel of *ka* begin to turn once more!" (III:232) To the beleaguered inhabitants of Mid-World, the aristocratic gunslingers are the knights of the White. In an unstable and violent present, they represent a stable and peaceful past, a kind of golden age. Roland's father, Steven Deschain, is often referred to as the last Lord of Light. Both the Affiliation and the ancient hero Arthur Eld represent the White, and yet the term means more than a particular political faction, allegiance, or social class.

The true meaning of the White relates back to the philosophy embedded in the Old Tongue, or High Speech, a philosophy of wholeness which seems to bear some resemblance to the Neoplatonic vision of the One. Just before Jake sees the Rose in the deserted lot at Forty-sixth Street and Second Avenue, he hears the voice of the White, which he finds indescribably beautiful:

> The humming grew. Now it was not a thousand voices but a million, an open funnel of voices rising from the deepest well of the universe. He caught names in that group voice, but could not have said what they were. One might have been Marten. One might have been Cuthbert. Another might have been Roland—Roland of Gilead.
>
> There were other names; there was a babble of conversation that might have been ten thousand entwined stories; but above all that gorgeous, swelling hum, a vibration that wanted to fill his head with bright white light. It was, Jake realized with a joy so overwhelming that it threatened to burst him to pieces, the voice of *Yes*; the voice of *White*; the voice of *Always*. It was a great chorus of affirmation, and it sang in the empty lot. It sang for him. (III:124)

The White is wholeness and unity. It is the tapestry woven from many interlocking *ka-tets*. It contains both good and evil, yet seen in the greater context of the White there is no gray or black, only whiteness. Like white light, the White contains all colors within its balance. Maerlyn's Rainbow is a breaking-up of this whiteness into a spectrum, many colors of which are troublesome. For example, the hungry, semisexual energy of

Maerlyn's Grapefruit (the Pink One) proves disastrous for any who stare into its depths.

WHITE TEA: A refreshing, non-alcoholic drink.   IV:184

WIDE-EARTH: One of Gilead's Fair-Days. See GILEAD FAIR-DAYS at the beginning of this Concordance. See also MID-WORLD HOLIDAYS in APPENDIX II.

WINE-BIBBER: A boozer.   III:61

WINTER: One of Gilead's Fair-Days. See GILEAD FAIR-DAYS at the beginning of this Concordance. See also MID-WORLD MISCELLANY in APPENDIX II.

WITCHGRASS: Grass that grows in the foothills of the Cyclopean Mountains.   I:118

WRISTBANDS: Handcuffs.   II:356

**YAR: Yes.

YEAR'S END: One of Gilead's Fair-Days. See GILEAD FAIR-DAYS at the beginning of this Concordance. See also MID-WORLD HOLIDAYS in APPENDIX II.

MID-WORLD SAYINGS

ALL THINGS SERVE THE BEAM: This is a Mid-World truism. III:406

**ANIMALS THAT TALK BE TOUGH: Don't eat anything that can answer you back. Their flesh isn't pleasant.

ARGYOU NOT ABOUT THE HAND YOU ARE DELT IN CARDS OR IN LIFE: This pithy phrase was written on a sign in the Travellers' Rest.   IV:171

BAD TIMES ARE ON HORSEBACK: Bad times are coming quickly. I:163

BEANS, BEANS, THE MUSICAL FRUIT. THE MORE YOU EAT, THE MORE YOU TOOT: We have this saying in Our World too. The raven Zoltan was very fond of it.   I:16

BEHOLD YE, THE RETURN OF THE WHITE! AFTER EVIL WAYS AND EVIL DAYS, THE WHITE COMES AGAIN! BE OF GOOD HEART AND HOLD UP YOUR HEAD, FOR YE HAVE LIVED TO SEE THE WHEEL OF *KA* BEGIN TO TURN ONCE MORE: Aunt Talitha of River Crossing utters this pronouncement.   III:232

BUMBLER GOT YOUR TONGUE?: This is the equivalent of "Cat got your tongue?"   III:327

CRY OFF: Renege. Stop.   IV:40

DISTRESSAL OF A LADY: In Eluria, this is a legalistic euphemism for rape.   E:151

DO BUMBLERS LEARN TO SPEAK BACKWARD? NO MORE THAN CATS CHANGE THEIR SPOTS: In other words, people don't change.   IV:251

**DO THAT I BEG YA: Please do it.

DON'T MAKE THE MISTAKE OF PUTTING YOUR HEART NEAR HIS HAND: Don't leave yourself emotionally vulnerable.   II:104

DO YER KEN: This is a term Gasher uses for "do you know."   III:297

**DO YOU KENNIT?: Do you understand?

**DO YOU SEE YOUR SISTER'S BUM?: This was one of Cort's sayings. It means "What are you staring at?"

FATHER, GUIDE MY HANDS AND HEART SO THAT NO PART OF THE ANIMAL WILL BE WASTED: IV:93

FAULT ALWAYS LIES IN THE SAME PLACE—WITH HIM WEAK ENOUGH TO LAY BLAME: This is one of Cort's sayings.   II:174

**FIRST BLOOD! FIRST BLOOD TO MY BOSOM: Cuthbert says this when Roland begins to best Cort. It's what is said when the first blood is drawn during a coming-of-age battle.

FOOL NOT YOUR MOTHER 'LESS SHE'S OUT OF FACE: In other words, don't lie.   E:183

FOOLS ARE THE ONLY FOLK ON EARTH WHO CAN ABSOLUTELY COUNT ON GETTING WHAT THEY DESERVE: IV:160

FOR A PRETTY: This doesn't have a direct translation. You often ask someone to do something "for a pretty." It seems to sometimes mean "please." It can also be a rhetorical statement added on to the end of a sentence.   I:29, I:198

FOR YOUR FATHER'S SAKE: This phrase is used frequently throughout the series. To do something for your father's sake is to do it for honor's sake. IV:22, IV:129

GOOD RIDDANCE TO BAD SWILL: The Pubes of Lud use this term instead of "Good riddance to bad rubbish."   III:324

GUNSLINGER LITANY: "I do not aim with my hand; he who aims with his hand has forgotten the face of his father. I aim with my eye. I do not shoot with my hand; he who shoots with his hand has forgotten the face of his father. I shoot with my mind. I do not kill with my gun; he who kills with his gun has forgotten the face of his father. I kill with my heart." It seems likely that the Gunslinger Litany was originally recited in the Tongue.   III:14, III:68

**I CRY YOUR FAVOR: I ask for a favor.

I CRY YOUR PARDON: I ask your forgiveness.   III:177, III:269

I HAVE FORGOTTEN THE FACE OF MY FATHER: This is a term often used by Roland. It is a phrase of shame. When one has forgotten the face of one's father, it means that one has behaved dishonorably. Mid-World is patriarchal, a cultural structure that is older than either the aristocracy of gunslingers (the Barons of Mid-World), or the kingship of Arthur Eld. When Eddie and Susannah visit the Cradle of Lud, they see the sculpted visages of "stern men with the harsh faces of executioners who are happy in their work." (III:343) We do not know whether these men were judges, justices, politicians, or legendary forefathers, but their sculpted faces, somehow reminiscent of busts of Roman senators, tell us something about both the pride and the unrelenting harshness of the Great Old Ones. Like the Romans, or our own culture, they were guilty of *hubris*.   I:97

I WILL SET MY WATCH AND WARRANT ON IT: I'll bet on it, or I'll guarantee it. It's damn true.   III:332, III:353

I WOT: "I believe so" or "I reckon so."   IV:104

IF IT'S *KA*, IT WILL COME LIKE THE WIND: If it's meant to be, it will be.   IV:157

IF YE'D STEAL THE SILVER FROM THE DINING ROOM, FIRST PUT THE DOG IN THE PANTRY: A famous saying from the Barony of Cressia.   IV:175

IT'S ALL THE SAME JOLLY FAKEMENT TO ME: This is a Lud term for "It's all the same to me."   III:297

**JILLY-COME-LATELY: A sarcastic comment about youth. An old woman can also look like a jilly-come-lately when compared to a much older woman.

*KA WAS A WHEEL, ITS ONE PURPOSE TO TURN, AND IN THE END IT ALWAYS CAME BACK TO THE PLACE WHERE IT HAD STARTED: This is another Mid-World truism. What you do comes back to haunt you. What goes around comes around.   III:394

LEAD US NOT INTO TEMPTATION: In Our World, this phrase can be found in the Lord's Prayer. It is another one of the raven Zoltan's sayings.   I:20

LEMON JUICE WON'T TAKE THE STAIN OUT OF A LADY'S REPUTATION: It's not easy to lose a bad rep.   IV:143

**LET'S SHAKE A MILE: Let's get moving.

LET YOUR SHADOW GROW. LET IT GROW HAIR ON ITS FACE. LET IT BECOME DARK: Wait until you're older.   I:172

LIFE FOR YOUR CROP: This is a Mid-World greeting. Roland uses it when he meets Brown, the Border Dweller.   I:15

LONG DAYS AND PLEASANT NIGHTS: This is a polite greeting used in Gilead.   IV:197

MANY AND MANY-A: A long time ago.

MAY YOUR DAYS BE LONG UPON THE EARTH: Mid-World greeting.   IV:141

MY LIFE FOR YOU: Richard Fannin makes Tick-Tock repeat this sinister saying.   III:389

NO ONE EVER REALLY PAYS FOR BETRAYAL IN SILVER; THE PRICE OF ANY BETRAYAL ALWAYS COMES DUE IN FLESH: The cost of betrayal is dear.

OH BITE IT!: This was Pat Delgado's favorite cuss.   IV:239

ONLY A FOOL BELIEVES HE'S DREAMING BEFORE HE WAKES UP: Don't ignore the situation, deal with it! Also, hope for the best and expect the worst.   III:59

PASS-ON-BY COUNTRY: Ugly country. The land between Pricetown and Tull is pass-on-by country.

PUT ON YOUR THINKING CAP: As in Our World, people in Mid-World tell puzzled children to put on their thinking caps. The story stems from the belief that the Guardians each carried an extra brain on the outside of their heads. They kept these brains in a hat. Actually, the "hats" were radar dishes.   III:40

RAIN, HEALTH, EXPANSION TO THE SPIRIT: This is a blessing used by Brown, the Border Dweller.   I:19

RIDE THE HANDSOME: To Ride the Handsome is a Lud euphemism for dying.   III:300

RITUAL OF RENUNCIATION: I CURSE THEE WITH THE ASHES! I CURSE THEE TO DARKNESS! YE LOST AND RENOUNCED!: Cordelia Delgado performs this ancient ritual and smears Susan with ashes. It is meant to dishonor Susan and brand her as an outcast.   IV:497

SHUT YOUR QUACK: Shut up.

SO FELL LORD PERTH, AND THE COUNTRYSIDE DID SHAKE WITH THAT THUNDER: "So Fell Lord Perth" is a line from a longer poem. The story, very similar to that of David and Goliath, goes as follows:

> Lord Perth was a giant who went forth to war with a thousand men, but he was still in his own country when a little boy threw a stone at him and hit him in the knee. He stumbled, the weight of his armor bore him down, and he broke his neck in the fall.

Tick-Tock becomes very angry when Jake mentions this "unlucky" story. Obviously, it parallels the interaction between the huge Tick-Tock and the very young Jake.   III:274

SCREW YOU AND THE HORSE YOU RODE IN ON: This is another one of Zoltan's favorite sayings.   I:16

SOME THINGS DON'T REST EASY EVEN WHEN THEY'RE DEAD: IV:98

SPARE NOT THE BIRCH SO YOU SPOIL NOT THE CHILD: Saying from the Great Book. Recounted by Roland.   III:13

STICKS AND STONES WILL BREAK MY BONES YET TAUNTS SHALL NEVER WOUND ME: This is a variation on a saying from Our World.   III:17

THE DEAD FROM THE DEAD: ONLY A CORPSE MAY SPEAK: We hear this saying in the Way Station's cellar, where Roland hears the Speaking Demon and then finds human remains in the wall. Speaking Demons may only manifest where there has been a death, or where there are the remains of the dead. In the new *Gunslinger,* this proverb has a slightly different form. It is, 'Take the dead from the dead; only a corpse may speak true prophecy.' I:91

THE LUCK OF THE GALLOWS: This is why Roland takes a piece of the hangman's tree when he sees Hax killed.   I:109

THE QUICKEST WAY TO LEARN ABOUT A NEW PLACE IS TO KNOW WHAT IT DREAMS OF: This is one of Roland's truisms. III:59

THE SUN IS GOING DOWN ON THE WORLD: This is Aunt Talitha's saying. It means the end of the world is coming. The world is dying. III:237

THE WHEEL OF *KA* TURNS AND THE WORLD MOVES ON: III:403

THE WISE THIEF ALWAYS PROSPERS: III:45

THE WORLD HAS MOVED ON: This term is used throughout the series. It means that things have changed, and that the world is now profoundly different from what it once was.   III:73, III:310, III:411, IV:426

THE WORLD WON'T MOVE ON TOMORROW: This was a term used in Gilead before the world really did move on. It means that there's time yet.   I:173

THERE WILL BE WATER IF GOD WILLS IT: If it is meant to be, it will come to pass.   III:26

TIME GROWS SOFT: Time has grown erratic.   IV:266

TIME IS A FACE ON THE WATER: Mejis saying. The world has moved on and time has grown strange.   IV:445

**TIME IS THE THIEF OF MEMORY: This is one of Vannay's sayings.

TO COME TO THE CLEARING AT THE END OF YOUR PATH: To die.   IV:124

**TO DRAW THE BLACK STONE: This is how gunslingers of old chose who would have to act as hangman.

**TO PULL LEATHER: To draw your gun.

**'WARE THE MAN WHO FAKES A LIMP: This was one of Cort's sayings. In other words, don't trust somebody who wants to be caught.

WE'LL HAVE TO MOVE VERY FAST, OR WE'LL FIND OURSELVES BASTED IN A HOT OAST: In other words, our goose will be cooked. II:136

WELL MET ("WE WERE WELL MET"): A lovely saying. We met, and that is important. It is good that we met, etc.   IV:158

WHERE ELSE WOULD I BE? THE WEST END OF THE WORLD?:
This is a Lud saying.   III:339

WHY IS A CROOKED LETTER AND CAN'T BE MADE STRAIGHT . . . NEVER MIND WHY: This is one of Cort's sayings. In other words, don't bother asking.   I:135

WILL YOU DRINK TO THE EARTH, AND TO THE DAYS WHICH HAVE PASSED UPON IT? WILL YOU DRINK TO THE FULLNESS WHICH WAS, AND TO FRIENDS WHO HAVE PASSED ON? WILL YOU DRINK TO GOOD COMPANY, WELL MET?: This toast is made by Roland in River Crossing.   III:234

YE'RE A FIERCE TRIM: This is a Lud term for "you're a tough guy." III:297

YOU MIGHT AS WELL TRY TO DRINK THE OCEAN WITH A SPOON AS ARGUE WITH A LOVER: II:304

YOU RUN WITHOUT CONSIDERATION AND FALL IN A HOLE: One of Cort's sayings.   IV:286

YOUNG EYES SEE FAR: IV:174

LANGUAGE OF THE LITTLE SISTERS OF ELURIA

Roland doesn't hear much of the Little Sisters' language, but what he does hear he cannot identify. It is neither low speech nor High Speech, and it sounds like no other language or dialect he has ever heard. Since the Little Sisters are not human, it seems likely that theirs is a demon-tongue. The following phrases are uttered by Sister Mary (Big Sister) when she and the others of her vampiric order feed on the unconscious, unnamed man in the Sisters' hospital tent in Eluria. The words are never translated. E:180–81

CAN DE LACH, MI HIM EN TOW

RAS ME! ON! ON!

HAIS!

APPENDIX II:
MID-WORLD MISCELLANY

MID-WORLD DANCES
**Commala (Sowing Night Cotillion or Sowing Night Cotil'): This was the name of Gilead's Spring Dance. The geometric steps of this dance were meant to mimic a courting ritual.
Pol-kam: This dance was popular in Gilead. It was lighter and faster than a waltz.   I:137
Quesa: A simple sort of reel. Danced in Hambry.   IV:209
Waltz: Waltzing was popular in Gilead.   I:137

MID-WORLD DISEASES
Blood-sickness: This one sounds a bit like blood-poisoning, but it could also be another blood-related illness.   III:248
Mandrus: A venereal disease found in Lud. It's also called Whore's Blossoms.   III:297
Mutation: Mid-World's many mutations were caused by the Great Poisoning. See MUTANTS in the CHARACTERS section. See also MID-WORLD ARGOT: THE GREAT POISONING in APPENDIX I.
Rabies: We have this one in Our World too.   III:296
Rot: This disease affects the Border Dwellers of the Mohaine Desert. It is a lot like leprosy.   I:15, I:18
Superflu: This one actually affects the alternate Topeka, not Mid-World. It is also known as Captain Trips and Tube-Neck.   IV:73
Wasting Disease: IV:307

MID-WORLD DRUGS
Alder-bark: Helps bad breath.   II:363
Graf: Strong apple beer.
Mescaline: A hallucinogen that helps gunslingers see and communicate with demons.   I:125, I:127
Pettibone: An alcoholic drink.   IV:251
Sugar: Good for energy bursts.   II:103–4

MID-WORLD GAMES

Castles: A game very much like Chess.   IV:191

**Croquet and Points: These games were popular among Gilead's ladies. In the new version of *The Gunslinger* we find out that Points is played with ninepins. It sounds a bit like bowling.   I:88, I:96

Faro: This is probably a betting card game, since Sylvia Pittston makes her followers repent playing it.   I:50

**Gran-Points: In this game you hold a bat and wait for a rawhide bird to be pitched. It sounds a bit like baseball.

**Mother Says: This children's game is similar to Simon Says.

Watch Me: This is one of Mid-World's card games. People tend to bet, and the games can get rather dangerous.   I:26–27

MID-WORLD HOLIDAYS AND CARNIVALS

All-Saints Eve: I:32

Barons' Year-End parties: III:50

Dance of Easterling: This great party marked the end of the Wide Earth and the advent of sowing.   IV:194

Easter Night: In the new version of *The Gunslinger,* the Easter Night Dance is replaced by the **Sowing Night Cotillion.   I:150, I:156

Fair-Day Riddling: Riddling was an extremely important game in Mid-World-that-was. Riddling was believed to hold incredible power. A good Fair-Day Riddling contest would ensure that the crops grew well.   III:281

Fair-Days: Here is a list of Mid-World's seasonal Fair-Days.   III:416
   Winter
   Wide Earth
   Sowing (New Earth or Fresh Commala)
   Mid-Summer
   Full Earth
   Reaping
   Year's End

Feast of Joseph fairtime: I:186

Glowing Day: Cuthbert liked this holiday because of the fireworks and the ice.   IV:185

MID-WORLD'S MUSICAL INSTRUMENTS

Fiddles: I:145

Guitars: IV:194

Way-Gog Music: This instrument, which is a bit like a bagpipe, isn't actually from Mid-World. It is played on the upper levels of the Tower. III:409

MID-WORLD RELIGIONS
In Mid-World, the Gods almost always seem to drink blood.   E:147
    Amoco, the Thunder God: I:154
    Asmodeus: E:147
    Baal: E:147
    Christian (general): In Mid-World, Christians are called "followers of the Jesus-man" or of the God o' the Cross.   E:147
        Methodism: I:34
    Guardian Totems: IV:222

MID-WORLD RHYMES
    1a. Rain in Spain (Original Version)
        The rain in Spain falls mainly on the plain.
        There is joy and also pain
        but the rain in Spain falls mainly on the plain.

        Pretty-plain, loony-sane
        The ways of the world all will change
        and all the ways remain the same
        but if you're mad or only sane
        the rain in Spain falls mainly on the plain.

        We walk in love but fly in chains
        And the planes in Spain fall mainly in the rain (I:71)

    **1b. Rain in Spain (Version #2)
In the new version of *The Gunslinger,* the second verse is replaced by the following:
        Time's a sheet, life's a stain
        All the things we know will change
        and all those things remain the same,
        but be ye mad or only sane,
        the rain in Spain falls mainly on the plain.

    **2. Fire Rhyme
In the new version of *The Gunslinger,* Roland says this rhyme before lighting his devil grass fire:
        "Spark-a-dark, where's my sire? Will I lay me?
        Will I stay me? Bless this camp with fire."

    **3. Baby Bunting
        Baby bunting, baby dear, baby bring your basket here.
        Chussit, chissit, chassit, bring enough to fill your basket.

MID-WORLD *SIGULS*

Christian Medallions: One of these saves Roland from the Little Sisters of Eluria. E:182

Coffins and Blue Coffin Tattoos: These tattoos are worn by the Big Coffin Hunters. Tick-Tock of the Grays wears a coffin-shaped clock around his neck. IV:155

The Dark Bells: The Dark Bells are the *sigul* of the Little Sisters of Eluria. E:184

The Eye: This is the *sigul* of John Farson, but it is actually the *sigul* of the Crimson King. IV:91

Fist and Thunderbolt: This is a lot like Mid-World's version of the swastika. III:275

Jesus-Man *Sigul*: A crucifix. E:153

Rose: The Little Sisters of Eluria wear the Rose on their habits. It is the *sigul* of the Dark Tower. E:165

MID-WORLD SONGS

"A Hundred Leagues to Banberry Cross" I:120

"Careless Love" I:86

"Captain Mills, You Bastard" IV:508

"Come on Over Baby" IV:213–14

"Ease on Down the Road" I:120

"Golden Slippers" IV:244

"Hey Jude" I:22–23, I:26

"I am a Man of the Bright Blue Sea" IV:445–46

"Onward, Christian Soldiers" I:34

"Play Ladies, Play" IV:268

"Shall We Gather at the River" I:48

"We All Shine On" I:191

"Woman I love . . . is long and tall . . . She moves her body . . . like a cannonball" IV:268

APPENDIX III:
POLITICAL AND CULTURAL FIGURES
(OUR WORLD)

The Dark Tower series contains references to quite a few historical figures from our *where* and *when*. Here is a list of those mentioned.

Actors and Stage Personalities: Humphrey Bogart, Walter Brennan, Gary Cooper, James Dean, Cecil B. De Mille, Clint Eastwood, Judy Garland, Robin Leach, Rich Little (comic), Butterfly McQueen, Marilyn Monroe, Paul Newman, Sidney Poitier, Jerry Reed, Burt Reynolds, Adam Sandler (comic), Jean Stapleton, Rod Steiger, Jimmy Stewart, Spencer Tracy, John Travolta, Jack Webb, Raquel Welch

Biblical Figures/Biblical Stories: Abednego, Adam, Daniel, David and Bathsheba, David and Goliath, Devil (Interloper), Eve and the Serpent, Isaac, Jeremiah, Jesus on the Mount, Jezebel and King Ahaz, Lazarus, Mary, Mesach, Moses, Saint Matthew, Saint Paul, Saint Peter, Samson and Delilah, Shadrach, Star Wormwood

Civil Rights Figures: Medgar Evers, Freedom Riders, Martin Luther King, Rosa Parks

Cultural and Historical Figures: Alfred Adler (psychiatrist), Attila the Hun, Bonnie and Clyde, Buffalo Bill, Eratosthenes, Incas, Reverend Jim Jones, Christa McAuliffe, Wiley Post, Jack Ruby, Jimmy Swaggart (preacher)

Film Makers: Woody Allen, Federico Fellini, Sergio Leone

Films: *The Craft, The Dark Crystal, Dr. Jekyll and Mr. Hyde, The Exorcist, Halloween, In the Heat of the Night, Gone With the Wind, The Last Starfighter, Mandingo, Old Yeller, One Flew Over the Cuckoo's Nest, The Purple Rose of Cairo, Rambo, Robocop, The Shining, Smokey and the Bandit, Star Wars, The Terminator, Three Faces of Eve, War of the Zombies, **Zorro*

Magicians: Harry Blackstone, David Copperfield, Doug Henning, Harry Houdini

Musicians: Allman Brothers, Anthrax, Hoagy Carmichael, Johnny Cash, Creedence Clearwater Revival, Bob Dylan, Duke Ellington, Billie Holiday, Marvin Gaye, Kiss, Led Zeppelin, Megadeth, Wayne Newton,

Olivia Newton-John, Tony Orlando and Dawn, Elvis Presley, Rolling Stones, David Lee Roth, Sex Pistols, Dodi Stevens, Barbra Streisand, Donna Summer, ZZ Top

Songs: "Buffalo Gals," "Clinch Mountain Breakdown," "Darlin Katy," "Dr. Love," "Double Shot (of My Baby's Love)," "The Hippy Hippy Shake," "Knock Three Times," "Love to Love You, Baby," "Oxford Town," "Paint It Black," "Sharp Dressed Man," "Tube Snake Boogie," "Velcro Fly"

Novel, Cartoon, Myth, Film, and Folktale Characters: Alice (in Wonderland), Barbara Allen (folksong), Frodo Baggins and Sam Gamgee, Bambi, Bobbsey Twins, Charlie Brown and Lucy, Buckwheat, Edith Bunker, Casper the Friendly Ghost, Cheshire Cat, Claribell the Clown, Donald Duck, Ferdinand the Bull, Hansel and Gretel, Mars Henry, Humpty Dumpty, Icarus, Jack and the Beanstalk and Giant, Janus, John Henry (folksong), Jove, Clark Kent, Keystone Kops, King Arthur, Little Lord Fauntleroy, Lois Lane, Philip Marlowe, Ronald McDonald, Travis McGee, Merlin the Magician, Narcissus, Oedipus, Old Yeller, Peter Pan and Captain Hook, Popeye, Puck, Rambo, Samson and Delilah, Scheherazade, Shane, Speedy Gonzales, Spider-Man, Superman, Thor, Tin Woodman, Ulysses, William Wilson

Political Figures:

Cuba: Fidel Castro

Germany: Adolf Hitler

Haiti: Papa (Poppa) Doc Duvalier

USA: Vice-President George Bush (Sr.), President Jimmy Carter, Barry Goldwater, President Lyndon B. Johnson, President John F. Kennedy, General MacArthur, Lee Harvey Oswald, President Ronald Reagan, President Harry S. Truman

USSR: Nikita Khrushchev

Vietnam: Diem Brothers

Radio, Television and Sports Personalities: Mel Allen (sports announcer), Athletics, Braves, George Brett, David Brinkley (news), Walter Cronkite (news), Dwight Gooden (baseball), Chet Huntley (news), Sugar Ray Leonard, Mets, Walter Payton (football), Royals, Yankees

TV Programs: *All in the Family, The Brady Bunch, Cheyenne, Dragnet, Gunsmoke, Hollywood Squares, Peter Gunn, Journey to the Center of the Earth, The Little Rascals, Miami Vice, The Rifleman, The Twilight Zone*

Writers And Artists: Richard Adams, Thomas Hart Benton (painter), Clay Blaisdell, William Blake, William Peter Blatty (screenwriter), Robert Browning, Edgar Rice Burroughs, Raymond Chandler, William Cowper, Salvador Dalí, Walt Disney, T. S. Eliot, William Faulkner, Chester Gould (cartoonist), Donald M. Grant (publisher), Alex Haley, Nathaniel Hawthorne, Robert E. Howard, Shirley Jackson, Roy Krenkel (artist), Michelangelo, George Orwell, Wayne D. Overholser, John D. MacDonald, Edgar Allan Poe, Frederic Remington (painter), Charles Schulz (cartoonist), William Shakespeare, Thomas Wolfe

Books, Stories and Poems: *Alice's Adventures in Wonderland, The Bridge of San Luis Rey, Catch-22, The Hobbit, King James Bible, Little Lord Fauntleroy, Look Homeward, Angel, Lord of the Flies,* "The Lottery," "The Love Song of J. Alfred Prufrock" (quoted by Blaine), *Mike Mulligan and His Steam Shovel, Peter Pan, The Plague, Punch* (magazine), *Roots, A Thousand and One Nights, Tom Sawyer, Shardik,* "The Waste Land," *Watership Down, The Wizard of Oz, You Can't Go Home Again*

APPENDIX IV:
MID-WORLD MAPS

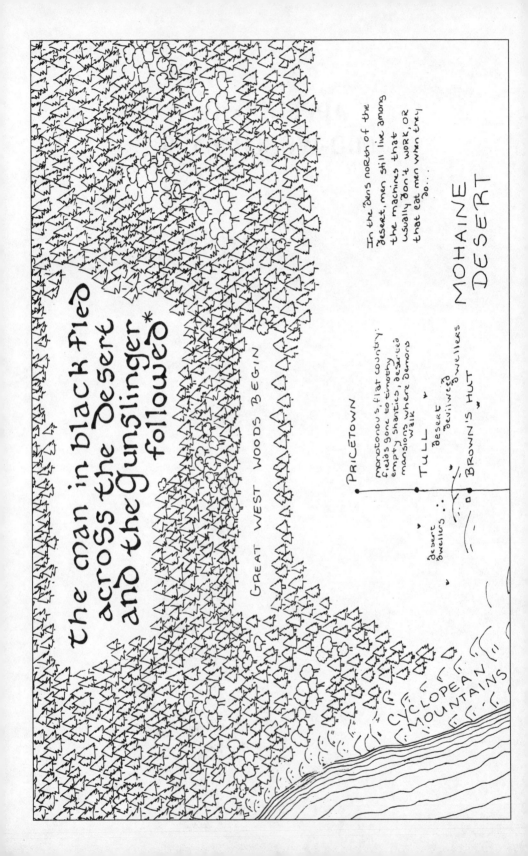

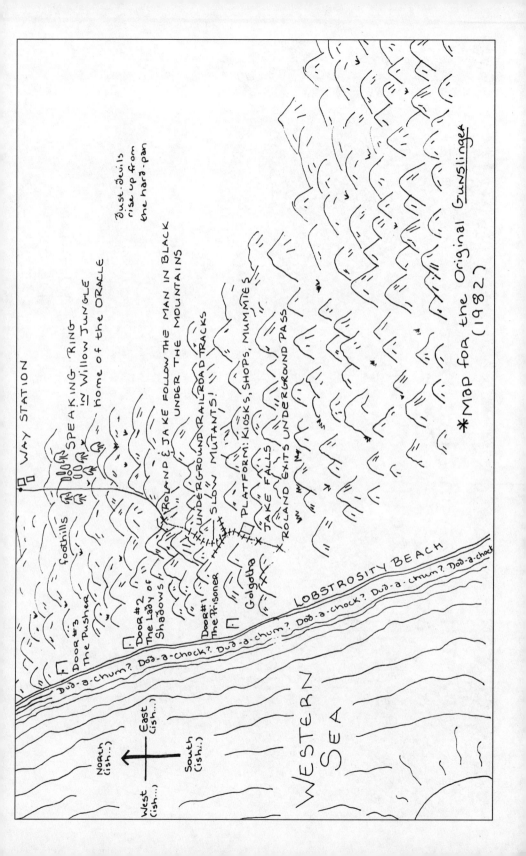

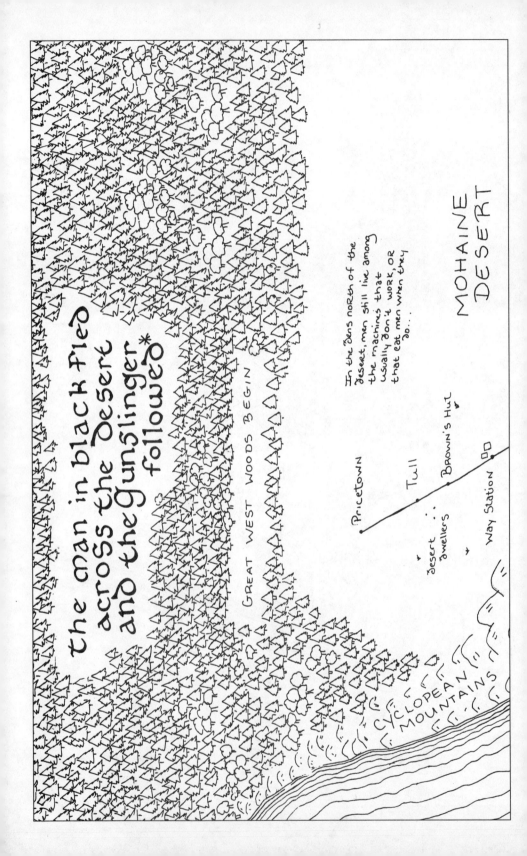

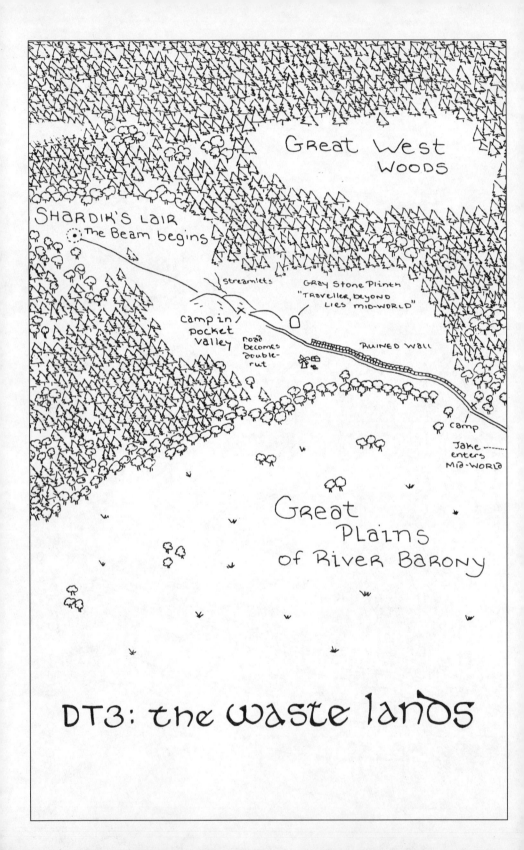

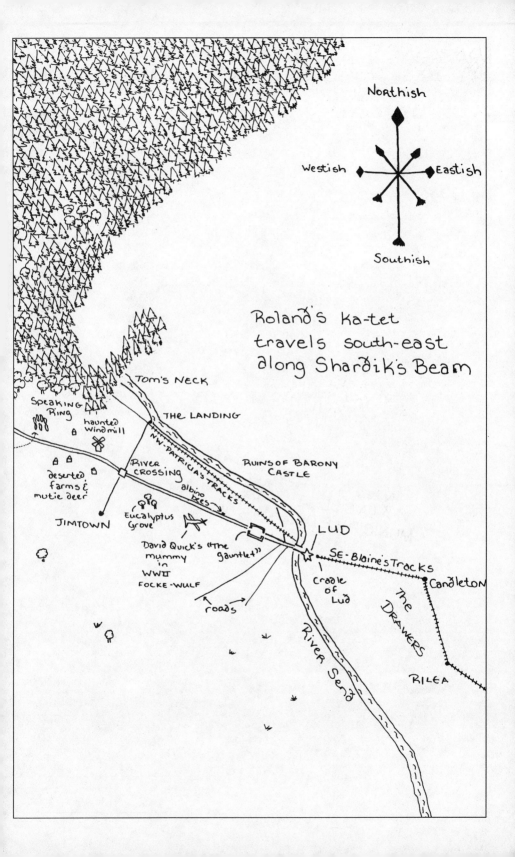